suffer a witch

MORGANA GALLAWAY

St. Bride's Press

This book is a work of fiction. Names, characters, places, and incidents are either products of the author's imagination or used fictitiously. Any resemblance to actual persons living or dead, events, or locales is entirely coincidental.

ST. BRIDE'S PRESS

815-A Brazos Street #637
Austin, Texas 78701

Copyright © 2011 by Morgana Gallaway

All rights reserved. No part of this publication may be reproduced, distributed, or transmitted in any form or by any means, including photocopying, recording, or other electronic or mechanical methods, without the prior written permission of the publisher, except in the case of brief quotations embodied in critical reviews and certain other noncommercial uses permitted by copyright law.

Cover image *Hecate* or *The Night of Enitharmon's Joy* by William Blake 1795, modified and used under public domain; file courtesy of The Yorck Project

ISBN: 978-0-9836989-0-6

First Edition, July 2011

*For my friends who helped me
craft this story:
Beth, Aliyah, Patrick,
Matt, and Adrian*

*and for Sybil, who was waiting
for me at the end of it*

The Thorn Inn

He began as usual. He used a silk rope because its softness reminded him of her skin, and its knots were like her calluses. It was midnight on a Friday and he knew what that meant. It was the hour of the black mass. It was the hour he was in their grip.

He tied the rope around the bedpost, while the other end was slipped into a simple noose. He put his head through it, already excited, heart pumping his black sinner's blood. He fell to his bare knees on the floor next to the bed, the supplicant's position, and the ligature tightened around his throat.

Into his own fervent darkness he fell, sweating, straining, crying.

In the last moments, as everything went coil-tight and starry-eyed, he heard the whispers, as he always did.

"*Dance-y, dance-y.*"

Her silken hands were relentless.

"*Master, faster, vow at-laster.*"

He was a sin-born little boy.

"*To you I say, I am a witch.*"

"I meet with him in the night—"
"—the night."
"I lay with him in the night."
"Meet me, circle plea, round and round and round we go! Witch, dee, scree, scry, scratch!"

They screamed and cackled and then he collapsed, exhausted from the fight. He barely had the strength to reach up and untie the knot, to free himself. He crawled into his cold bed with a murmured prayer, trying to remove the flush of shame, the knowledge of his unclean beginnings. "I am of God's flock, and God hates you," he whispered back to the fading voices.

Sleep came.

After hours of vague and threatening dreams, he swung his feet over the side of his down-stuffed mattress and hit the wood floor with a thud. He always got up on the right side of the bed. The left side of things was *sinistra*.

Above all else, Matthew Hopkins made sure to wake up the godly way.

He broke the thin cover of ice in the washbowl and splashed once over his face. It did little to dispel the sheen of his skin, oily from sleep. He stared at his reflection in the gloom, reminding himself there was nothing enchanted, nothing unusual about his face this morning: dark eyes, pointed nose, solid cheeks, a trimmed beard on his chin, brown hair with a few streaks of lighter ash. No warts or boils.

Hopkins reached over and pulled back the curtain, eager to see the light of day. Below him was the high street of Mistley, Essex. Roofs competed for space and beyond them was a stretch of watery fenland and woods. They were close to the sea here. Ships sailed up the estuary of the River Stour for trade and transport, but despite this the town had a grim, provincial feel. Its people did not trust foreigners much these days. In times of violence it was best to keep to one's loyal neighbors.

England was in the midst of a civil war, and this was the

heart of pro-Parliament country, reformist men and women who'd had enough of the decadence of kings and aristocrats and Catholics. Hopkins counted himself as one of the free thinkers who yearned for a simple, strict, pious life.

At the foot of his bed, his dog stirred, always waking up with her master. Her name was Elspeth, a fine greyhound, but marred with a fight scar on her left ear. She'd come to Hopkins as a pup two years ago. He petted her on the head and then pulled on his shirt, breeches, and his doublet jacket, doing up the tiny buttons in a straight line all the way to his throat. He brushed his cuffs into place, adjusted his collar, and made sure his white shirt was visible through the slashes in the doublet's fashionable sleeves. Right foot first, he pulled on his boots, polished black leather turned down in a bucket top style.

Peering out the window once more and seeing the barest layer of icy dew on the ledge, he decided in favor of his short cape of black wool. Satisfied, he was dressed and ready for the day.

He didn't stay in the best room at the Thorn Inn—that was reserved for visiting dignitaries or rich men—but it was the second-best, because Hopkins owned the place. He'd bought it two years ago after coming into an inheritance, and in that sense Elspeth and the inn were tied together in his life. He owned another house as well, a small but well-kept cottage down the street.

The kitchen downstairs was cold and empty. He took a moment to shout at the old cook who was just hanging her cloak, late and full of excuses. He told her that constant hard work was a Christian duty and she had better get busy.

Irritated, he caught a tin mug from the shelf and dipped it into the water bucket. The cool taste reminded him of baptism, and of the purity required of God's servants. He wondered if his father was looking down from his place in Heaven, waiting for his youngest, most problematic son to prove himself.

Hopkins sat down on a bench and leaned his elbows on the oak table. A sigh of ennui overtook him. Twenty-four years old, and he owned this inn, but that could not be all there was to life. *Faith,* he told himself, *have faith.* Rather than following his brothers to Cambridge, he'd hesitated, and fumbled around, and ended up being sacked from the one position he'd managed to procure.

It had been a legal clerkship in the city of Ipswich that had lasted but a few disappointing months. He'd worked for a lawyer who said his skill with letters was fine, but that he was stubborn and self-righteous, and that his sermonizing drove away clients—criticisms that stung to this day. Swallowing, he pushed the memory back into one of the dusty cracks of his mind. *Faith.*

The wooden door creaked on its hinges and an old man entered. With him he brought the first drops of rain from an iron sky.

"Sir Grimston," said Hopkins, stepping forward and bowing. "Greetings."

Sir Harbottle Grimston was the kind of man for whom the best room would be reserved. He was a landowner and a Member of Parliament, and he'd taken a mentor role with Hopkins. "Nasty weather," Grimston said, shaking off his fine wool coat. He had a beefy constitution which made him seem younger than his seventy-some years. He also never hesitated to denounce the evils of the world, which he did when he learned there was no breakfast to be had.

"I have already admonished the cook," said Hopkins, nervous of being ill-judged.

"Hmmph," said Grimston. "Sit, my friend. There's been an incident at Lawford. Something wicked is afoot."

A tiny thrill ran through Hopkins. He knew well the voices on his Friday nights. "Good sir, tell me."

Grimston sat down and hoisted his foot onto a stool. "The

gout is returning," he grumped.

Hopkins tried to wait with patience.

While Grimston re-adjusted his posture and the tie around his neck, and ordered the cook to fry eggs, Hopkins could wait no longer. "Please, sir. What incident in Lawford?"

Grimston pursed his lips. "A goodwife, who was with child, collapsed during the church service. She then birthed a stillborn babe . . . I'm loathe to say it . . . but the babe was deformed. It was witchcraft, no doubt."

Hopkins leaned in closer. *Witchcraft*. A vision of blazing pyres and cloven feet quivered in his mind's eye. He had met witches before. "Who has done this against an honest man's wife?"

"There have been many years of troubles in Lawford," said Grimston. "Murders, unexplained illness . . . and of course last year, the good Richard Edwards was cursed! He lost several livestock and then his own son fell dead in a fit."

Hopkins remembered. If witches had the nerve to curse an established gentleman, what was next?

Grimston continued. "There are repeat offenders," he said. "Like old Elizabeth Clarke, that beggar and widow of a scoundrel. Once, she made the sign of the evil eye at me when I refused to give her coinage." He shuddered. "With this war on, we cannot find justice in the courts. No one in London cares about witchcraft afflicting us here. 'Tis our duty to maintain the rule of law ourselves. Hopkins, with your background in jurisprudence, I would have your help in this matter."

Enthralled with the idea of prosecuting witches, Hopkins nodded, perhaps too fast. "I am your servant."

"What do you know of laws and techniques? I must have experts here, mind you. The matter is too grave for amateurs."

Hopkins was no amateur. He believed in knowing one's enemy and was better-read on the subject of witchcraft than anyone he knew. "But of course," he said. "I have made a study of the laws and procedures of witchcraft trials."

At Grimston's impressed nod, Hopkins told his mentor how witches' lies might be unraveled by depriving them of food and rest for several days. Godly women could endure such hardships, while witches would confess. Hopkins lowered his voice, arriving at the most interesting tests. "Physical proofs include unnatural marks, protrusions, and teats on the body—evidence of the imps that suckle their blood for nourishment. Test them by pricking with a needle or a sharpened bodkin. If it does not bleed, it is proof." Hopkins licked his lips. "Often these witch's teats are found near her privy parts, for demonic copulation is part of the pact." An image flickered through his mind of a woman with a red-eyed animal suckling between her legs. It caused an uncomfortable rush of blood through his body.

Grimston was likewise appalled and shifted in his seat. "Indeed, a pious woman would have no cause for the unusual on her body, which is created by God."

"And there is the way advocated by King James, which is the swimming. If she floats, she is light on morals indeed, and rejects her baptism."

Grimston slapped his knee. "I'm convinced, my boy. There is none better than you to help me." He stood up. "Ride with me to Manningtree later this week. There is someone you must meet, another godly man who is willing to be a witch-finder. I shall introduce you."

After Sir Harbottle Grimston had eaten his breakfast and taken his leave, Hopkins's heart fluttered in his chest. This could be his calling. His *cure*.

He quit the Thorn Inn for his nearby cottage and flung open the door, taking two long strides to the bookshelf. He pulled a favorite out of its place. Penned by King James I himself, it was a guide to the work of the Devil in England: *Daemonologie*, it was called, and within it was the key to hunting witches. He could smell his destiny in the book's instruction.

He sank into a chair and sighed relief. There was an explanation for his suffering. On Fridays—according to his texts, the day of the witches' unholy sabbat, their orgy with demons, the day of their malefic workings—he had heard their whispers. The strange urges that passed through his mind, the nameless deeds that he was compelled to perform . . . this report of witchcraft meant there was nothing wrong with him. It wasn't his fault. No, it meant he had a gift for detecting witches.

His fingers brushed the rough edges of *Daemonologie*. The book told of something called the Devil's Register, a list of all the witches in Christendom. When they became witches, they signed the list, giving their souls over to Satan.

He knew of at least one woman whose name was on that Register. Long to Hell she may have been, but her sisters still haunted him.

If he discovered something so evil, and brought it into the waiting arms of justice, perhaps he could begin to pay off the debt on his soul, inflicted by the weight of his unlawful parentage. Perhaps the urges would stop. *Father, I will prove I am your son, equal to the others,* he prayed . . . not to the Lord, but to his dead human father.

He coughed. He would attend church. Then he would be ready.

THREE GIRLS SPIRITED through a wood at dawn. Their pace down this familiar pathway was sometimes leisurely, meandering; other days, like today, it was with strong purpose. This was in part because of the morning chill. It was the beginning of February, in the Christian year of 1645, and the ground was frozen from a long winter. The thaw, the girls hoped, would begin soon.

There was no color to be found amongst the bare branches

and frosted floor. The girls' dresses and cloaks were dark, plain wool, although one of them had a delicate white lace collar. Their hoods were pulled tightly over their linen head caps. Sturdy shoes protected their feet. They did not speak until deep in the forest, because even at this early morning hour, someone might overhear them.

"Almost there," said Philippa, known to her friends as Pippa. Her hazel eyes seemed to kindle with excitement. Her grin was wide and unrestrained.

Sybil, whose blond hair escaped in wisps from under her cap, giggled. She skipped through the trees rather than walked, always a little off the path from the others.

Alice, the third, gave a bashful smile to Pippa, blinked with gentle brown eyes, and clutched a small clay jug close to her chest.

Past a brook, around the trunk of a wizened warty oak, and through a cluster of boulders, they reached their destination: a small grove of apple trees with a slight depression in the center. Here the ground was charred from fires previous. "We must call the spring," said Pippa. This outing had been her idea.

"Ash Wednesday today and the feast of St. Bride, for the unreformed," said Sybil, her voice angelic like her pale gold hair.

"Maybe this year we shall be brides," said Alice.

"Not if we don't light the fire." Pippa produced a small sachet from under her winter cloak. "This be all we need, if Alice brought the milk."

Alice nodded and held up the clay jug. "I had to milk the cow meself," she said.

Sybil shuddered. She was afraid of cows.

"'Twasn't terrible," said Alice. "But I feared it would make a noise. Me father will wonder who done Daisy so early today."

Pippa winked. "We need twigs. Oh, Sybil, you've already started!"

Sybil had wandered off into the trees, bending every so often to choose a thin stick of fallen wood. She hummed to herself, a song on the chilly wind. The other two followed. Pippa stripped off her mittens and chose the best and driest pieces to begin their fire. Glancing up at the sky, she saw heavy clouds closing in, and nodded her head in satisfaction. Tradition held that bad weather now would mean an early spring.

Firewood gathered, the girls built a pyramid of sticks on their usual spot. Always the fire-starter, Pippa struck a flint, and a bright spark danced and caught on the dry moss inside. A tender lick of flame took hold of a piece of kindling. From there it spread, growing in strength, until it was time to place larger pieces on top. The golden glow was like a splash of sunshine in the grey forest. The girls smiled at their accomplishment.

Pippa then brought out a handful of herbs from her sachet, preserved over the winter: dried primrose and poppy seeds. "All of us," she directed, holding out pinches for the girls to take. They tossed them into the fire and watched as they were consumed, crackling.

Alice uncorked the jug of milk. "Ready," she said.

They joined hands and walked around the fire in a deosil circle, the same direction as the hands of a clock. Pippa began to chant a made-up rhyme. "Men, sin, kin, din, win. Baby, lady, baby, fate-y." The others joined, singing.

"Milk for the earth," Alice said, and tipped the jug forward. A white, foamy stream fell to the ground, following the circle they carved with their feet. Tiny wisps of steam came off the milk, still lukewarm from the cow.

"Take our offering, Lady of the Forest," said Pippa. "Great Lady, fair Maiden, we implore you. Send us husbands this year!"

Alice glanced upward. "Lady Mary, mother of Jesus, hear us."

"Winter goes to sleep," sang Sybil. "Spring, ring, thing,

wing."

They danced their circle. Pippa laughed and threw her linen cap to the ground, releasing a tumbled mass of wavy dark hair. Faster and faster they circled the fire until they were dizzy, laughing, and gasping with breath fogging around them.

"Look into the fire," Sybil pointed, "and see their faces!"

"Whose?" asked Alice.

"Our husbands," said Sybil with a firm nod. Her pale eyes lost their focus as she stared. Sybil saw things that others did not.

"What do you see?" Pippa giggled.

"A dark man," said Sybil.

Pippa raised an eyebrow. Their neighbor Thomas Radcliff had dark hair, but he was away.

A tiny crease appeared between Sybil's eyes. "He has a hat, and a cape, and boots," she said. "He has a dog? He looks... oh, I've lost it." A breathless laugh escaped her.

"Dance for the spring!" Pippa declared, throwing her arms in the air and twirling around.

"Look, look," Sybil exclaimed. She pointed at the earth.

A small bright green snake had emerged from beneath a slushy pile of mud and leaves. It slithered toward the fire, perhaps drawn by the warmth or the vibrations of the girls' feet. Alice stepped back. She was gentle, afraid of snakes and spiders.

Pippa reached impulsively for the creature, but it was gone before she could touch it. "Spring is upon us!"

Then came the downpour of bad weather. The girls shrieked as sleet pelted their heads, and their ritual fire was extinguished behind them as they hurried home.

Mid-week, on the day that the extravagant Catholics would have begun their Lenten fast, Matthew Hopkins rode with Sir Harbottle Grimston the short distance to Manningtree. His dog Elspeth ran at the heels of the horses. Hopkins was eager to meet the other man who shared his knowledge about the plague of witchcraft. When they were almost to the town, they spotted another figure coming from the other direction. Grimston raised a hand in greeting. "That's him," he said.

The horses drew to a halt beneath the spiraling hulk of a diseased chestnut. Its drooping branches made Hopkins nervous. The tree looked like it was melting and it had spots on its bark. On the trunk, someone had carved a rune-like symbol. *Witches,* Hopkins thought, and the side of his face tingled. They were everywhere.

The other man hopped off his palfrey. He was of small stature, with excitable hands and eyes that burned. "John Stearne," he said.

"Stearne, meet Matthew Hopkins," said Grimston. "He knows much of identifying witches. He has read the *Malleus Maleficarum,* have you not, Hopkins?"

Hopkins nodded. Along with *Daemonologie,* the *Malleus Maleficarum*—the "Witch's Hammer"—was a text that had been used for hundreds of years to prosecute the crime on the Continent. It had been written by two monks who, Hopkins figured, must know what they were dealing with.

"There's a rot here in Manningtree," said Stearne. "We'll cut it out, by God's will."

"By God's will," Hopkins agreed. He could see that Stearne believed as he did. "We will need Christian women as searchers, so we don't contaminate our own souls by searching for the imps' suckling marks on the bodies of fallen women."

Stearne bared his teeth. "Indeed."

"With so much happening, the King, the armies on the move . . . we cannot afford these troubles," said Grimston. "It is as you say, John. Witchcraft is a disease that has infected us. It explains the plagues, the violence, the odd signs in the skies. These times have driven the people into the arms of Satan."

"Let us begin with the Widow Clarke," said Stearne. "She has harassed her neighbors for too long. We shall put her in her place."

Hopkins was hungry to find the fallen women. If he could discover them . . . if he could *destroy* them . . . their *black-bear-evil* thoughts would cease tormenting him. He could find God's peace. He smiled at his mentor and at John Stearne. Their presence told him he was doing the right thing.

PHILIPPA WYLDE SAT IN CHURCH, fidgeting. She couldn't help herself. Sermons made her restless, the wool of her dress made her skin itch, and the square bonnet pinned atop her head was not sturdy enough to contain her mass of hair. She tapped her shoes on the floor in a drumbeat pattern, earning a glare from Mrs. Radcliff several rows ahead. She sent a vicious grin and continued tapping her feet softly, gently, on the hardwood floor.

Beside Pippa sat her mother, Elizabeth, whose hearing was not good enough to notice the noise of her shoes. Lillibet, as Pippa called her, was fifty-four years old and what she lacked in hearing, she made up with gimlet eyes.

From the pulpit, the voice of the Reverend Peter Yates sailed through the rafters of the church. He was a soft-spoken man in daily life and had to project his voice with intent. As a result his tone was inconsistent. In Pippa's opinion this fit with what he preached, logical inconsistency. She was not old enough to remember the time before Puritan ways had taken hold in East Anglia, but her mother was. Church had not always been so strict.

There was, however, just one parish church for the forty or so families who lived in and around the country hamlet they called the Vale, so they had no choice but to attend.

Pippa's gaze wandered along the pews. She picked out the

important people. Near the front was her friend Sybil Yates, the Reverend's daughter, and Sybil's elder sisters. All were fair, but the other two had none of Sybil's odd, effervescent manner. Their mother had died in childbirth with Sybil, leaving their father to raise them with the help of a house-woman.

Pippa could sympathize. She'd been three years old when her father had died of heart failure after riding on a hot summer day. Lillibet, already almost forty years old at the time, had been left to raise her alone.

Pippa didn't usually miss the father she'd never known. Lillibet was her idol, often more of a mentor than a mother, and Pippa wanted nothing more than to be just like her someday.

On the other side of the aisle from Sybil sat the Radcliff family. They had a daughter about Pippa's age, named Winifred, but they were a wealthy merchant family, reserved and snobbish, and kept to themselves. She didn't envy their seats in the front pew, however. The Reverend had a tendency to spit when he said words like penitence, punishment, and propriety.

Winifred rubbed her eye after the Reverend said "com*punc*tion." Pippa held back her giggles.

"There be no reason for feast nor fast," Yates was saying. "In God's eyes are all days equal, and so there be worship on all days, and on all days do we glorify God and His Son . . ."

Pippa was distracted as Lillibet knotted and unknotted an embroidered handkerchief, marred by a few small stains. The hands, too, were knotted and stained with age spots. Many times Pippa had admired their skill when gutting a river fish, or chopping herbs, or knitting.

In the row at a diagonal to her sat Alice Baxter with her parents and four younger siblings. Alice did not notice Pippa. She was too busy wiping the nose of her eight-year-old brother with a cloth, and then nudging her sister to pay attention to the sermon.

"And so God sayeth to Job . . ."

Pippa turned forward again and peeked at the well-formed head of Hugh Felton. The view of him was blocked by old Widow Moore and the exuberant rolls of her chin. How disappointing. Church was the only time Pippa was guaranteed to see Hugh. Her heart and body ached for the man who had been her childhood friend . . . but he sat at the front, with his family, and she sat toward the back, only a few rows ahead of the beggars. Pippa turned her eyes away from Hugh, her most desperate dream, and willed the service to be over. Her feet continued to tap. Her thoughts continued to wander. She had too much energy to be contained in the long day of services.

At last, people were standing up. Pippa was poked by her mother.

"Work to be done," said Lillibet.

"That chicken," Pippa remembered with a low groan. They'd had a bounty that week, a chicken in payment for a willow bark tea that Lillibet had made for Lady Felton, who suffered headaches. The chicken was meant as a Sunday roast and it was Pippa's job to kill it and then pluck it. She did look forward to the meat, though. Sustenance in the Widow Wylde's house was often in the form of less expensive eggs, milk, nuts, or tripe.

Outside the plain wooden church, the villagers gathered to chat, the most sociable time of the week. Lillibet spoke in a low voice to newly-married Margaret Howell. She could be overheard to say, "If ye rock the cradle empty, ye will have babies plenty . . ." Lillibet was the only bishop-licensed midwife in this fold of countryside. It often ran through the maternal line . . . along with Lillibet's other calling.

They were known as cunning-folk, and it meant that witchery was in their blood.

Pippa inched away from her mother, unnoticed, and joined up with Alice and Sybil.

"I h-h-h-hear you have a chicken f-from the Feltons," said

Alice. She had a stutter, except when she was in the woods with her friends. Alice almost never spoke to anyone else. Even now her body was turned inward, shying away from her neighbors who might tease or judge.

"Mmm," said Pippa with a smirk.

"Is it up to you to pluck it?" asked Sybil.

"Mmm."

"Cannot be shy with chickens," said Sybil.

"Or F-F-Feltons," said Alice, laughing.

"I don't know what you mean!" Pippa laughed too, secretly pleased that her friends had reason to tease her about Hugh's family. "But you must be excited, Sybil. I heard something about a letter from the Americas. Your father?"

"Yes, he's begun correspondence with one of the ministers from the Plymouth Colony. Sometimes I wonder if he would move there himself, were it not for my sisters and our home here."

"How th-thrilling!" said Alice, clasping her hands. "Such a n-n-new place. It must be f-f-frightening there."

"I hear there are savages," said Pippa, "who run naked through the forest."

"Shhh!" Alice admonished her.

"Did I hear something about savages?" Hugh Felton approached. He tipped his buckled hat at them. Its brim created a deep shadow on his face, but the light still reflected from his bright blue eyes.

"The Americas," said Pippa.

"My father soon anticipates the company of a minister from the Massachusetts Bay colony," said Hugh. "I hear he's returned to convince others to join them. He would tell us the truth about savages, naked or otherwise."

Pippa blushed to hear him say the word "naked." It set her mind off into places that were indecent for a seventeen-year-old virgin girl. "I do not know anyone from the New World."

"He'll be at the textile market at Lavenham," said Hugh. "We're going with the Radcliffs this week. Winifred is always good company. Ah, my mother is gesturing at me. A good day to you all." He tipped his hat once more, lingering an instant longer on Pippa.

As soon as Hugh stepped away, another girl intercepted him: Elizabeth Yates, Sybil's oldest sister. Elizabeth gazed up at Hugh, and there was a voracious gleam in her pale eyes. Pippa noticed how fresh and white Elizabeth's expensive collar was in comparison to her own. It made Elizabeth's skin look clearer than it was. Hugh complimented her; Pippa could tell by the way she blushed.

Many villagers said that Hugh was courting Elizabeth. Some—like Goody Brewer, that old gossip—said that he'd made her an offer of marriage.

Looking wistfully after Hugh, Pippa wished that she, too, had a reason to go to Lavenham. All she could think of was that they were almost out of poppy seeds for the pantry. Lillibet would be proud of her for thinking ahead, but it was not enough of an errand to take the full day at the market. Besides, she didn't want to run after Hugh. He might tire of her if he saw her every day. "We do need poppy seeds, though," she murmured to herself.

"Shall we make cakes?" Sybil suggested. "With the seeds?"

"That wasn't my purpose," said Pippa, startled at how Sybil paid so much attention. She noticed that Elizabeth was walking away from Hugh, her skirts swaying around her ankles, and he was watching. Sighing and turning away, Pippa explained, "Sugar is far too expensive to waste on a cake!"

"Oh." Sybil did not keep track of prices on things, or numbers of any sort. "Whatever you do with poppy seeds, will you teach us?"

"I'll ask Lillibet," said Pippa.

The girls fell quiet when old Joan Buckett and her daughter Anne passed by. Joan held her wooden charity cup with a claw-like hand. It was a Sunday and thus people were made uncomfortable whether they gave Joan a spare coin or not. Sybil moved to give her a penny, but recoiled when Joan Buckett leered at them. Anne waved, then spat into her hand with a half-cackle, half-cough.

The girls edged away. Alice whispered, "Sh-sh-she scares me!"

"That's only because she used to shake her stick at us when we were little," Pippa said, but she still craved a safe distance. When the threat had passed, no one dared look back for fear old Joan would speak to them, or perhaps whisper a hex to steal their youth and beauty.

PIPPA SAT UNDER THE SHADE of an ancient yew tree, scrubbing out a cauldron. The ground beneath the yew was dead ground because of its poison. Lillibet adored the tree, not least because it kept her from weeding that section of yard. Pippa liked the tree too, because in all her years it had never changed, nor would it change for centuries more. The yew tree was immortal.

The snake at their secret fire festival had been wise to come out of hibernation. Winter was done and it was now late March. On the small grassy knoll next to Lillibet and Pippa's cottage, bright yellow daffodils clustered, their heads tipped towards each other in joyful conspiracy to keep growing.

Their property was set apart from the rest of the village as though hiding from its neighbors, its door turned to the northeast instead of a cardinal direction, and its roof beginning to sag at the beams. There were three small windows set in the rough stone—one for each wall but one. The door was plain wood and on the lintel above it, scratched marks could be seen along with a dried bunch of vervain herb: sigils of protection.

The yard was fenced with wood planks. It kept the large

creatures like chickens, geese, goats, and pigs in or out, although rabbits still molested the lettuce in the garden. Pippa had suggested that they acquire a dog to protect the beds, but her mother had said, "Having pets don't look right." Perhaps a stone fence one of these years—it would be more permanent, *and* keep the rabbits out.

The property was called Wylde-Wood Cottage by the folk, for it had belonged to Lillibet's family, named Wood. Lillibet had been their only child and when she married John Wylde, the property had passed to him.

Pippa's father had been a prosperous yeoman, a free landholder with farms and tenants. His life had been the only thing to hold up the finances of his wife and daughter. When Wylde died, everything changed. They'd moved out of their stone farmhouse and into Lillibet's old family cottage. By arrangement, all of Wylde's land had gone to his neighbor Sir John Felton, including Wylde-Wood Cottage.

Sir John was kind and refused rent from his friend's widow, but it irked Pippa to be beholden to such charity from Hugh's father. It reinforced their inferior position, but there was nothing she could do about it, and she had to be grateful.

A break in the skittish clouds sent a tentative beam of sunlight to the rise of farmland opposite the Vale. A team of oxen could be seen pulling a plow. That field belonged to Sir John, like so much of the land in and around the village.

Pippa paused her work to wave goodbye to the Goodwife Brewer, their nearest neighbor, who emerged from the cottage after a consultation with Lillibet. Goody Brewer sneezed into one hand and clutched a handful of chamomile flowers with the other.

After the cauldron was clean and set upside-down to dry, Pippa went inside and climbed the ladder to the loft, her tiny cave of a bedroom, and took off her work apron. She owned three frocks: a best one of thin black wool for church and special occasions, a house dress of blue wool, and her work garment of brown linen. Likewise she had three collars: white linen edged with lace to go with her best frock, and two square beige collars that were admirably humble.

Back outside, she found Lillibet preparing to leave.

"I'm off to deliver these," said Lillibet, waving a cloth sack full of clay jars at Pippa. They were filled with potions and tinctures. "Stay out of trouble, and work on those bottles." She gestured at a pile of rustic pottery in the yard, jars of varying sizes and shapes, sorted by function. The folk called them witch-bottles, for the ingredients of spells would go inside, and it would be Pippa's job to paint the symbols on the outside. Happy to be trusted with the task, she nodded and grinned.

When Lillibet was out the gate, Pippa pinned on her apron once more and dragged the rocking chair outside. The vernal air was sweet in her lungs and she drank it in. Using a brush and a bowl of homemade ink of blackberry and toad's blood, she settled a large bottle on her lap and began to draw the horned face of the Devil. One swipe for his brow, another for his curved mouth, two more for the horns . . . then feathered strokes for his whiskers. This bottle was to protect against Satan's influence. It would be filled with nails and thorns to bind him and then buried in a hearth or chimney. It was a well-known magical technique: when the Devil saw his face reflected back at him, he would go elsewhere. This bottle was for one of Felton's new tenants.

She had moved on to a similar witch-bottle when she heard distant thunder across the hills. "Hmm," she said, wondering if there would be an early storm.

Then, it was thunder in the yard, stamping feet and huffing breath: eight-year-old George Pye, one of Farmer Pye's sons. "Pippa! Where's Lillibet! We need help!"

"What's the matter?" She jumped up, spilling the crimson ink onto the dirt. Hannah Pye, the mother, had just given birth to a girl, and Lillibet had delivered her. What if there was something wrong with the babe?

But it wasn't the infant. "Me twin, Francis," gasped George. "He been bewitched. Where's Lillibet?"

A twin-pronged jolt of fear and excitement coursed through Pippa. Bewitching! She'd never seen it directly, and had only made charms for general defense against it. Taking a deep breath and trying to act like Lillibet, she was calm with George and asked him to tell her the problem.

It seemed that Francis had been about his usual chores that morning when he began to convulse. He'd dropped the plate he'd been washing and it had shattered on the floor. His eyes had rolled back into his head, and his teeth had clattered so hard that he'd bitten off a tiny piece of his own tongue.

"God Almighty preserve us," said Pippa. The prayer was real, but at the same time she was overcome with desire to solve the problem herself. She'd never been allowed, but Lillibet was gone . . . Pippa thought she knew how to break a hex. Once, Lillibet had explained the process, and she had mostly paid attention. She could prove herself now.

The same thing must have occurred to George. He glanced over the bottles and the symbols that Pippa had been drawing. "Wait . . . wait, Pippa, you're cunning, are you not? Can you come?"

Pippa snapped to a decision. "Yes! I'll fix it for you! Wait here."

George waited in the yard while Pippa dashed inside the cottage and dragged an iron horseshoe out from under Lillibet's bed. She changed from her brown, muddy work clothes into her blue house dress.

"Come," she said, seizing George's hand and latching the gate behind her. "Let us make haste."

The walk up to Pye's farm was a long one and Pippa and George both were breathing hard by the time they reached it.

"Goody Pye," Pippa dipped to Hannah Pye.

"Oh, Heavenly Father, what has come upon this house!" Goody Pye ushered her in. "What can be done?"

The scene that greeted Pippa was normal in the physical realm. Neat rows of pots and pans. A clean-swept wood floor. The newborn babe rested in a cradle next to a rocking chair. A teapot of water simmered over the fire, almost ready to hiss. A brass lantern clock adorned the mantle, and the hands told the hour: almost three o'clock in the afternoon.

"They say that Jesus rose at three o'clock," said Goody Pye, nodding to the time.

It was thus the best hour to neutralize ill will.

"He's upstairs," George whispered.

Pippa was led up the steep staircase to the loft-like space where the twins slept. Francis was laid out on a mattress with a wool blanket up to his armpits.

"Hello, Francis Pye," she said. "You know me. Pippa Wylde."

"Hello," Francis whispered.

"Now," she said, kneeling on the floor next to him. "Let's see what's the matter with you."

With firm hands, she felt his chest and his heartbeat, and dipped her ear to listen to his breathing. All seemed well. But then . . . she looked into his eyes. "Hmm!" she said.

The pupils of Francis's blue eyes were larger than usual. It was as though he was seeing a darkness that was not there. It was a sure sign of bewitchment.

Goody Pye, at the door, said, "Oh, Heaven help us, and God be with us, and . . ."

"I will remove the curse," said Pippa.

Goody Pye looked ready to kiss her.

And then, Pippa was at a loss. She couldn't remember what happened next. She tried to recall Lillibet's precise technique. Gulping, she closed her eyes, feeling Hannah's eyes upon her.

What if she failed? "Er," she said. "Um . . . I must . . . the horseshoe! We . . . um . . ."

Goody Pye stared at her.

She could hear Lillibet's admonition in her head: "*If you do magic without confidence, it will not work.*"

"Right," said Pippa. "I need a pot, large enough to hold this," she said, holding up the horseshoe. "Take a lock of Francis's hair, and he must piss into the pot. We boil it away, and the hex will be removed."

Goody Pye nodded. "George, bring a pot for your brother."

Meanwhile Pippa stoked the fire downstairs and moved the teapot out of the way. Into a small iron cauldron went the horseshoe, the urine—an impressive amount for a small boy—and it was set to boil.

They waited.

The sharp scent of the urine filled the room. "Open the window," Pippa said, remembering more. "If a person or a stranger is drawn to this, they're the culprit."

When the urine was good and boiling, Pippa tossed the lock of Francis's hair into the mix. All was quiet for a few tense minutes and Pippa began to wonder if there was a more mundane cause for Francis's fit. She was also nervous that Lillibet would find out what she was doing, march up here, and scold her in front of their client.

There was a knock on the front door and both women and George jumped at the sound. Pippa drew a deep breath before nodding to Goody Pye to open the door.

"I be selling eggs," came the hoarse voice.

"We need no eggs," said Goody Pye shakily. With a hand she waved at Pippa to come over.

"Anne Buckett!" exclaimed Pippa. Speaking her name was to control her power of malice. "Get yourself elsewhere. You may not come here again."

"Who be you, perky girl, to tell me what to do?"

"Leave!" said Goody Pye shakily, pointing at the cattle road that led to the house.

Anne lingered and waved the eggs at them. Her stringy hair hung about her face, already lined with hardship at the age of thirty, and there was a blemish on the corner of her mouth. Her father, the wretched husband of Joan Buckett, had abandoned them and then died of consumption. They had no power to earn their living but from begging, petty thievery, and the occasional selling of eggs or milk.

It was not until Francis's urine had completely boiled away that Anne Buckett ceased her pacing outside, quieted her pleas for them to buy eggs, and headed down the road. It was obvious that Anne's ill intent had been toward Francis. Pippa left the Pyes' with the satisfaction that the hex had been lifted, and also with a shilling in her pocket as payment from a grateful Goody Pye. The threat of thunder had drawn closer; from the southwest, a storm front approached the Vale.

When Lillibet returned at sunset, Pippa decided to tell her straight away about Francis Pye. Her mother had an uncanny way of finding things out, so it was best to be honest with her. "I did something you'll be proud of!" Pippa said, taking Lillibet's shawl from her shoulders.

"Oh?" said Lillibet, her mouth curving into a smile.

Perhaps she already knew.

Pippa plunged into the story. "He was bewitched, young Francis Pye! And I did just as you said that one time, I brought the iron horseshoe, and boiled his urine, and discovered it was Anne Buckett! She brought a hex on him. Who knows why, I imagine the boys were harassing her, but . . ." she trailed off at the look on Lillibet's face.

The smile had faded, replaced by a crinkle of consternation. "Oh, Pippa. I hope you did not charge her for it."

"Well, she was so relieved, Goody Pye was. She paid me a shilling! Is that not what we do?"

"Did Francis have spasms, with darkened eyes?"

"Yes . . ."

Lillibet sighed and eased herself onto her chair. "Start the fire, me bones ache. And you're to return that shilling to Goody Pye."

Pippa couldn't understand what she'd done wrong. Swallowing a sudden urge to cry, she was silent as she gathered up the kindling and struck the flint.

"Pippa," said Lillibet, taking her by the chin and looking into her eyes, "that curse has been with the Pye family since their grandparents' generation. You broke no hex by Anne Buckett, for Francis's grandfather had the same affliction, long before the Bucketts lived in the Vale. I've done all I could for the family in me day, but it seems to be in their blood. You cannot accept payment for what you did not do."

"But Lillibet, it was so obvious! Anne came round just at the time the mixture boiled, and seemed unable to leave until it was finished . . ."

Lillibet shook her head. "A chance event."

"You say there's no such thing as chance."

Aged, wise lips pressed together. "Did you believe you broke the hex?"

"Yes!" Pippa cried.

"Well, perhaps it will give Goody Pye some relief, to believe the same thing. But if Anne Buckett is innocent, 'tis not right to put this thing on her. You must return the coin and tell them that the service was free of charge, if they will remember our kindness someday in return."

"But —"

"No arguing. Pippa, you should have come to me, not gone crashing around yourself, without any knowledge of curses or the history of the family!"

"I'm sorry," Pippa muttered. How was she supposed to become cunning if Lillibet wouldn't teach her? And how would she convince Lillibet to teach her, unless she could somehow prove herself? Scowling, Pippa chopped turnip greens for their stew, attacking the vegetables with firm, angry slices of the knife.

The Green Man

The next day, Pippa was over her sulk and she knelt at her mother's feet, hoping for instruction. "What today, Lillibet?"

"Tincture of St. John's Wort," she said.

"For?"

"Edmund Renshaw."

Pippa raised her eyebrows. Edmund Renshaw was in middle age and owned the village inn and public house. He had a wife and a grown son, Will. St. John's Wort was taken by men to re-ignite passion . . . why did Renshaw need it?

"I know what goes through your head," Lillibet warned. "'Tis not our place to judge."

"Did I say anything?" Pippa asked, but she still smiled to herself as she brought out the alcohol and stoked the fire.

Midday, Pippa was delivering the tincture to Goodman Renshaw when she saw a small parade down the Vale's only proper road. She picked out Hugh Felton right away, admiring how well he rode a horse. Accompanying him were his father and brother, and the Radcliff girls on a wagon. She remembered

Hugh saying that they were going to the Lavenham market.

"Good morning," said Hugh, tipping his hat, courteous as always.

"May God bless your journey," Pippa said to the whole party, eyes still lingering on Hugh's expert seat.

The Radcliff girls ignored her. They'd never liked Pippa, and she'd never liked them.

The wagon and horses rounded the bend. Pushing away the image of Winifred—who would be spending the day with Hugh, she with her pearl cuffs and gleaming chestnut hair—Pippa turned toward the pub.

She paused at the wooden carved sign that hung above the door. The Green Man, it said, and his innocent, leaf-lined face was a familiar friend to her: round eyes and a broad smile, childlike yet knowing. Years of weathering had washed away most of the paint on the sign, but the essence of his oak leaf headdress remained. To Pippa, he was more of a living divinity than the cross that adorned the top of the church.

Giving him a tiny wink, she walked through the open door.

The pub's interior was almost as old as the Vale itself. The inn was the first building in the village from the days when this was a better-used thoroughfare between Lavenham and Bury St. Edmunds. The inn had been followed by cottages and farms and a tiny roundabout with a maypole.

The white-washed church was the most recent construction. Before the Reformation and the strict theology that accompanied it, the people of this area had walked to nearby Brettenham for services. But then Calvinist doctrine had spread through the land and the plain undecorated church had been built. There had once been a grove of very old yew trees there, but they had been chopped down to make way for the church building.

Aside from new velvet curtains in the Green Man, little had changed in a hundred years. The floor was packed dirt.

The windows were thin stretched vellum. There was a carved oak bar, barrels of ale and bottles of wine, several rustic stools and benches and tables, and a fireplace made of fired bricks. Candle wax had dripped into fantastical shapes on the mantle and inside the sooty lamps. At this early morning hour, there was only one patron inside, Old Man Ashley. He was a drunk with one leg, but he'd been in the wars.

"Mr. Renshaw?" Pippa called out.

"Pippa?" Goodwife Renshaw emerged, wiping her hands on her greying apron.

"From me mother," said Pippa. She showed Mrs. Renshaw the small clay vial containing the tincture.

"Hmm!" said Mrs. Renshaw, taking the vial and peering at it.

Did she even know about her husband's problem?

Mr. Renshaw walked in the door with a straw broom in his hand. "Ah, my thanks." He fished in his pockets and produced ten pence, the fee for a strong tincture. "For strength," he told his wife.

Well, Pippa thought, *that was one way of putting it.*

She sat down next to Old Man Ashley, who peered at her with his one good eye. The other eye had a cataract.

"Hello, Ash," she said.

"Pips," he said, raising his cup. "Can ye bring me any news?"

"The Feltons are visiting the market at Lavenham today."

"Not that kind of news, ye silly gilly." He swatted at her. "News of the armies! Of the King! Of Cromwell, may God protect 'im."

"Oh. I know not." Pippa knew there was a civil war raging in England between King and Parliament, but it didn't concern her as long as the battles were far away.

"Bah! What use are women?" Ashley took another gulp of ale. "I tell ye, Pips. That King'll march 'is army straight down this way. His eye's on these counties."

"Would the King fight for the Vale?"

"Bah! No! But Cambridge, or Bury, or Ipswich 'e'll damned well fight for."

"Your language, Ashley!" Goodwife Renshaw bustled out of the kitchen. "Girl, you'd better get on home. Listen no more to this wicked old dog, he's a bad influence on your ears."

Before Pippa had a chance to take her leave, the door behind her creaked open and she swiveled to see the silhouette of Reverend Yates. "I have heard," the Reverend announced, "that there have been cases of witchcraft abroad. In Essex."

"Witchcraft!" Mr. Renshaw's voice cracked with fear.

A thrill of alarm made Pippa's hands tremble. *Witchcraft*! She had a sudden vision of herself, weaving spells of protection with smoke and flame against a horde of oncoming black witches, protecting those she loved . . . her friends, Hugh . . . her mother praising her skill . . . in one hand was an open Bible as she read aloud the verses Jesus used against the demon legions, in her other hand was a torch of cedar wood, wrapped with holly berries and oil-soaked cloth . . . the witches fell back, screaming, and she was triumphant. Pippa snapped out of her reverie as the Reverend spoke again.

"I've brought pamphlets for distribution. Terrible, and in these uncertain times . . . the moral laxity of the people must be prevented."

"Couldn't agree more!" Old Man Ashley chimed in. The Reverend gave him a sideways look.

"I was deep in study this morning," said Reverend Yates, "reading the wisdom of the Old Testament. There are strident warnings against anything that reminds of idolatry, which after all leads to worship of ungodly things, and devilish things, and to consortium with Satan."

Pippa shifted in her seat.

"Indeed," said Mr. Renshaw. "Indeed."

"I was in prayer," Yates continued. "I began to contemplate the ways that we people of the Vale might improve our ways toward God. In dress, in manner, in thought . . . there are always areas that need purification."

"It reminds me of old Brewer's process," said Mr. Renshaw, "that makes his ale the best in this country. He strains the ale, you see? He uses cloth to—"

"Yes," said Yates, "but that's just ale. Our *souls* are at stake."

To Renshaw the innkeeper, there was little difference between ale and souls, and perchance the two were intertwined.

"You live here at the crossroads," said the Reverend. "Keep your eyes open for the doings of witchcraft. That part of Essex has long been troubled by it. We must make certain it doesn't infect us here." He glanced toward Ashley, slurping down the last of his ale.

"Here, now. Do you say that my inn is ungodly?" Mr. Renshaw asked. "That I be of lax morals for owning it?"

"No, no, my good man. Not at all. All I say is that we must take care not to attract thoughts or individuals who do not take their authority from the Bible. As they say, prevention is better than affliction."

The talk unsettled Pippa. With one hand she felt at the band of her petticoat. Tucked against her skin was a charm against evil influence. Alice and Sybil had identical ones. They'd made them together, writing nonsense rhymes on old paper to confuse bad spirits, and adding rosemary.

"Beware," said the Reverend in a high-handed tone as he set a stack of flyers on the bar. Pippa and Ash peered over one and she shuddered at the illustration: several ragged women surrounded by sneering imps, unnatural creatures with the bodies of animals and the faces of men. It said, "Trying of witches in Manningtree . . . by the gentlemen Stearne and Hopkins . . . witch-finders."

Pippa wanted to stay and discuss these new developments,

but Ashley had become preoccupied with his drink again, so she bade him good day and went home. There were always chores to do, like sweeping the yard, feeding the two hens, and picking wild comfrey that grew on the hill. Her mother was on a house visit to Margaret Howell and her unborn child.

Even in so small a village, there were always clients for the cunning-folk.

The Wylde women were exactly what the Reverend would call pagan, ungodly . . . a white witch was still a witch.

Sighing as she labored, Pippa wished that Lillibet would bring her along on her rounds. *She must let me do it someday,* Pippa thought. *I'm going to be a midwife just like her. And my cunning will show, just like hers.* Pippa made up the forest rituals, mimicking Lillibet, but deep down she knew it was just a girlish game.

When she was finished with her chores, she let her hair down and brushed it one hundred times with the fine-tooth comb that had belonged to her maternal grandmother. It was kept in the locked chest beneath her mother's bed, along with the other treasures of the house, except for their coins which were behind a loose stone in a random spot high up the northwest wall. Thieves always looked in and around fireplaces for hidden treasure. It would not have been very clever to keep their hard-earned shillings there.

The ashes from the morning's fire were in piles amid a few glowing coals. Pippa took the iron poker and began to draw idly in the grey remains: spirals, stars, and then the *other* symbols, sharp-edged and strong, the ones her mother had taught her, the ones that spelled out wisdom older than the trees.

THE INSTRUCTIONS WERE CLEAR in *Daemonologie* and the *Malleus Maleficarum* on how to identify a witch. An idea had occurred to Hopkins, inspired by *Daemonologie*, that if he could find the Devil's Register itself, the entire list, there would be no stopping him from bringing God's justice down on the witches. He would have their names. Already he was thinking, plotting, on how to find this demonic artifact.

He'd been more than happy to share his learned techniques with his new friend John Stearne. Their mutual benefactor Sir Harbottle Grimston was committed to purging his sphere of witchcraft and to this end, Hopkins and Stearne became a team. For the past several weeks they had scoured the countryside, the towns, the villages. Mutterings of suspicion had been drawn to the surface to be examined in the light of righteousness.

The yield had been surprising.

On a cold night in March, the men found themselves in old Widow Elizabeth Clarke's hovel. The room was chilly with a single window open to the elements. The noises of night-time could be heard on the other side of the wall. Hopkins waited, along with Stearne and their search-women, because Clarke was going to call her imps.

Imps. All witches had familiars, demons that appeared to be farm animals. Hopkins had some protection from the spirit world in the sleek form of Elspeth, but she was tied up outside the gate for fear she would make the imps too nervous to approach. Everyone was on edge. A low fire burned in the crooked fireplace and the crusted remnants of pottage soiled a tipped-over cauldron on the floor. Hopkins raised a lip in distaste. Cleanliness was the neighbor of godliness and Elizabeth Clarke was neither.

The old lady sat on a rickety wooden chair. She was one-legged, decrepit. Her eyes were bright as though glazed with illness and she kept licking her dry lips. Everything about her posture spoke of desperation, which was proof to Hopkins of her moral lassitude. Hopkins felt the fear of such creatures, fallen into the sin of which their sex predisposed them.

Suckle and touch me, bathe me, enslave me, said the voices. Hopkins blinked.

It was always women. The few cases of male witchcraft could almost always be traced to the original sin of a woman. Hopkins fought the twinge of the black desires that plagued him . . . those thoughts in the night of hot flesh and a long-haired woman, moving like a serpent above him. Of women using him, placing their clawed hands around his throat and holding him tight. Of women's whispers, carried on the wind of a Friday night. Of the many-eyed, many-legged things that lurked in forgotten corners of his mind.

"Shh," said Widow Clarke. "He be here, back from 'is work."

The silence in the room was so heavy it pressed on Hopkins's temples. He strained to hear the noise of imps. He suppressed the urge to cough.

Clarke gave a rasping laugh and rocked back and forth on her chair.

The motion made Hopkins want to slap her. Filthy old woman.

In that silent and stuffy room the watchers could hear their own breathing, the buzzing of their own thoughts, and then . . . a fluttering, a movement . . . jaws clenched tight as the *thing* approached the door.

"Sacke and Sugar," said Clarke. That was the imp's name. "Me blackie Sacke and Sugar, 'e'll rip ye apart."

The grass outside the widow's door rustled and Hopkins's heart pounded against his ribcage. The watchers peered into the moonlit yard and beheld "Sacke and Sugar."

It was a rabbit. The rabbit made leisurely hops and appeared interested in a discarded piece of rotten cabbage.

"That be 'im!" said Clarke, still rocking.

"The Devil takes many harmless disguises," whispered Hopkins, his eye still on the rabbit.

"Clarke has the teats, there's no doubt," said Mary Phillips, one of the search-women. "And now here is the imp."

"Proof is had," said Stearne.

And the Widow Clarke was arrested.

It was with triumph that Hopkins returned home alone in the night, skittish Elspeth at his side. The charges ran through his head. To name them gave him a sense of control over their horror. *Witchcraft. Satanic pact. Intercourse with the Devil and the suckling of his creatures on her body. Ill will against her neighbors and against holiness itself.*

In the feisty March winds, Hopkins shivered and coughed. There was something in the air that made him feel feverish. Elspeth's hackles were up. On the dark road, his feeble lantern cast an inadequate circle of light around him.

He spun around and was startled by his own shadow. The voice of caution spoke. To go against witches was to invite their attack. The witches had secret ways of communicating, Hopkins knew, else how could they coordinate their sabbat meetings? At this very moment they could be warning one another of his presence.

The fear began to press inward. "Come, Elspeth." He meant it to sound authoritative but it came out as a rasp. "Heel."

The dog whined and with her ears flat against her head, she slunk next to Hopkins. He thought he saw shapes moving behind the line of trees, black-and-white shapes like Sacke and Sugar. The imps of other witches could be following him. *Oh, dear Lord, preserve me*, he thought. The night had eyes, thousands of eyes, and without further regard for his dignity he bolted towards home.

He could not bear to look around his yard at the *blackie* shapes masquerading as bushes. The key was in his hand when he reached his front door. Elspeth barked and Hopkins's fingers shook—*open, open*, he prayed—and then he and Elspeth were inside. He slammed the door behind him, slid the iron bar across it, lit all the candles in his bedroom, and opened the Bible that lay on the table.

Murmuring a familiar verse, Hopkins began to calm down. Sweat tickled in his mustache and beard. He was doing the work of the Lord Jesus Christ on this flawed earth. He had no business losing faith and giving in to fear. The weakness in his blood would not triumph over the Holy Spirit in him . . . as long as he worked hard to purge it from himself. This was the lance to the boil of his beginnings. His father's words echoed: *"Work hard . . . remain strict . . . overcome the stain . . ."*

The law, too, was on his side. On Judgment Day, he, Matthew Hopkins, would be remembered for using the laws of man to enforce the laws of Heaven.

He'd found a witch and discovered her name. She would be jailed because of him. No matter what happened to scraggly Elizabeth Clarke after this, she was on his master list. The relief was a warmth throughout his body, a restless and wild jubilation.

I'll remember you, Clarkie, he thought. Inspired, he opened his leather bag and pulled out one of the bodkins used for testing the Devil's teats. Hopkins held it by the wooden handle and twirled it in his hand, watching the bright glint off the tip. *One witch, two witch. Deborah, Elizabeth.*

Panting, he took the bodkin in a hard grip and began to scratch at the wood beam on the wall. *Shush, scritch.* The point dug in to the hard seasoned oak. Tiny flakes fell off. One long line, up and down, up and down. Another shorter line, back and forth, back and forth. That was for the original witch. That was the scratched cross that Hopkins had to bear.

He scored another cross next to hers, for Elizabeth Clarke. It was off-kilter, crooked; the grain of the oak was tough to rub against.

Two witches named. Two crosses to mark the work he had done for Heaven.

After recording his success, he felt strong enough to ignore the creaking timbers of the house and the groaning wind outside. With trembling fingers he undressed for bed . . . then he had Elspeth curled at the foot of his bed, and the covers tucked up to his nose.

The next morning, however, contained the comforting promise of spring. Birds sang in the sunshine, new grass made the landscape bright, and the shrubs outside his window were just shrubs that waved in the breeze. It put Hopkins in mind of the Book of Revelations, and the new earth that would be made after the Apocalypse.

He breathed a little easier. There was good work to be done.

PIPPA WAS IN HER house dress, which she did not want to stain, so she stood a foot back from the cauldron. With a long wooden spoon she stirred what was inside. The window shutters were closed, as was the door. *A shame*, thought Pippa, for it was a nice day. Lillibet was careful about who saw them about their business.

"Why must we be so secretive, Lillibet? Everyone comes to you for remedies."

"Pippa, you must learn discretion. Here, 'tis time to add the horsetail." Lillibet measured out a scoop of the dried herb and poured it into the cauldron. It hissed in response. Lillibet sighed. "Knowledge is not always good. People don't understand our ways. The traditions of our mothers are being lost to those who think we do evil."

Pippa scoffed. "How could you be evil?"

"They don't know the land as we do. The old ways are called witchcraft, and we cunning-folk are driven to caution."

"But I cannot understand! Even this," Pippa gestured at the bubbling concoction, "is at the request of Isabel Moore. She cannot conceive again, and so she comes to you to brew her a potion."

"That is because she has no other choice," said Lillibet. "If we advertise ourselves, we become open to attack."

"You have the midwifery license."

"No license to be cunning-folk. 'Tis a deeper thing. It must be kept quiet."

They were interrupted by a soft tap on the door. Pippa dashed over, knocking down a wooden cup that fell to the earthen floor.

"Careful, child!" Lillibet said.

"Who goes there?" Pippa whispered through the door.

"'Tis us," said Sybil Yates's voice. "Alice and myself. We've brought the cream.'

Pippa pulled the door open to admit her friends.

"Oh! The s-s-smell is . . . in-interesting," said Alice.

Sybil grinned and twitched her nose.

Lillibet glared at Pippa. "What are they doing here?"

"They want to help! Don't worry, they'll never tell. This is a bound secret, just like our times in the forest." Pippa gave meaningful looks to Sybil and Alice.

"Please, Lillibet?" added Sybil. "We want to be cunning, too."

Lillibet sighed. Sybil was a favorite of hers, and Pippa had heard her say that Sybil had a gift. And Alice was quiet and kind, the last person to judge the ways of others. "All right. And may God bless you with children, Alice, so that you never need brew it for yourself. I know how you adore the care of little ones."

Alice smiled, dipped her head, and then peered into the cauldron.

"The cream is added last," said Lillibet. "It masks the pungency of the herbs. Cream and milk . . . both represent the nursing of children. Go ahead, Alice. Pour in four of these." She handed over a pewter cup.

The cream was poured with a cautious hand and allowed to bubble for a few more minutes.

"Now," said Pippa, hoisting up her skirts and snatching a small clay jar shaped like an hourglass, "the vessel."

"This is important because it births the idea of fertility," added Lillibet. "Here, Sybil. Use this to draw a spiral upon it." She produced a fine horsehair brush and an inkwell.

Sybil sat on the floor next to Pippa and stuck her tongue out of the corner of her mouth, concentrating as she dipped the brush into the inkwell. With a few quick strokes on the jar, she drew a spiral where a woman's stomach might be.

"Seed takes hold, the child grows," Pippa murmured the rhyme. Her mother nodded approval.

The ink was brushed into a spell, into further spirals and waving lines. When Sybil was finished she blew lightly over it, to help it dry. "Ready," she said, holding it out to Lillibet.

"Now we pour it in," said Pippa. "May I?" she asked Lillibet. She wanted to have the important job.

Sybil passed her the jar. The potion was taken off the fire and Pippa used a ladle to pour the mixture into the vessel.

"This is the proper look," said Lillibet.

It was dim inside the cottage but the cracks of light through the shutters was enough to show the pale liquid. Sybil said, "I feel confident should the need arise. Thank you, Lillibet."

"But not for you!" said Pippa.

"No." Sybil laughed. "I fear my sister Elizabeth may find difficulty in her marriage, whoever the unfortunate man shall be. Her manner is hostile to growth of any kind. Perhaps this would sweeten her womb!"

They all laughed. "Here, take some hot water," said Lillibet, using a cloth to take a smaller pot off the fire. "Good for your selves." She sat in her rocking chair and took a long, slurping sip. "Do take heed of this charm cast, for it be the same I cast upon meself for the birth of Pippa."

Pippa sat down slowly to hear her mother speak, careful not to spill the scalding water from her cup. Then she took too big a sip and burned her tongue.

"Yes," Lillibet reminisced, "I was too old, so they said, but John and I wanted a child, and prayed so many times for God to grant us a little one. But the Lord helps them that help themselves. At the height of summer I set to bring meself fertility, and the planting of a child, and used these same herbs and charms, and so it worked. Nine months later, in the spring, when the lambs were birthing their own, Philippa arrived in the world. I be using this method ever since, and never has it failed."

Lillibet's eyes held light when she spoke of Pippa's origins. She had been the miracle baby, the one so unlikely, and Pippa was glad that Lillibet had someone to carry on her knowledge. Sometimes Pippa felt more like an employee than a daughter, but she enjoyed the honest banter and hard work she shared with Lillibet, rather than someone else's idea of how a mother and daughter should be. She even called her mother by her given name, and that made her feel closer, as though they were not just kin, but friends by choice.

Later, as the girls were leaving, Lillibet said, "Please, young misses, say nothing about your time here. I've explained to my Pippa that women's knowledge must be quiet knowledge." Lillibet's fingers were laced together, drumming anxiously against each other.

"I sh-shall say n-n-nothing," said Alice, "f-for I have no others to t-t-tell."

"I only talk to my friends and my dolls, and the trees," said Sybil. Her voice was high, like that of a much younger girl, or a songbird.

"God bless, then, children," said Lillibet. "And Sybil, take no advice on matrimony from your sister Elizabeth!"

Sybil, laughing again, departed down the path toward her

own home with Alice's arm linked through hers.

"I'll be taking this to Isabel Moore now," said Lillibet. "Open the windows, this place needs air." She paused. "Pippa, I mean this. Discretion. Discipline. You may someday regret sharing this part of our lives."

"But, Lillibet, they're my friends! You said yourself that Sybil is . . . different. And Alice, though she hardly gets time away from her work, has the kindest heart of us all."

"You should have asked my permission before inviting them."

Once again she'd stumbled into disapproval from Lillibet. Sighing, she resolved to do better next time, and ask permission for things. Although Lillibet was so strict about their magic, Pippa couldn't be upset with her.

While her mother was gone Pippa ate a piece of buttered brown bread as a lunch, swept the floor and cleaned out the cauldron, and pinned her hair up into its coif. She wanted to take a walk and would need to look proper. "If only I could wear my hair as a man," she said to herself. Men cropped their hair short and did not need to fuss with it.

Her mother's errand did not take long—the Moores lived down the lane—and on Lillibet's return Pippa asked permission to go for a walk. The lively air was like a restless spirit, and the woods and fields called for attention.

"Go, child, go!" said Lillibet, waving her off with a smile, her mood passed.

Strong legs took Pippa across country. She wandered with the brook for awhile and skirted the woods. The trees sighed contentment in the breeze. The buds of new leaves tipped the branches. The fields, plowed and seeded, showed exuberant shoots of green. Pippa was careful to tread along the edges of the new fields. When a family of rabbits emerged from their warren near an oak tree, she greeted them with a loud call.

"Ho, there, rabbits!"

She broke into a run downhill toward the main road. Errant strands of hair escaped her Dutch-style cap but she did not care. Beneath her petticoats her legs were bare and free.

When she saw the figure walking on the road ahead of her, her heart stuttered.

The man stopped when he saw her, and she stopped a few paces away, breathing heavily.

"Hugh Felton," she said. "Good day." She made an absurd curtsey, with her hair half-tumbled and her skirts awry.

"Pippa." He might have tipped his hat but he was bareheaded, burnished gold hair shining in the sunlight, and in working clothes. A pale wool shirt rested on his broad shoulders, and his dark breeches were tucked into muddy boots. He walked with an air of casual ownership for this road, this land. That was something Pippa liked about Hugh: he was a wealthy landowner's son, but he took involvement in the everyday working of that land.

There was a moment of silence, lightened by the chirping of birds, and then Pippa was startled when Hugh burst out laughing. "My apologies," he said, bent over with his hands on his knees, "but you're ridiculous! What are you doing, running like the Devil's at your heels?"

"Perhaps the Devil is," she said, laughing too and trying to get her hair back up. *Oh, those horrid pins,* she thought. She'd lost several of her wooden hairpins while running. "I hope I don't frighten you with my mad pace."

"You don't," said Hugh, taking a step closer. "Walk with me? I'm to the smithy. Father's needing a new bit for one of the horses."

He wants to walk with me! she thought. "Gladly," said Pippa. "Thank you."

"Do you know," said Hugh, "my mother was speaking the other day about decorum in young ladies. She thinks they have too much."

"Indeed?" Pippa didn't have much decorum. Perhaps Lady Felton would like her, if only she knew her.

"Yes. A very proper young woman from Lavenham refused to greet my brother. Later it emerged that she felt it would be imprudent to speak to a man. Any man. Too much piety at the sacrifice of Christian hospitality."

"She's not used to our country ways," said Pippa. It was a recognized fact that country people were friendlier and more casual about things. She doubted that she could walk with Hugh in a city. "Or, your brother's not used to the ways of towns."

"I prefer country ways," said Hugh with a sidelong glance at Pippa.

Something inside of her soared.

"Were you at the new field?" Pippa asked. The Feltons had cleared and plowed what had once been fenland after purchasing tracts from smaller farmers. Using stronger equipment they were able to make fertile what once had been unsuitable. The Feltons' new grain fed their fat cattle. It was making them land-rich, for in these uncertain times fewer families had money to spare for new enterprises.

"I was," said Hugh. "I must confess I find it exciting."

"Plowing?"

"Overturning virgin soil," he said.

A furious blush overtook Pippa. "I know not what you mean." But she turned her head to look up at him from under her eyelashes.

Hugh smiled. "But you *do* know how invigorating the outdoors can be. You're the only girl I know who runs free across the fields."

"I like my freedom. It must be taken when it's there."

"I agree," said Hugh. He stopped walking and looked hard at her. "Do you know . . . I think perhaps we are alike. We *are* country folk, with country values. I care nothing for what my Christian brothers in the towns and cities find important. Not money, which is different from wealth, the wealth of the land. Not prestige, not even religion. Not," he paused, putting a thoughtful hand to his mouth, "not that I don't value piety."

"Your idea of it is just more natural," suggested Pippa. She was, as always, impressed with Hugh's command of his ideas. He was educated further than she, who could not even read beyond simple things. Her heart pounded at his serious words. Perhaps it meant he took her seriously, too, as more than a friend or acquaintance or pretty girl with whom to flirt. Once again, Pippa dared to hope that Hugh might choose her above all the more eligible girls with whom he flirted, too . . . That he wasn't really engaged to Elizabeth Yates, that he didn't really prefer Winifred Radcliff . . . She blinked once to ground herself and paid close attention to his speech of philosophy.

Hugh took long, slow, deliberate strides as he walked. "I feel to be close to God is to do His work with humility, to help the poor, to do good and be joyful. Not to deny oneself but to embrace all of this as God's creation, and safeguard its virtue." His eyes, azure like the sky, scanned the fields and trees that surrounded them, and came to rest on the white timber church a half mile down the road.

"And virgin fields? Are they to be safeguarded too?"

"They are to be cultivated," he said. His eyes moved from the church to pause on Pippa's lips.

Pippa laughed and skipped ahead of him. "Catch up with me!" she shouted over her shoulder, and then as though they were children again, they raced to the village. As she flew along the road, Hugh holding his pace at her heels, she flung her arms outward and closed her eyes, remembering the first time they'd done this. When they were children, before all the burdens of class and marriage and expectation, she had always been a few steps ahead and leading the way to wildness, and he would always catch up to her.

Pippa was six and Hugh eleven when they married. It was midsummer, the brightest and longest day of the year, and the forest was bursting with green. Pippa, tall and gangly for her age, skipped past a rock where a lizard basked in the sun; she paused to say hello. The lizard's emerald eye regarded her with patience. Giggling, she glanced behind her for Hugh. She knew these woods better than he did and she could hear him crashing through the bushes down the path.

Today they were playing gypsies. "If you're a warrior, you have to hurry," called Pippa.

"I'm a king today. And I stopped to present you this royal gift," said Hugh, stepping from behind a tree and presenting her with a branch of blueberries.

Pippa's eyes widened. The berries were large, round, and the deep indigo of perfect ripeness.

"Come," said Hugh, seizing her hand, "and tell my fortune in the apple grove!"

When they played gypsies, Pippa was always a fortune-teller.

They ran together, ducking beneath branches and twisting around the trunks of trees. When they emerged into the rosy glow of the apple grove, they stopped to catch their breath. Hugh flopped backward onto the grass. His eyes matched the sky above him.

He was the only friend of Pippa's who was a boy. She was often called strange by the other boys of the village, and she knew it was because of her mother, but Hugh treated her differently. He said she was quite normal to him.

Pippa wondered what Hugh would think if she was cunning like Lillibet.

Wandering around the clearing, snacking on the blueberries that she knew would turn her mouth dark, an idea struck her. "Let's play something different today."

Hugh lifted himself onto one elbow. "What shall we play?"

"Let's play married," she said. "A gypsy wedding!"

His eyes widened. "Well . . . I suppose. I can't tell any of the lads I'm married, though."

"Of course not," said Pippa. "It's a secret wedding because . . . um . . . because you're meant to marry the evil witch daughter of the enemy king! But you decide on the fortune-teller instead, because she sees the future."

Hugh grinned. "And why do you decide to marry me?"

"Because you're the good king, of course."

He stood up. "How do people get married, anyhow?"

She bit her lip. "I don't know. We'll have to make it up." Stepping toward Hugh, she felt a shimmer, as though the air gasped. "Let's stand facing each other."

They stood solemnly, Hugh a head taller. "All right . . . close our eyes," said Pippa.

Hugh closed his, but she peeked up at him. He had a nice face, a kind face. She liked the way his fair hair laid across his forehead. He was too young for it to be cropped yet.

Pippa thought in her head, We are married. We are married. Then she said aloud, in a firm voice, "I take you, Hugh the Brave, to be my husband." She stared at him and raised her arms to the sky.

He opened his eyes. His features were like stone, held in a trance, an enchantment that flowed from Pippa's mind.

Around them, an eddy of wind swirled, and apple blossoms began to fall like snow into the clearing. Thicker and faster, the flowered, scented cloud engulfed them.

"Take me as your wife," Pippa coaxed. The words seemed to come from someone much older than six.

Hugh stood frozen, staring at her. After several moments, when the fallen blossoms were caught in their hair, he whispered, "I take you, Pippa the Cunning, to be my wife."

Pippa wasn't sure what to do after that, and so she held out her palm for him to kiss. She felt the tickle of his lips and it made *her giggle.*

That seemed to break the spell, and she cried, "Now here comes the evil king to avenge his daughter!" she pointed at a spot in the trees, and they broke apart, and seized long sticks to use as swords against their imaginary enemies.

PIPPA SMILED TO HERSELF as she thought of her inadvertent charm on Hugh. They'd never spoken about that day, but ever since, he'd paid all kinds of special attention to her ... more than was due a girl of her lowered station, from a man of his high station. Now that they were old enough, who knew ... they had always been friends, but from the way he sometimes looked at her, so speculative ... Pippa prayed their relationship would take a different turn.

"Pippa, stop," he said in her ear.

They thundered to a halt at the crossroads. Something out of the ordinary was happening at the inn. The Green Man sign had been taken down, the Renshaws stood in deep discussion with the carpenter, and their son Will was taking apart the bracket that held the carved sign. Overseeing all of this was Reverend Yates.

"Hile, Will," said Hugh.

"Hallo, Hugh Felton," said Will. "And Pippa. Good day."

"What are you doing with the sign?" Pippa asked, pointing.

"Don't be forward, girl," said Reverend Yates.

"Oh!" she cried as the carpenter took a hammer and chisel and split the old sign down the middle to loose it from the bracket.

The Green Man's wide eyes seemed upset by what was happening to him. To Pippa it was as though a family member had been struck in the nose. The Green Man was not just for the inn. He was in the woods, in the trees. She'd seen his face in the gnarled oak near the clearing. She'd seen him in the morning inside the mulberry bush below the kitchen, and in the yew tree when the sun hit it just right.

"The inn is being renamed," said the Reverend. "To something less pagan. There is wickedness abroad and we must guard our own souls with greater vigilance."

Hugh looked troubled. "Has this to do with the rumors of witchcraft to the south?"

A small shiver went through Pippa. She remembered the pamphlet from Essex. But then she remembered that she knew how to defend herself against black magic. Her mother knew ancient tricks. The Reverend might even call them pagan. Still, she was certain that white witchcraft was not a crime.

"Have you decided, Papa?" Will asked Mr. Renshaw. "On the name?"

"Yeh," he said, "from now it be called The Charter Inn, seeing as we have a charter from God to provide refreshment to this village."

Reverend Yates looked satisfied with this. So did the carpenter, for whom it would mean a commission.

Pippa took a quiet leave from Hugh and the others. Her legs felt weak all of a sudden, as though the destruction of the Green Man had done something to her own spirit.

The Cunning-Folk

All was quiet in the house of the Reverend Peter Yates. It was the hour after dinner and the minister was in his study, writing the sermon or studying the Bible. It was always one or the other. His two eldest daughters were in the room they shared, speaking in low voices. The house-woman had gone to sleep. When the Reverend's wife had died many years ago, Martha had been hired to cook, clean, and do the things that a woman was needed to do.

This routine left Sybil Yates alone to pursue her own strange designs. This evening it was an embroidered handkerchief. She'd forgone the usual border of flowers or initials. Instead her quick fingers flashed in the gloom and, thread by thread, she stitched a colorful bird perched on a bare branch. The bird had bright red tail feathers and blue-green wings and a crest of yellow at its head. It had taken Sybil a long time to gather up the colors she would need and there was no room for error.

The low light of the candles was no hindrance. She had the entire bird in her head: its motion, its plumage, the sound it made when it sang. Whether there was such a bird in life did not matter . . . perhaps it existed somewhere in the tropics. Sybil's imagination often took her to the borderlands between myth and reality. She murmured to herself, "Ladybird, ladybird, this knot I knit. Ladybird, ladybird, this knot I cross . . ."

She tilted the fabric toward the candle and smiled at it. She was almost to the exciting part: the bird's eyes. *Those should be . . . green,* she thought. *Green as a newborn grain.* She stuck the needle in the safe place between her lips and her pale thin fingers searched for the correct thread to set aside; she would hate to lose track of it.

Sybil always seemed to lose things. Hairpins, needles, buttons, and even larger objects like her hairbrush and her favorite petticoat. She wondered if she was plagued with mischievous fairies. Perhaps Pippa would know what to do about it. They could make a charm together, or even offer something to the fairies to end their thievery.

Under her breath she sang a soft hymn to the spirits. Her mother was with her tonight and appeared as a bright white light that danced in Sybil's peripheral vision. Whenever she tried to pin it down with her gaze, it zipped away. "Oh, Mother," she said. "I miss you. So does Father. He takes too much solace in the Good Book—not that he cannot find solace there—but I fear he does not pay much attention to his daughters. To *your* daughters."

That wasn't all the way true. Sybil's father often warned them against the evils of the world. He also found special rapport with Elizabeth, Sybil's oldest sister. Elizabeth shared his passion for religion and they discussed the Bible together. Sybil found herself ignored in this, for she found it difficult to memorize things from the Bible or any other book, and her attention wandered from one thing to another.

"You make no sense," Elizabeth often told her, no matter what it was Sybil had said.

Sybil remembered the first time she had tried to explain

things to her family. It had also been the last time. Since then, she had kept her conversations with her mother a treasured secret.

THE FIRE CRACKLED *and popped, and Sybil's five-year-old eyes watched the pulsing of the red-hot coals at the bottom. It was like a beating heart, the fire, and it warmed the parlor where she and her sisters listened to their father as he read aloud from the Bible. He told the story of Jesus and Lazarus. Raising the dead was nothing tricky to Sybil. Her world was made of fairy tales and magical deeds. She believed the Bible to be true just as she believed the legends of King Arthur.*

They'd adopted a tiny kitten last week and Sybil had suggested the name of Galahad. He would be raised to hunt mice in their house.

Elizabeth, nine years old, dangled a piece of yarn in front of Galahad's tiny, playful paws.

Catherine, seven, sat on the sofa, curled up, watching and listening and quiet as always.

Glancing up at her father, Sybil noticed that the glowing white light was back. It hovered at his right shoulder. The light smiled and winked at Sybil.

"Hello, Mama," she said.

Papa stopped his reading, mid-word.

"What did you say, Sybil?" Elizabeth asked, dropping the yarn into Galahad's waiting grasp.

"She's here," said Sybil, wanting to share with her family the things she saw. They didn't seem to understand and, struggling to find the correct words, she said, "Our mother. She's here."

Papa frowned and closed the Bible, keeping his place with a finger. "Sybil, child, your mother is in Heaven with God."

"No, she's not! She's here in this room!"

Elizabeth scowled. "Stop imagining things and listen to Papa's story."

Catherine blinked and looked from one person to the other.

"Papa, don't you believe me?" Sybil asked.

Her father sighed. "Elizabeth, do not scold your sister. She's young and doesn't understand." He made a petting gesture at Elizabeth, telling her to relax.

But Sybil did understand. Her family could not see the glow of Mother. She followed the light as it bobbed and danced. Smiling, her own heart swelled. Although her mother had never known her, and had held her but once before passing away, Sybil knew that she was loved.

"What is she smiling at, Papa?" Elizabeth asked.

"Sybil."

Papa's soft, stern voice tugged her away from the light.

"Sybil."

Breaking contact with the spirit, she turned her wide eyes onto him.

"It is a temptation," he said. "For you, especially, daughter. If it comforts you to know that your mother watches us from the arms of Christ, far away in Heaven, then doubt it not. But Christian spirits stay not with us on earth. Don't claim it, for you upset your sisters."

Sybil closed her eyes. Perhaps if she listened very hard, her mother would speak through her. It had happened before. Then her family would believe her.

A voice moved in Sybil's throat.

Images played across her eyelids. A smiling woman, a young Reverend—Papa—with a gift of apples in a basket, and then the words erupted out of her mouth.

"She says hello to Petey," Sybil said slowly. She didn't know who Petey was, but it was not a message for her.

Her father sat straight up in his chair.

Sybil said, "She remembers the apples. There was a note in the apples. The reddest apples from the best harvest. She polished that one special for you. Then she baked you a pie."

The Bible fell from Papa's grasp and hit the floor with a great thud.

"How—" he croaked.

"She says it was her time to die and that she was sorry to leave. She didn't mean to hurt you, Papa. It wasn't her fault. It wasn't my fault, either, she says."

The Reverend stood up, shaking with rage. "Stop it!" he shouted at Sybil. "Stop it! This is—wrong, it's unnatural, this is an invention! Stop!"

But Sybil couldn't stop the force that moved her lips. On the brink of tears, she said, "'The white dove sat on the castle wall. I bend my bow and shoot her I shall. I put her in my glove, feathers and all.' She says that was what you said together."

Elizabeth and Catherine stared at her, horrified, and Sybil cringed under her father's burning gaze. This had been a mistake. She should never have said it aloud . . . *Mother,* she thought, *they don't want to hear you.*

A feather-light caress moved across Sybil's heart and the presence was gone.

Sybil clamped her mouth shut. She resolved to keep her mother to herself from now on.

"Get out," Papa whispered. "Go upstairs. Get out. You are a necromancer."

Sybil didn't know what a necromancer was, but it couldn't be good.

"You are a cursed child. Go. Go."

Shaken, she scrambled up and darted out of the room, away from the circle of fire-warmth and into the cold dark hall. How was she supposed to know he would react in such a way?

She heard him tell Elizabeth, "Tuck your sister into bed and return here. We will continue our reading."

Elizabeth appeared in the doorway and seized Sybil's hand, dragging her up the stairs to her child-size bed. "You are a stupid child," Elizabeth hissed. "Why do you say such stupid, bad things?"

"I didn't—"

They reached the bedroom and a light flared as Elizabeth struck a match for the single candle. "Into your bedclothes," she ordered Sybil.

Sybil spun around as she changed. She liked feeling dizzy.

Elizabeth's face hovered in front of her. "You did not see Mother," she said.

"Yes, I did."

"No, you didn't! I've never seen her, and if I can't, neither can you. She would visit me first. I was her first child and she loved me. You killed her."

Sybil wondered why her sister told lies.

Elizabeth bent closer. "Did you know you were born without a face?"

That was another lie. It wasn't possible. Sybil blinked at her and said, "No face?"

"Papa's right. You are cursed. I saw you myself, the day you were born. There was something strange over you, a veil, and you haven't been right in the head ever since. Mama died just after. 'Twas you who took her away from me. Now don't you feel bad?"

Curious, thought Sybil. Elizabeth seemed so convinced, yet Sybil knew the truth, had felt and heard her mother's love. Shrugging, she climbed into bed without answering Elizabeth.

Elizabeth blew out the candle. The last thing Sybil saw that night was her sister's face filled with a peculiar envy.

THE WHITE LIGHT THAT was Sybil's mother glowed in the northeast corner of the room. Sybil's eyes flashed over to her, but the light flashed away faster. "I fear that Father and I grow apart," she said aloud, but quietly, because no one should overhear these conversations with the dead. "But my friends, Mother, they're my true sisters. I don't wish to cast away the bonds of my shared blood with Cathy and Elizabeth, but in soul, 'tis Pippa and Alice that I love. They understand my oddity. They know I see things that others cannot. Lillibet, Pippa's mother, calls it the Sight."

She paused because she heard the creaking of the floorboard outside her bedroom, but then she heard the soft "meow" of Galahad, the old cat, their mouser.

"My dreams are full of visions, things so real I can't tell when I wake and when I sleep. Sometimes, Mother, I think you send them to me. Do you?"

There was no response. Mostly Sybil's mother liked to listen, not answer.

"Others might call it devilry. But how could it be, when it helps people? The other day I looked into my face bowl and saw a sheep lying down in pain, near the copse on Baxter's hill. I told Alice, who told her father, and they found a sheep in that very spot. It was in a breech birth. The lamb and mother both were saved, because Goodman Baxter got to them in time to help the laboring. So the Sight has done good."

Sybil felt the familiar hand of sleep begin to tug at her mind. "Goodnight, Mother." She set aside her embroidery, blew out the candle, and had a rather frightening dream that a grey dog with bared teeth chased her down the road.

THE NEXT MORNING OVER breakfast porridge, Sybil relayed her disturbing dream. Perhaps her sisters knew of someone who owned a greyhound.

"Are you afraid of dogs, Sybil?" asked Catherine. Her hair was a dirtier shade of Sybil's silvery ash blond and she was strenuous about keeping it beneath a coif.

At this early hour, Sybil's hair was still hanging about her face. Her scalp was sensitive to her hair being tugged into place.

"No, dogs don't frighten me," said Sybil. "Except that one."

"Dreams mean nothing," said Elizabeth. "To put much stock in them is to believe your own self more capable than God of revealing mystery."

"Did not Joseph . . . um . . . interpret the dreams of Pharaoh?" asked Catherine. Her question trailed off toward the end, as if she'd lost her nerve halfway through.

"The land of the Egyptians was an impure place," said Elizabeth, "and the Pharaoh an ungodly man. Joseph never tried to interpret his *own* dreams."

"How do you know?" said Sybil. "Perhaps his own dreams helped him interpret others'."

Elizabeth looked down her nose.

Catherine poured her sisters a second cup of tea. It was bought from the Dutch traders and its complex taste made Sybil think of the hot foreign slopes on which it grew.

"We are blessed to have this," said Elizabeth. "Most families cannot afford it."

"Providence has blessed us," said their father, entering the room dressed for the day. "I'm glad my girls enjoy the tea. I am not a man of fashion—the French drink excessive amounts of tea—but I do believe it fortifies our constitutions."

"May I?" asked Catherine, holding up the pot to pour him a cup.

After their father drank his tea and retreated back to his study, Elizabeth said, "'Tis a shame that Winifred's brother Thomas Radcliff is away at Oxford. He would be sought after here. But 'tis a necessary thing for a man to have letters, and an education toward the ways of God."

"Do you like Thomas, Elizabeth?" asked Catherine.

Elizabeth pretended to contemplate. "Though he's a year younger than I—him twenty-one—I think I should not object to him. Perhaps he'll surprise us all by returning for a visit at the end of his term."

"I think not," said Sybil, who knew Thomas would not be

home, because he was not at Oxford at all. He was fighting in the King's army. That was a secret Sybil would keep.

The Radcliffs were Royalists, but amongst neighbors who all favored the Parliament, General Cromwell, and the New Model Army, the merchant family kept their politics carefully hidden.

"Sybil, what would you know about Thomas Radcliff?" Elizabeth said. "He pays no attention to flighty girls."

Sybil tilted her head and shrugged. All this talk of Thomas—Tom, as she knew him—pulled her away from the present moment. In her mind's eye it was last year, last winter, when Tom asked her to tell him silly stories and when she knitted him a crooked scarf. "'Tis meant to be crooked," she said, "it folds easier about your neck." She'd showed him how it worked. Then he'd kissed her, first on her red nose, then on her lips. "Hmm," she said to her sisters, "is it not strange how in winter, tea and hot beverages warm us? And how in summer, when the air is hot, the same thing with a sprig of mint can cool us?"

"You make no sense," said Elizabeth.

"No sense," said Catherine.

"Thomas aside," said Elizabeth, "I expect other matches might be made this summer. Winifred's cousin Jonas Martin is visiting soon, from Stowmarket, and will bring his family connections. They're in the printing business, Bibles and such. A virtuous man."

Elizabeth and Winifred Radcliff were great friends and shared this sort of thing with each other, often with quiet Catherine listening to their chatter.

"There are fine men to make husbands in the Vale already," said Sybil.

"Hugh Felton," said Elizabeth, and sighed. The eldest Felton boy was the true aim of Elizabeth's acquisitive heart. He called at the house on occasion. It could even be called courting. Hugh and Elizabeth went for walks around the village common in full view of their watchful parents. After these evenings, Elizabeth was always flushed and excitable, the same way she got when she was about to win at marbles.

"Do you see," said Elizabeth, "how that girl throws herself at him? What is her name? The cunning-woman's daughter."

"Pippa," spoke up Catherine. "They call her Pippa. That's what Sybil calls her." She pointed across the table as though this were a sin on Sybil's part.

"*Philippa*," Elizabeth's voice dripped across the table. "Just as well, it is. She'll fall on her face for him and be reminded of her proper role in society."

"But wasn't her father a yeoman?" said Cathy.

"He's dead," said Elizabeth. "So she's nobody."

"Unless you have a baby someday," said Sybil. Her fingers traced the rim of her teacup and she peered inside at the black swirls of tea leaves at the bottom. "She will be a midwife like her mother and her grandmother."

"I'm quite sure Isabel Moore will receive the license. She's much more respectable."

Isabel Moore thought she had knowledge of midwifery on account of having three children. Sybil remembered that Isabel had purchased a conception potion from Lillibet, so she must not be everything she claimed.

Elizabeth continued, "It disgusts me how brazen Philippa acts around Hugh. He is the son of Sir John Felton! He'll take an upright wife into his family." Elizabeth clucked and bristled in her chair. Sybil was reminded of a snooty hen. Elizabeth continued, "I predict that girl will go the way of Anne Buckett. Quite lewd."

"I hear a redbreast," said Sybil, standing up with a clatter. "Do excuse me!" She twirled out the kitchen door and into the garden, where the tittering laughter of her sisters was just another faint sound on the breeze. She swung herself around the trunk of a tree and slid down it to wait. A few minutes later the robin redbreast landed on the thorn hedge and trilled at her. She smiled. "Greetings, Robin!"

Through the window she could see the figure of her father, hunched over the large English-printed Bible, and his head was in his hands as though despairing.

Sybil was untroubled. She watched the billowing motion of the laundry, the white sheets that Martha had hung on the line, and she wondered if that was what men at sea witnessed when they traveled to far-away places. Her thoughts were likewise carried away on the wind.

THE SUN WAS JUST PAST its zenith in the sky when Sybil meandered down the lane from the Baxters' farm. She'd gone to visit Alice, helped her with chores, and played a clapping game with the younger girls. Sybil liked to invent such games with rhythm and rhyme. As she passed the back garden of the Radcliff house, she could not help peering through the hole in the fence. She'd done this when Tom was around and they would whisper confidences through the boards.

The tidy, well-kept garden was not empty. Winifred, Tom's sister, was bending over to pick a lone weed. She winced and shifted her posture; the whalebone point on the bodice was not designed for gardening.

Closer to Sybil's spying eye, a fat red ladybug chased the season's first aphids on a strawberry plant. Chamomile had been planted to ward off evil spirits—Winifred knew a great deal about gardening—but ladybugs were the best cure for the tiny black pests.

Winifred stopped to smell an odd, foreign-looking plant and wrinkled her nose at it. Then she got a speculative look on her face. Sybil felt sympathy for such a look. It meant Winifred was swimming in the pond of ideas, fishing for something.

Then the rich girl took a long, deep breath and ran an impatient finger under the tight cuff of her sleeve. The cuff was lined with tiny pearls.

It was a bit silly to wear such fine clothes for gardening. Sybil might have warned Winifred that it was just the sort of thing a Royalist would do. The Radcliffs tried very hard to fit in as Puritans, but they were not, and Sybil knew it all too well.

Winifred's brown hair gleamed beneath her head cap as she turned and went inside. Shrugging, Sybil skipped home, wondering if Winifred would ever be her sister-in-law . . . if only the civil war would end, and Tom would come home, and the Radcliffs wouldn't have to be so tense and awkward and full of secrets.

Later, as Sybil sat in her own less orderly garden, she heard voices drifting through from the parlor. Winifred had come to call on Elizabeth. They called on each other often. Sybil flinched at the sound of Elizabeth's strident greeting, and at the superior tone in Winifred's. She wished that her future sister was not so much like her current one.

Unaware that Sybil was listening through the window, Winifred said, "I saw your sister running off to visit that farm. Baxter, is it? Rather low for her."

Elizabeth sighed. "She gets worse all the time. There's something wrong with her. She's always saying the oddest things."

"I don't know how you put up with her," said Winifred. A tone of eagerness crept into her voice. "What is the last thing she said?"

"This very morning she jumps up from the table, cocks her head like a bird, and then leaps practically out the window, all arms and dancing legs. 'Coo! Coo! I hear a redbreast!'"

"Chirp, chirp!" Winifred added. "We ought to fashion her some wings as a gift, since she likes birds so much. Birds of a feather . . ."

"And then tell her the wings work, and she ought to try

jumping from the roof," said Elizabeth. "She's silly enough to believe it."

Winifred giggled. "It would be a tragedy."

"A tragedy?"

"For the shrubberies below!"

Elizabeth's laughter rang louder than she usually allowed herself.

A silent tear had formed in Sybil's left eye, but it didn't fall. Not yet.

Elizabeth called Martha. "Bring us two slices of that cake," she ordered. "Winnie, can't we eat outside?" She claimed that sunlight cleared the spots she sometimes got on her face.

"No, I'll muddy my hems," said Winifred.

Sybil frowned. Winifred hadn't seemed worried about her hems earlier, pulling weeds in her own garden.

"Fine, let us open the other window, at least. I'll have Martha do it." Elizabeth sighed and Sybil could hear the creak as she sat down onto a chair. "I wish I might have new cuffs like yours."

This was the beginning of a familiar conversation. Sybil had overheard it several times before.

"I wish the shape of my ears was as nice as yours," said Winifred.

"At least you have a bosom to speak of," said Elizabeth, undoubtedly looking down at her own meager chest.

"I wonder who speaks of my bosom!"

"I wish someone would speak of mine!"

By "someone" Sybil knew Elizabeth meant Hugh Felton.

Winifred said, "But really, Elizabeth, I expect that you and I are the prettiest girls in the Vale. Certainly the most sought-after."

"By far," Elizabeth agreed. "Hugh comes calling almost every week now."

"And my cousin Jonas will be visiting from Stowmarket in

a fortnight," Winifred said.

"Yes, that's right! I suggested that he should know my sister."

Winifred laughed. "Oh, really?"

"Humble Cathy, not Sybil! Good Lord. No one in their right mind would marry that creature. I don't believe she's truly related to me."

Blinking quickly, Sybil dashed away the second tear that sprang up. They didn't know, and she didn't want them to know, about the boy she loved. *And he loves me, too.*

"A changeling," said Winifred.

"I imagine so. I would dread to think the same qualities were in me."

"I don't think you have any of Sybil's qualities," Winifred reassured her friend.

"I certainly have better taste in the company I keep," said Elizabeth.

"Sybil's friends are so unsuitable," said Winifred. "I saw them running barefoot a few weeks ago. They're practically feral."

"And unclean."

"Downright threadbare."

"Horribly madcap."

"Wallydrags!" said Winifred. "Ninnies!"

Elizabeth's voice was full of the hysterical tears of laughter. "Ne'er-do-wells!"

"Barking skullduggers!"

Their howls must have brought Martha into the parlor, for the door opened and the older woman murmured, "Your cake, Miss Yates."

"Set it down on the table. And open that other window."

Martha's footsteps retreated and the door closed again.

Winifred giggled.

Elizabeth said, "Lewd beasts."

There was a long, somewhat awkward silence and Sybil heard the sounds of forks and plates and chewing. Their words reverberated in her head. She felt winded, giddy, like after falling from a tree. Her intuition told her that Winifred wasn't cruel, just carried away into Elizabeth's mean streak. Still, Sybil didn't know what was worse, to be genuinely malicious or to follow along with someone who was.

Winifred was speaking again, and Sybil stayed quiet and still as she listened. "Did you see the hole in that Philippa's collar in church the other day? It looked like a moth had eaten through it. How dreadful."

"W-w-would you help me c-count the sheep?" Alice asked Pippa one day on Baxter's hill. "I g-get so distracted thinking about each one, r-r-r-remembering who was taken with a cough last year and wh-who had a lamb the y-y-year before."

Pippa smiled. It was so like Alice to make friends with the farm animals. And counting sheep with a stutter could not be easy. "Do you still name them as you did when we were girls?"

"No," said Alice with a blush. "Well, n-none but Esther." She pointed to a ewe with black ears who had a small lamb by her side.

"Why Esther?"

"Because she was m-m-mated to the king of Farmer Pye's herd. 'Tis like the story of Esther in the Bible."

"I suppose it is! Here, we'll sing the trick as we count them. The old way of counting sheep, you remember?"

"N-n-not all of it."

"It'll bring good fortune to them." Pippa clapped her hands together and shouted at the sheep. "All right, all of you! Into the pen!"

Alice's younger brother Ralph—who worked as shepherd boy during the time he wasn't in his grammar lessons—used his stick to prod the animals forward. "Oy! In ye go!"

The sheep bleated in protest.

"Say it now," said Pippa. "With me!" As the sheep were herded by Ralph one at a time through the gate, she began, "Yan. Tan. Tethera. Pethera. Pip. Sethera. Lethera."

Alice joined in. "Hovera. Dovera. Dik. Yan-a-dik. Tan-a-dik. Tethera-dik. Pethera-dik."

The chant seemed to calm the sheep, as though somewhere in their collective memory they knew this was the rhyme of shepherds. There was a break in the thick clouds overhead and the hill lightened. Pippa loved the vantage point from here. She could see down to the Green Man Inn—like many of the other villagers, she refused to call it by its new name—and the road and across the Vale to the forest. She could even see her own home with a thin plume of smoke rising from the stone chimney.

"A R-Radcliff c-cousin is coming for a visit," said Alice when all the sheep were counted and the gate locked behind them. Although she and Pippa did not associate with the Radcliffs, their news was village news.

"Oh, who?"

"F-F-From Stowmarket. J-Jonas Martin, the Bible p-p-printer."

"I doubt he's as nice as their Tom," said Pippa. Sybil had told them everything about her beau, and Pippa knew him to be a good sort of person. Yet Mr. Radcliff had hidden politics, not that Pippa cared, and so the Radcliffs' more Puritan cousins would improve their suspicious reputation in the village. They probably wanted this cousin to be married to a Vale girl. She said so to Alice.

"That b-be the truth," Alice replied.

Weddings always made for interesting conversation.

"I w-w-wonder wh-who the older daughter will marry," Alice said. "The one j-just above our age. W-Winifred."

"I don't like her, she's a toad," said Pippa. "To her, we don't exist." She would never say so to Alice, but Pippa also didn't like that Hugh was friendly with girls like Winifred Radcliff and Elizabeth Yates. It made sense for Hugh to marry one of them, for wealth was attracted to wealth. The thought of Hugh with either of those prim, proper girls made her feel very sour.

"T-True, she's not like our Sybil," said Alice. "F-For wh-wh-whom station don't matter. We are glad to have her as our friend, our s-s-s—"

"Our sister," finished Pippa. When the girls were ten years old, they had made a bond of sisterhood by pricking their fingers with a sharp blackthorn branch and sharing blood. Even these seven years later she could feel the strength of it in her veins. Nothing could break their love. Pippa took Alice's hand and kissed the back of it. "I must run," she said. "I'm to fetch yeast from Brewer's."

"Oh! What are ye m-m—?"

"Making?" Pippa finished again. "Birch wine."

Alice's face lit up. Lillibet's recipe was a well-loved and well-kept secret.

Pippa left Alice and walked the familiar way home. She knew every leaf, every stone, every cottage, every family and their history. Past the roundabout, she looked with disdain on the new swinging sign at the pub, which said "Charter Inn" and had a scroll painted on it. She continued up the footpath towards her own home and stopped at the Brewers' cottage, her closest neighbor.

"Hallo, Goody Brewer!" she called.

The Goodwife Brewer was sweeping her stoop with a rough broom. "Good day."

"I'm meant for a bit of yeast."

"Ah, ye're making that birch wine." It was known that Goodwife Brewer was jealous of Lillibet's wine. One year she'd even tried to steal the recipe by peering in the window.

Pippa laughed. "Worry not, we've not a mind to take over business. 'Tis but once a year we harvest from the birch."

"Hmm," said Goody Brewer with a low grumble to herself, and with ill grace handed over the sackcloth of yeast.

"Thank you, Goody."

At home, Lillibet and Pippa hung linen over the windows so Goody Brewer could not spy on them. The ingredients for the wine were ready: a sack of plump raisins, several pounds of sugar, a few bright lemons, the yeast, and a bucket of birch sap. While the sap was set to boiling over the fire, the sugar was added until it looked right according to Lillibet. It was a thick mixture with small, slow bubbles that fought their way upward. Using thick rags to protect their hands from the hot iron, they moved the cauldron off the flame to cool.

"Now we wait," said Lillibet. "Until?"

"Until it's the warmth of blood," Pippa recited.

"Mmm. Good. But there are things you're yet to learn, child, before you know all the ways of we cunning-folk."

Pippa exclaimed, "Then teach me! I'm seventeen. I'm ready to know what you know. I should learn before I marry and leave."

Lillibet cackled. "Marry! I think you have a few years yet if your eye's on that fickle Hugh Felton. He's not serious about you or anyone else, I seen the way he's kindly to all the girls, and most richer than you. I hope you're not set on him."

"I never said it!" Pippa cried.

"You didn't have to. I've seen the way the both of you look at each other."

"He's not fickle. He's just slow to make an important decision."

"He'll be wanting more from you before he promises anything. I know the type, these *gentlemen*. Think they own your body just because they own some land. If your good father was still alive, it'd be different. It'd be proper for Hugh to come courting. But as it is, you must be wary."

"Still," said Pippa, eager to change the subject before she received a lecture on being careful with boys. She'd received that one before. "I do feel I'm ready to learn your ways."

"That's because you're an impatient girl," said Lillibet. She sighed. "You have trouble following rules, Pippa, and everything about the cunning is rules. You must be disciplined, cautious, and wise. You are none of these things yet."

Pippa disagreed with vehemence. "How will I prove myself if you give me no chance? I'm ready, Lillibet, I promise!"

"Just watch and learn for now," said Lillibet with a gentle smile that said she'd made up her mind. Dipping a wrist into the bucket, she said, "'Tis ready for the yeast and lemons."

Pippa twirled her pinky finger into the sap-sugar mixture and tasted it. "Mmm!"

The yeast was added, and Pippa sliced the lemons in two and squeezed them over the bucket so the juice dripped in. Lillibet stirred it in with a wooden spoon and put the lid over top.

"Three days," she said. "Then we strain it, and for two moons it ferments, in time for May Day."

To Pippa, eager to taste the sweet wine, it seemed like ages away.

The Dark Places

Matthew Hopkins emerged from the dank pit that was the gaol at Colchester Castle. John Stearne was at his side. Hopkins was sweating and troubled, although he maintained his personal decorum in front of Stearne, who was similarly agitated. If one of them broke in front of the other, they might lose their resolve altogether.

Once Hopkins was in the fresh rain, the steady light, he regained himself. They'd conducted an interview with a seventeen-year-old girl. Her wicked mother had sold her to the Devil and initiated her into the ranks of witches. She had given him details, so many details . . . of imps, of congress with the Devil, of orgiastic sabbat gatherings, of the many times she'd plagued her neighbors with bewitchings. She'd told him that she was wedded to Satan himself.

He imagined their wedding—*black and orange and cream of flesh, riding the night*—and shuddered, pushing away the wickedness, focusing on the task at hand.

They had offered the young woman a plea bargain. If she confessed and gave details on the other witches, the law would spare her the hanging sentence and instead she would spend her life in prison.

Hopkins and Stearne continued on their walk through Colchester. It was a busy industrial town, full of weavers and textile markets, and their associated businesses such as dyers and tanners. The Dutch influence was strong but the Reformist influence was stronger. It was a place primed for the casting-out of witches.

They passed a parish church and Hopkins was pleased to see that the vivid stained glass in the windows was being smashed out by workmen in favor of plain glass. God's heavenly light should be beauty enough. *Icons, idols,* he thought, and turned away as a bright yellow and blue and red sunburst was shattered.

"Now that we have testimony for Grimston, what next?" Stearne asked. He was a head shorter than Hopkins and had twice the energy—he had a swinging gait and hands that never stopped gesticulating.

"This is not the last of the witches," said Hopkins, pointing with a backwards thumb toward the castle.

John Stearne was nodding. "'Tis as though we've tugged at a small root of a great tree that spreads across this land." His voice began to rise in pitch. "Now is our chance, Hopkins! When these particular women are long after the hangman, we two shall be hunting others still."

"Two men, acting on the will of God, can affect great change," said Hopkins. Stearne's excitement infected him. It took shape in his mind, a campaign across all of East Anglia, and then throughout all the counties of England. And Scotland! And perhaps even Ireland—those people were Catholics and not far from witches themselves. While the armies of the King and Cromwell tangled, Hopkins would be a different kind of soldier. He was in the battle for his soul, and for the souls of all good Christians.

He felt at the purse full of coins at his belt. Like any soldier, he was within his rights to earn a living from his work.

The clock on Colchester's guildhall struck four o'clock. Hopkins was startled at the time. "I must be going," he told Stearne. "While our good Sir Grimston continues to ferret out witchcraft on his estates, we can extend ourselves further."

"Not too far," said Stearne, "Agnes is with child again and I promised to stay within a few hours' ride of her." Stearne, unlike Hopkins, was married and had children.

Hopkins fetched Elspeth from the ragamuffin he'd paid to watch her while he was in the gaol. Within an hour he was on the road toward his own home, Elspeth racing along beside him. The rhythmic pounding of the hooves made his head hurt and a refrain echoed in his head. *Sunset is coming. Sunset is coming.*

It was Friday.

Hopkins dreaded being on the road tonight. The sights and smells of the gaol clung to him, and the soft whispering voice of the girl as she told him of unspeakable sin. The witches' imps could be anywhere, their empty animal eyes watching him from the side of the road, noting his progress and direction.

They might catch him, and use him, and he might like it.

Only one thing could cleanse him of this fear. Once the bad women, the witches, were gone, he could rest.

Elspeth's pink tongue lolled out of her grinning mouth as she trotted alongside him.

"Good girl," Hopkins told her. "Good dog."

Past forests and fences, huts and manor houses, past mud puddles and over meandering streams, it was a grey early twilight when he reached Mistley. "At last," Hopkins said aloud, as though wearied from the journey and not from his own imagination. He slowed the horse to a gentle canter and pulled to a stop in front of his Thorn Inn. The windows were glowing and it was crowded with men, friends and strangers, drinking foamy pints of ale.

The room was so warm and congenial that Hopkins drank more than he intended. He stocked good ale at the Thorn. A pleasant relaxation suffused his body. There was nothing to threaten him when he was in good company. He lifted his mug in a toast to Parliament, a toast to America, a toast to Sir Harbottle Grimston. But, as always, the pub emptied and Hopkins retired home to his cottage with Elspeth and fumbled at his collar and took off his boots.

He paused to add five more scratched crosses on the oak beam. "Manningtree," he muttered. Seven of them now. Seven little witches.

The room was lit by a single candle in a handheld lamp and the shadows flickered around him. Elspeth whined and curled up on her rug at the foot of his bed. Everything was tip-tilted and Hopkins knew he'd had too much to drink. "To bed," he muttered, "to sleep."

He should not have blown out that candle. He should have let it burn down after he was safe in the realm of a solid sleep.

"*Blackie. Beetle blackie!*"

"No," Hopkins moaned.

"*Shhh, shhhh.*"

"*Heeper reaper, little peeper. Listen up and listen well to all the things I have to tell.*"

Original witch, original sin. Born of sin, they're *bad bad bad like me.*

Somehow Hopkins fell asleep, cowering, and then in the soft envelope of darkness, her lizard's glowing face told him what to do. Smooth scaly green skin, a sickly light in hollow lizardly eyes, a toothless grin. "*Sator rotas,*" she said. "*Friday, Friday, the witch flies high. See and smell, her shadow's in the sky. Special time, Matty, I love you most. You belong to us!*"

"No. Yes. Please."

He was on his back. She writhed above him so fiery warm.

"*Slave to me, slave to us, arch now upwards, born of lust!*"

In the circle they danced and sang. They laughed and pointed. He was humiliated and he liked it. "*Drink, drink,*" they implored him. "*At midnight on a Friday, use a silver sickle and prick thyself, Matty. Let us drink of you, and you will drink of us. Down your throat, warm blood, your head between our legs. Suckle, little merry boy. Listen up and listen good. We know you'd join us if you could.*"

"*At midnight on a Friday.*"

"*Silver sickle.*"

"*Read the book, chant the rhyme, call the Master, you are mine . . .*"

"*Read the list.*"

Hopkins awoke in a throe, a sweating fit, an aching pleasure and tears streamed down his face as he mumbled aloud his instructions. "Read the list. The Devil's list . . ."

ONE OF PIPPA'S CHORES was the cleaning of the chicken coop. Her nose wrinkled at the sharp odor while their two hens fussed about her feet. She nudged them away. Pippa had no great love for chickens other than the way they tasted. "Go on. You too, Eli."

They had a new piglet they'd named Eli, payment from a farmer after Lillibet had cured him of a boil. The piglet believed it had a right of abode not in the shed, but in the house with Pippa. Whenever she was in the yard the creature trailed after her. As she looked down into its beady, intelligent eyes, she had to admit a fondness. "Shame we must eat you someday," she told it.

She hurried through the chicken job, ending with a snort of disgust. Eli trotted after her, trying to nose his way into the house, but Pippa closed the door before he could. She set to work scrubbing the kitchen table. Residue and stickiness could not be allowed to build up; Lillibet was strict about not contaminating different herbs. Pippa gritted her teeth and scrubbed hard, figuring if she was strong about it, it would make up for her haste.

Lillibet said from her chair, "Take your time, child. No need to rush through life."

"Yes, Lillibet." But she moved the brush all the harder. She wanted daylight left to work on her collar. Sybil had given her some threads and although Pippa's needlework was nowhere near the artistry of Sybil's, her designs were interesting enough. Her embroidered flowers were often so jagged and impatient as to be passed off as exotic.

Red and blue, she decided for the tiny flower she would stitch on her linen collar.

"Oh, begone," she snarled at a stubborn patch of honey in the crack of the table.

"Shh," said Lillibet, holding up a hand.

Pippa noticed the aged perfection of that hand, the way it held still, the freckles and the knobs. Her mother's caring hands could heal with one touch.

She stopped her scrubbing. A drop of water plinked onto the dirt floor where it was absorbed.

"Is someone crying outside?" Pippa asked.

"Your youthful ears can hear better than mine," said Lillibet. She stood up and peered through the tiny square window. "So there is." She opened the door.

Standing with her head down was Sarah Ford, a dairymaid from the other side of the Vale. She trembled and tears streamed down her pale young face, and her hands were pressed against her flat belly. "Please," she said, dropping to her knees at their door, "please, cunning-woman, help me."

"Stand up, come in," said Lillibet, snatching the broom from the corner and using it to prod Sarah inside. "Make not a spectacle. Pippa, get the door, so that pig don't try to come in."

Pippa bolted the door. "Sarah?"

"Stop that crying," said Lillibet. "Take this brew, sip it nice and slow. That's right. Hush, now. Whatever your problem, there's an answer."

At first Pippa wondered if Sarah was under magical attack. There were few physical aches or pains that could produce such extreme distress for a young person. She sat down and, although still scrubbing the table, she went quiet about it so she could listen.

"Now," said Lillibet, taking the pewter cup from Sarah, "tell us what ails you."

Sarah wiped her face with the cuff of her sleeve. "I missed me monthlies."

Pippa ceased her scrubbing.

Lillibet made a low noise. "Have you ever missed them before?" she asked Sarah.

The girl shook her head. "No, never."

"You been regular, right along with the moon cycle?"

"Yes."

"And when did it happen?"

"When did *what* happen?"

Lillibet gave her an unwavering glare. "The thing that makes you be with child. During what time of your cycle?"

Sarah sniffled. "At—at, well, I know not."

"It was more than once?"

What terrible immorality, thought Pippa, although she was consumed with curiosity for what Sarah knew and she did not, although they were both unmarried. She also wondered how it could have been allowed. Sarah's parents were God-fearing people who would surely whip their daughter, or even cast her out. Pippa had once seen a public whipping of an adulteress in Lavenham.

Sarah refused to say anything more, and so Lillibet pressed further.

"You must tell me, child, so we know what to do. You were supposed to bleed at the dark moon, and did not?"

A nod.

"The first bleed missed?"

Another nod.

"And you lay with a man around the full moon?"

Hesitation, then a nod.

Lillibet pressed her lips together. "That's four weeks on, if you're with child. Onto the bed, flat on your back, so I may determine the situation."

At first Pippa wondered if her mother was going to inspect Sarah's privy parts, as had been done when Pippa first started her monthlies at the age of twelve. Lillibet had checked her and pronounced her normal, and it had been horribly embarrassing for Pippa at the time. But was there a way to tell pregnancy just from looking at the exterior of a woman?

It wasn't what Lillibet was after. Instead those knobby hands patted Sarah on the forehead as though to soothe her, and then she touched Sarah's belly. Lillibet closed her eyes and began to hum. She closed her eyes and her face was transported, her brow quivering as though seeing something behind her eyelids, her lips moving barely. Then, her mouth turned into a frown.

"There's a spirit with you," Lillibet told Sarah after several moments. "You're with child."

A fresh sob escaped Sarah's lips. "No! What am I to do? I'm ruined. Me life is over."

"Calm thyself!" Lillibet was not impatient, but she always countered others' emotions with stern calm. It had seen the old woman through Pippa's tempers, which could be considerable.

Pippa added, "Listen to her, she's seen everything. I doubt you be the first village girl to have this problem."

This made Sarah hiccough and say, "I'm not?"

"Of course not," said Lillibet. "Why do you think so many babes be born a month early in a new marriage? Now answer me this. The man who's planted 'is seed in you—will he marry? Has he the means? If so, be wed with haste, and no one need ever know that the consummation came before the contract."

"I cannot," said Sarah. "He cannot."

"Don't be stubborn, girl. You've got yourself in this situation, 'tis up to you to make him marry you."

Sarah caught her lip with her large teeth.

"May as well tell us, we know much already," said Lillibet.

But Sarah would not give a name. Instead she buried her head in her hands. Then with an anguished wail she said, "He's already married!"

Pippa sat straight up. Married? She knew that in theory, married men could dally with unwed girls, just as single men did, but that it was happening in her own village was a shock indeed. She desperately wanted to know who it was.

Lillibet on the other hand looked unsurprised. She sighed and said, "So be it. Ye have two options, Sarah Ford. The best, and the right way, is to admit the mistake and raise the child. Perchance in the future a good man will come along and marry you anyway, seeing as your fertility is not in question."

Sarah shook her head. "Ye don't understand. Me father will murder me. Already me sister had to be sent away, for she lain with a man, though she didn't fall with child."

The Fords, it seemed, had an issue of female discipline in the household. Pippa thought again on Sarah's parents: they were strict to excess and sometimes the red welts of a strap could be seen on the backs of Sarah's hands. She remembered there had been talk that they might go to the New World.

"I know!" Pippa burst with her idea. "Sarah, did your parents not think of going to the Massachusetts Bay Colony?"

"They did . . . ?"

"So if you can convince them to go, you may be able to start a new life. Say that you were married and then widowed just after, no one will know. There'd be no shame for anyone to see."

Lillibet smiled approval at her daughter.

Tears began welling up in Sarah's eyes again. "I cannot. Do you not see? It's me own father that I'm most a-feared of. Is there not something to be done? Something to . . . to . . . make the baby go away?"

The exuberant energy of springtime seemed to wilt and retreat from the windows. A dove that had been calling to its partner in the yard ceased its cooing. The piglet—who had been drinking from the trough—paused. Pippa could hear it.

Lillibet said, "That's your other option. A way to set loose the babe that grows in you."

"I didn't know that!" Pippa cried. "How?"

"There never was a need to tell," said Lillibet. "And, in God's grace, there never will be for *you*. You wait until a proper marriage before letting a man touch you, Pippa, do you hear?"

"But how?" Sarah asked.

"An old way. A way that only cunning-women know. And only women must know! Do you understand, Sarah Ford? If I do this thing, and if you whisper a word to any living soul, I'll kill you with me own carving knife. Do you vow silence to me, here, now?"

"I do," said Sarah. She nodded her head over and over. "I do, I do."

"So be it. And I've not decided that I *will* do it. I'm . . . considering. Leave us, go home, say nothing, and come back in the morning. Then I give my answer. Be ready for a good size fee."

Sarah, looking frightened by the cunning-woman's flashing eyes, stood and ran out the door. Her retreating steps were soft on the spongy footpath.

Subdued by all of this, Pippa said, "Lillibet? I feel it's wrong to kill a babe in the womb, especially in the springtime. Is it not . . . is it not to break the Commandments? Is it not murder?"

Her mother sighed. "Or is it murder to let her carry to

term? If Sarah's cast out, Pippa, she's good as dead, and would lead a life of degradation and poverty. 'Tis not up to us to decide. If we help her not, she may try something herself to lose the babe, a way even more dangerous."

That was true. Sybil had once told Pippa a story about a girl from Bury St. Edmunds who'd fallen with child and thrown herself down a stair. The baby had died, but so had the girl.

"Pippa. Be a good girl, go to the wall and bring me the coin satchel."

Pippa caught her slender pinky finger in a hidden notch and the loose stone in the wall slid out. It was all the savings of the household. The soft leather satchel was lightweight in her hands. She opened it, pawing through and counting the coins. "Lillibet? There's so little!"

"I know. The cost of everything goes up every year, and we're not making up for it. So often the farmers pay in grain, or cheese, or piglets—" Lillibet gestured out to the yard, "—but those things don't pay for rare herbs and the spirits we need to make tinctures. Or sugar, or shoes, or cloth. We need coins. They keep through the winter." She paused and put a hand on Pippa's cheek. "I'll do this thing for Sarah. You will not burden yourself with it. I know the ways. I'll do the gathering, the brewing, the casting."

But Pippa wanted to become as her mother. "No," she said. "I'll help you. I want to learn—no, I *must* learn. I do take that same vow put upon Sarah Ford. I'll never tell a living soul these secrets, 'cepting of course my own daughter, should I be blessed."

Lillibet took her hand. "Watch and learn, then. This is what it means to be cunning: to know the secrets of life and death. 'Tis no light burden. I . . . I hope this will not return to haunt us. I hope this is the right thing, that we will not be punished by God for what we're about to do . . ."

Pippa had never heard such reluctance in Lillibet's voice

before.

Her mother wrung her hands as though drying off the worries. "I hope that someday you know the joy of children, not the liability."

"Just not without a husband first!" said Pippa. They laughed together, but the state of the money sack was sobering, as was the thing they would do to put some weight in it.

Sarah Ford returned the next morning, her face drawn. Overnight she looked aged by several years. "I still want this."

"Twenty shillings," said Lillibet.

Sarah gasped. "What? How'm I supposed to pay that?"

"'Tis your business to pay. 'Tis my business to cure your condition. I'll not be having this moral burden on me without recompense."

Sarah nodded. "Then I'll have him—er—I'll have the fee for you."

Curiosity piqued, Pippa stared at Sarah, wondering again who the father really was. He was married, he was the sort of man to dally with a dairymaid, he would pay twenty shillings to avoid the consequences. Perhaps Goodman Renshaw at the inn? He had an eye for pretty young things—she'd caught him staring at her more than once—and could explain away twenty shillings as business expenses.

Then she remembered the tincture of St. John's Wort that she'd delivered to him . . . for masculine strength!

Her eyes widened with the possibility. *Hmm.* It seemed there was much more beneath the surface of the Vale than she'd known.

"Start with these berries," said Lillibet, handing Sarah a handful of fresh blueberries. "Eat as many of them as can be found on the hills. This'll prepare you. 'Tis not a certain thing. If the herbs don't work, it'll damage the babe inside—you must be ready for other means."

Pippa shuddered. The night before, Lillibet had told her dreadful things about other women and what might be tried by quack doctors—things about shears or wires with hooks on them. By then it was often too late anyway, for the girl would have started to show a rounded belly and large breasts, and the stain on her honor could not be removed.

"Also," Lillibet warned, "it'll not be pleasant. You may get sick and the bleeding, when it begins, may go for weeks. You could turn yellow for a time and feel very poorly. Ready still?"

A resolute nod.

When Sarah had gone with her blueberries, they closed up the cottage and set out to the west, where the land was wild and many things grew on the slopes and in the forest meadows. "Look for a strong showing of mugwort," Lillibet said. "We must pick it in the light of the full moon, but in the meantime 'tis best to know where to go. Errands made at night should be swift. Find angelica, as well, and that we can take right now."

Angelica was easy to spot, for it was tall and had a compound bloom of white flowers on the top. Pippa found a good patch of it in the high grass near one of Felton's fields. Using a sickle-shaped knife carved from bone, she took four stalks and thanked the plants for sharing with her, just as she'd seen Lillibet do.

They also harvested fresh pennyroyal from the banks of the gentle brook behind the cottage. Its strong minty scent made Pippa sneeze. The pennyroyal would be used in a tea, Lillibet said, to stimulate the womb into contractions. It was the most harmful of the ingredients. "Once," said Lillibet, "my mother told me of someone who took pennyroyal tea, too much and for too long. It wasn't working, see, and she felt that continuing would loosen the babe. But instead, she became all cold and sweaty, and her innards ached, and she died. That's why we'll give Sarah enough tincture for five days only. If it don't work . . ." she shrugged.

Pippa had no idea that familiar herbs as mugwort and pennyroyal could do such a thing. Once in awhile she drank mugwort tea to bring on strong dreams. "It'll work," said Pippa, confident in whatever Lillibet chose to do.

Lillibet laid the collected ingredients on the kitchen block. It had taken three full days to prepare the mixtures and the charm.

When Sarah Ford arrived, she looked like a woman with a death sentence. Her hands were clasped in front of her. She wore a maroon dress and the same plain collar as before. A folded cap covered her mousy hair. Every stitch of her garb suggested humility, surrender.

"Ready?" Pippa asked.

Sarah nodded once.

"Come in, then."

Lillibet had strict instructions for the taking of the herbs. "Have you been eating berries?" Lillibet asked the unfortunate girl.

"Yes, Goody."

"Now you make a tea with these leaves of angelica and mugwort. Make it strong, steep it until the color is settled. I've measured it out for you, day by day, see? Then add a small spoonful of the tincture to the tea and drink it." Lillibet waved the little brown bottle with the clear tincture of pennyroyal inside. "Do this three times a day for five days. On the third day, take this—" she handed Sarah three small bouquets of fresh picked parsley, each tied with a long string, "—and put it up inside thy privy parts."

"What?"

"You heard me, child. You're no stranger to things bein' a-put there. The parsley should bring on bleeding. Whatever you do, don't stop taking the tea, no matter how poorly you feel. Then come back to me." Lillibet gestured at Sarah. "Now sit."

Sarah sat down and Lillibet asked permission to lift her dress up to her belly. "All women here, don't be shy, this will help the child depart now." Lillibet pushed the woolen dress up so that Sarah's navel was exposed. She left the other petticoat intact for the girl's modesty. "This'll make you right as rain, see? Now close your eyes." Lillibet began to murmur a rhyme. With her special paintbrush, dipped in the blood of a bat, she wrote a sign on Sarah's white skin. It was the rune for the thorn, to prick and to bleed, to reverse the growth of the life within.

Pippa listened carefully to the words Lillibet spoke. "Christ who died on the cross. Christ with the crown of thorns. A hedge is formed around thy womb, the child from the womb is shorn." Pippa closed her eyes. It was as though she could see inside Sarah's skin to a hot, wet, weightless place, to a secret cave, where the first stirrings of a doomed life listened to a mother's gentle voice. Lillibet whispered to it, "She's not ready for you, little one."

When the spell was cast and Sarah vanished into the rain, Lillibet turned to Pippa. "You've done good, child. You did your job and did not judge the failings of others. I'm proud of you."

"Thank you." Pippa dipped to her mother. She continued with her chores for the day, and tried to focus on the compliment, but she couldn't help feeling like she was about to cry. She wondered if they'd done a dreadful wrong. Somewhere in that rain, a new life would be flushed away, and they had new coins in their satchel because of it.

That night, Lillibet sat Pippa down at her feet, near the fire, and told her old stories of babes born in the Vale, and their various complications. "Life," Lillibet said, "is a funny thing. Sometimes it takes, sometimes it don't."

Lillibet was wise, and Pippa listened.

The Speaking Raven

On the night her friend Pippa was learning new things, Sybil too was in an unfamiliar land. She writhed and muttered deep in her sleep, on her feather mattress, and was not herself. No one witnessed this, for there were three bedrooms in the Yates house—it was a graceful old place—and Sybil got the single room because she was prone to talking in her sleep.

She flew on a broom. It was between her legs and this felt nice somehow. In the sky all around her was mist, fog, white cloud . . . although she could not see through it, this was a comfort, because something about flying on a broom was transgressive and Sybil did not want anyone to see.

"Not that way," said a voice.

Sybil glanced over to see another figure on a broom, a man. He was dressed as her father, in black with a conical hat, but he had the face of Tom Radcliff. The wind ruffled the short hairs around his ears and he smiled at her. "I will meet you at the end," he said, and then veered off in some other direction.

"But I don't know where I'm going!" she tried to shout at him.

Her words came out tinny and ineffective. It was as though the wind had stolen her voice.

The air grew warmer. Then the clouds in Sybil's head formed a tunnel. They spiraled in front of her, a clear path forward, and Sybil was yanked along it.

Faster and faster . . . then she opened her mouth to scream. She emerged above the Vale and could see the fields and the village and forest as though she was a bird. And in the center of her view was a fierce vortex that spat lightning and sucked everything into it: cows, pigs, houses, people. Her sister Cathy flew past her, dress flapping in the wind, and vanished into the maelstrom.

Then, Sybil felt the tug on the broomstick, and she began to drop towards the whirlwind, too. The force of the wind on her clothing made her collar constrict around her throat, choking her.

A bird croaked.

"No!" Sybil tried to shout. She tried to tug herself away but to no avail.

There was the croak again. She turned her head to see a baby blackbird struggling to fly alongside her, but it tumbled away, not into the vortex but toward the forest.

Closer, closer, and then the twister morphed into a living creature, a writhing worm, black and segmented and rising from the earth. That conquering worm opened its maw lined with silver bodkin teeth. She fell towards it.

She gasped awake.

From the light behind her curtains, it was almost dawn. Relaxing, she flopped back onto her pillow, and scrabbled underneath her mattress for her dream charm. It was a tiny cushion into which was sewn a sprig of valerian and a bundle of spiderwebs, to catch bad dreams. Spiders were the guardians of sleep because they came out at night. Sybil remembered gathering the webs for the charm with Alice and Pippa—they'd found fresh dewy webs and had carefully moved the spiders off their homes before gathering the web into a tiny ball.

The thought of her dear friends did not calm Sybil, however . . . it made her more anxious for fear they were having nightmares of their own inside a black cloud. She tried to fall back asleep for a few hours, but it was interrupted when Elizabeth clattered down the stairs at dawn.

Later in the morning after her breakfast, and after she'd helped Martha with sorting the laundry, Sybil buttoned up her leather shoes—she'd dabbed a dot of red paint on each black button—and climbed up the long hill to fetch Alice.

She found her friend finishing up the hours-long task of churning butter. Her sight wandered to a place above Alice's head where she thought she saw a pointed finger. It turned out to be the shadow of a branch through the window.

Alice released the churning stick, flexing her fingers. "Mama? M-May I be excused?"

"Yes, yes," said Goody Baxter, waving at the girls. "But come back soon, Alice, I need you this afternoon."

Together they walked to Wylde-Wood cottage. Pippa's home was an off-kilter sort of place. Sybil had always liked it. A thin plume of smoke rose from the crooked chimney, the chickens wandered about the yard picking at seeds, and Lillibet could be seen dusting the windowsill. She spotted them and waved.

"Good day!" the girls returned.

Sybil said, "Is Pippa about?"

There was a clatter inside the house and then Pippa emerged in her house dress and an apron covered in flour. "Hello!"

"Have we interrupted?" Sybil asked.

"No," said Pippa, "I've just put the loaf in. I'll clean up. Come in!"

Lillibet added, "Take a cuppa tea to revive thee."

Sybil laughed because she adored inadvertent rhymes.

The three girls sat down with hot cups of herbal brew while Lillibet went out to the yard, sat by the brook, and washed her feet.

"'Tis fortunate we have that brook," said Pippa. "The water is cleanest here before it finds the river."

That, thought Sybil who had once been to Bury St. Edmunds, was the benefit of the deep countryside. It was unpolluted by other people's thoughts.

Pippa sipped her tea. It was too hot and so she hissed it through her teeth. Alice was more patient and took tiny sips. Sybil did neither and let it cool. For a moment she forgot she had it; she was watching the throbbing glow of the coals in the hearth.

"We need to go into the forest," Sybil blurted.

"Wh-Why?" said Alice.

"There's something to be found there."

Pippa stared at Sybil. "What do you mean?"

"A dream I had," said Sybil. "I dreamt . . . well, it was rather bad. There's a storm coming here to the Vale. I was in the air, and I saw a great black cloud, right over the village. And there was a baby blackbird trying to fly, but it fell into the forest. I think we'll find it there if we go today. We should rescue it."

Both Pippa and Alice looked troubled. Pippa said, "This dream cloud. What was it about?"

"I know not. But it sucked everything into it. I never saw a cloud like that in my life. It touched the ground at the crossroads . . ." But Sybil paused, remembering. "No. That's wrong. It touched down at the church. And at my house."

"There's but one way to find out if it will happen," said Pippa, finishing her tea. "We go into the forest and look for the bird."

"Alice can nurse it back to health," said Sybil. Deep in her bones, she was sure they would find the blackbird.

Alice, who loved baby animals, nodded eagerly.

"Lillibet!" Pippa stood and called out the window. "If we go for a ramble, I'll change the straw later! Alright?"

"Alright," came the reply. "But don't you be neglecting duties! Be back for evening. I'll take the loaf out of the oven."

"Thank you!"

They headed for the forest. Sybil took breaths of the air scented with seed. It was invigorating and she understood why young people were implored to be physically active and healthy. She had frailer health than most—she'd suffered intermittent fever when she was young, and the doctor said she had too many sanguine humors—but she felt most alive when she was with her two spirit sisters. They did not fuss over her or make her feel strange the way her blood relatives did. She was a cheerful and true being around Pippa and Alice.

"Hear that!" she said. Above the sounds of pigs and chickens they could hear lively shouts.

"The boys," said Pippa. "There was a game of football to be played on the common today. Roger Felton was playing, and Will Renshaw, and some others."

The woods enclosed them and Sybil's feet danced along the old pathways. She hummed to herself. The world sang back to her. She forgot the sense of impending doom from her dream. Instead her mind reached feelers into the trees to find their new friend, the blackbird.

Sybil stopped mid-twirl. "Listen! There!"

The other two stopped.

Indeed, there was a feeble croaking. Sybil pushed through the branches of a young birch. "There you are," she whispered.

"Oh, dear! Look at it!" Alice appeared at her shoulder, distressed.

It was a baby raven, scrawny, its feathers dull and in that middling stage between downy and glossy. Its wing was at an awkward angle. A bald patch on its head gleamed, and its mouth was open in an attitude of terror.

"Broken," said Pippa, kneeling on the ground. "Poor thing."

"Cry no more," said Sybil to the raven. She slipped her

fingers underneath the bird and cradled it. She could feel the quick pulse of its tiny heart. "We heard you."

The bird seemed to sense that all was right, for it stayed quiet and stopped quivering in Sybil's hands.

Alice promised to find a box and some straw for the bird. "I'll feed it porridge and worms." She glanced up from her new charge. "Wait! Is it a boy or girl?"

Pippa reached out a mischievous finger and tickled it. "A girl!"

"We should give her a name," said Sybil.

"You tell us, for you dreamt we would find her, and knew where to look," said Pippa.

For a moment Sybil thought about names she liked. There were some she wanted to reserve for her own children, but that could be far in the future, so she said, "Ursula!"

"Ursula the raven," said Alice.

On the way back from the Baxters, where they dropped Alice and the baby bird, Pippa said, "But, Sybil! This means the rest of your dream will come true."

"I'm not worried," said Sybil. She felt they'd found a fourth to their circle, and that was something to be joyful about. Storms and worms didn't matter. She didn't even notice the church, the epicenter of her dream, nor did she notice her father's thunderous expression until he stood in front of her, arms crossed.

"Idle girl . . . Where have you been?" His voice was quiet, at odds with his anger.

"In the forest, gathering herbs for the stew," said Sybil.

"Oh? And where are these herbs?"

Oh. She might have thought of that. "Erm . . . there were none to be found. Someone has already taken the best of the rosemary, I suppose."

Peter Yates narrowed his eyes. "Are you telling me a falsehood? If you have been wandering about, endangering your health, letting the day pass in lassitude . . . You must stay indoors, child. You have neglected your studies. Get thyself inside and finish the reading from this morning." He pointed an unwavering finger at the door of their house.

"But, Papa, I —"

"No more lies! Imagination is dangerous. Sometimes I wonder not that it killed your mother when you were born. Let your mind take you instead to godly ways. Take your example from your sister Elizabeth. She is reading at this moment and you will join her."

Sybil smarted from his soft-spoken words. And she despaired of reading from the Bible with Elizabeth, who often scolded her for lack of paying attention. But with her father in this mood, there was no way around it, and so she darted inside for her indoor education.

Pippa was on the shaded slope near the forest on a sunny afternoon, weaving a doll of twigs and lavender stems, when she heard the uneven clunk of a wooden leg. She peered toward the path and saw Old Man Ash limping toward her.

She sighed and put the doll aside. It was for one of Lillibet's spells—it would be dressed in fine lace to represent a bride, a charm for a village girl who wanted a husband. Pippa was assigned the hand-worked construction of it because of Lillibet's arthritis, but Lillibet would do the charming, as usual.

Pippa waited for Ash to finish wheezing and speak to her. It was unusual for him to seek her out, for his best friend was the drink.

"Pips," he said.

"Good day!"

"What ye workin' on there?"

Pippa had hidden the doll behind her. "Something for Lillibet. 'Tis not for you."

"Ah, well." Ash's bones creaked as he lowered himself to sit on the grass near her. He rubbed his rough-shaven chin and his eyes darted around.

"What's bothering you?" Pippa asked. If he had a physical malady, she didn't know what he was doing here with her. It was always Lillibet who healed, no matter how much Pippa wanted to try. Other peoples' health was a great responsibility, her mother always warned her.

"Well," said Ash, "I—uh—I seem to be out of funds."

Pippa raised her eyebrows. Everyone in the village knew that. Ash's money went straight into the innkeeper's pocket. "I'm sorry to hear that, Ash."

He turned to her. "Pips, I want to ask you for this magic, seein' as you know me best."

"What magic?"

Ash whispered, "I want you to find me a treasure!"

"A treasure! What do you mean?"

"I mean, use your cunning, your witchery, and I'll share it with you. When you find us some treasure, I'll give you a quarter of it, for your services."

Although Pippa knew what Lillibet would say—that treasure-seeking was not a proper way to use cunning powers—she was tempted by the thought. This would be her triumph, and if she just closed her eyes and manifested treasure from the earth, there would be no doubt in Lillibet's mind that it was time for her real training. Plus, such techniques could secure them in the future. If Pippa had a nose for discovering lost riches, they would never again be forced to do a thing like with Sarah Ford.

"I'll do it," she blurted to Ashley. "We'll have to wait for the growing moon, though." She might not be Lillibet, but she had absorbed the basics: to gain things, use the power of the growing moon. To be rid of things, act during the vanishing moon.

"So you know what to do, then?" Ashley asked her. He must have been hard up for ale, because his hands shook and twitched.

Pippa thought about it. To find a treasure . . . she could make a dowsing stick out of rowan and attach wealth rhymes to it. That might work. "Yes!"

"One quarter yours," Ash reminded her.

They spat into their palms and shook once to seal the agreement.

She helped him back on his feet and contained her squeak of excitement. This was a trifling thing, but if she succeeded, Lillibet would be so proud! The new moon couldn't come fast enough for Pippa. After May Day, then she could prove her ability.

She grabbed the bride doll-to-be and skipped home.

The girl who wanted a husband, a plain-faced village maid named Susan, was already at the cottage with Lillibet when Pippa walked in. "Ah, there," said Lillibet, eyes alight on the doll. She took the poppet and gave it to Susan. "We've made ye a charm. Listen close to what I have to say." She waved at Pippa to sit down and listen, too.

Susan was wide-eyed with excitement.

"Did you bring the lace?" Lillibet asked.

The girl nodded and brought out a scrap of gorgeous fine blue Dutch lace. "'Twas all me savings toward the lace and your fee," she said, producing several coins for Lillibet.

Lillibet smiled at her. "Well, I'll just have to craft this charm the strongest for you. I'll make sure it works."

Pippa watched the frothy folds of lace as Susan fashioned it into a tiny wrapped dress for the doll. *When I find the treasure for Ash, I'll be able to buy a scrap of lace for myself,* she thought, and squirmed with excitement as Lillibet took the doll and held it between her hands. Marriage spells were always fun to watch, for their results were dramatic.

Closing her eyes, Lillibet chanted, "Hunter, lover, good Christ brother, draw, draw, draw. Husband, man, friend and father, draw, draw, draw. By the Son and Holy Ghost, by the Father's heavenly host, draw, draw, draw. For Susan a good husband, a goodly man of England, draw, draw, draw." Lillibet's voice trailed off into a rasping whisper. The aromatic twig doll seemed to hover between her careful hands. She opened her eyes and said, "Now. Take this token and bury it at a crossroads at full moon, near May Day. I recommend the village common, by Renshaw's inn. This way the spirits will notice it. But make certain that none see you and uproot the doll, for that would annul the spell."

Susan nodded quickly, her mouth pressed tight, eyes shining with anticipation for the as-yet-unknown husband.

Pippa, for her part, tried to recite the incantation once more in her head. She could use it herself once she had money to buy lace. She could use it on Hugh Felton . . . *Hunter, lover, good Christ brother, draw, draw, draw.*

ALL WAS SILENT IN THE YATES HOUSE except for the soft pitter-pat of mice feet in the wall. Sybil lay awake, head resting on one hand, and through her open east-facing window she could see the bright morning star just above the horizon. Dawn would follow it.

When an acorn with a ribbon attached to it sailed through her window and landed on the soft down quilt, she was not even startled. A lover was calling her—the God of May, the God that lived in the forest. Lillibet told folk tales about him and all the forms he took . . . stag, warrior, king.

Sybil was already dressed. She stepped up to the window sill. Pippa and Alice were in the yard below, nudging each other to be quiet. Alice had brought the healed baby raven, and Ursula rested on her shoulder. Waving at them, Sybil snatched up a bottle and a small pile of red ribbons, with a peach-colored flower embroidered on each. Gifts for May Day.

She met her friends outside and they ran with light feet toward the forest. A thin mist curled close to the ground. It was going to be a fine, sunny morning. Other figures could be seen at that early hour—other women in cloaks. They three were not the only ones to gather the dew on May morning.

Alice handed over the raven to Sybil. "Y-Y-You k-keep her now," she said. "I w-was happy to be her n-nursemaid." Alice gave her a shy smile and Sybil dipped her shoulder down so that Ursula could hop on.

On the way they stopped at the Wylde-Wood cottage, where they found Lillibet fastening her cloak. It was lined with pockets, each holding a tiny clay vial and stopper. Every year she gathered enough dew for her stocks.

"The wives will be happy for today," said Sybil. Mrs. Radcliff, Lady Felton, and Goody Renshaw all bought the youthening drops from Lillibet.

"It's me own secret," said Lillibet, patting her own cheeks, which were soft and wrinkle-free in comparison to her hands . . . and her age. "And if you girls keep the dew collected as maidens, forever you'll have the pretty look that you do today."

They set off. Ursula made tiny squawking noises from Sybil's shoulder.

From inside a fold of her sleeve Alice produced a pale wriggling earthworm. Sybil stared at the way it moved in Alice's fingers, blinking as she recalled her dream about the storm, the conqueror worm, the mouth that ate her. But Alice, untroubled, chewed up the worm and then spat it back into her hand. One bit at a time, she placed the mashed-up worm down Ursula's throat.

"It's like having a child," Alice said. They were in the woods now and her stutter had vanished, along with her normal veil of shyness.

"Dear Ursula," said Pippa, tapping Ursula's tiny bird head

with a gentle finger.

They found the large leaves of a horse chestnut gathered with beads of precious, glistening dew. They ran fingers along the stalks of wild grass, careful not to slice their fingers, and ran the drops into their vials. Pippa shook the dewdrops off the leaves of a birch tree to pool in Alice's palm; they peered into it.

"For eternity we be young," said Pippa. Her smile flashed so white in the newborn dawn that Sybil believed it to be true.

"Young in spirit, at the least," Alice said. "We ought to go to the grove, and leave our hairs for God."

This was a tradition that the girls had invented. On May morning they left a piece of themselves—a lock of hair—to the forest.

As they walked, Alice asked Sybil, "Why do we do this? I'm never quite sure. Is it for God the Almighty, or his Son? Or is it something else, like nature?"

Sybil pondered, her head tilted to one side, listening to Ursula's input. She'd always had a hum living in her left ear, a noise both tinny and deep. Sometimes she wondered if it was an earbug like people talked about. Now, with Ursula sitting on her shoulder, the noise made sense, as though the raven's presence translated it. "God created all the earth for the benefit of mankind, and all of this is His creation. So, it must be that we are offering to God Himself. But God takes mysterious forms. He was a burning bush to Moses."

"Yes," said Alice, "but are we not also told that Jesus died on the cross for that?"

"It's more like prayer," said Pippa. "God is in everything."

"Even in our hairs," said Sybil, and they all laughed.

They reached the grove of apple trees. The blossoms were fresh and damp, the same rosy white as the girls' English skin, and the first kiss of sunshine pierced through the forest from the east.

Pippa had her tiny knife. She cut an inch-long lock of her

own dark hair, then cut Sybil's blond, and then Alice's fluffy light brown. They were placed in a careful circle amidst the short grass and clover. "For God," she said, "and we are your brides today."

Ursula made a noise that bore an eerie resemblance to a human voice, though in what language no one knew.

Alice must have felt the need to make things a bit more Christian, and she began a few words from the Book of Common Prayer: "Oh heavenly Father, who hast filled the world with beauty, open our eyes to behold Thy gracious hand in all Thy works; that, rejoicing in Thy whole creation, we may learn to serve Thee with g-g-g-gladness."

A shiver of something unnamed went through Sybil, and Pippa too, and they stared at Alice.

She'd never stuttered in the woods before.

The Fevered Land

It was a warm rainy day when Matthew Hopkins and John Stearne crossed the River Stour. Elspeth sat next to Hopkins, her tongue hanging out. A drop of drool gathered on her fang and then stretched down to hit the deck of the ferry, and was lost in the rain.

Hopkins's heart stopped pounding quite so fast once the ferry was across the river. Water made him nervous, especially when it had a strong ocean-bound current. He could just imagine being swept out into the vast, cold North Sea.

His boot-clad feet stepped off the dock and onto solid ground. He clasped Stearne's hand. "Brother," he said, "I bid you Godspeed."

"And you, brother," said Stearne. His tiny brown eyes danced with emotion. "As planned, I take the west road, you take the east road. Between us all this county will be cleansed."

They crossed the river now, while summer loomed, and while the King's army was driven back after the Battle of Naseby. All of Suffolk was open to a witch hunt. Hopkins would have the undivided attention of the populace.

With purpose, he mounted his horse and made ready for the road. Others may go to the New World, some may fight in the armies, but Hopkins was forging into the ultimate unknown: the territory of the supernatural. The tiny boy inside of him quaked, but in the daytime it was easy to shut him up, to be a man, to take a stand.

Stearne, too, was spine-stiff with excitement as he swung up onto his horse. "Fare thee well, friend!" said Stearne, raising his hand.

Something occurred to Hopkins, and he said, "What if we should meet by chance somewhere in the middle, before Bury?"

"Then it be a sign that the infestation is particularly bad, and will need our combined strength to root out," said Stearne.

This made sense. Hopkins nodded once. "Right, then. Farewell!" He dug his heels into the horse's flanks and leapt forward, undeterred by rain or wind or storm. He hunted the voices. He saw not countryside of grain and sheep, but the landscape of Heaven and Hell and the souls therein. Most especially he saw his own soul, both the glory and the blight, and knew that he would go down deep before he was cleansed.

"*Tan-a-dik.*"

"*Flim flam flum.*"

"*At midnight on a Friday, we meet. The Master meets us. Follow us into the woods, and you will find our book.*"

Hopkins remembered what he'd been told.

THE HIGH PULSE OF LATE SPRINGTIME had taken over the Vale. Farmers and laborers took advantage of the growing hours of daylight to work, with muscles swinging and backs bending over their plows. Some of the women, too, worked in the fields. Despite the extra sun there was never enough time. The Brewers likewise did a strong business, for hard labor raised a great thirst.

Pippa was busy from dawn until dusk. Now was the time to grow and harvest herbs, to gather certain fruits to be preserved, to treat aches and pains and babies being born. The scent of life was rubbed deep into her skin—the mineral earth, the pungency of herbs, the coppery wet of birthing blood. For the first time she'd watched Lillibet at work, attending Margaret Howell for the delivery of a fine healthy girl.

The elements of her life were falling into place, for the moon had turned and it was time to find a treasure for Old Man Ash.

The morning was young when Pippa met Ash on the road outside her house. She had gone about her morning chores as quietly as possible and then muttered to half-awake Lillibet that she was off to gather fresh nettle. Unsuspicious, Lillibet had nodded and turned back to sleep.

The air was crisp ahead of the heat that Pippa knew would develop later. It seemed full of promise, perfect for divining treasure. She'd hidden her dowsing stick inside a hedge and she retrieved it on the way to Ash, checking it over. The branch was made of rowan wood, also called witchwood or mountain ash, and both names led Pippa to choose it for this project. It was whittled into twin points, like the forked tongue of a snake, and she'd carved three crosses into the branch.

In her mind she rehearsed the incantation to find treasure in the earth. She'd heard Lillibet say it once, many years ago, when they were having a slow year and needed a few extra shillings to pay for essentials. Lillibet hadn't found money, but she did find a patch of wild poppy flowers and harvested them for their valuable seeds.

Pippa had a good ear-memory, but still hoped she remembered the rhyme correctly.

Ash swayed on his good foot, waiting for her, and gave her a dubious look when she reached him. "None's going to follow us, are they? If we find a big treasure, I don't want to share it."

"No one's awake yet," Pippa reassured him. "Besides, we'll not be staying in the village. That would be too easy."

Pippa wasn't certain how to proceed, so she stepped with Ash into the field next to the road and said, "We'll start here." She remembered something about walking around a fire three times to say the charm, but it was daylight and they had no fire, so Pippa faced the rising sun instead. It was the most powerful fire of all.

Closing her eyes, she held the dowsing branch in her hands and chanted, "Panthon, Craton, Muriton, Bisecognaton. Siston, Diaton, Maton, Tetragrammaton."

She could feel Ash watching her. The more mysterious the rite, the more credit she would receive when it worked. Feeling the warmth of the sun on her face, she continued. "Sorthie, Sorthia, Sorthios. I conjure you three sisters of fairies, Milia, Achilia, Sybilia, by the Father, by the Son, and by the Holy Ghost, Amen."

For a moment Pippa wondered if Sybil was indeed a fairy-sister and she giggled to herself. They were three friends, after all. But no, it was just a coincidence in the rhyme.

Pippa spun three times around and stretched her arms. Taking off in huge strides, she allowed the dowsing branch to lead her forward.

Ash scurried after her, complaining. "Slow down, gilly!"

Pippa marched across the field. The dowsing branch had a mind of its own. Right, left, forward. It jerked this way and that. "Oh, here!" she called to Ash as he struggled to follow her meanderings.

They were led through the field, along the brook, through a muddy ditch, up into a fallow field made of weeds. The spirit trail led south, bordering the road to Lavenham, and then up a rise.

Pippa jerked to a stop.

A thin layer of sweat tickled her neck. Ash was far behind

her. She could just see the patched-up roof on the row of hovels where the Bucketts lived. Thin curls of smoke rose from their early morning fires. Pippa felt safe from being watched, for the Vale was just rising. She beckoned at Ash to hurry up.

The ground at her feet was balding, free of grass. A perfect place to dig. The dowsing stick did not seem to want to move anymore and it hung from her hands, pointing straight down.

"*Here*!" she mouthed at Ash, gesturing.

He wheezed up next to her, leaning on his cane.

Kneeling, Pippa scrabbled with bare hands at the earth. The soil was loose and dry. Deeper and deeper she went, finding nothing but a few earthworms and dead roots. Pippa felt the first shadow of disappointment, and then her fingers brushed against something that wasn't supposed to be there.

A piece of leather.

"There's something here," she muttered.

Ash bent over, blocking the sun's rays. "What is it?"

"Just . . . one . . . moment . . ." Pippa excavated the object and held it up in triumph.

A money sack.

Ash's eyes gleamed. "You done it! You really done it!"

Grinning, Pippa tore open the string and turned the sack inside out, counting the heavy coins in her hand. "One . . . two . . . two pounds and fourteen shillings! 'Tis a fortune!"

It was not the money that grew wings on Pippa's heart. It was success. At last her cunning had worked! *I have what Lillibet has.* She must have remembered the charm perfectly. She turned to Ash. "This is yours," she said, beaming with pride as she handed over the results of her first independent act of cunning.

"And this is yours," said Ash, counting out seventeen shillings for her.

They shook hands for their success and Pippa said, "Don't

give it all to Renshaw at the inn!"

"I intend to go to Lavenham with this," said Ash, jangling the coins. "They've got the whisky I been yearning for, no country ale."

It was not for Pippa to judge what Ash spent his money on. She had her commission, and that was the fair deal. "A nice day for a walk," she said.

"Walk? I'll be hitching a ride with me new fortune!" said Ash. He pinched her cheek. "Thank you, Pips. You've brought happiness to an old man today."

"Remember it," she said, patting his arm.

She carried her dowsing branch home. Lillibet was up and about, and Pippa meant to draw out the story of her spell, to tell it with suspense, but she couldn't resist blurting her triumph. "Lillibet! I did it! I found a treasure!"

Lillibet, in the middle of slicing bread, turned to her, astonished.

"I didn't tell you because I thought you would disallow me. That it would not work. But it has! We found a treasure this morning, and I did it with this!" Pippa held up the branch.

"Why . . . Pippa, what are you saying? That you cast a charm and actually found a treasure?"

"Yes!"

"Well, my goodness . . ."

"And I brought us our share of it. Seventeen shillings." Pippa fished the coins from her apron pocket.

Lillibet reached out to touch the coins. "Where did you find this treasure?"

"On the rise next to the road. It was buried in the earth, the branch led me to it. A satchel of coins."

Lillibet turned a shade paler. "Oh, Pippa . . ." she said.

"Why don't you sit, Lillibet? I'll make us that mint brew. With this money we'll be able to afford everything for awhile."

Hand pressed to her heart, Lillibet sat in her rocking chair.

Pippa decided her newfound abilities must have come as a shock to her mother. *It shouldn't,* she thought. *Runs in the family, it does.*

Pippa was halfway through brewing the mint and recounting the details of her treasure-hunting when someone pounded on their door.

"Lillibet! Help me! I been stolen from!"

Alarmed, Pippa jumped to the door and opened it to find Joan Buckett, her grey hair standing on end, her papery cheek smudged with dirt.

"What is it, Joan?" asked Lillibet. There wasn't a trace of surprise in her voice.

"I went to check on me savings this morning, as I always do," Joan stammered, her voice filled with outrage. "Someone's dug it up! Everything I saved!"

For a moment Pippa was upset, too. Who would steal an old beggar's life savings? And then, the awful truth dawned on her.

She had stolen it.

Gripping the herb strainer, Pippa stared down at the floor. It couldn't be . . . Joan Buckett was an impoverished old woman. There was no way she could have saved over two pounds. Every time Pippa saw the Buckett women, they were haggard and begging for more. Who could have known that Joan had savings?

No, she's impoverished now, admonished Pippa's inner voice. *Thanks to you.*

Lillibet patted Joan on the shoulder. "I'm truly sorry. I'm the one who told you it would be safe to bury it away from your hearth."

Pippa understood why she'd been led to that spot. If Lillibet knew of it, Pippa must have accidentally picked the information from her mother's mind, for they were connected. Shamed, she reached into her pocket for the few coins that remained of Joan Buckett's life savings.

Joan muttered in a torrent of curses.

"Now, there must be something to be done," said Lillibet. She reached her upturned palm to Pippa. "Let us help you with as much charity as we can spare."

Wordlessly Pippa placed the coins in Lillibet's hand.

"Here, take this for now," said Lillibet. "We'll see about retrieving the rest." She pressed Joan's coins into her quivering hands.

"You'll track down the thief for me?" Joan asked.

"I'll try," said Lillibet.

Still muttering, Joan shook her finger once at Lillibet. "See that you do! 'Tis your fault I ever agreed to put me treasure out of sight."

When the woman was gone, the silence in the cottage was too much for Pippa to bear.

"I'm so sorry," Pippa murmured.

"Where is Ashley? At the inn?" Lillibet asked.

"He's gone to Lavenham, said something about buying whisky . . ."

"The money is truly lost, then," said Lillibet. "Oh, Pippa."

"I'm sorry!"

Lillibet pressed her fingers to her temples. "I don't know what to do with you," she said, more to herself.

"Teach me, Lillibet, please! It worked, I did find a treasure, even if it wasn't mine to find."

"Sit, Pippa." Cradling her cup in her aged hands, Lillibet looked weary. "You have done a grievous wrong. You have destituted Joan Buckett. You must pay her back over time. I will disguise it as charity, for we can't have you charged with theft. That's a hanging crime. How could you do this? Why did you not come to me before charging off on this . . . errand?"

"Why will you not let me be independent?" Pippa said, but she knew the answer. It was because her bumbling ways just brought trouble.

"You've made a real knot of things," Lillibet said.

"But —"

"I think," said her mother with deliberation, "it would be best if you refrained from attempting spells. You have no focus, and you wield your ability unwisely. There is no good in cunning-ways, Pippa, if you know not the results of your actions. You are like a bull thrashing about a kitchen. You must learn to harness yourself. This is why I've not allowed you to work on your own. 'Tis the little bit of knowledge that be a dangerous thing."

Pippa's eyes swam with tears of defeat. She had failed in the eyes of Lillibet, the one person whom she'd hoped to impress. She was not cunning, she was stupid and hasty and impetuous. Whatever power she had was being misused. The worst part was that Pippa didn't even know where to begin learning what Lillibet called wisdom. She didn't know what it was, or how she would know when she'd found it. "Are you angry with me, Lillibet?"

Lillibet paused before answering. "Yes. No. I'm disappointed in you, Pippa. I thought I'd set a better example."

"'Tis not your fault! I'm the one who acted badly. I'll never do magic again. I'll be good, I promise."

"The day may come when you find your wisdom. Until then, I daresay you will stop these attempts to misuse what I've taught you." Lillibet leaned back in her chair, lips pressed together, her decision final.

But Pippa knew she would never be like Lillibet, hard as she tried. It was not in her nature to be patient, wise, and calm.

"I'll sweep the floor, then," said Pippa, awash in self-pity. For the first time the cottage had become a mundane place. Pippa's function here was to cook and clean and sweep and chop herbs for Lillibet's work. There was nothing for herself.

Lillibet looked sympathetic, but she did not ask Pippa to

help her as she began to stitch a charm into an old shoe intended for the wall of one of Felton's new tenant cottages.

THE TREASURE-HUNTING DISASTER was not the last time Pippa did magic. A week later, when the full moon approached, she resolved to cast one last spell, one last chance, just to see if God would grant her one last wish.

In the dead of night when the moon lined the world in liquid silver, Pippa crept into the yard and stood beneath the yew tree. From a heart-shaped knot on the trunk, sap coursed like blood in rivulets and globs, shining in the light. For a moment she was tempted to taste that heart's blood of the yew, but she knew better. It might kill her.

Somewhere a confused bird chirped. In the bright of the full moon, some creatures thought it was still daytime.

Pippa tilted her head upward and gazed at the moon, a crisp white circle against the black sky.

"Illuminate me," she whispered.

She reflected on Lillibet—her mother who could heal a fever, and birth a baby, and break a curse, and divine a husband for a young maiden. Lillibet held the power of birth and death. Pippa wanted that power, too.

From her pocket she tugged a single piece of red ribbon. It was the gift from Sybil on May Day, with a flower stitched on the end. Clutching it in one hand, Pippa held it up to the moon. "God . . . Jesus . . . whoever's out there, please hear me. Make me into whatever I'm supposed to become."

At that moment, Pippa did not hold herself in high regard. She'd misread a curse on a child, Francis Pye, and cast a phony hex-breaking; she'd stolen the life savings of a beggar-woman and given it to a drunk. It was hardly a road to happiness and success. But even now, Pippa wanted to walk through that door to magic, if it remained open to her. Gritting her teeth, she didn't care how it happened, only that it did. If it took reading and hard work and prostrating herself to her mother's mercy, she would.

She tied the ribbon in a firm knot around a strong branch. Murmuring soft and low, she repeated her request, talking to the tree.

"Please, please, please. Give me the key, open the door. Make me cunning and wise. Send *something* to me in this small village, this small cottage, something to make me strong and powerful and famous. Make Lillibet proud of me. Make Hugh want me, and let his family want me as their daughter above any other. I'm tired of being a child. Make me into a woman." She rested her forehead against the branch. The yew was the tree of immortality, and its smooth, solid arms pulsed some terrible evergreen force.

It was known that if a person made a wish and tied something red about a branch of yew, the wish would come true . . . as long as it was not a trifling thing. The yew was too old and too wise to be bothered with frivolity. Lillibet had done this before, praying to heal a lump that had grown in her breast near the pit of her arm. Within two months the lump had gone away—a relief, for it could have been that wasting disease that sometimes afflicted people, and turned them grey and pale and weak until they died.

If it worked for Lillibet, it might work for Pippa.

In the moonlight the red ribbon was the same color as the glistening sap.

Pippa regarded it and felt . . . nothing. The world had not changed. The bewildered bird chirped for a morning that was hours away. The yew was still, the moon was white, the land remained in its well-known curves. Perhaps her wish was too vague or too much. Dissatisfied with the anticlimax, she shuffled back inside, resigned to the power she would never have.

Weeks passed. Pippa waited for a divine omen, but her days were filled with chores instead: feeding the pig and the chickens, preserving berries picked from the forest, sweeping the yard, running up the hill to the Baxters' farm to buy milk. She sometimes helped Alice watch her younger siblings, and they took walks in the forest, but never for girlish rituals anymore.

Pippa wondered if such would be her mundane life. Sybil and Alice would find men to marry, and they would all have children, and Pippa doubted that any of them would have time to dance in circles around a fire after that happened.

Another of Pippa's jobs was errand-girl, carrying things for Lillibet whose bones ached in the heat. One day she'd carried a bottle of tonic up to Pye's farm for the son, Francis. It was to calm his nerves. He'd had another seizure. The curse was strong upon the family. As payment for the tonic, Goody Pye had given Pippa a young rooster. The noisy bird would be bred with their hens.

The late afternoon was hot and weighted with tension. This weather bred discontent and Pippa stretched her back before setting off down the hill with the rooster in his basket tucked beneath her arm. She walked through a frenetic cloud of tiny insects and one got stuck in her eye. Sighing, she paused to pluck it out.

Never had she been so bored.

Then, she heard the pounding of steps behind her. It was Alice, intercepting her from the direction of the Baxters' house.

Alice couldn't speak for several seconds, instead making frustrated noises. "I-I-I-S-s-s-F-f-f-G-go!" Alice's normally neat hair was in disarray and there was something approaching terror on her face.

"What is it? For God's sake, Alice! Tell me! Is it Lillibet?"

"N-n-no. 'T-t-tis Sybil. She's—she's fainted and d-d-deadly ill."

"What!?" Pippa was already tearing down the lane, Alice catching up a few seconds later. The rooster gave a terrified squawk from inside his container. A prayer escaped Pippa with the sparest of spare breaths: "Oh, Lord, keep her and heal her, let her be all right."

A mere faint would not have been so worrisome. Sensitive Alice was known to have them during her monthlies. Sybil, however, had been very ill once when she was a girl. She was frail in body—it was a thin thread indeed that kept Sybil's roving spirit tied to the earth.

"Is Lillibet with her?" Pippa shouted over her shoulder at Alice.

A shake of the head.

The dust scattered as Pippa ground her heels to a halt outside the Yates house. A curtain flapped in an open upstairs window. She dropped the rooster on the front stoop and knocked. They were admitted by Martha, the servant. "She not be havin' any visitors," said Martha. "Miss Radcliff is already helping."

"Miss Radcliff? Winifred?" Pippa was puzzled. What could she be doing here, nursing? Sybil needed her dear friends about her, not her mean sister's mean friend. Annoyed, she said, "Well, if Winifred Radcliff is here, then we can assist her."

"Well . . ."

"Thank you, Martha." Pippa pushed past the servant and up the stairs.

Alice hissed, *"Pippa!"* but Pippa paid no heed.

Sybil's door was closed and Pippa knocked twice, softly. Winifred Radcliff opened it.

"Yes?"

"We've come to see *our* friend," said Pippa. "We've come to heal her."

"Only God can do that," said Winifred. Her eyes were narrowed in dislike at Pippa and Alice, yet a wrinkle of worry split her smooth forehead.

Pippa peered over Winifred's shoulder and saw the vague shape of Sybil beneath white bedclothes. "Why are you here?"

Winifred's brown eyes widened, then blinked. "Elizabeth is my friend," she said, "and Sybil is her sister. As a dear friend of the family, I have as much Christian duty to help as I can. She needs godliness and cleanliness. I rather think you two don't qualify."

Pippa almost snarled with anger. This was ridiculous. Stupid Winifred with her bejeweled head cap knew nothing of Sybil and her needs. Pippa was about to knock the girl aside with a firm arm when Alice spoke.

"W-W-Where is the R-R-Reverend?" Alice asked Winifred kindly.

"At the church, praying for her until the doctor arrives." Winifred's voice was low, throaty, cool.

"And h-her sisters?"

"Keeping vigil in their father's study, reading from the Good Book. They were told not to come in the room lest it be catching."

"But you're here," said Pippa.

"I've never had a fever in my life," said Winifred with a touch of haughtiness. "I don't intend to now."

"Fever, you say? We'll see," said Pippa, suspicious of a laywoman's diagnosis. She would only trust whatever Lillibet said about Sybil's condition. Losing all patience, she pushed past Winifred only to stop short inside the room.

Sybil was pale and the color of her lips had leeched out to pure white, as though stained by the horseman of death. Cold dread slithered into the pit of Pippa's stomach. "Oh, Sybil," Pippa whispered.

"When the doctor arrives, he will bleed the bad humors away," said Winifred.

"Bleed her?" This sounded like the wrong idea to Pippa. Sybil already seemed bloodless as a ghost. "She doesn't look like she has any blood left in her!" With a steady hand she felt Sybil's forehead. The skin was hot—the fever consumed her. Winifred had been correct. "We must get Lillibet." Pippa looked out the window and groaned in frustration: Lillibet's slightly hunched figure was on the slow climb up Pye's hill to find her.

"What h-h-h-happened at P-Pye's?" Alice asked. "F-f-for them to p-pay the rooster?"

"I'll not say here," said Pippa. To speak of hexes might bring similar onto Sybil and push her over the edge. "I must fetch Lillibet. I'll be back soon." She ran out the door and snatched up the basket with their rooster.

Then, it was more running, more pounding through the dirt. Sweat soaked her collar and ran down her legs. The bird hindered her progress. "Lillibet, Lillibet!" she shouted. "Lillibet!"

A few seconds later she reached her mother and gasped out the emergency.

"But, child, did the Pyes receive their tonic —"

"Sorted," panted Pippa, holding up the rooster. "Walk with me to Sybil, and I'll tell you what happened." They turned back at a slower pace, for it had been many years since Lillibet could race around like Pippa. "Sybil has the fever. I felt it burning in her blood."

"She's in a sickroom?"

"She's in her bed, windows closed to this bad air."

The rooster was left on the Yates's front porch once again, and Lillibet was hurried into the house by Martha, who whispered, "The Reverend don't want you here. He don't believe in cunning-ness. But he be at the church, so it waren't me who let you in, if'n anyone asks."

Lillibet muttered, "Cunning-ness do better than doctors," and followed Pippa up the stairs to where Alice and Winifred sat on the narrow bench at the end of Sybil's bed. Inside that bench was where Sybil kept her embroidery and needles.

Lillibet pushed at Sybil's eyelid with a gentle finger. Pippa noticed a yellowish stain on the thin skin below the eyes.

Sybil had a tiny bout of shaking that made her bedclothes ripple like a cloud.

"Talk to her," said Lillibet.

"Sybil?" Pippa said. "Sybil, darling, we're here. Can you speak?" She held Sybil's hand with loose fingers.

Sybil's pink tongue darted out to wet her parched lips. "Water," she managed.

An instant later Alice was there with a spoonful of water that she edged between Sybil's lips.

Lillibet asked, "Is thy neck stiff, child? Does it hurt to look down?"

"No. Just . . . my . . . my head," said Sybil. The pain was in her eyes, for she was too weak to make a facial expression.

Lillibet nodded and stepped away. Speaking in an undertone to the girls, she said, "Ague. I'm certain of it now, with the headache."

Ague. A hammer had descended on them. It was middling-to-common in this hot, moist weather—the ague, the intermittent "marsh fever." It was what Sybil had contracted as a child, for it was known to come back later in life. In those of weak constitution, it killed.

"Oh, no," said Winifred. "Oh, Father of mercies, God of all comfort! Oh, Lord help her!"

Pippa glanced at the interloper. She didn't think Sybil needed to hear dramatic religious declarations.

"The Lord can help. We must pray to Him," said Lillibet. "But in the meantime there is something else to be done. Move that rug." She pointed down at the knotted rug covering the wood floor. A small piece of chalk appeared in Lillibet's wrinkled hand.

Bending to the floor, she scribbled a protection square underneath the bed, nonsense letters that would confuse the fever spirits that tormented Sybil:

```
SATOR
AREPO
TENET
OPERA
ROTAS
```

From the corner, Winifred watched, eyes wide. Sybil's condition must be serious for Lillibet to cast so openly in front of a stranger.

"Winifred Radcliff, can you fetch me a paper?" Lillibet whispered.

Winifred paused, disapproval written on her face.

"Do you want to heal her, or not?"

"Yes, yes, of course." Nodding once, seemingly to herself, Winifred darted from the room and returned with a pencil and a scrap of paper. The paper was printed on one side, an old news pamphlet about the movement of the royal army. "This?" Winifred asked, holding it out.

"Thank you, dear," said Lillibet. She scribbled on the paper and Pippa saw it was another protection cipher, the most powerful of them all, a triangle of letters that read the same in every direction:

```
abracadabra
 bracadabr
  racadab
   acada
    cad
     a
```

Lillibet folded the charm and tucked it against Sybil's chest, beneath her nightgown. Then she held Sybil's hand and murmured prayers, reciting from the Book of John.

The air in the room was heavy, like a tomb. Alice and Winifred fell to their knees beside the bed and prayed. Feeling helpless, Pippa put aside her resentment at Winifred's presence and joined them.

When the casting was done, Lillibet bade Pippa to leave with her. "There are further workings," she said.

They waited until the half-moon had gone to sleep over the western horizon in the small hours of the morning, then fired up the cauldron. They said a prayer and decocted a powerful liquid opiate from Lillibet's store of poppy seeds. The poppies grew wild in the fens and were cultivated by some. "'Tis fitting," said Pippa, "that the cheerful bright poppy flower should restore Sybil to health. The flower is like her."

"'Tis," Lillibet agreed. "Here, the stopper. Don't you lose a drop of that."

"Will she be all right?"

"If God wills it. But God be more willing to aid those who would use his natural blessings toward the healing. In some places, brewers add these seeds to the ale, in the marshes and near the still waters." Lillibet sighed. "But, the moon's growing, and 'tis not a fortunate time to banish a fever. Instead we focus on restoring health."

The next morning Sybil was unimproved, or so said Martha at the door. "The Reverend's in with her," she said. "Ye'll have to wait."

"How long?" Pippa danced from one foot to the other, clutching the vial of medicine wrapped in cloth.

Martha just shook her head.

Discouraged, Pippa set off to wait at the village common. She sat next to the pond, took off her shoes, and dipped her feet into the water, watching the ripples, one eye on the Yateses' front door. The pond water was warm, just like the sticky summer air. Pippa watched the lazy paths of minnows and mosquitoes through the reeds. Sybil lived so near to this deep, still water . . . perhaps it was a danger to her health? It was said that stagnant waters led to illness. Pippa kicked her bare feet harder, trying to dislodge the sluggish pond, and watched as the ripples sped across and hit the reeds on the opposite side.

Some while later the Reverend Yates emerged from his house, looking serious in black and wearing his slouched hat. Pippa waited until he was gone, then made her move, pulling her shoes over her wet feet and dashing back across the road. Martha let her in and informed her that the doctor was unable to come for two days. "There's outbreak of the cholera at that school in Lavenham, 'e's hemmed down by it. That doctor canno' make no special allowance when so many young ones are taken ill."

In Pippa's opinion, the longer Sybil went without being bled by the doctor's leeches, the better. But it also meant the burden of their friend's health was square on their shoulders, or so it felt.

"Sybil?" Pippa pushed open the door. Catherine Yates sat on the bed, dabbing Sybil's forehead with a wet cloth. Elder sister Elizabeth sat in the chair, knitting. And there was Winifred Radcliff again, murmuring verses aloud from an open Bible.

Pippa felt a twinge of unease at so many people in the room, especially judgmental Elizabeth. It couldn't be restful for Sybil. She glanced from one to the other and finally met eyes with Winifred. It could have been her imagination, but she thought she saw the same worry in the rich girl's earnest brown eyes. She hadn't expected to find anything in common with such a snooty person. *I'm imagining things*, she decided.

"It's the ague," said Catherine in a quiet mumble, hard to hear even in the stillness of the sickroom, "so we've been minding her. Ague is not catching."

Pippa wondered if Sybil had been cursed, and the fever

brought by someone who wished to do her harm. She exchanged another look with Winifred, who surprised Pippa further by saying to the Yates sisters, "Bless you both. Would you give us a moment so that we may pray over her?"

Elizabeth nodded reluctantly, and beckoned Catherine to come with her. With them gone, the atmosphere lightened just a little. Sybil's eyes flickered open.

"Have something for you," said Pippa. "This'll make you all better." The opiate potion was poured into a large silver spoon. "Drink up, now." She nudged Sybil's lips open.

"There's a good girl," added Winifred as Sybil swallowed the first spoonful. It tasted terrible but in such a state, it was unlikely Sybil noticed or cared.

Another spoonful. Then another.

To Pippa, the common purpose with Winifred felt awkward. Why did Winifred care so much about Sybil all of a sudden? She must be true friends with Elizabeth to take such care of her under-loved sibling. Pippa wasn't sure she trusted Winifred with the potion, or to overhear the charm she wanted to say over Sybil.

Winifred's hands were steady as she measured the potion into the spoon that Pippa held. "I don't pretend to know what you do, but I know your mother's methods work," she said.

"Oh?"

"Once, my younger sister Jane was taken very ill. She was five years old, you might not remember, but your Lillibet did heal her. Whatever it is you need to do for my neighbor—for Sybil—I shall help you."

Pippa turned to stare at Winifred. There was no lie in her frank declaration, but Pippa thought she did see a trace of something approaching guilt. How odd. Perhaps Winifred felt responsible for the cruelty of Elizabeth and herself. Everyone knew that ill thoughts and ill words could be considered a curse.

"She is my friend's sister," Winifred explained. "If you are truly Sybil's friend, you know about that sort of bond."

"I do know," said Pippa, although she could not pretend that *she* would tend Elizabeth Yates with such care, were Elizabeth to fall ill. "Thank you, then. If you be true."

"Of course I am," said Winifred.

Sybil shook her head weakly against another spoonful of potion.

"How do we make sure she takes the rest?" Winifred whispered to Pippa.

"We'll pour it into her drinking water, here," said Pippa. She poured the remaining liquid into the jug of water on Sybil's bedside table. "Then her sisters will feed it to her without knowing."

"The water won't dilute it?"

"Nah. 'Tis a strong potion." Pippa held Sybil's hand through another bout of shaking. She would have no choice but to share a touch of Lillibet's method with Winifred. Taking a deep breath, she said, "Lillibet gave me a charm for her. Now we say it three times over. Like this: God's Son climbed over the hill. God's Son rose under the hill. Vein to vein, banish heat and pain, we pray God will make thee well again."

Winifred joined in after listening to Pippa once through. "God's son climbed over the hill . . ."

THE LIGHT HAD GONE from the sky and the candle flickered in the corner. The light was the color of flesh. It lived in the corner. The shadows chased it, approached it, retreated. They were the loam, the black of earth and of throats. Her sisters were gone . . . what were their names? Pippa and Alice and Winnie. The door opened and Sybil was helpless to who entered . . . in this case, Elizabeth. She looked frightened, although Sybil sensed it was not because of the illness, but rather something else. She tried to speak her gratitude when Elizabeth spooned some water into her mouth, but her throat was too dry and hot.

Her head throbbed. Her skull was swollen. Every breath was an endless expansion. Every breath a crushing contraction. Her head was not supposed to do that.

Sybil knew she was very, very sick. She knew it was the ague, for she remembered Lillibet coming in and touching her and saying it aloud. That made things better, for to name a thing was to reduce its power over her. *Ague. Ague.* She'd had it once before. She would come through this, too. If only her head would stop crushing her.

Elizabeth left and her father entered, and he murmured prayers over her, his Bible open in his hands. Sybil knew the words, and did not know them. Those words were alien in this land. They were bumblebees that were lazy and low and droning. They stuck to the wall that melted like hot treacle.

Cotton wool in her eyes. Cotton wool in her ears.

Christ climbed over the hill, Christ rose under the hill.

"When will the doctor come?" Was that Cathy? Or had the door creaked?

"Day after tomorrow. 'Tis an ill time. Those children in Lavenham."

It was the door talking. "Father, I must speak to you about something. Not in front of her."

The weight of the sheet on her skin was a stone, a miller's stone, the kind that crushed grain. She was a grain, a shaft of wheat with rough arms and legs branching outward, about to be crushed, about to be harvested. She was a hand-stuffed doll made of wheat, made of grain. The cotton rubbed her like a thousand tiny knives. *Breathe in, breathe out.* Good girl. Take your medicine.

Sybil watched the candle in the corner. She was comforted by its steadfast light. A halo surrounded its flame, its flesh. A circle of candle in a square room. A circle of Sybil in a square bed. She could see a star through the wavy glass of her window. It was unmoving and cold. She was in her bedroom and everything was all right. Martha popped her head in to check on her but did not linger. Like an animal, Sybil needed to be alone so she could find her way through the hot, sticky darkness. Or, she wanted her sisters. Pippa and Winnie.

She slept and did not sleep. The hours peeled away. It was so very dark but for that candle. It did not seem to be burning down. Perhaps it was a newfangled kind of wax from Holland?

Sybil breathed in cotton wool. With eyes of sandpaper, with eyes that were heavy spinning marbles, she traced the corners of her room, mapping them out, making them normal. Square room. Round-doll Sybil. There was the white-painted wall. There was the door, open just a little. There was the window and the curtain and the dark wood post of her bed. There were her feet, hidden under the pale covering sheet, making a little tent. There was the skeleton sitting on her bed to her left.

The skeleton regarded her with empty eyes.

Sybil regarded the skeleton with equal calm and wondered who had let it in the house.

Christ rose under the hill. Hey, diddle diddle, the cat and the fiddle.

Around the skeleton's shoulders was a wreath of snowy white flowers. Sybil tried to identify them but she couldn't; they were not earthly flowers. They were from Heaven. A thousand tiny knives were the stems of the flowers.

"Who let you in?" Sybil asked.

The skeleton grinned a bleach-white smile, a smile of sharp polished moonlight.

You're a happy dead lady, aren't you.

The cow jumped over the moon.

Sybil closed her eyes. She was so very tired. It was safe to rest for a little while, but then she had a great deal of work to do. She had to save the raven. She had to finish her embroidery. She had to do her Scripture lessons.

The cow kept jumping over the moon.

Sybil wished it would stop doing that and let her sleep.

Hey diddle, diddle. The cow jumped over the moon. Christ jumped over the hill.

She tried to bolt up out of bed. If she didn't keep a careful eye, the dish would run away with her spoon, and she couldn't drink her medicine! But then, the skeleton was still there. It would take care of that dish.

"Sybil? Here, take some water."

Sybil tried to ask Cathy if she could see the skeleton too, but the skeleton shook its head at her and raised a finger to its rows of teeth in warning.

The shivers overtook her after she swallowed the teaspoon of water that was a river. It disappeared down the loam-black hole of her throat. *Shiver. Ague.* When she moved her head in the throes of that shiver, her hair plucked at her scalp. Every hair she could feel. Her hairs were a thousand tiny knives growing into her.

Many years later, Cathy left and the candle was still burning and the skeleton was still there. Sybil's voice had returned. In fact, she spoke out loud with ease, and wondered if she was through the worst of it.

"I'm all better," she told the skeleton.

Out of the gaping black eye of the skull, something crawled. It was Ursula! She'd come to visit Sybil. Ursula had grown up—she was large, the shape and glossy black of an adult. Even in the dim light the raven's feathers shimmered a rainbow.

Ursula said, "Tan-a-dik."

"Count the sheep," added Sybil. "The cow jumped over the moon."

"Hey, diddle, diddle. Beware the man with the grey imp."

Vein to vein. Sybil wondered why the sheet had to be so

heavy. Who had let that skeleton in, anyway? Her father didn't like her to have friends over.

"Will you do my Scripture lesson for me? Elizabeth will burn my bacon if it's not done."

Instead of answering, Ursula plucked a glowing white flower off the sharp white skeleton and ate it, stem first, so that for a moment the petals erupted out of her beak.

Tooth to tooth. Scripture! Oh, God, the lessons! *An eye for an eye. Two eyes. Two empty eyes.* The skeleton sat on her bed and this was important.

"I know you," she said to it. "I like your flowery necklace."

"We are all children," Ursula told her. With her beak she tugged on the flowers until the wreath tightened past the horned clavicle, around the skeleton's laddered bones of a throat. The jaw dropped.

The door opened. It had been open. Elizabeth had been standing there, staring at Sybil, who was sitting straight up. Elizabeth's jaw dropped. "Who are you talking to?" she shrieked.

"The cow jumped over the moon!" Sybil tried to raise the alarm, but it came out as the faintest of whispers.

The Meeting of the Roads

For thirteen hours Pippa slept. After giving Sybil her potion and then going to the church with Alice to pray, she had returned home where Lillibet force-fed her a heel of fresh bread and a hearty rabbit stew. Then she'd crawled up the wooden slats to her loft where she collapsed onto the straw mattress, pulled a wool blanket over herself, and let her soul rest. She did not dream, the night passed in a blink, and it seemed that she'd no sooner closed her eyes than opened them again to lilac shadows of the pre-dawn light.

"Psssst! Pippa!"

Pippa's loft was open to the rafters and the thatch roof, and the dried mud filling the cracks on the eave wall was thin. A person could whisper through it.

"Who's there?" she hissed back.

"Hugh."

"What time is it, you daft man?"

"An hour before dawn. Come out and talk with me!"

All of a sudden, Pippa was wide awake.

"No," she said, "I don't want to alert the rooster. Come

through here. What are you about?" She unlatched the square wooden hatch in the wall where the sloping sides of the roof met in a triangle.

Hugh stood on an awkward tower of a barrel and an upside-down bucket. He put his elbows on either side of the window and heaved himself through, landing with a soft thud on the straw. His nearness made her heart do loops in her chest. Her imagination raced, wondering what he had in mind . . . would he ask to court her? Had he decided that after all this time, despite his courting of other girls, it was Pippa Wylde he'd loved all along?

Hugh grinned at her. "Hello," he said, a little too loud.

"Hush, lest Lillibet awake!" She was glad for her mother's dim hearing, but Lillibet was also notorious for sleeping at odd times, and wandering about in the night.

As a precaution, Pippa closed the thin cotton privacy curtain. She took a long drink of water from the cup she kept by her bed.

Then Hugh grasped her around the waist and rolled her onto the mattress. Surprised, she giggled, muffling the sound on his chest.

"I pray I did not wake you," he said.

"No . . . I've overslept as it is." His face was so close to hers. His hands were warm and firm on the curve of her waist. She felt like she couldn't breathe.

"You must have needed a good heavy rest."

"What are you doing here so near to dawn, anyway? My mum will murder me if she finds us out."

Hugh leaned out of their embrace and propped himself up on one elbow. "I came to tell you. Sybil Yates is through the fever. I heard from a farm-hand, who heard from their housewoman Martha, who was up very early indeed to fetch her some milk."

Liquid relief made Pippa collapse backward. "Oh, thank

God above," she murmured. "Thank you, Lord."

Hugh smiled. "I thought to tell you first. I knew you'd want to know."

"That's very . . . thoughtful of you, Hugh."

With her worries lifted, Pippa became even more aware that it was the quiet hour of morning, and that Hugh Felton was in her loft. With her. Alone. So far, he'd been considerate, telling her about Sybil, nothing out of the ordinary—except for the way his hands had lingered, the way he'd tackled her like a playful animal.

As she glanced down at the way his hand rested, palm upward on the straw, she felt the air change. *He must care for me*, she thought, and lowered her eyes.

Hugh reached out, tilted her face toward him, and kissed her on the lips.

Pippa had no idea it was like this. The triumph over every other girl in the Vale who fancied Hugh was swept away into the moment when his hands caught in her tangled mess of hair. They fell back together and she kissed him in return, awkward and not quite sure what she was doing, but it didn't take long to find a rhythm.

All kinds of new feelings bubbled up from a hidden cauldron within her. She pressed herself up against Hugh, the long length of him. His hands roved over her, feeling through the thin cloth of her nightgown. His breathing was heavy and . . .

"We must stop," he gasped. "We must . . . stop . . . 'tis not right outside the laws of God."

"No, keep . . . well . . ." Much as Pippa did not want to stamp out the fire inside, she thought of Sarah Ford's recent predicament. She sighed. "You're right."

Hugh kissed her on the forehead and rolled away. "Best I get home."

"And I'll visit Sybil. I'm so glad." Her words disguised her inner turmoil, still aflutter from her first kiss, still not quite believing what had just happened. *Why? Why is he here?*

When Hugh had backed out of the window to stand on the bucket, and the pale orange of the sun began to peek over the horizon, he paused to seize Pippa's hand. "You might just be my favorite person, Pippa. I want to be with you."

"With me?" she breathed. She was aroused by his words, but troubled, too. What did he mean? Was he aiming to use her? Would he ever ask her for marriage? He kissed her, and now he was ready to leave. He said this, but in what way did he want her? Suddenly Pippa wondered if she knew Hugh at all.

"Yes," said Hugh, sounding absolutely certain of himself. "You." He leaned forward and kissed the tip of her nose.

A dozen questions hovered in her mind. She wanted to know why, if he wanted to be with her, he walked with Elizabeth Yates and spoke to Winifred Radcliff after church and mentioned merchants' pretty daughters in Lavenham. Perhaps Lillibet was right. Perhaps Hugh was fickle and she should abandon hope of a commitment from him.

Clasping Hugh's hands in the gloom, Pippa knew one thing for certain. If she didn't use whatever power she had over Hugh now, in this moment, her dream of him as a husband would vanish. With a yearning that burned through her blood, she leaned over and kissed him, her tongue grazing over his. Her throat burned with the beginning of a strong bout of crying. *Ask me, please ask me to marry you*, she thought, the pleading in her kiss.

But Hugh didn't. Instead he gave her a brilliant smile to match the sun rising behind him and he clambered down from the loft.

Disappointment flashed through Pippa and tears moved up to tickle behind her eyes. The worst of it was the pain of knowing she wasn't cunning like Lillibet. All her life, her spells had never worked . . . not even the heartfelt enchantment of a pretend marriage, cast when she was six years old and had no idea what she was doing. Perhaps this was the only cause and effect she would see: the light in Hugh's eyes when he looked at her. Perhaps this was the only weak magic she was ever meant to work.

If she couldn't make a living as a cunning-woman, she would have to do something, and she wanted to live as Hugh's wife and secure her future and be kissed every day. There was nothing else for her. But the unfortunate fact was that her wish to the yew tree, the red ribbon spell, had not worked. The weeks had passed as a blank. Pippa had no hand in healing Sybil except caring. Her magic was defunct. Hugh might kiss her, but would never marry her. She, the failed folk magician and daughter of a dead father, stood no chance against wealthy, proper, well-dressed girls like Elizabeth Yates.

As she watched him retreat into the shadows cast by the newborn sun, she knew that she did love him . . . she just wished it might bring a measure of happiness, not the twinge of loss.

ANOTHER TOWN, ANOTHER ROAD, another inn. Matthew Hopkins was not weary, however. He'd scoured the eastern part of Suffolk for weeks, interrogating as he went, and giving evidence for a string of indictments. The guilty women—and, in a few rare cases, men—were taken to the larger gaols at Ipswich and Bury St. Edmunds. There would be an assizes, a court day, in August and the cases would be tried and, he prayed, convicted.

The list of names in his pocket grew ever longer. Every time he found a witch, he felt the joy of hard work, a job well done, a tilting of the balance toward his salvation.

On the walls and beams and bedposts of the inns where he stayed, he left a trail of crooked crosses, etched with his bodkin. One for every name. He never forgot to leave his mark.

It was a hot day and the wind fought against him from the south. It threatened to knock his hat straight off his head.

"Bugger this," he finally said under his breath, and carried his hat in front of him. But then, the sun high above beat him down and made his eyes sting. There was no way around the discomfort in one form or another.

The way of the road, he thought to himself, *the way of God's lawyer. I should not complain, even in thought, about what He hath created. My resolve remains true.*

Hopkins threw his head back and pretended to welcome the sun's harsh rays.

Behind him, the cart carrying the Essex search-women and their supplies plodded along the road, raising a cloud of dust. All were matrons or widows, respectable as they came. They brought a case full of sharp instruments with them, used for pricking witches: needles, pins, knives, and wooden-handled bodkins, filed down to glinting points.

It was deep countryside through which they moved. He'd taken a south turn from Bury and, according to his maps, there were several small farming settlements along this route. Old places full of old hatreds, people who were ignorant of the laws that could protect them from the supernatural. Hopkins looked forward to educating them.

His horse crested a rise and spread before him was a crinkle in the landscape that cradled a village and a thick wood. Hopkins eyed the wood with suspicion: forests were wild and wanton places that concealed evil doings. But then, there was also strong cultivation happening here, and he looked with approval on the ordered squares of field, cow pasture, and the fluffy white dots of distant sheep.

Reaching backward, he fumbled around his map case for the rolled paper that would tell him the name of this place.

The lines of the map were heavy in some places, weak in others, as though the ink itself was inconsistent. The name of this village was cramped alongside its road. Hopkins read it aloud. "Another Vale." From here it looked a quiet, sullen place. *This could go one way or another,* he thought. Either the villagers were devoted to worship, or their isolation had driven them to less civilized ways. Even here in East Anglia there were pockets of Royalist sympathy and of Catholicism. *Satan's workers,* he thought. He would keep an eye out for them, too.

As he descended into this unknown territory, a familiar knot formed in his stomach. It was like a fist of power inside him. His gut was his supernatural nose in detecting witches.

Elspeth panted hard and raised her elegant narrow snout to sniff the air.

"Smell them, do you?" Hopkins said. "Yes, as do I. There's at least one witch here."

From the south he could see another dust cloud approaching and he wondered who he was about to meet.

THE CROPS WERE THICK AND HEALTHY at midsummer, a relief to the people of the Vale, for the margins were thin with the burden of wartime taxes. It looked to be a fine harvest if there were no unexpected storms. The animals went about their forest business and many a goodwife swept bold rabbits away from the fenced rows of lettuce and cabbage. The cats hunted the mice, the dogs guarded the sheep, the leaves were thick and green on the trees. All was in order, and Pippa stood with Sybil next to the duck pond on the village common.

Sybil was pale still, but the fever's grip was two weeks in the past, and with diminishing doses of Lillibet's opiate she regained her strength and color every day.

On Sybil's shoulder sat Ursula the raven, who had thrived under Alice's care and lost her baby feathers. The bird now had a thick glossy black crown and glinting eyes that carried a sharp intelligence. Ursula's wing would hobble her from flying, but she was well-fed by the girls.

Pippa wore her severe black church dress. She would be attending the women's Bible study at the Yates house, but had arrived early to take recuperating Sybil for a short walk outside.

"I wonder who approaches," said Pippa, spotting a dust cloud in the distance on the road from Lavenham.

Sybil whispered, "The imp."

"What?"

"I said nothing," said Sybil, but she looked suddenly pale.

"Let us go inside," said Pippa, though still curious about the approaching visitors. "Bible study is about to begin, anyway." Pippa took Sybil's arm and they walked inside, letting Ursula off in the back garden.

Bible study was not Pippa's normal mug of ale, but Lady Felton was there, and Pippa wanted to present herself as a fine good Christian. With the career of the cunning-woman falling away, Pippa had to make herself respectable so that she might secure a good marriage. When she saw Hugh's elegant mother in Reverend Yates's sitting room, she felt the desperate tug of hope that she might be granted a miracle. That Lady Felton would like her, that Hugh Felton would marry her instead of a more suitable girl.

She hadn't been alone with Hugh since that morning, weeks ago. He was of the right age to marry, and everyone said he would make a proposal soon, and it made Pippa sick with anxiety to think about it.

The Bible study began and Pippa swallowed her distaste at keeping company with so many women who'd never liked her.

Elizabeth Yates asked her to read aloud a passage from Galatians and Pippa, whose letters were of a more practical bent—herbs and inventory and numbers—struggled with it.

She could hear the low muttering of the other women, felt their impatient expressions, and flushed with shame and irritation.

Winifred Radcliff in particular looked at Pippa with hostile speculation, her eyes pausing on the berry stain on Pippa's cuff. Whatever goodwill had formed between them over Sybil's illness had since vanished.

However, when the Bible study was done, Lady Felton said to Pippa, "I like your spirited voice, Philippa Wylde. Study your letters more diligently and I'm certain you would be a fine reader."

Pippa smiled suddenly, her heart lifting. "Thank you, ma'am." She knew that Hugh loved his mother, and now she knew why—the lady deserved the title in her kindness.

The group of women emerged from the rectory. What Pippa saw made her smile vanish.

Two dark silhouettes were in the road, the sun a bright torch behind them, their faces in shadow. Fat flies buzzed around a pile of horse dung near their booted feet. Both men wore fashionable wide-brimmed cone hats. A sleek grey dog skulked at the heels of the taller one.

Pippa turned to look up at Sybil's house and she saw her friend's slight figure peeking out from behind a curtain, like a ghost.

Reverend Yates went to the strangers first, speaking in low whispers. They all shook hands. Then the Reverend turned to the curious group. "Lady Felton, good women. These men are here to help us. They are Matthew Hopkins and John Stearne. They are appointed by law as witch-finders!"

Something quaked inside Pippa. When she tried to pin it down, it slithered away. She was troubled by witches and their powers of evil, else why would she learn the defense against them . . . but there was something else, too. Some sort of inner warning, like a church bell ringing in a fog. She edged to the back of the crowd, trying to conceal herself from the attention of the two men.

"Providence!" said Winifred. "We've been afflicted in this

village. Just this spring was young Francis Pye bewitched. And they say that one of Felton's cattle fell to a hex, as well."

"Is that true, your ladyship?" asked Goody Renshaw.

"Yes," Lady Felton replied, with a quick glance at Pippa. "The cow was tested and found to be under the influence of a hex."

Lillibet had been the one to do the testing by making a cut on the animal's ear, rubbing its blood in patterns, and it was rumored that Old Man Ashley, at his usual place in the pub, had complained of an earache at the same time. Hugh had told Pippa about it, although he was not convinced that witchcraft was the cause of the animal's behavior, and rather suspected stomach worms.

"Fear not," said the shorter man. His voice was high and reedy. "I, John Stearne, and my partner Hopkins have much experience in such cases. We've brought professional search-women with us." He gestured to one of the carts parked in front of the inn, where two primly dressed women sat. "It was Providence that brought us here in your hour of need."

Recognition flashed through Pippa after hearing their names again. The pamphlet about witches in Essex. These were the gentlemen Hopkins and Stearne. They were here to help. Although Pippa could not see the men's eyes—*Must the sun be so very bright?*—she sensed someone looking at her. Reverend Yates, perhaps, who knew that it was her mother who had thus far done the job of detecting witchcraft.

But, perhaps these other men would say that it took a witch to know a witch.

Pippa wanted to go home. Lillibet always told her to listen to the "small voice" and so she did, moving behind the group and skirting around the pond instead of going the way of the inn. She found her mother scattering feed for the chickens.

"All's well?" Lillibet asked.

Pippa almost told her about the witch-finders, but discovered that she didn't want to name them or talk about them. Her throat felt constricted. Instead, she just nodded.

"Get thyself to the kitchen, then, and prepare for tea."

It was with thoughtful hands that Pippa chopped an onion with some herbs. They had a large eggplant, gleaming purple, and it was to be stuffed with stale bread crumbs and vegetables. The kitchen work calmed Pippa. Lillibet was the cleverest person she knew and her mother would keep them safe.

The summer wind was unrelenting and Pippa laughed when Lillibet lost her cap and had to chase it, cursing, across the lawn.

SOMEWHERE IN THE NIGHT, a dog howled. Elspeth's ears perked and her nails clicked on the wood floor as she danced in agitation. Night had fallen over the Vale and Matthew Hopkins was in his room at the Charter Inn with Stearne, inspecting a local map drawn for them by Goodman Renshaw, the proprietor. Like most innkeepers, Renshaw was full of useful information.

From his east-facing window Hopkins could see the moon on the rise, a fat moon growing, and this made him nervous. Anything to do with nighttime made him nervous. But Stearne was there and they had several large candlesticks to light the room, and so Hopkins was able to focus on the task at hand.

As his first impression had allowed, the Vale was an average farming hamlet, if a bit isolated. There was a manor house owned by a noble family called Felton, and a few large homes at the crossroads. The other prominent family in the Vale was called Radcliff, involved in textiles; Mr. Radcliff was often away in Lavenham, Colchester, or Ipswich. "But it be the son that's the puzzle," Renshaw had told them. "They say he's away, studying a' some university. But none's seen him for well on a year now. Mrs. Radcliff comes from gentry and they say the family has sympathies for the King."

It was most intriguing.

Radcliff, Hopkins thought, *Royalist?* He spread a hand over the map. "Farm laborers, yeomen, a smith, a brewer . . . all good folk, on the surface," he mused.

"A few beggars in their hovels," said Stearne. "Passed them on the way in. Grim little places along the road, so filthy I could scarce distinguish them from a lump of mud."

"Such people often resort to witchcraft," said Hopkins. "Their tendency is toward knavery and theft. A small leap to consort with Satan. We shall ask about them first."

"Indeed," said Stearne. He smiled. "All along this way have I found evidence of the evil pact."

"As have I," said Hopkins. In his travels since he last saw Stearne, he and the search-women had rooted out a witch at nearly every stop. His purse had grown fat with his commissions. "How was Lavenham?" he asked his companion.

"A fair number of ordeals uncovered it. All the accused have been sent to Bury ahead of the assizes."

"And here we've met, both at the same village. There must be a real coven here," said Hopkins. His own words frightened him. He imagined a group of witches cavorting with their imps around a fire . . . dancing, drinking . . . bare breasts and loose hair . . . monsters with a thousand teeth, sharp as knives . . . every sin committed and *Oh, Satan himself in attendance. Oh, I am there, too.* He blinked his eyes to clear his mind.

"My guess is on the beggars," said Stearne. "A place as small as this cannot have much room for the lazy and insolent."

"Yes, it will be a good place to start," said Hopkins.

Later, when Stearne had left for his own room—the Charter Inn had but two guest rooms, and the search-women were sleeping on mattresses in a curtained area downstairs—Hopkins tried to sleep. His mind wandered to the forest nudging against the Vale. What a perfect meeting place it must be for witches. He reminded himself to ask about it.

In that middling place between wakefulness and sleep, his mind wandered, his defenses down, and he was snatched back into a time when he hadn't known to be suspicious.

MATTHEW HOPKINS, AGED NINE, *crept into the kitchen to find their house-woman, Deborah, spinning in place, her generous hips rolling, her skirts twitching around her ankles. She was a buxom woman with a narrow waist, a ready smile, and eyes that were every bit as dark as his. Deborah was the same age as Matthew's mother Mary, but the two women didn't get along. "What are you doing?" he asked.*

"Dancing," said Deborah, reaching out to seize Matthew's small hands and twirl him with her.

He giggled. In the back of his mind, he knew his father would disapprove of dancing, but his bond with the servant was special and she allowed him to see her private, joyful moments. They became Matthew's moments, too.

The dawn's light made the kitchen seem silvery, like they were underwater.

As the room went topsy-turvy, he saw a grouping of stones and flowers laid out in a pattern on the plank table. He pointed, looking up at Deborah with the question in his eyes.

"Shhh," she said, placing a finger on her pretty lips. Then she smiled, the kind of smile that meant it was all a great secret.

When they stopped spinning around the kitchen, Matthew's head felt all wobbly, like he was one of those wooden-bob dolls. He focused on the table, where a bunch of dried herbs were placed inside the stones that formed the outline of a heart. Deborah had picked the stones from the brook, for he recognized their color and their soft roundness from the caress of the water. He touched one, the pinkish one at the bottom point of the heart.

"No," she whispered. "These are my special stones."

"What's special about them?"

"In a manner all and some, into my wound of love do come," Deborah recited, *and a wistful look passed over her as she gazed down at Matthew. In a more even voice she said,* "They are to bring love back into this house."

"You love me, though, Deborah?" *He meant it to be a statement, but it came out as a question.*

"Yes, you are my darling," *she said.*

She always called him darling. Although she was just a servant, this made Matthew feel above his brothers, whom Deborah did not like nearly as well.

"Love for who?" *he asked.*

She shook her head. "You ask a great many things, my little questioner!"

Matthew loved to find things out. Adults told him he asked too many questions.

"Go on, get thee to work. Your father said he wanted you and your brother John to pick the early apples from the yard. Hard work is godly." *The last sentence was said out of habit. The Hopkins household was strict, for Mr. Hopkins was the minister, and he brought his sermons home to the point where even the servants quoted him.*

Matthew wrinkled his nose. He didn't mind work, but his older brothers bullied him and foisted the worst jobs onto his small shoulders and teased him for the wavy curls of his hair. They called it "girlish." Matthew couldn't wait until he was old enough to crop his hair. He didn't understand why his hair was not straight like his brothers'; no one else in their family had untamed locks.

"Come 'ere," *said Deborah, pulling Matthew into a tight embrace. He was shoved up against her soft breasts and he wrapped his arms around her comfortable, familiar waist.* "If you do your work hard," *she said,* "and come in dirty, I'll give you a bath myself. We'll have our special time."

Deborah often took it upon herself to bathe Matthew. It was one more way that she made him feel loved.

She spanked him on his way out the door to the yard. "Get to work!" *she said.*

When he turned to look at her on his way out the door, he saw that she'd taken the bouquet of herbs from the middle of the heart and was pinching them between her fingers, and sprinkling them into the family's porridge.

PHYSICAL HEALTH HAD RETURNED to Sybil. She was able to walk and do her chores and her lessons. The fever circles beneath her eyes receded. Her eyes lost their jaundice around the edges and were clear white and blue once again.

There was a shadow in her, though, a remembrance of the places she'd gone when she was ill. Sybil knew that the world was not quite as it seemed. In the fevered state of mind, things were real and yet unreal. She remembered what they had told her.

Beware the man with the grey imp.

Two days ago, when Matthew Hopkins came to her father's door with that grey dog at his heels, she'd known fear. Folding, twisting, sharp fear. It was him. The dark man who had haunted her visions. He wore a short cape, and a hat, and expensive bucket-top boots. And when those terrible blank eyes rested upon her, it had taken all Sybil's strength to resist fainting dead away.

Elizabeth had nudged her when their father introduced them to the visitors from Essex. "Sybil!" she'd hissed.

She'd remembered to dip a greeting, and gave her knees the command to bend just a little, and not succumb to the bone-limp weakness radiating from her core.

"Do pardon me," she'd said right after, and she heard Cathy making an excuse about her recent illness.

Then, her father had told them that the men were witch-finders, bound by law to sniff out witches, and that the Vale would not tolerate any more wickedness. "'Tis been many years since a proper trial's been held here," he'd said, and Sybil knew that somewhere in his quiet demeanor, her father thirsted for such a thing. Losses must be accounted for. Justice must be done. His flock must be protected from the spiritual wolves that preyed from the feral forest.

"Oh, Tom," she sobbed to Thomas Radcliff, to her pillow, on Thursday night. "I wish you were here. I wish I was yours to protect. I wish there was no war. We might have escaped this."

For all of her doziness, and for all of her flights of fancy, Sybil was not stupid. She knew how this would go. She knew, and there was nothing she could do about it, and so she was a cloud pushed by a wind. She was a girl-woman on a broomstick drawn into the maelstrom.

Sybil knew Matthew Hopkins. She knew his fabric. He was like a tangle in her embroidery, the kind that never loosens, the kind that hinders and unravels all the threads around it.

Worse, he was a lawyer.

Even Jesus denounced lawyers in Scripture and called them hypocrites. Sybil thought that was in the book of Matthew, but she would have to ask Elizabeth, who would know for sure.

"I will confess my relief," said Catherine at the breakfast table the next morning. "With the witch-finders' help, things will seem less frightening."

"Some of us have not guarded our spiritual well-being," said Elizabeth, pouring a generous amount of honey into her porridge and stirring it. "There is no escaping God's justice."

Sybil wanted to protest Elizabeth, to wheedle her, but her deeper voice told her it was too late for all that. Elizabeth refused to meet Sybil's eyes. Since the relapse of the ague, Elizabeth had become coy, as though afraid to cross words with Sybil. It had been a welcome relief from the usual nagging and ridicule, but Sybil knew a suspicion had grown like a weed in her sister's mind. It was possible she'd said something in the throes of fever that might be . . . misinterpreted.

Lillibet, knowing the girls went into the forest to work their girlish magic, had always told them to keep quiet. That others would not understand the difference between black and white.

At midday Sybil brought Ursula inside from the garden and tucked her safely in a box under the bed, with a bit of water and fresh grain should she get hungry. "Stay silent," she warned the bird, for Martha did not approve of wild creatures in the house.

On the way into the church that afternoon, Sybil reminded herself that evil witches there may be, but she was not one of them.

The mood of the country folk was curious, and a little fearful. Many had never seen a witch trial and didn't know what to expect. For months there had been rumors from other, presumably more wicked places, but none had thought it might afflict the Vale. The neighbors gathered at the church: Widow Moore, her daughter-in-law Isabel with three children in tow, and the Goodman Moore, the widow's son, who wore a perpetual expression of bafflement.

There was Goodman Powell, a young man with a strong face and still unmarried.

Old Man Ashley, already quite drunk, swaying in the back.

There were the Pye children with their parents. The infant girl was in her mother's arms. The twins both appeared in good health, despite their recent brush with witchcraft. They would have something to say at this hearing.

The Baxters were in attendance, all seven of them. Alice carried one of her youngest brothers, still in diapers.

Next to Sybil, Elizabeth sat straighter: the Felton family was here. Elizabeth had a predator's instinct for the things she wanted, and she wanted Hugh.

The Radcliffs entered, along with Jonas Martin, their visiting cousin. "Do you suppose they've seen a great many witches?" Winifred could be overheard whispering to her mother as they took seats behind the Yates girls. "Will they be taking accusations today, do you think?"

"Witch," Sybil whispered, "ditch. Snitch. Pitch. Tar and feather them."

"Are you feeling all right?" Catherine asked, looking at her sideways.

"Fine," she whispered, "I'm fine." She turned around and saw Lillibet clutching Pippa's arm. The older woman's face was grim. Pippa, on the other hand, looked annoyed at having to be in church on a Friday afternoon.

A light breeze drifted through the open windows. The movement of air was a slight relief on sweaty brows and necks.

The church was the only building large enough for group meetings, so it also served as the hall where village business was conducted. For a moment Sybil gazed at the plain altar with its white candles and simple wooden cross. Cutting into her vision of the holy altar were the two witch-finders, dressed officiously, arms crossed.

Sybil's father stood in front of his flock. "Good people, this meeting is not for worship, although we stand in God's house. We do His work today through earthly laws. I turn the floor to Matthew Hopkins and John Stearne, Witch-finders."

The small crowd was hushed and leaning forward, ready to hear more.

"Worry not," Pippa told Lillibet. "Cunning-folk are in every village. This is all a spectacle because the summer's heat breeds boredom."

"You know nothing of it, Pippa. Every generation this happens. Women are never safe from the accusation of immorality."

"But you're the midwife. The bishop gave you the license." Pippa considered that Isabel Moore might try to move in on the position. Midwifery was an occupation that always made men nervous—women's mysteries were outside of their theology or understanding. It was important to some that midwives be the most scrupulous in matters of Christian belief, above all criticism.

Isabel thinks herself as such, Pippa thought sourly, glancing at the Moores.

Reverend Yates introduced Matthew Hopkins and Pippa got her first proper look at the witch-finder.

Something about him made her uneasy. His stance was dominating, confident, and his rich doublet coat was tightly buttoned up to a strong-muscled neck. There was a sheen of sweat on his white skin. He wore a sharp goatee beard. His eyes scanned the crowd.

Then there was his colleague, Stearne. The little man was shifty and energetic, as though his feet could not keep still inside his boots.

"Good people of the Vale," Hopkins began. His voice was quiet, but then he projected it in a burst of alarm. "There is a plague upon you! You are under attack from Satan himself! In your hearts you know it to be true."

A murmur grew.

"Think, good people. Think of the unexplained evils you have suffered. Think of the blight on your crops, the war in this land, think of your illnesses and ailments. These are not the doings of the Lord who loves you . . . no, they are the work of the witches who live amongst you!"

A few people began to nod. It had always been problematical for Reverend Yates to explain why evil things happened to faithful people, if God truly did love them. Hopkins offered a tidy explanation.

"These witches are in league with Satan himself. They work to sow discord amongst you!"

"I been bewitched once, 'tis true!" someone from the back

called out.

Hopkins paused and then, *sotto voce,* unrolled the terrible truth. "The witches are amongst you. I guarantee that witches are right here, in this room, defiling God's church. They attempt to hide behind godly faces."

The congregation shuddered as one. Heads turned from side to side. Hands were clutched, and children whimpered.

"Look around you!" Hopkins said. "You have not been imagining this spiritual attack! In the dead of night, when fear takes you, that is God's own voice telling you to be vigilant. The Bible warns us of the insidious danger. *'And thou shalt not suffer a witch to live*!'"

"Book of Exodus," added John Stearne in a whip-thin voice.

"And I am here," said Hopkins, spreading his hands, "to root out this disease that lays waste to our spirits. I am trained in the most modern techniques of discovering witches. Master Stearne and I have vast experience in interrogation, and in separating the good from the guilty. Trust us in this task, for we are—like you—godly men on His earthly errand."

Some of the men were staring at Hopkins and Stearne with open admiration. It took a brave soul to not only stand up to witchcraft, but to make a life's work of stamping it out.

Stearne said, "We have traveled far and wide across this country. In Essex, in the towns of Colchester and Ipswich and Bury St. Edmunds, in the countryside, hundreds are being found out. There are none but us who can lay claim to such experience."

Reverend Yates stood. "I, too, can vouch for this process. I have spoken at length with these two men and they are gentlemen, pious to the utmost. We should be honored to have them."

"No problem of the supernatural is too small for our notice," said Hopkins, bowing to Yates. "With every witch convicted the world is made purer."

"Ask in your hearts for the answer from God," Yates told the crowd, "and let that knowing be your guide."

Hopkins cleared his throat. "This is an open hearing," he said. "We are a country ruled by a Parliament, a representation of the people, and so it is you—the people—who will participate in the course of justice. I will open the floor to hear your concerns."

A tentative hand rose in the front: Robert Pye, the farmer. "Welcome, and thank you, sirs. As my family has been the victim of a foul hex, I wonder how the guilty are found out?"

"I am troubled to hear of your misfortune," said Hopkins. "You ask a fair question, and I tell you, there are laws governing the interrogation of witches. These laws have been written by wise and virtuous men, even by kings. They are foolproof. I am but a humble questioner, the one who finds the witches. Their conviction is left to courts and the magistrates in this jurisdiction—in your case, Bury St. Edmunds. After I give my evidence, it is in the hands of the law. But fear not, our ways have proven reliable in the past. Justice will be done."

"God bless you," said Farmer Pye, and sat down.

"Any others?" Stearne asked.

Pippa's heart skipped when Hugh Felton stood up. "I wonder," he said with a trace of disdain, "what are the fees for your services?"

Good question, thought Pippa, cheering inwardly for Hugh.

Stearne, smooth as cream, said, "A just concern. Our fees are modest in comparison to the work we do, and the risk to which we are exposed. Remember that we look upon the very face of Satan's minions."

"But how much?" another man asked from the back.

"For each interrogation—which is an involved process—the fee is twenty shillings per witch-finder and his team."

Another murmur, this time of consternation. Twenty shillings was a large sum, especially if the number of accusations was high.

"But worry not," added Hopkins hastily, "if an accusation be made in jest, or out of pure spite without prior evidence, we accept it not . . . wages are not our aim, for we're gentlemen already. This fee covers our general costs and the upkeep of our helpers." He paused, hand to his mouth, looking over the congregation. "This reminds me of another point. As many of you know, we brought with us four experienced search-women. But they will train volunteers—devout women in this village—in the same techniques. We will need your help. Are there any women who would learn to be watchers?"

Pippa almost raised her hand. She figured there was no better way to avoid being "watched," whatever that meant, than to become a watcher herself. But Lillibet snatched her hand back down, hissing, "Draw not attention!"

"Matrons," Hopkins specified, "for the . . . nature . . . of this searching is not for maiden eyes."

This time it was a tremor of titillation that spread through the crowd. It was not often that such things were touched upon in this clean white building.

A young farm laborer had the cheek to call out, "What sort of things? What nature?"

Hopkins lowered his eyes. "'Tis terrible," he said slowly, and the people stretched their ears to hear what came next. "Witches consort with Satan. They *copulate* with him. They allow their imps to suckle their bodies and gain nourishment, and so there can be found unnatural teats which reveal this allegiance."

An older woman—Sarah Ford's mother Mary, devout to the point of prudish—fainted away at the mention of "teats" in church.

Pippa wanted to giggle and had to bite the side of her lip to keep quiet.

Several matrons rose and offered to be watchers—the Widow Moore was one of the first. She was nosy on a normal day, so an actual license to pry was too tempting to pass up. Several other women stood up, including Goody Brewer.

"And none may be watchers who have accusations to make," warned Hopkins, "lest there be an unfair bias."

Lillibet scoffed.

"Why don't you do it?" Pippa whispered. "You're a matron."

"'Tis the search-women they will investigate first," said Lillibet. "They would take a single look in our cottage and know we are cunning!"

"And *not* the same thing as witchcraft! For Heaven's sake! How many of this village have you cured, how many babes brought into the world . . ."

"I will keep myself low," said Lillibet, "and I don't want to hear another word about it." She crossed her arms and turned her face away.

When there were six women standing at the front, including a recovered Mary Ford, Hopkins said, "Good. Very good. Humble people, I understand how difficult it is to come forward with an accusation of witchcraft. You fear supernatural retaliation if you point the finger here in public . . . I know what it is to be afraid. Thus, I will be available in the Reverend's study at his home, or found at the inn, for all who wish to come forth. One of us—myself or Mr. Stearne—will be in one of those places at all times."

"What if we wish to accuse now?" asked Robert Pye.

"This is a public hearing, you are welcome to speak," said Stearne. "Who has done this thing against you?"

"Anne Buckett!" Pye declared. "She—"

An eruption of cries, of agreement and fear, drowned the rest of what he said.

"Decorum, good people!" Reverend Yates called. "Goodman Pye, please continue."

"She bewitched me son—Francis. He fell in a fit. Tests revealed Anne Buckett to be the culprit! Me wife was there to see it, and the children. Shortly after it happened Anne Buckett came round the house, wantin' to sell some eggs. We told her we weren't in need of eggs, but she refused to leave. She was drawn by her wicked spell!"

"Anne Buckett, step forward!" Stearne said.

But Anne and her mother Joan were not present.

"The accusation has been made and noted," said Hopkins. "We shall interview this woman. Are there other stories about her?"

A chorus: "She gave me the evil eye." "She sold me milk had gone rotten." "When I gave her an apple out of me garden, she stood outside me door and stared for three days."

The beggary of Anne had grown unpopular, surpassing the charity the Vale was duty-bound to give.

Pippa heard young Jane Radcliff speak up and say that Anne Buckett was a witch. Jane was excitable. The talk was influencing her young mind.

"Anne Buckett is just a poor woman," muttered Lillibet. "Her manners may be ill, and her person filthy, but that don't make a witch."

Pippa swallowed guilt. It was partly *her* fault the Bucketts were on hard times. But unfortunately for them, Joan Buckett and Anne lived up to the idea of witches: warty, stringy-haired, bony-handed, bitter, and husbandless.

"It makes me nervous," said Lillibet, "this notion of secrets. If folks haven't the courage to say it aloud in front of all, then it shouldn't be said."

Pippa, however, doubted that many people would go so far as to accuse their neighbors. There were always conflicts and tensions between neighbors, but they were all Christians. Judging from the overwhelming opinion that Joan Buckett and Anne were witches, that was all that would come of this nonsense. Once the village had their scapegoats, all could go back to normal, and Pippa could work on charming Lady Felton into wanting her as a daughter.

When the people filed out of church together, the green haze of gossip and tension surrounded them. Lillibet looked wary, her arms crossed defensively against her chest. Pippa felt relieved.

"Do pardon me," said a voice, hoarse but compelling.

Pippa turned to find the witch-finder, Matthew Hopkins, standing behind her. "Sir," she said, curtseying once.

"I was hoping you might speak with me for a moment. I was told you are the midwife in this village?" He looked at Lillibet.

Lillibet sniffed and turned away.

"She is," said Pippa. "My mother. How might we help?"

Hopkins nodded toward an empty area on the green. "Walk with me."

Pippa skipped along next to him, Lillibet trailing behind, her face filled with shadows. Pippa had a feeling she would get shouted at later for speaking with the witch-finder.

"I saw you leaving the women's Scripture study," said Hopkins to Pippa. "Your name?"

"Philippa Wylde."

"Miss Wylde, you and the other young ladies who attend the Bible studies . . . you are my best hope for righteous voices during my investigation. I would implore you to tell me anything you know about the doings of witches in this village."

Pippa stopped walking and looked earnestly into Hopkins's eyes. They were rich, filled with the shine of hope, or the shine of fever. Letting out a long breath, she knew she must follow Lillibet and stay far away from this man . . . and yet she wanted to help discover witches, too. Who else was better qualified? "Master Hopkins, if I hear anything, I shall come to you," she said, settling for compromise. "But I think the Buckett women are a likely place to start."

His lips quirked into a smile. "God bless you, Miss Wylde. I should hope that all the young women of this village are so lovely."

Pippa felt a not-quite-comfortable tingle in her solar plexus. She couldn't tell if she was pleased, or if her intuition was trying to warn her off.

When she dipped her head and took her leave, linking her arm through Lillibet's on the way, she turned around to see Matthew Hopkins staring at her with a fresh gleam of speculation in his dark eyes.

8

The Discovery

The smell of fear was ripe in the Vale. Hopkins knew. Hopkins was long familiar with fear and the way it went *scritch scratch* in the night.

On Sunday morning, Hopkins dressed for church. He was eager to hear Reverend Yates's sermon. Now there had been an unexpected kindred spirit. The Reverend was well-versed in the Puritan views, and he had been much humbled by personal tragedy. He was highly encouraging of the work of witch-hunting.

As Hopkins buttoned his doublet, an idea occurred to him to write a book. If it were to be published and widely read, he would be exalted as the true Witch-finder General, not just of East Anglia but of all England. Perhaps the Parliament would even create a special position for him.

Just past dawn, the bare-bones church—the style Hopkins approved—was packed with worshippers. With Stearne on one side and followed by their four search-women, Hopkins took a seat at the front. Families filed in around him. All was quiet except for a few coughs and throats clearing as the Reverend stepped up to the pulpit, heavy Bible in hand.

It was balm for Hopkins's soul.

"The Bible is clear on the subject of witchcraft," said Yates. "It is a mortal sin. It guarantees damnation. Witches are the very tools of Satan's design and are beyond hope of reparation.

"But let not images fool you. Witches are women, but witches can also be men. And those who call themselves cunning-folk are also to be avoided! A white witch is still a witch. True redemption comes from simplicity and humility."

The Reverend's eyes fixed on the back of the room. Hopkins turned and saw several parishioners, *women*, looking uncomfortable.

As the service wore on, the air grew heated, and it was a meager breeze that drifted through the windows. Languid flies and summer gnats buzzed around faces. Women waved fans woven from brook rushes. The words were familiar, a low drone at the back of Hopkins's awareness, and his mind wandered into a vague prayer. *Give me the strength to continue, the prosperity to continue, that I may be your humble worker on the earth. Let me cleanse myself of the original sin that created me. Sin, sinner, bad like me. I am bad, I am special.*

And then, as though following the beckoning imp, he wandered down the crack in his mind. He'd been fourteen when he discovered what a wretched soul he was. That day had changed everything.

"Matty! Matty! Come in *and take your elevenses," Deborah called to fourteen-year-old Matthew from the door of their manor house in Great Wenham. He was reading in the shade of an oak, sitting upright in a wooden chair amongst the carpet of early autumn leaves. Glancing up, he waved at her to leave him alone, but Deborah grinned and came bouncing out to fetch him anyway.*

As she approached, Matthew watched the curve of her breasts, visible at the top of her bodice. Her sleeves were rolled up for kitchen work, exposing wrists that were strangely delicate for a servant. He'd been noticing such things more lately.

"Come on, then. I've made the fresh bread ye like so much." She ruffled his hair and he glared at her, for he preferred a tidy appearance . . . yet her touch made the heat rise on his cheeks.

"After I finish this verse," Matthew ordered, his new adolescent voice cracking. He was reading the Book of Samuel from his own copy of the Bible, given as a gift from his father.

Deborah retreated.

Just as Matthew was ready to stand up and go inside for a thick slice of bread with a generous dollop of honey, his older brother Thomas appeared. "She favors you," said Thomas, nodding toward the kitchen where Deborah worked.

"Just as Father favors you," said Matthew.

Thomas smirked. "Yes, well, he knows that I'm his son."

Something about this sent a note of alarm down Matthew's spine. "What are you talking about?"

"Just think it's about time you found out. I'm not supposed to know, and you're not supposed to know, but if you're going to be a man, Matty, you'll have to prove you're a real Hopkins."

"What are you saying?"

Thomas shrugged. "Just that you're not our mother's son."

A squirrel scrabbled out of a hole in the trunk of the oak and snatched an acorn from near Matthew's feet. He stared at the creature, feeling his own heart stolen. Thomas was goading him, he had to be . . . his elder brothers loved to tease him. That was because he was the youngest. But Father treated them all with the same stern discipline.

"You're fooling," said Matthew. "You don't know anything."

"But I do," Thomas whispered. "I overheard them talking about it. Mother and Father. They were talking about how you're Deborah's son, that she had in sin. And then Mother said, 'I can't look at Matthew without remembering how you betrayed me.' See,

Matty, I think Father laid with Deborah."

Knowing how egregious this was, Matthew sat there, stunned and speechless. "I—I'm not Mother's son?" Unspoken was the other thing. Deborah? *A wave of shame rolled over him; he'd had such thoughts about her . . . she, his mother?* Father laid with her, he thought, and was shocked by the bite of jealousy that nipped on the heels of his shame.

"Don't worry, though. Father's taken care of your inheritance, just the same as us real sons."

Matthew didn't want to hear any more. He was violently glad that older Thomas would be leaving for the New World soon. He never wanted to see his brother again. Leaping up, he shouted back at Thomas, "Don't ever talk to me, ever!" and pounded into the house. He paused to see Deborah, hovering near the stove in the kitchen. Her hair was tousled, coming out of its pinned cap, and an apron was tied about her round backside. Matthew stared at the sloppy tie of her skirt, and at the creamy skin at the nape of her neck. Something warm and uncomfortable slithered through him. *This, his true mother? This . . . loose woman?* Horrified, he took off through the house, ignoring Deborah when she asked, "Matty? How much honey?"

He found his father in his study, preparing a sermon for Sunday.

"Matthew, come in," said Mr. Hopkins. "What troubles you?"

He hesitated around the question, but the agony forced it from his lips before he could word things properly. "Is Deborah my real mother?"

For a few moments, there was only the ticking of the lantern clock on his father's desk. Then Mr. Hopkins lowered his head. "Who told you that?"

"Thomas."

"Matthew, you are my son. But it is true, you came from Deborah's womb as a result of my temptation. My generous wife agreed that we should raise you as our own, for I could not aban-

don you for a fatherless bastard, and we could not admit my sin of the flesh to the outside world. For these years you have been my cross to bear. You are my reminder that, as a minister, I must stay true to righteous ways. I've tried to raise you the same, so that you will not make the mistake that created you."

"Why have you not gotten rid of her?" Matthew demanded. "Why is she still here?"

A grimace twisted his father's mouth. At once Matthew saw that Deborah still had some kind of a hold over him. "You must understand," Mr. Hopkins said, breathless. "She has . . . powers. I was bewitched by her. I fear she has bound herself to this family, and if I were to release her, she would . . . retaliate."

"Retaliate?" Matthew asked.

His father lowered his voice. "She has what is called the cunning. Son, she is a witch. If I were to act against her, she would curse us, or worse! I can only hope that you, my greatest mistake, can redeem yourself of your origins."

Matthew felt nauseated. The room swam in front of his eyes. He was a mistake. A sin. A reminder of the lust and temptation of Satan. He might as well have been the Devil's own child. He gazed into his father's remorseful eyes and discovered that he was furious . . . not at his father, but at Deborah. She was the whore of Babylon. She had seduced his father out of the holy bonds of marriage and . . . and . . . bore him as witness! "A witch?" he whispered, his voice quavering.

"I am weak," said Mr. Hopkins. "I am afraid of her. It was all her doing, hers and her true master, Satan. It is a plot to destroy our devout family . . . And yet I cannot break the spell she has cast upon us all."

"There must be a way to break such a thing!" Matthew said. "Do you not say that prayer is the cure? What am I supposed to do!" He felt something splitting, as though someone had taken an axe to his soul. He felt betrayed by himself, by his very nature, and he suddenly understood the lustful thoughts, the dirty thoughts, that

had so tormented his body of late.

"I am sorry for this burden," said Mr. Hopkins. "But I see the potential for godliness in you, although you are at a disadvantage to your brothers. Perhaps if you work very hard, and remain strict in your heart, you will overcome the stain. Matthew... son... speak not of this to anyone. And worry not about your share of the inheritance—for that intent, you are the child of James and Mary Hopkins."

There was nothing he could say. He wished his father had abandoned him rather than raise him under such pretenses. Staring at the carpet, Matthew murmured, "Yes, Father." He backed out of the room and fled the house.

Images flashed in his head as he walked. Deborah, grinning and blinking through heavy lashes. His father, falling into a pit filled with imps. His father and Deborah together, tight in a sweaty embrace, with Satan looming over them with a pointed smile under a hooked nose. He envisioned his birth, a squalling and red child ejected from the corrupt womb-waters of Deborah... Deborah... not Mother. There was poison in his veins. And then he pictured Mother, who was not his mother, her lips moving in the vile lie to hide her husband's sin... calling Matthew her son.

He hated them all. Father, Mother, and Deborah, a hideous trio who'd conspired to shame him. And his thoughts toward Deborah... she'd bewitched him, just as she had his father.

He was halfway along the lane that led into town, next to the thorn hedge, when Matthew realized he was crying. Never, he vowed, never will I lay with a woman. *He didn't know what precisely that entailed, except that it was what he wanted most of all.* They are evil, every last one of them. Never, never, never. *He chanted it over and over to himself. He would not hand himself over to their power. They were weak, they were damaged, they were* bad, bad, bad, *just like him. He was* their *fault.*

Hopkins gasped as he struggled out of the memory of his father's revelations. Despite the sermon in the background that should have been a comfort, despite that he was surrounded by people in the white-washed house of the Lord, he was utterly lost. He knew that his soul was blotched and sinful. He knew, and yet he could not help but remember she who had caused it all. The original witch, the original sin.

"No," he breathed. "Not here. Not allowed." If it killed him he would regain control. The only sign of his struggle was the pulsing of a vein on his temple. Gritting his teeth, he focused on the Lord's Prayer. This was familiar. He knew this. He made his own voice louder in his recitations. "And lead us not into temptation . . . but deliver us from evil!"

He was perturbed and his suspicions aroused. How could he have been so stricken in the middle of worship? Was there a witch under this roof with him, working her spells, pretending to be of God? Church was meant to be his solace. He wetted his lips with his tongue.

There was some strong evil here in this Vale.

After six hours of worship, the service broke for three hours. There were farm animals to check on, and the stomachs of children were rumbling for their mid-day meal. Hopkins was pleased to learn that there would be a further Bible study from mid-afternoon.

As the villagers dispersed, some to the green where they'd brought picnic lunches and others back to their houses, Hopkins found himself alone on the road. Sweat trickled down his neck and back and under his arms. He coughed once—this air was no good.

A girl tugged on his sleeve. "Excuse me, Master Hopkins." She was about thirteen, and her accent was not as countrified as the rest.

"Yes?" he said.

"I'm Jane Radcliff. The Reverend said to speak to you. I want to say that there are offensive people round here, that Anne Buckett, she frightens me. And Old Man Ashley swears a terrible lot. Even in church I hear him take the Lord's name. He has the gout in his one leg, but that's not a reason, is it? My cousin Jonas is very strict and I want to marry a man like him someday. My sister Winifred says it would be good for me."

Hopkins had stopped listening. Chattering girls did not interest him, unless they had something useful to tell. He almost turned to her to say that empty, idle speech was sinful, but then she said,

"I know not how my sister Winnie does it. Goes all by herself into the woods! I'd be too scared, especially seeing as there are real witches that might hurt her. What if she got bewitched? But then, those other three girls go there, too. They don't seem afraid . . ."

"What other three?" Hopkins asked.

"Why, Alice Baxter, and Sybil Yates—the Reverend's daughter, I don't expect a witch would dare with her—and Pippa."

"They go into the woods? On Fridays?"

Jane thought hard about this. "I don't know about Fridays," she said, "But they've gone now. Not my sister, but the three strange girls."

Hopkins turned toward the east. The forest gained the look of a closet, a cellar, a place of hiding. He remembered his initial thought. *What a place for witches to meet.*

"Where do they go in the forest?" he asked Jane.

"As though I would be allowed!" she said, pouting. "I'd probably be bored of it, for trees never *do* anything but stand there. Still . . ."

"You've done well, Jane Radcliff," Hopkins told her. "Be thee my ears. Tell me of anything you hear, from your sister or anyone else. Can you do that?"

"Why, yes," said Jane, perking up. It was likely the first

time anyone had paid serious heed to her.

"How do I get to the forest?" he asked.

Jane pointed. "That lane's the fastest way. Follow the brook, it goes all the way through to the other side."

It occurred to Hopkins to bring Stearne with him, but he wasn't sure where his colleague was, and he was overcome with curiosity. It was a Sunday and this gave him renewed courage. He had overcome himself already in the church. No matter what lurked out there, he had already brought himself back from the brink. The Lord was with him and he would be fine.

The narrow footpath led past the Charter Inn and away from the main road. He passed what was obviously a brewer's residence to his left—the smell of ale was strong, and there were a few rows of imported hops growing behind it—and a few other small cottages. The last one before the fields was at a crooked angle and set away from the rest. Its roof needed repairs and there was a piglet guarding the door. The brook ran behind the cottage, just as the girl Jane had described.

Hopkins had to admit that he shrank from the country life. It was so very dirty.

His feet, sweaty inside his boots, took him along the tinkling brook and toward the forest. The trees swayed, their vegetation in full green, and from somewhere he heard the scraping caw of a pheasant.

A part of him wanted to take off his boots and walk barefoot on the soft earth, but that would be unbefitting a lawyer. Instead he left heavy tracks.

When he plunged into the forest, it was like entering a cool room with walls of leaves. All was at peace . . . all but Hopkins himself, whose mind raced with what might hide in the bushes. *Give me towns and churches and streets any day,* he thought. This forest was too disordered. It obeyed not the laws laid down by man or, Hopkins felt, even God.

He clasped his hands for a moment to apologize for the

blasphemy and for his own fear. *I am not to judge what He hath created.* Then why did he feel that God was absent from this wildish place? During his walk, which had now exceeded thirty minutes, he contemplated the task ahead.

He was doing a good thing in the Vale. It was isolated. It needed the stiff yoke of pure Biblical law. Otherwise its people might descend into pagan ways.

"*Dragon's head, dragon's tail!*"

Hopkins halted, clutching onto the limb of an oak tree.

"*Alpha, omega, head to tail!*"

There was the sound of feminine laughter, disembodied, hearty with wickedness.

Heart thudding, Hopkins moved to the beat of his own terror, slowly through the trees and toward the brook.

It was from behind the glossy leaves of a mulberry tree that he glimpsed them: three girls, dressed dark and humble for church, on the banks of the water. It was with utter normality that they ate from a loaf of bread and a broken-off wheel of cheese, and drank from a shared jug of ale. They rested on a grassy slope, and there looked to be a small swimming hole where the brook paused at a rock dam.

He recognized Sybil Yates, the minister's daughter, who sat plaiting the light brown hair of a second girl, plain and poor.

That left the third, dark-haired and pretty, who stood examining a leaf and eating a bit of cheese. *Philippa, her name is Philippa.* He remembered meeting her outside the church. His breath grew shallow.

Hopkins remained still as he listened.

"That's a rhyme Tom taught me," said Sybil. "He knows Latin from . . . university."

"Mmhmm, *university*," said Philippa. "Is that what they call the army these days?"

"Dragon's head, dragon's tail," said Sybil. "I wish to see a dragon, like in the old stories." She closed her eyes as though to find it behind her eyelids.

"Dragons are frightening," said the one with light brown hair.

"But Alice, they're exhilarating!" said Philippa. "I would love for Hugh to rescue me from a dragon."

"I don't know of any dragons in the Bible. I prefer the tale of Daniel in the den of lions," said Alice.

Hopkins thought Alice must be the godliest of all these girls.

"I've never seen a lion," said Sybil. "Only drawings of them."

"'Tis good there are no lions in *these* woods!" said Alice. "Pippa, you would fight them off for us."

Pippa laughed. It was her laugh that Hopkins had heard before. It sent a thrill of fear through him, and longing.

"There's no doubt, 'tis hot as a dragon's breath right now." She glanced up at the sun through the trees. "Time for a swim. Who would join me?"

"No, Pippa!" Alice said. "You'll get all wet, and won't be allowed into church."

"I'll pin up me wet tresses," said Pippa, and to Hopkins's alarm, she began to unhook her collar and then her cuffs. Her feet were bare and she skipped over to the edge of the brook and put a white toe in. She giggled. "Cold!" she said, flicking droplets in the direction of her friends.

"Aaah!" Alice shrieked and ducked. "I'll push you in from behind!"

"Don't!" said Pippa, laughing. "Lillibet will have me for good if I spoil me church dress."

With a mouth gone dry, Hopkins watched as Pippa's fingers opened her collar and then reached behind her to unhook her bodice. Her friends paid her no heed, as though accustomed to such behavior. *Immoral, she is immoral,* thought Hopkins, but he could not tear his eyes away as the black cloth dropped to the ground, leaving her standing in a pale petticoat and chemise.

"If someone spies you, Pip, 'tis your own fault," said Sybil.

Hopkins was startled. The girl couldn't know . . . but no, Sybil was teasing, for she had a smile on her face.

Pippa said, "But someone *is* watching me." She paused in her disrobing and turned to her friends. "You two gillies!"

They laughed.

"And the Green Man," she said. With deliberate hands she cupped her breasts through the fabric and stuck a playful tongue out at a spot somewhere to the left of where Hopkins lurked.

The brazen, horrible girl unhooked her petticoat and stood in bare legs and loose chemise. Then she grasped the hem and pulled it over her head . . . a painful rush of blood to places south of his heart made Hopkins dizzy . . . he could not help the aching lust that overwhelmed his rational thought. The sunlight was dappled over her fair skin. With a graceful leg, a taut body, and breasts that moved freely in the air, she walked into the pool and slipped into the water.

Temptress, thought Hopkins, *harlot, Deborah, that fallen woman, she's not real. She is Satan's creature.* He wrestled with the base self that wanted to touch her, to . . . Such thoughts should be reserved for a wife within the boundaries of holy matrimony, not stolen by this girl, naked in the wild forest! Hopkins had an acute sense of violation. Would he never escape the sin that had created him? This was his weakness . . . this yearning so secret he could not face it . . . how he wanted her, and hated himself for it.

And his breeches were not loose enough, and he was in agony.

Pippa flung her head backwards and wet her hair. It snaked around her shoulders, it *writhed*, she contorted her body in the water and flipped over and vanished into the mirrored pool with a small splash.

Hopkins remembered to breathe for the moment she was gone, but then she emerged again, laughing and sputtering. "Come, Alice."

No, thought Hopkins, *no!*

"No," said Alice, "I'll be needing dry clothes for the day, as me others are quite dirty."

"Sybil? It feels heavenly!"

Hopkins wanted to object. *She* would never know Heaven. He had found his first witch in the Vale! How could he ever have asked her for help, believed her godly? She had infiltrated the Bible study, made him think she was good, bewitched all in this village with her pretense at piety.

Yet, he could not stop staring at her bare backside, and the curve of her hips under the water, and the way that wet dark hair writhed.

Tie me, bind me, you belong to us! Hopkins's eye twitched. *God, no, not here.* The images poured forth, swimming in the water with Pippa. Of himself, naked, back against a tree . . . hands bound . . . laughing girls, laughing witches, circling him . . . and *she*, the dark-haired one, flying through the air, mounting him, ordering him to please her . . . and he, obliging . . . *This is our special time, Matty. Show me that you love me.*

Sybil raised her petticoats and dipped her feet and lower legs in the pool.

Blinking away the terrors that danced and mingled with reality, Hopkins licked his lips once, gripping onto the smooth leaves of the mulberry that concealed him. *Watch, just watch. Don't think.*

It inflamed him to know that these girls watched their friend, saw her as he did. The very way Pippa moved was, to his mind, unnatural—sinuous and joyful and unaffected.

He prayed. *Lord, give me strength to face this creature of Satan, this woman. She is the very essence of Deborah . . . er . . . Eve. She must be stopped. Lord, Almighty Father, I am your humble servant, I am your lawful enforcer, I am your pure and repentant heart, I am—*

"Alpha and omega, head to tail!" the girls chanted, interrupting him.

Pippa dived forward to touch her toes and did a full circle in the water. "Ah," she said. With a childlike abandon she splashed her way toward the bank and climbed up. Hopkins squeezed his eyes shut. He heard one of the girls say, "Here, dry off with the blanket."

When he looked again, Pippa had the ground blanket wrapped around her. She pulled her chemise back over her head, then tugged the petticoats over top, and then piece by piece was restored to decency.

Rescued from his temporary torment, Hopkins took a step back, and with great care retreated from his spying-place. *Witch. Witch.* He knew what they wanted. They wanted him as their suckling imp. This girl—no, this witch, this hag in disguise—wanted to use him for her own lustful purposes.

And in the deep, sticky, salted depths of himself, he wanted it, too.

A familiar shame burned his cheeks. He was a man, not that little boy in the bath with Deborah's too-sweet hands. It was part of his demonic nature to have these feelings. Taking a deep, quiet breath, he thought, *Are we not all sinners? Christ can still redeem me. I must focus, accomplish my task, find the list, find the Register, name the witches.*

Then I will be saved.

The slow return of sanity corresponded with the retreating voices of the girls at the brook. The further away he got, the better he was able to think.

Never had the Bible's admonitions against false ones and sorcerers made more sense. Never had he been more convinced that evil could put on a face of respectability. The Reverend's own daughter!

Often during these hunts Hopkins let the townspeople reach their own conclusions about who was guilty within their community. His job was not to accuse, but to discover proof of that accusation. In this case, though . . . he must take a more active hand. He must fight her. *Pippa.* It made his nether regions twitch again to think of that girl jailed, chained, restrained. He thought of her jerking and swinging at the end of a rope.

Oh, but he had to get out of these woods, before he did something to himself he would regret.

THE YATES HOUSE WAS stuffy, dark, and the shutters tight. The flies knocked up against the walls from outside. The front door opened and closed, opened and closed. The muffled sound of voices from the hall reached Sybil in the garden. She sat in the shade of a rowan tree and mashed its red berries into a mixture of hartshorn gelatin. It was a pretty, glossy stain for the lips.

Ursula was with her, out for some fresh air. The bird sat on a branch of the rowan tree, watching Sybil, occasionally squawking in that gravelly voice so like an old hag. So like old bones.

Inside Sybil's father's office, Hopkins and Stearne received a stream of townspeople. They were either united in force against someone in particular, or there were a great many single accusations. Either way was bad. Either way made Sybil sick to be under the same roof with it. In and out, a parade of fear, and in they went to point their fingers and out again, feeling safer.

When she was finished mashing berries, she went through the back door to the kitchen to clean the mortar and pestle, and to bottle the smooth mixture.

Sybil peeked into the hall and saw that the door to her father's office was an inch ajar. Voices drifted out, serious voices. She could not help her curiosity. The floorboards creaked as she approached. Sybil's hearing had been a little off since her fever and she could not quite discern the words or the speaker.

The door opened and she jumped to attention. It was her sister Elizabeth, hands folded in front of her, all piety. Elizabeth's eyes were cast to the floor but as she passed, those eyes curved up to meet Sybil. They were sly. They were knowing. They went back toward the floor as though nothing had happened.

But Sybil knew. The betrayal was a clinging stench around Elizabeth.

Sybil climbed the stairs, slow and feather-light. Knocking on her sisters' door, she found the other. "Cathy?" she asked.

Catherine sat in front of the window, patching up a torn sleeve cuff, and refused to look at Sybil.

You too, Sybil thought. She glided back downstairs and sat in the garden with Ursula on her lap. With thin fingers she stroked the bird and sang.

Ursula said, "Win."

"Winifred Radcliff?" Sybil asked. "She stopped by, I know not why."

"Why."

The sound of footsteps pounding up the stairs was loud enough for Sybil to hear from outside.

"Danger!" said Ursula, hopping down onto Sybil's shoulder, talons clutching onto Sybil's sleeve.

The window to Sybil's bedroom overlooked the garden and so she was able to see the hand that flung it open, and hear the voice of her father. "Well, then, let the light show us! What's underneath?"

There was a scraping noise. The bed.

A hush.

Then footsteps again, down the stairs, through the house, out the door. Sybil hurriedly set Ursula back on the tree branch and stood to face her father.

"Sybil," he said. His voice was quiet, as it always was when he wasn't preaching.

"Yes, Father?"

"Come here." He beckoned with a finger and they went upstairs to her room. A swooning sort of panic overtook her. The bed and the woven rug had been moved to reveal the sigils and charms scratched in chalk on the floorboards.

"What is the meaning of this?" the Reverend asked.

"I . . . Oh . . . Has someone bewitched me? I know not!"

"You are a liar and a deceiver," he said. His voice was calm. It was as if he were talking to a wayward parishioner, one who was not his daughter, and one whom he did not love.

Sybil said, "It must have been during the fever. I was not myself."

"No," he mused, "you were not. Your sisters heard you speaking to someone. Your sisters heard the Devil reply."

How you must have waited for this chance, Elizabeth, Sybil thought. *How you must cherish it now.*

The late afternoon sun had vanished behind the bulk of the church next door, leaving the room and her father in shadow. "I cannot be a hypocrite," he said. "There has always been something about you, child. I have wondered on occasion about your very parentage. Your peculiar birth. Your mother who—" He stopped and shook his head. "I cannot have the cast of suspicion on my house, not when honorable men are working to find the witchcraft at work here. You must remain in your room until I decide what to do. Martha will bring your meals."

"But, Papa, I—"

He held up a swift hand. "*Do not* argue." He stepped toward the door and, half-turning, said, "And attempt not to contact your coven of friends. They are a wicked influence, especially that Philippa Wylde."

The door closed behind him. There was no lock on it, for no lock was needed. Where was Sybil to go? There was nowhere to hide. She had no one outside of the Vale. Her prison was made of air and roads and houses and, most of all, made of people. And so she stayed in her cage, and held on to the charm from beneath her mattress that she had sewn for herself, and waited.

The Watchers

Pippa was in the yard and there was a large pile of grain in front of her. A mountain of long, dimpled grey-brown ovals. Rye, thought her dreaming self. She was supposed to sort it into two bowls: a large wooden one on the right, and a smaller bowl of solid gold on the left. When she began to pick through each grain, she saw that some of them were black with the ergot fungus. The black grains she placed in the gold bowl. The normal ones went into the wooden bowl.

"Work harder," said Lillibet, looming over her, wearing a black dress.

Pippa's fingers picked through the pile fast as they could. If she let the wrong grain into the wrong bowl, something bad would happen.

"Hurry," said Lillibet. "Not much time."

The sun was going down and soon Pippa would have no light to see the difference in the grains. Slowly, slowly, the pile began to diminish and each bowl grew to full. Pippa became quick at laying her hand flat so she could pluck out the black ones and set them into the gold bowl. The rest were tossed into the wood bowl.

One after the other, in handfuls.

The blazing arc of the sun had just slipped over the horizon when Pippa rushed through the last of the grain. There! It was done.

Lillibet crouched in front of her. "Well done, child. But you can take one bowl only. Which one will ye have?"

Pippa thought hard. On the one hand, the wooden bowl was large, and held enough healthy grain to make a great deal of bread. It would last her awhile, but not forever. On the other hand, the small bowl was itself a golden treasure, and if she ate the ergot she would either see a vision of great magnitude or she would die in agony.

"Beware," said Lillibet. "Choose the gold and you must hide, or someone will steal it. Choose the wood, and you must forget the gold ever existed."

Pippa was reaching for the gold bowl when her eyes snapped open. It took her a few moments to realize she was awake, for everything was dark.

A hand clamped over her mouth, and she screeched in alarm.

"Hush! Say nothing! Get dressed!"

Lillibet took her hand off Pippa's mouth and retreated, scuttling down the ladder like a spider, and Pippa scrambled into an upright position. "Lillibet? What's happening?"

"Do as I say." Then her mother mumbled and knocked over an empty jug in the kitchen.

"I had the strangest dream," said Pippa, still trying to process the difference between waking and dreaming.

"Hurry, child. 'Tis almost midnight, and there's something I must show you."

Frowning, Pippa climbed into her bodice and skirt. Normally Lillibet liked discussing dreams. Something was very wrong. *What if Sybil's fever has recurred?* she thought, and the fear of it spurred her into action. Tying up her bodice and buttoning her petticoat, she clambered down the ladder after Lillibet, who was readying her cloak.

"What's happening? What's wrong? Lillibet, please, speak to me!"

Her mother stared out the open door in the direction of the forest. In the candle's circle of light, pale drops of rain glinted.

"The witch-finders," Lillibet said. "I have something to show you—something that I know you're not prepared to see. But my way is forced. I must pass along the secret, for I have a terrible suspicion that . . ."

"That what?" Pippa whispered.

Lillibet rounded on her. "Put on your cloak. Take off that white collar, and leave your cap. No one can see where we go. We'll not even take lamps." Lillibet's hands roved over Pippa's arms, tucking the white parts of her cuffs beneath her sleeves so they did not show. Then Lillibet dashed over and closed the shutters on the window. She tucked an errant strand of hair behind her ear. Her mouth was set tight.

Pippa had never seen her mother so agitated.

"We must be especially vigilant tonight," said Lillibet. "We have enemies in the Vale, and they will be watching movement." She sighed. "At least there's a rain. Forces the people to stay inside and hides the noise of our feet."

"You really don't want anyone to see us!"

"Pippa." Her mother reached her hands up to Pippa's taller shoulders, gripping like talons. "What I'm about to show you can never be revealed to anyone. 'Tis a secret place. And if anyone sees you going there, and follows, and finds it, then an accusation would be made."

Pippa was wide-eyed, edgy with anticipation. "Accusation of . . . what?"

"Witchcraft."

A shiver of a premonition skated through Pippa's mind.

"Not much time," said Lillibet, and Pippa recalled those

very words from the dream she'd just had.

The door swung open, Lillibet blew out the candle, and she was into the beckoning night. Pippa followed. Their cottage was at the end of the footpath so from there it was into the woods along the tracks left by animals. At first it was the same route to the apple grove. Others would have feared the landscape at night, but Lillibet and Pippa knew every stone, every tree, every blade of grass, every hole where an unwary person might twist an ankle. The soft rain broke up to reveal the glow of a half-moon, to Lillibet's apparent dismay. "Too much light," she muttered. Then they were safe, out of the fields, into the forest. In the deep shade of the trees, in the tangle of holly and oak and ash and thorn, in the gentle rustling of their new leaves and old branches, the forest itself seemed a third party to their errand.

Sure-footed as a young doe, Lillibet followed some hidden path. Pippa could see her only as a silhouette against the dappled white of moonlight that penetrated the forest canopy. Lillibet's words had lit a fire in her mind. *Enemies in the Vale. Witch-finders. Accusations. Surely Lillibet can't be afraid of those two charlatan men?*

"Do you know where we are?" Lillibet turned, interrupting Pippa's thoughts, and she spoke in a whisper so low that it was almost indistinguishable from the soft sighs of an oak tree next to them.

"Yes." *On the path to the grove.*

"Now, I show you the sign." Lillibet's ghostly hands reached outward. She came up against the smooth grey trunk of a small rowan tree. "Here." She seized Pippa's hand and held it against the wood.

At first the trunk felt normal, a hard, smooth curve. Then Pippa was startled by the deep groove of a carved sign. It was a straight line—no, several lines—and Pippa, blind, traced her fingers over it. After several minutes she knew what it was: the old symbol, the pentagram, a star-shape inside of a circle. It was for protection.

The rowan tree was powerful, for that same tiny symbol could be found on the tree's red berries. The wood could repel hexes from black witches. Pippa had used it for the treasure-hunting rod, and she flushed at the memory.

"This rowan tree is where we turn," said Lillibet. "Remember it." Her voice was whisper-quiet and yet made of iron.

Pippa was surprised she'd never noticed the symbol before. She must have walked past this very tree in broad daylight many times. Then again, the carving was behind a curve in the trunk and might be shadowed even in the sunshine. Excited by this discovery, she followed her mother through a tiny archway of prickly holly leaves. They plucked at her clothing and their sharp edges scraped her exposed face.

"Twenty-two paces," whispered Lillibet. She paused and glanced around, the bones of her neck standing out. Satisfied, she beckoned to Pippa.

They arrived at a cluster of large boulders overgrown with moss. The moon lined the edges in silver. A lime tree grew out of the crack between two stones, its twisted roots snaking over the ground and flowing in between smaller things. She had never seen this fold of land before. It looked doubly alien in the night.

And then, Pippa felt upside down, and had the peculiar sensation that she was no longer in the modern world . . . that she had stepped into a time long past. *Ridiculous,* she told herself, for she was in her very own forest, the trees that she knew as old friends. Yet, she felt as though that dear old friend had pulled off a mask, showing a face different from what she'd always known.

"Where are we?" she whispered.

Lillibet said nothing. She felt along the ground in front of a round boulder and tugged. The boulder moved. Then it rolled off to one side, aided by Lillibet. A tunnel yawned behind it.

Somewhere nearby an owl hooted.

Pippa had thought the forest was dark, but she hadn't known what darkness was until she gazed into that tunnel.

"All's well," said Lillibet, anchoring Pippa back into the present. "You feel this place? Its power?"

"Yes. Yes, I feel it."

"Good. Come with me." Lillibet ducked down and they were a few feet inside when Pippa heard the scraping of something on a rock. A spark flared and burst into light—there was a candle waiting near the entrance. "Now we close the door," said Lillibet. She pushed aside a fern and showed Pippa the indentation where the boulder rested. A smaller stone held it in place; if the small stone was removed, the large stone would slide back. The inner side of the boulder was carved into a rough-hewn handle, so it could be pushed back open from within the cave. It was a simple mechanism and Pippa could not imagine how long it had been there.

"Who built this?" she asked as Lillibet removed the small stone and the boulder glided into place against the night.

"No one knows," said Lillibet. "'Tis been here since I was a girl, and before that when me grandmum was a girl, and before that. Old as the Vale itself, older than the trees in the forest." She paused. "Perhaps our old yew tree knows who built this."

In the confined space, Pippa could smell their damp clothes, but beneath it was the scent of age and herbs and earth.

Lillibet crouched her way through the tunnel, which was much shorter than it had first seemed, and they emerged into a space the size of their cottage's living area. There was room for one person to stand, but the walls—cracked, crinkled stone—sloped downward and it was more comfortable on hands and knees. Lillibet used the first flame to light a candelabra full of candles, all dripped into a single grotesque waxen sculpture. With the light to see, Pippa sat up and looked about her in awe.

One side of the cave was packed with jars, bundles of herbs, bottles full of strange liquids and, in a few cases, pickled animals. Pippa gazed at the bloated corpse of a green toad magnified in the curve of glass. She didn't need to be told what they were—spell ingredients.

Along another curve of wall was a small wooden shelf crowded with odd things. There were a few rolled-up parchments that looked like maps, there were seashells and bones, and there was a hand-sized piece of black obsidian, highly polished, carved like a shallow bowl.

A stack of books rested on one end of this shelf, covered in a thick layer of cave dust. Pippa read the imprinted lettering on the top book: "*Book of Secrets,*" it said, and then beneath, "*Albertus Magnus.*" It looked bursting with those secrets and Pippa itched to hold it and see what was inside.

She reached out for it and Lillibet made a noise to stop her.

Disappointed, Pippa remembered that she hadn't been ready to know of this cave, and that this was an emergency. But, rather than feeling unnerved by this magical place, or afraid that the witch-finders would find it and use it to condemn, Pippa felt at home. This was a safe haven. Even Lillibet, despite her worried frown at Pippa, seemed calmer than before.

In the center of the room was a fire pit blackened with old charcoal. Pippa looked upward and Lillibet nodded.

"There's a natural crack in the cave. As a chimney it spreads the smoke to escape through the hill. The fire should be lit only with dry wood. Else, others might see the smoke coming from beneath the ground and would guess what's beneath. During the day a pinpoint of light comes in and moves across the floor." With a bony finger she pointed to a wall, where someone had carved the track of the sun and marked the turning of the seasons with faces. For Easter and springtime Pippa saw his face again: the Green Man, wide-eyed and surrounded by leaves. After him was another male face, one with horns, and this horned man seemed to merge with the face of a young woman. The icons were hard-edged, primitive, the faces that lived in the deepest part of the mind.

In the hush of enclosed stone, Pippa heard another noise, a trickling of water. She glanced around and saw a ribbon of water in a crack in the wall. It gathered in a natural rock basin on the floor. There was not enough water to sustain more than one adult, but it looked pure. Crawling over for a closer look, she gasped.

Beneath the surface of the water was a rainbow of color, glimmering in the refracted candlelight. Stones, polished . . . crystals, raw and sparkling . . . even, Pippa could see, a small faceted ruby. She only knew what a ruby looked like because Sybil had seen one on a court lady in Cambridge and told them how it was like a drop of blood. The one at the bottom of the pool must be valuable.

"Offerings to the cave," said Lillibet. "By giving to her, she gives back to us."

Pippa bit her tongue—she was about to suggest they sell the ruby. As she gazed into the pool she knew that would have been a sin. This cave was beyond the mundane. She wondered which of her ancestors had offered the ruby, and what they'd received in return. A Bible verse from the book of Job ran through her head, that "the price of wisdom is above rubies." And then she understood what might be gained here. Excited, she turned to Lillibet.

"This is where you learnt so much of what you know!"

"When I was ready," Lillibet corrected her. "But, yes, it's true. Me mother taught me when I was grown, as I would teach you. There is a book where we keep our records, and the knowledge of every result of every magical action." Lillibet reached to the shelf and pulled off a large, rough book bound in blue leather. "You may read this sometime. Not tonight.

But sometime." With a loving hand she caressed its spine, and then as though remembering something less pleasant, her head snapped up. "Do you understand why I brought you here? That I show you only in case . . . in case something happens to me? Do you know what would happen if it was discovered?"

"I know," said Pippa, thinking of how Reverend Yates had insisted the Green Man Inn be renamed to remove its paganness, and how the witch-finders were, at this moment, sniffing out what they considered ungodly ways in the Vale. Imagine if they knew of this!

"'Tis unusual to write down the knowledge of we cunning-women, but we have this hidey-hole. For a long time nothing was written. For a long time, no one knew how to write."

A different world existed beneath the surface of the routine world Pippa had known. There was more magic than she'd dreamt, and yet she was still cut off from it. Lillibet would give her a taste, just for the sake of passing it along, but Pippa could not read the books. She didn't even know how to use the power of the cave.

So, she sat in silence with Lillibet's worry as company, watching the candles.

THE NEXT MORNING WAS overcast with clouds that were pale and rainless. Pippa was sweeping the yard with eyes closed, memorizing what she'd seen in the cave. Lillibet said she would not be allowed to return there for a long time.

The sound of boots at the gate, squelching in the drying mud, interrupted her, and her eyes opened. "God bless," she blurted.

It was the two witch-finders, Hopkins and Stearne, along with the constable and Goodman Brewer. At first Pippa thought they were here to consult Lillibet about the many curses and hexes she'd removed for the villagers over the years. But something on their hard faces made her stop sweeping and clutch onto the broom handle. The cave hovered at the forefront of her mind and it was dangerous. What if they had been followed last night, after all?

"May I help?" she asked.

"This is the cottage of Elizabeth Wylde the cunning-woman and her daughter Philippa?" The question was from Stearne. It was a silly question, considering their closest neighbor stood with him.

"I'm Pippa, as you well know."

The lawyer, Hopkins, stared at her with those beady dark eyes. She met his gaze and was discomfited by it. He choked as though holding back a cough.

Pippa wondered if she should offer him a chest poultice.

"Is Lillibet here?" the constable asked.

"She's inside . . . why? Have you need of her?"

Stearne produced a piece of paper. "You, Philippa Wylde, and your mother, the Widow Wylde, are to come with us to the village common."

"Why?"

"Don't be difficult, girl," Hopkins spoke up. "Fetch your mother."

But Lillibet had appeared at the door. "Harass us not, we have no business with you!"

"Ah," said Stearne, "but *we* have business with *you*. Constable?"

The constable took Pippa by the elbow.

"Unhand me! Don't you touch me!" She tried to shake him off but his bruising grip was relentless.

Something in Lillibet's posture collapsed as she stepped forward. Goodman Brewer shoved her from behind. "Get moving," he said.

"Tom Brewer, I've know you since we was children. What are you thinking?" But her tone was surrendered.

They were frog-marched down the lane—Pippa cried out to shut the gate, lest the chickens escape—and to her surprise, Hopkins closed it behind him. She felt humiliated and annoyed. To be paraded down the street like this, like a criminal, just to visit the village common! But as she rounded the bend at the crossroads she saw a crowd on the green, and her stomach seemed to fall through her knees at the sight of raw wood: newly-built stocks. It began to dawn on Pippa that she and Lillibet were not meant as witnesses against witchcraft . . . that someone must have pointed the finger at them.

"Lillibet!" she whispered, and pried her arm away from the constable to reach for her mother. The first tears blurred her eyes.

Lillibet was too far away to touch Pippa's fingers.

The constable wrenched Pippa's hand behind her back.

Also set up on the green was a wooden platform where a row of search-women waited—the foreigners and the locals.

"Alice!" cried Pippa, for her friend was also held by the elbows by two farm laborers.

Alice, however, was so frightened that her stuttering could not form a complete word in response.

Pippa stood up straight. This was too ridiculous. She had been worried at first, for to the uninitiated the cunning-folk might be considered witches, but seeing Alice standing under the same suspicion made her feel better. Alice was no witch. There was nothing to prove any such involvement, unless walking through a forest was a crime. All of this would be cleared up.

Hopkins stepped up to the wooden platform. His boots made clunking sounds on the fresh lumber. "To all the assembled of this village," he said, reading from the same piece of paper that Stearne had waved at the cottage, "the following are hereby accused of the most evil crime of witchcraft: Joan Buckett. Anne Buckett. Alice Baxter. Philippa Wylde. Elizabeth

Wylde. Sybil Yates. Ashley Potter."

Pippa's first thought was, absurdly, *who's Ashley Potter?* But then she saw Old Man Ash, tottering on his feet, his arm held behind him by Goodman Powell.

Then the full import of it was like a slap in the face. Her breath grew shallow, squeezed. She was named as a witch. So was her mother, and Alice, and *Sybil!* Of all things! This was no joke, no mere annoyance or misunderstanding. The witch-finders and the search-women were serious about the charge. Sybil was not present; Pippa wondered where she was. Being kept at her house? A few hours ago, in the routine strength of her friendships and daily chores, aware of the secret cave in the forest, Pippa had felt infallible, an audience to this sideshow of witch-finding in her village.

A spark of indignation flared. It was like being wrongfully accused of lying—it was impossible to prove a negative. Fear of her was written on the faces of her neighbors. She wanted to shake them by the shoulders, and scream, *It's me! It's Pippa! I've done you no wrong!*

"There are tests to show a witch, and means of extracting confession," Hopkins told the assembled. "In three days we will have conclusive results. Any other accusations should be made now, for Master Stearne must leave on business in three days, and myself in five."

Business, thought Pippa, *more villages to harass, like this one?*

John Stearne was on the platform too. "On the matter of fees, it has been decided that as a village matter, this will be a parish cost. The burden will be deflected amongst all, and from each according to their ability to pay."

"Say now! What's going on here?"

Pippa almost fell over with relief. It was Sir John Felton, with Hugh and his brother. All three looked baffled by the proceedings.

"The witches, your lordship!" said Goodman Ford, pointing. "They be witches!"

"Now, now," said Hopkins, "no one is convicted yet. These are accusations only." But he had satisfaction about him nonetheless. He was expecting proof of guilt in every case, and he would receive his fee for the searching whether there was a conviction in the end or not. "But," Hopkins said with horrible slowness, "There's no cause to give them opportunity to run away. Put them in the stocks!"

There was a cry of agreement from the villagers. Someone spat on Anne Buckett's tattered shoes as she was dragged, cursing, toward the wooden slats. Alice was catatonic with terror and Pippa tried to hold her gaze, to reassure her, but then she heard her mother's rancor at Goodman Brewer.

"Get your hands off me! You're me neighbor, don't do this, don't do this!"

Brewer kicked Lillibet's knees and made her stumble, then dragged her by the armpits toward the stocks.

"Lillibet! Let her go! Oh—" Pippa paused to swat at the constable, who attempted to push her forward.

"Stop struggling," he hissed in her ear, and then she cried out as he bent her arm backwards and a sharp, twisting pain lanced her shoulder. "Hugh!" she cried. "Hugh! Stop them! Tell them!"

"Pippa!" Hugh was elbowing his way through. "What—how—why —"

"Tell them." Her whisper carried through the commotion. "Tell them I've done nothing!"

Hugh flushed. He looked as though he could not quite believe what he saw. "Now see here," he said, turning on his heel to approach Hopkins on the platform.

"Nothing I can do but perform the ordeals," Hopkins said. "Worry not, they are a fair measure of witchcraft or innocence."

"There's nothing fair about it!" Pippa cried. "He lies!"

"Attack not the Witch-finder General," Stearne interrupted, "or you will prove thyself guilty in this very moment! He does God's work, you ignorant child."

"Speak not to her that way," Hugh protested, but it was feeble, as though he couldn't be certain of Pippa's guiltlessness.

"The law is on our side," said Stearne. "Trust the law to find the truth, young man."

The constable released Pippa only to draw her arms forward and thrust her head into the hole in the stocks. The wood clamped down around her neck and wrists and she stooped there, bent over, disgraced. Tears dampened her face. "Lillibet," she whispered to her mother, trapped on her left.

"Fear not, child," Lillibet choked. "Pray to God. Just pray."

For awhile the people milled around, watching their neighbors. Several of the young boys threw poison-apples, tomatoes, at the Buckett women. They were objects of universal scorn and accustomed to such treatment. Old Man Ashley moaned in pain as he struggled out of his morning intoxication. Alice was crying softly. Her brother Ralph approached with a ladle of water and then crept back away as though her condition was contagious.

Hugh bent down on one knee to speak with Pippa. "Fear not, Pippa, 'tis as the man said. The law will clear this up. I hate to see you like this, I say . . . I'll demand you recompense for this indignity. Fear not."

Pippa was speechless, but Lillibet rasped, "You are but a boy, Hugh Felton. You've not seen what this is. You not know what the ordeals of a witch be."

"Well," said Hugh, brow knitted, "is it not a questioning, and a search for evidence—Pippa, like how you discovered that . . . *Anne Buckett . . .*" his voice dropped to a whisper, "bewitched Francis Pye?"

Lillibet gasped out a bitter laugh. "No," she said. "I hear rumors of what they call swimming. And I know a tale of a woman being made to think she would drown, until she gave a confession. 'Twas a false one, of course."

"Surely not," said Hugh. "These men are acting on the law. This Hopkins is a lawyer!"

"Just because it be a law of man," said Lillibet, "it don't follow to be a godly law."

Hugh shook his head, as though a persistent gnat flew around inside. Pippa could tell he had trouble grasping the idea that the authorities of church and state might act in a way completely contrary to God's will. A surge of irritation overtook her tender feelings for him. What good was he if he would not act to help her?

"I'll ask my father what to do," said Hugh, further enraging Pippa.

She could say nothing, though, for she didn't want to antagonize him and drive him away.

"Pray for strength," said Hugh. "I won't give up on you when you're innocent."

As she watched his retreating back Pippa had to wonder what he meant. Did he think her innocent already? Or would he help her only if she was *found* blameless of witchcraft?

The angle of her body was so awkward that no matter how she moved, something was being pressed upon or tugged or pulled. If she stood, her back and neck were sore; if she tried to kneel, the wood dug into the base of her spine and neck. Poor Lillibet . . . and with the prospect of hours of this, it seemed impossible to imagine what would become of them.

THE WALLS OF SYBIL'S BOWER seemed to be pulsing again. She'd thought they only did that when she was ill. Then again, the room was full of people, and that made everything seem askew. On the edges of Sybil's vision, panic crept in waves, but she held it away. In her core she was calm. Something told her it was that peaceful inner space that would survive all of this. The rest might be stripped away.

The witch-finder, Hopkins, filled her vision. No man had ever set foot in her bedroom except her father. Sybil was suddenly sorry that she hadn't let Thomas Radcliff kiss her more before joining the army. She didn't want this dark man to shape her bedroom thoughts.

At Hopkins's shoulders stood one of the search-women he'd brought with him from Essex. Sybil thought her name was Mary Phillips. Also in the room were her sister Elizabeth, the fat Widow Moore, and pious Mary Ford. They had come to question her. The night was fresh and the candles burned high and bright, making all their eyes a-glitter.

Sybil sat on her chair, waiting.

Hopkins spoke first. "Have you a pact with Satan?"

What a silly question, thought Sybil. "Why would Satan bother with me?"

"Excuse me?"

"I said, no Devil would bother with me. I'm a Reverend's daughter."

The search-woman huffed and Hopkins gestured at her to be quiet. There was something about him that was very patient. He reminded Sybil of the cat waiting for the mouse to make a mistake, knowing that sooner or later, it would. The way he held his shoulders was stiff and self-disciplined. Closing her eyes, she imagined him bound up by ropes of his own making. For a moment she almost felt pity. Almost.

His questions assaulted her, so fast she was dizzied, and the room spun and her throat closed up.

"Are you a witch? Have you made a pact with Satan? Have you entertained him? Are you a witch? Do you have knowledge of Satan?"

"No. No."

"Who are your imps? What are their names? Have you

copulated with the Devil? In the night, does he come to you? Do you lay with him? Do you allow him into the house of the Reverend, betraying your earthly father, your Holy Father?"

"No!"

Hopkins clenched his fist. "You will say for us the Lord's Prayer."

"I can say that forwards and backwards. I'm a Reverend's daughter." In fact, Sybil tended to think backwards.

"You say the Lord's Prayer in reverse?" whispered Mary Ford, aghast.

"I—"

"'Tis the sign of a true witch," said the search-woman, Mary Phillips.

"Say the Lord's Prayer for us, Sybil Yates," Hopkins interrupted. "Say it now. The *correct* way." He stepped closer.

A tremor of fear shook her into stammering out the first line. "Our F-Father, who art in Heaven, hallowed be Thy Name. Thy kingdom come, Thy will be done, in earth as it is in Heaven. Give us this day . . ." Sybil continued the prayer, the words coming in a rush of remembrance. As she spoke she thought of Alice and her stutter. She would never pass this test. She prayed Alice wouldn't have to endure it. "For Thine is the kingdom, and the power, and the glory, for ever and ever. Amen." Her breath came in quick gasps.

Hopkins was still as a statue in front of her.

"Are you in league with Satan?"

Sybil turned her face away, but could not help the hysterical bubble of laughter that escaped. Sybil knew that Hopkins was ignorant of his deeds. He thought he did God's work. *What a dreadful God you must know,* she thought, swinging her eyes back upon him.

"She laughs," said Hopkins. "She laughs." He snapped his gloves across his hand. "Watch her." He swept out of the room, his short cape flapping behind him.

The women acted fast under the orders of Mary Phillips. It was Elizabeth who brought the plain wooden chair from downstairs and placed it in the middle of the floor. It was Mary Ford who had the rope. It was Widow Moore who said, "Take off your clothes, girl."

Sybil shook her head and crossed her arms. "That's not modest."

"Ye should have thought of it before consorting with the Devil," said Mary Ford.

The women held her by the arms and stripped her bare. It was summer, so there was no bother of cold, but Sybil shivered anyway.

"Sit," said Mary Phillips, pointing.

She sat and her arms were tied backward to her ankles so that her back was bent at a hard upright angle.

It was very strange. The women sat on her bed and on her bench. Elizabeth passed around cups of ale for them. It was as though Sybil were a silent spectacle.

They waited and they watched.

Tiny muscle spasms crept along Sybil's arms, stretched as they were. The hours passed. Elizabeth thumbed through her Bible, murmuring to herself.

"Anything comes in," said Phillips, "say so at once. It could be one of her imps."

"What are you watching for?" Sybil asked.

"You know very well," said Mary Ford. "They will come to you. The imps cannot go long without suckling."

Outside, the twilight bled into full night, and the sky filled with stars. More hours passed. The candles flickered on the bedside table. The women ate bread and sausages, brought to them by Martha. Sybil's stomach growled at the sight, for she'd not been given tea or dinner.

"Elizabeth, might I have some ale? I'm so thirsty."

"Hush," Elizabeth said, and turned back to her Bible.

Martha hovered at the door, curious. "What you be doing?"

"Watching for the girl's imps," said Widow Moore, and belched after swallowing a mouthful of bread.

"Imps!" Martha drew back. "Demons, like?"

"Imps be demons in disguise," said Mary Phillips. "Take the form of animals and insects, they do. They do a witch's bidding and return to her for their nourishment."

"Oh," said Martha. She hesitated and there was a frown's wrinkle on her broad forehead.

"Something to say, Martha?" asked Mary Ford, leaning forward eagerly.

"No . . . well . . ."

Sybil prayed. *No, God, please, let her walk away . . . Martha, do you not love me?*

"She does have a-a blackbird," Martha said, looking both sorry and fearful. "I seen it in a box in here, and in the garden. I do believe the bird is lame, and Miss Sybil helped nurse it to health again."

"Nurse it?" Mary Ford screeched.

"A bird, as a pet?"

"So that explains the odd noises I hear from this room," Elizabeth said, standing up, triumphant.

Sybil prayed that Ursula had possessed the good sense to hop away from the back garden. If only her wing was not hobbled. If only she could fly away.

Elizabeth swept out of the room with Martha. "I will see if it's to be found in the garden," she said. From out the window behind her, Sybil could hear a ruckus, and Martha exclaiming, and the sound of flapping—skirts, or wings.

"Got 'im," Martha could be heard to say.

Her, thought Sybil.

There was a watchful silence when Elizabeth reappeared in the doorway clutching Ursula. The search-women stared at the raven. Ursula—who knew no better, and was used to being rewarded for speech—opened her beak and said, "Sybil!"

It was a ringing imitation of Sybil's own name in Sybil's own voice.

Elizabeth screamed and dropped Ursula, who flapped her one good wing and careened to the floor.

"Oh, Heaven help us, God be with us!" Mary Ford grabbed at her chest and her eyes rolled in her head.

"Devilry!" Widow Moore cried. "Devilry!"

Mary Phillips was white in the face. "I never seen anything so unnatural," she said. "Not ever. This be no bird. This be an imp."

The women stared as Ursula hopped over toward Sybil. Tied helpless as Sybil was, she could not even nudge her pet away. *Please go,* she tried to tell the bird, *save yourself.*

It was quite silly, how much Sybil cared about what might happen to Ursula, above concern for herself. Closing her eyes, the darkness behind her lids swirled in jeweled colors around her, and she thought again of Tom Radcliff and where he was. In a battle, perhaps? Fighting beside the King, or perhaps with a noble?

"There be next to no doubt," said Mary Phillips. "But we must make sure. We must prick her."

Sybil's eyes fluttered open again. A long sharp bodkin had appeared in the stranger's hand.

"We will find the Devil's mark on her. When it don't bleed, or when she don't jerk in pain from the needle, then 'tis proof that Satan has marked her as his own."

The women clustered together on the other side of the room. "Here, you women use these, as well" said a whisper. They had opened Sybil's sewing box. As one, they turned, and the wavering light of the candles made grim shadows of their noses and eye sockets and half-open mouths. Sybil noticed how Mary Ford's tongue darted in and out of her mouth, lizard-like.

They approached her. The last thing Sybil saw before she

fainted in a rush of heat was the sharp gleam of her own sewing needles.

Hopkins had learned several interesting tidbits from Renshaw the innkeeper. The first was that Philippa Wylde's mother Elizabeth—or Lillibet, as she was called—was not only the village midwife, but also the cunning-woman. How easy it was to extend those activities into witchcraft. A young woman and her mother, living in that cottage alone, no man to protect their morality . . . just the sort of women Satan chose to do his divisive work.

Renshaw also told a story about the year Philippa was born. There had been plague, and a mysterious disease that felled entire families of cattle. And that was the year Lillibet Wylde, already in her late thirties, had given birth to her first and only child. She and her husband had been desperate. Then this miracle babe was born to elderly parents. Renshaw whispered that Lillibet had discovered a secret charm to create pregnancy that she now sold to other barren women. Some said that Lillibet lay with the Devil in exchange for a child. Then, of course, a few short years later her own husband had died quite suddenly. It all pointed to evil-doing.

Of course, Hopkins needed no proof to know that Pippa was a witch, but he could hardly give *that* sort of testimony to the magistrates. What he did do was make sure he was present during the official watching of Pippa and the Widow Wylde. They were just the kind of witches to convince others to sign the Devil's Register, to weave them into their plots, spiders at the center of the Vale's web.

Perhaps they have the Devil's Register itself.

Of all the witches he'd met, these might be the most powerful, and he was tantalized and terrified. He would press them about the Register's location.

Pippa's name was already written in his own notebook. What he'd seen in the forest was enough for him. On a wooden beam in his room at the inn, there was already a single tiny crooked cross made in haste during a long night. He'd done it with the bodkin.

He liked to scratch things.

So it was that Hopkins, along with Priscilla and Mary, his searchers from Manningtree, and two more local women sat inside the cunning-est cottage he'd ever seen. There was a cabinet full of mysterious herbs. A magic cipher was inscribed over the door—not carved in this generation, for it was worn-away, but this had been a family dwelling for a long time—and upon a search of the place, a box had been found with the odd accoutrements of Lillibet Wylde's work. Horseshoes, iron nails, cuttings of hair and feathers, small clay jars—witch-bottles, they were called—and even what Hopkins suspected to be the pure white feather of a swan.

Also in the cottage, resting on a shelf next to the Bible, was a book on midwifery. Hopkins flipped through, blushed at the illustrations, and hastily replaced it.

"Do you know your letters?" he'd asked Widow Wylde.

"Well enough to read me Bible," she'd said cheekily.

The sun was at a low angle in the sky, and the cottage's southwest-facing window allowed a solid shaft of light to break through the stuffy air. It was a perfect condition to search their bodies for the Devil's marks. It was time.

Pippa was spitting mad, Hopkins could tell, and this pleased him. Perhaps she could be goaded into confession.

"'Tis time for the searching," he said to the search-women. "Priscilla, you will be the pricker."

Pippa stared at him with murder in her eyes.

Hopkins had the urge to order all the other women out of the cottage, to embrace Pippa, to squeeze the truth out of her. Instead he murmured to her, "Look at me not with that ill aspect. I am but doing God's duty." He wished that he was allowed to take to the needle and the bodkin, but that was only for male suspects. He would prick the accused man, Ashley Potter, when his watching was scheduled in two days' time. For now, he had to wait outside.

To see her bare flesh again would be too much for him to bear.

When the door closed behind him, he could hear the shrieks of protest from inside. "Let me alone!" was the old woman. The words of the daughter were somewhat more ripe, although not past the limit where it might have been a demon's influence.

She is cunning, that one, Hopkins thought. *Both of them. They have thrived as cunning-folk.* Many cunning-folk were men, and tended towards a literate, or at least semi-literate, trade or artisan background. They were difficult to prosecute on charges of witchcraft so Hopkins most often left them alone. Too much risk they would counter-sue. However, these women were without a man, and still they kept their cottage with food on the table. Their relative success could only stem from a Satanic pact.

Find the book, he thought.

He closed his eyes and inhaled the scent of earth, grass, manure, smoke . . . but there was something peculiar in the smoke from the cottage behind him, an herb that gave it a sweet smell. He wrinkled his nose and coughed.

And coughed again.

He'd always been prone to coughs and colds since he was a boy, but this particular ailment had a stubborn hold on him. He was not worried, however. He prayed hard and often for the cessation of his cough, and God would provide him with the long health necessary to do his work.

Squinting his eyes, he wondered what the setting sun touched through the window . . . the bare skin of two women, one young and one old . . . the illuminating shine on parts that belonged to the night.

Hopkins wished that he could resist, but he couldn't. He took slow, quiet steps toward the door, and leaned in toward the crack in the door jam, and stole a glimpse inside. He wished he wasn't drawn forward from the low place in his gut, like an imp beckoned by its dark mistress. He wished he didn't see Pippa, naked and bent over at the waist by the hands of the search-women, her inky hair hanging like a curtain in front of her face. How he hated that woman. She was every part of his nightmares, every part of his dreams.

He backed away from the door, boots crunching in the dirt and the remnants of long-ago broken pottery.

From inside the cottage, there was a gasp, and another one, and another. A small squeak of pain. A muffled sob. The pricking had begun. Hopkins smiled to himself as his mind's eye saw that haunting white flesh pierced with sharp metal.

For a moment his vision was marred when he heard that hag, Lillibet Wylde, protesting at them to use the kitchen knife and please, not that rusty old nail. "Not that, please. Not the nail, put it down, not the nail!"

"Stop, stop it," he could hear Pippa beg, and knew that it was for her old mother she spoke.

Prick.

Some time later, when the dark terminus of the east encroached on the sky, Mary Phillips the search-woman opened the door. She said, "The searching for unnatural teats, and the pricking thereof, is complete, Master Hopkins."

He whirled to face her, hands clasped behind his back. "Excellent," he said, and stepped across the threshold.

Pippa and Elizabeth were fully dressed again, but he could see tiny splotches of blood seeping through their linen bodices . . . just drops, really . . . a constellation of guilt. They both looked at the floor. Hopkins thought it was in shame. *Good,* he thought, *good, we're getting to them.*

"The findings?" he asked, bringing out his pencil and notebook to record the testimony of the search-women.

"On the old woman, there was found an unnatural protrusion near her privy parts, that did not bleed when pricked, a sure sign of a Devil's teat," said Priscilla.

"No such thing," the old woman whispered. "'Tis a simple hemorrhoid. Have ye not ever seen that before, in all your fumblings about the privy parts of strangers?"

"All of us saw the teat, and agreed upon its nature," said Goody Brewer.

Hopkins peered down at Lillibet. "Have you anything to confess?"

"I'm no witch," she said.

"We have evidence," he said. "Lies will not save you. Only a confession before the law and before God will save you from sure dwelling in Hell."

"And you'd help me arrive at that afterlife, wouldn't you," Lillibet said with equal contempt. She stared at him with the hazel gaze of a raptor. "I know what you're about. I know what you fear, what haunts your dreams. You cannot hide from the eyes of an old woman like me."

"Shut your mouth," he snapped, avoiding those knowing old eyes. He scribbled in his notebook, *"Devil's teats found"* next to the name. "And the other one? What marks did she have?" Hopkins's pencil was poised over the book, ready to elaborate on Pippa's guilt, to *scritch scratch* her name, her sin, into his registry.

The search-women paused. "Well, sir . . ." began Goody Brewer.

"Well?"

Priscilla spoke. "We couldn't find anything unnatural on her," she said.

Hopkins narrowed his eyes. How could the search-women fail him so? "Are you certain?"

… free of blemishes. Surprisingly so," she added.

He bit down on his own tongue, relishing the pain, counting in his mind to stop himself from shouting. "She must suckle her imps in an unknown fashion," he muttered. "From a sore in her mouth, perhaps?"

"I've no sores in me mouth," Pippa said. "Nor anywhere else, thank you."

He refused to look at her. "You have concealed yourself with a glamour charm."

She scoffed. "How can you believe any woman or man has such power?"

"This is the law!" Hopkins shouted at her. "And I am the lawyer, and the judge of what is valid evidence or not!"

"Sir, she goads you," Goody Phillips said. "No good woman would do such a thing."

"No good woman would *not* object to treatment thus!" Pippa retorted.

"Hush," Hopkins said. "'Tis true that her attitude is that of the guilty. And worry not about the lack of marks. I feel certain with a long period of watching, the truth will reveal itself." He snapped his notebook closed and poured himself a cup of ale from the kitchen table. "Bind them." He eased himself into the rocking chair near the hearth of that sweet-smelling herb fire and leaned back.

Priscilla and Mary, the experienced searchers, tied Pippa first—her arms angled backward and her feet stretched upward against the chair, and secured together by a rope. The old woman was next, and Hopkins could tell she was in pain already at the wrists. The old ones often had trouble with their joints. The sooner the pain was unbearable, the sooner the confession, but his fee was the same no matter how long it took.

Hopkins witnessed a familiar descent. At first the two women were strong and silent. They would twist their hands or attempt to adjust their position. An hour passed; he stoked the fire. In his experience as Witch-finder General, Hopkins had seen every manner of reaction to the long wakefulness. Tears, resignation, laughter, pleading . . . or, as in the case of the young woman, a sort of flippant denial.

He stared at Pippa's reddened wrists, at the sight of the rough ropes rasping against her delicate skin.

The front door was open, as were the windows, so that imps would be free to enter. The sounds of nighttime were a back chorus to the human noises in the cottage . . . the breathing, the shifting, the occasional snort or cough from the older women. The slurping of ale. The breaking of bread. It took sustenance to stay up all night and confront the spirit world.

Goody Brewer stood up. "I'll bring tripe sandwiches from me house," she said, "and a jug of fresh ale." One of her tasks was supplying food and drink to the searchers. She was being paid two shillings a day to do it.

It was eleven o'clock. The small hourglass on the table finished its whispering cycle. Hopkins felt the sand in his own eyes, dropping them closed. The Widow Wylde, he could see, was also starting to fade into a twisted nap, and he clapped his hands at her.

"Then I'll sleep with me eyes *open*," she said.

Hopkins just smiled and settled back into the chair.

A half-hour later, Goody Brewer reappeared with a plate and a jug. Hopkins saw Pippa's hungry look. Her most recent meal was probably her breakfast.

"Confess," said Hopkins, biting into a sandwich, "and you shall have something to eat."

She pressed her lips together and averted her eyes.

The food revived his energy and he clapped his hands again at the drooping Widow Wylde.

"I want to sleep," she mumbled. "Want . . . sleep . . ."

"No sleep until a confession!"

Another hour slid by, measured by the sand. Somewhere far away, a dog barked. It was approaching midnight, the witching hour. Hopkins felt a thrill to wonder if an imp would come. He was not afraid now. He had people around him and the room was lit with candles and the fire. The mundane sandwiches and ale were an anchor. He had done this many times now, and had seen many an imp before: flies, gnats, cats, birds, mice.

Nothing came through the door, however. A fleeting thought crossed his mind that the herb burning in the fireplace was meant to keep insects away. If that be the case, then the imps might just come up to the door. He said, "Keep an eye on the windows and doors. These witches may communicate the danger to their imps, and the imps merely approach without touching them."

Sometimes the definitions had to be loosened a bit.

He brought out his Bible and began to read from the book of Exodus. His favorite verse was 22:18, for it was the direct command to do his work. He also found comfort in the stories of God's commands to the Israelites, and the trials they suffered. He knew what trials were like.

It became clear that Pippa and her mother would require a great deal of softening before they admitted to anything. As the night wore on, Hopkins's thoughts turned increasingly to the feather bed at the Charter Inn. He stood. "Keep watch. I'll send Master Stearne in a few hours."

"Yes, Master Hopkins," said Priscilla, yawning.

Elspeth waited for him at the gate to the yard. As always she was not allowed inside for fear she would frighten away the imps. Still, Hopkins was happy to see her, and grateful for her protection as he held his lantern in front of him and walked down the rocky, unfamiliar footpath. "Good girl," he told her when they reached the inn.

No one inside was awake. The Renshaws lived in the rooms in the back, and there was a curtain dividing off the main room, behind which the other search-women slept. Hopkins made a fair amount of noise climbing the creaky stairs to the first floor. On a normal night it might have taken him several hours to fight the shadows in the corners, but not tonight. He was too exhausted.

He'd barely taken off his boots and blown out the candle when he fell back onto the pillow, fast asleep.

"The Devil," Hopkins told Lillibet and Pippa Wylde the next day, "has the knowledge of thousands of years. He knows mankind. He has letters and sciences in his armory of knowledge. He knows of human physiology and its weaknesses. It is thus that Satan convinces idle women, such as yourselves, that they know better than God how to heal and cure the ills of man."

The two accused women were still kept from sleep, being walked around their yard by Goody Brewer and the constable, with Hopkins alongside.

He inspected his hands and removed a fleck of dirt from underneath his thumbnail. "I have proof against you. Testimony from one of your victims."

"Who dares?" Pippa hissed. Her voice was hoarse and her eyes bruised from lack of sleep.

"There is a good man and his wife who have proof that you poisoned their daughter. They say she went to you for a headache and was ill for weeks afterwards, bleeding as a woman bleeds, and that she was seen drinking a toxic tea of your own brewing that made her thus."

"She was not ill!" Pippa said.

"Ah! Then you admit knowing of such a woman, and that you gave her herbs!"

"You understand not the ways of women, *Master* Hopkins. She —" Pippa was interrupted by a croaking noise from her mother.

The Widow Wylde was shaking her head.

"Conspire not!" Hopkins said. He took hold of the end of rope that was tied to Pippa's hands and yanked on it, causing her to stumble away from her mother. "I see why you hold out. When they are tied up on their chairs again," he said to Goody Brewer, "be sure they face away from one another. They have secret language to communicate."

"Yes, sir!"

"Since the serpent tempted Eve," Hopkins continued, "has it been clear that Lucifer's knowledge is for the ultimate corruption of the soul. I am troubled . . . very troubled . . . not by your failure as midwives, but by your success. According to many interviews, this village is unusually healthy."

"Hardly," said Pippa. "Else we would not be so well-off as you accuse us."

"Still," said Hopkins, smiling, "I have an account of one woman who refused *you*, Widow Wylde, as a midwife. She later died in childbirth, and her child is believed to be a cursed one, a changeling." He paused, waiting for the old woman to break, to admit to the act.

Pippa spoke instead. "If you speak of Sybil Yates, 'tis true that her mother refused midwifery. But Lillibet would do no such thing as curse. 'Tis not in the power of humans. Mrs. Yates was in the hands of God." She licked her lips and glanced with yearning for the clear brook that skipped through the field, several paces away. "Can I not have a drink of water?"

"Grow accustomed to the thirst," said Hopkins, "for it is the way of damnation."

Somehow, Pippa managed to collect enough saliva in her mouth to spit at him.

"Inside," Hopkins ordered quietly. He walked away from the cottage, for there were more interviews to conduct, and he had a mind for a fresh pie from the inn. Goody Renshaw was a fine cook. As he walked away, he could hear the clanging of a kitchen pot, the clamor to keep the witches awake.

IN THE LONG HOURS OF THE second night, Lillibet collapsed. Pippa could not see it, for she was made to face the other way, but she could hear it and she bit her lip against crying out.

The watchers included Mary Ford—Pippa could have thumped her for accusing them of sickening Sarah. If only she knew what immorality her own daughter had committed under her nose! Then there was Goody Brewer, who for a mid-aged woman had a sudden energy when it came to harassing her neighbors.

All over a birch wine recipe.

In the many hours that Pippa had been awake, her mind had raced along endless circular corridors, always ending in the same place again: disbelief. Co-mingling with denial was an increasing sense of worry for Lillibet, who would not speak, and whose lips were cracked and starting to bleed with thirst.

She, Pippa, had strength left. She clung to it, and recited rhymes and charms in her head to keep herself alert. The ways of these witch-finders were to weaken her and make her delirious. She wondered if it was possible to take tiny naps unnoticed. *Yan. Tan. Tethera. Pethera. Pip. Sethera. Lethera. Hovera. Dovera. Dik. Count the sheep to fall asleep.*

Mid-afternoon and the smell of the stew over the fire was driving her mad. Drool gathered in the corners of her mouth. It had been so many hours since she'd eaten that her stomach had contracted into a hard fist inside her, but the smell of chicken stew made it hope. Had they killed one of the hens? The rooster? She tried to raise an objection, but she was too tired. Too tired.

She closed her eyes and it was an eternity, and then she was startled awake again by a pair of clapping hands.

"No sleeping," said John Stearne. He glared at her, a whirlwind of energy in this peaceful cottage. His high voice was loud, strident, as he gave what sounded like a sermon, recounting his experiences with other witches. Pippa only half-listened. *He's putting notions in your head, girl,* said a voice in *her* head. *Listen not.*

She thought about her friends, and where they might be.

She wondered why Hugh did not come to rescue her from these old women, these old dragons who watched her as prey.

Her head fell forward. She would not, would not succumb to the sandpaper on her tongue, the ache in her stomach, the spinning of her head and the fuzzy eyes of exhaustion.

The Turning of the Worm

It was midnight on the third consecutive night when Lillibet began to murmur things to herself.

Pippa and Lillibet had been given water beginning on the second day of the watching, but it was unnoticed against the deeper desire to sleep. That need went unquenched. Pippa could not remember how long she'd been awake, or even why, or who these people were.

Human shapes, and animal shapes, and the edges of tables and chairs and bed and door, all swam in her vision, upside-down. None had any real meaning.

Do not give in, said a voice. She had been listening to that voice for some time now, and doing what it told her. *Say nothing.*

But then Lillibet began to speak.

Hopkins leapt at her. "Speak up, woman, tell us what you've done."

"High on the hog, yarn in the bog."

"Did you bewitch the Reverend Yates's wife when she refused your help as a midwife?"

"Sator rotas," Pippa whispered. It was a mere scratch in her throat, nothing audible to the witch-finder. For some reason it was all she could think of for her mother. For Lillibet.

"Did you bewitch Mrs. Yates?"

"Yes," Lillibet whispered. "I bewitch. I be a witch."

The significance of this was lost on Pippa. She wanted to sleep . . . or was she already asleep? She could be dreaming. In fact, she suspected that she was.

"What else have you done? Is the strange child Sybil Yates a changeling? Did you steal the real babe and give it to the Devil?"

"Devil, he lived. Live, evil."

"You admit you are evil? That you have had relations with the Devil?"

"Yes. I know 'im well." Lillibet's speech was slurred and low.

"In what form does he come to you?" Hopkins's pencil was active on paper. He licked his lips, tasted the words.

"In me dreams. A dream."

"At night," said Hopkins.

"A man in the house. He visits me Pippa."

Rounding on Pippa, Hopkins loomed over her. "Be this true? That the Devil came to you? *Seduced* you? Did you copulate with Satan?"

Since there was no difference between the men in her dreams—her carnal dreams, of which she never spoke—and Hugh who'd visited her in the hours before dawn, she nodded her head.

Hopkins huffed. "Say yes or no to the question!"

But Pippa just nodded.

"Yes or no!"

A nod. Her head bobbed and nodded. Her neck was a limp stem supporting a wilting flower.

"You must *say it*!"

Everything was on the edge of her tongue. The magic she'd done, the theft from Joan Buckett, everything she'd done wrong. The cave in the forest. If she confessed, she could sleep, and all she wanted was to sleep . . .

"Where is the book?" Hopkins bent down so they were face to face. "Where is the book of witches? The list! The Register of your names! I know that you know!"

"Book . . . what book . . ."

He seized her by the shoulders. "The book of your secrets!"

Book of Secrets, she thought. Pippa knew where that was . . . *the cave in the forest, just tell him where it is and he'll leave you be* . . . but no. She was not supposed to tell. The secret was an iron weight on her shoulders, or was it the witchfinder's hands? In the haze, Pippa was frightened of saying the wrong thing, of betraying the part of herself that held back, that stayed silent . . . She opened her mouth.

"Master Hopkins, I believe the widow is trying to speak again."

In a voice so clear, so rational, that even Pippa was roused out of her stupor, Lillibet said, "I be a witch. I fornicate with the Devil every Friday night. He gives me unnatural energy and power for a woman of me age. He wanted me daughter, me Pippa, but I tell him no, not until she's of age. In exchange I did do his evil work. Here comes me imp now."

Lillibet must have looked toward something outside, because all the watchers were on their feet, clustering at the front door.

"I knew there was something unnatural about that pig!" said Goody Brewer. "I heard 'er talking to it like it was human. She calls it Eli Pilly."

"Is this true?" Hopkins asked.

"Illy Pilly, willy nilly. He's me imp. Eli Pilly and Yewberry."

"And what are the names of Pippa's imps?" Hopkins asked Lillibet.

"I tell you, she have no imps. She not be one of us witches . . . yet."

In the sudden blank space of her mind, within this temporary sanity, Pippa understood what her mother was doing. "No, Lillibet," she said, beginning to cry. "No . . ."

"Yes, hide no more," sang Lillibet. "I confess. I confess!"

"And you," Hopkins said, hovering again in front of Pippa, his pale face with heavy eyebrows and brown beard on the chin. "What have you to say? Do you admit to the names of your imps?"

"No . . . imps . . ." she said. All the world was fuzzy again. *No imps,* repeated the voice in her head. What madness had come into her home? Even the flames in the hearth looked unknown.

"No imps does not make her innocent," said one of the Vale search-women. Pippa had forgotten their names.

"Yes . . . that is true . . . there is one more test," said Hopkins. The look on his face was one of frustration, or at least it seemed to Pippa, before she fell asleep, eyes wide open, for a few seconds. She snapped awake, confused.

HOPKINS'S EYES WERE TRAINED on the rickety shed where a witch awaited him. This was the girl he'd thought pious, Alice Baxter, and she had been watched through the night by the search-women. The Baxter home was crowded with children and chores, and so Alice, their eldest, had been placed in the shed for the investigation. Behind the shed was the green rise of a hill and a cloud-like scattering of sheep.

Hopkins had received a message this morning that a biting fly had landed on her dry lip, and she'd bled from it, and admitted that the imp was hers.

"Be warned," his search-woman had told him, "she has a frightening disability in her speech. There is a devil inside her."

Cracking his knuckles to set his mind aright—he was disturbed by deformities and wondered if her tongue was misshapen—he knocked once on the door and opened it to find the desolate girl tied up and staring at him. Her soft brown eyes were huge and she reminded him of a trapped rabbit. A tender part of his heart squirmed in pity for her; these uncomfortable feelings sometimes arose when the witch in question did not live up to his picture of evil. He remembered how Alice had quoted the Bible in the forest. She hadn't had a stutter then. *Hmm.*

Elspeth panted in the sweltering heat of the wooden shed. Hopkins loosened his collar. He would try to make this quick. Alice was ready to break, he could tell, and he took out his notebook to be ready for her confession. His boots thudded on the packed earth as he walked towards her.

The girl flinched.

Hopkins turned over an empty barrel and sat down. Elspeth curled at his feet, her sharp eyes staring at Alice.

"Alice Baxter."

She closed her eyes.

"Alice," he said more gently. "You are a witch. The evidence against you is strong. Have you a confession?"

"M-m-m-m . . ."

So she did have a stutter! It sounded as though the forces of good and evil battled for her soul, and her tongue was caught in the struggle. He'd never encountered this before. "Speak to me, girl. Tell me the truth and there may be mercy for you."

"M-m-mercy?"

Hopkins took off his hat and sopped up the sweat on his brow with a handkerchief. "There is a coven of witches in this village. I have proof of it. I know what happens when you meet. Satan comes to you, does he not?"

She looked confused but said, "Y-Y-Yes. He d-does."

Hopkins stared at a place above Alice's head, tilting this

way and that as he listened to the voice that directed him. *She is a weak witch. Turn her, and discover the others. She will lead you to them.* Elspeth sniffed the air as though investigating the scent of Alice's fear.

"Do you know what happens to witches?" Hopkins asked.

She shook her head, appearing on the brink of tears.

"You will be taken to the gaol and thrown down a stinking pit with the other witches. There you will languish with the fallen, and then you will be brought before the magistrates. Do you know what happens when you are hanged?"

Her spine seemed to melt as she panicked and flung herself down on the ground, sobbing. "P-P-please! N-No! D-don't let it happen to m-me!"

"You will be taken to the gallows and a cloth is tied around your eyes so you cannot see. The last thing you will feel is the roughness of rope about your throat. The last thing you hear is a crowd of godly people cheering for your death. But that is not the worst of it. For you are a witch, and to Hell you will go. There will be no burial for you, no lifting of your spirit on the day of Judgment . . ."

The pitiful creature was his to mold. Switching his voice into quiet, calm authority, he said, "There is a way out."

"W-W-What?"

"If you confess to me, and if you give me the names of your coven, I might overlook your guilt."

"M-my coven?"

"The group of witches with whom you consort. Tell me who, tell me where, when, and tell me about the magic you've worked."

"I-I-I cannot." Yet Alice's voice wavered.

"You can. If you confess on behalf of others and agree to testify at their trials, I will grant you safety from prosecution." Hopkins peered at her, waiting with patience. This was how he'd turned that girl in Colchester against her own mother.

"Perhaps you are . . . innocent . . . in all of this. Perhaps you have fallen under evil influence and can still be saved. If you cooperate."

"S-Saved?"

"Tell me," Hopkins crooned. "Testify. Testify and I will say no more against you. You might be saved from the gallows, and you might spend the rest of your days in prayer to make up for this youthful mistake. Tell me."

Some internal wall seemed to break inside of Alice. When she raised her eyes to meet his, Hopkins could see their surrender, and their guilt, and their complete belief that she had done evil. Again he felt sorry for this hapless girl; he suspected she'd had no idea how she'd sinned, and now wanted to repent. It was further proof that Biblical education was the best defense against Satan in these backwards country villages. If Alice worshipped more, she would not find herself in this situation.

"We-we meet in the w-w-woods," Alice began. Hopkins sat back and listened around her stutter. "It b-b-be myself and Pippa Wylde and . . . Sybil Y-Yates."

Hopkins's pencil scratched across his notebook, familiar names on his master list.

Alice, in starts and stumbles, told him about Pippa and her knowledge of the old ways and her cunning mother. About how Sybil liked to dance in the forest and make up songs and rhymes. The way the girls tied ribbons and charms beneath their petticoats. About their learning of herbs from Lillibet, and their dance to change the seasons, and most of all about the face of the man in the woods. The Green Man. Apparently, he was a god older than God to whom Pippa in particular liked to pray.

Hopkins shuddered when he thought of his foray into the woods, and remembered Pippa's pink tongue, held out in a tease, and how she'd said that the "Green Man" watched her.

Green Man. Face of thorns. Face with demon's horns.

Alice's creeping secrets were unveiled for Hopkins. His pencil had stopped moving and he could but stare, aghast. Never had he imagined such degradation. This place was turned over to Satan, and he was glad to have Stearne and the search-women with him, for he could not do it alone. Not when the Devil had such a strong hold.

"Anything else? Anything about the Radcliff family?" he asked, his shallow breath eager. He'd remembered what innkeeper Renshaw had said about them, the rumors of their politics, that they seemed like Catholics even though they attended church.

"R-Radcliff?" Alice pleaded. "T-Tom?"

"Tom? Would that be Thomas, the son? What about him, is he a witch?"

"N-No, no! He be . . . away."

"Away *where*?" Hopkins hissed. He could see the light of knowledge in Alice's eyes and he hunted it, stalked it to the end, eager for what she held back. "Tell me . . ."

"In the army," she blurted.

"Which army?" Hopkins said, gleeful.

A tear squeezed out of the corner of Alice's eye. "The K-King's army, sir."

Royalists. Beautiful. Hopkins scrawled the name in his book. If the boy was away fighting against the righteous cause, then perhaps Hopkins could accuse someone else in that family of witchcraft, someone to draw them out . . . it could net him an even greater confession, one of treason against Parliament. Licking his lips, he put his notebook away. How he would be rewarded for this! And how he could taste sweet relief!

At the end of Alice Baxter's confession, Hopkins allowed her a cup of milk and heel of bread, and then brought out his pen and a small jar of ink.

"Sign here," he said, pointing at the bottom of his ledger.

With unsteady fingers she gripped the feather and made an

"X" next to her name.

It was helpful when the accused witches didn't know how to read.

Hopkins, recovering from the terrors of the night that Alice had stammered out loud, left her with a few parting words. "You are now beholden by law to come to the trials and testify in public. Do this not, and you will be hanged. Do you understand, Alice Baxter?"

She hung her head in shame and said, "Y-Yes."

Clicking his fingers for Elspeth to follow, he turned his nose toward the Radcliff residence.

When Pippa awoke, the first thing she remembered was the cave in the woods. She wanted to run away, to hide there, to ride out the storm. It was an island beyond the world and there she would be made safe. That was impossible, though, for she was curled up with Lillibet on the mattress, and her arms were tied. The end of a broomstick was poking her in the ribs.

They had been allowed two inadequate hours of sleep, watched over by the Brewers. Goodman Brewer was sipping on a cup of herbal tea made from Lillibet's own kitchen, and his wife was the one doing the broomstick-prodding. "Get up, you both," she said.

"Goody Brewer, please, let us rest," murmured Pippa. The firm hand of sleep was on her shoulder and she wanted to fall back into it.

"No. 'Tis time for your ordeal."

Lillibet muttered to herself. She looked fragile and dried out as an old leaf, her eyes empty and fluttering. There seemed to be more white hairs on her head.

Satisfied that they were awake, Goody Brewer nodded and marched outside. "I'll inform Master Hopkins," she told her husband. "Keep watch, man!"

"Please, Goodman Brewer," Pippa said once the other was out of earshot. "A small cup of tea for Lillibet? Just to help her waken. Please, it's only fair."

Goodman Brewer hesitated and glanced toward the door. His salt-and-pepper mustache obscured the tilt of his mouth, but there was some sympathy in his eyes. He held out his cup of tea.

Pippa helped Lillibet to sit up and brought the hot liquid to her lips. She swallowed in tiny gulps. It was peppermint—good for energy. The moisture of the steam in Pippa's nose was enough to rejuvenate her. "That's better," she whispered to her mother. "Much better."

Goodman Brewer allowed most of the tea to be drunk and then he leapt forward, seizing the cup. "That's enough," he said.

Goody Brewer was back with the constable. "The Witch-finder General says to bring them to the common."

Out the front door was a different world, a hostile world. The weather had grown cooler, the summer's heat tempered by a wind and the underside of a cloudy brew. Eli the pig looked forlorn as he watched Pippa and Lillibet being led out the front gate. Pippa supposed someone would steal him while they were away, unknowing that he was supposed to be an imp.

Pippa's head was woolly from exhaustion. She tried to think of what might be coming next but all of the witch-finder's methods were nonsensical. She knew witchcraft better than he did. *That Master Hopkins couldn't lift a curse if his life depended upon it.* They passed the Green Man, and time peeled forward when Pippa saw that it said "Charter Inn."

The day is July 8, the year is 1645, she thought, fairly certain she was correct. *I was accused on July 5. It has been three days.* Who could have known that forever was the same thing as three days? *The day is July 8.*

A buzzing crowd had gathered on the common. Pippa sleep-walked toward the crowd of friends, neighbors, and old enemies. She didn't see Hugh Felton.

Matthew Hopkins stood on the wooden platform that had been specially built by the carpenter. Pippa noticed a large cart in the road next to the common—it was covered with a wooden cage, the sort used to transport prisoners. A stranger sat at the top, scratching his unshaven jaw, and seemed disinterested in the activity around him.

Glancing about, Pippa also saw Hopkins's horse saddled. One of the village boys was holding its reins. Did that mean the witch-finder would leave them alone at last?

Pippa and Lillibet joined a small group of the accused at the base of the platform. Pippa was shocked to see elegant Winifred Radcliff amongst them, looking bedraggled, her brown eyes brimming with confusion. *This must be a joke*, Pippa thought. Who would ever accuse prim and proper Winifred of such a thing? Pippa would have guessed that Winifred would be the first to point the finger, bosom friends as she was with Elizabeth Yates.

Then again, Winifred's father was away from home, on business in Holland. Her cousin Jonas Martin had ended his visit. Her brother was in the army. Without a man to defend her honor, it was no wonder she was vulnerable to accusation.

There was no joy in Winifred's sudden fall, however. Pippa was too worried for herself.

Clinging near Winifred was Sybil, her face white as a sheet, her arms limp at her sides. Pippa had never quite realized how very young Sybil looked for her age. With those large blue eyes, that fair hair, and the small mouth, she might have been a girl of twelve instead of seventeen.

"Alice?" Sybil said, turning around. "Come stand with us."

But Alice just stood several feet away, shook her head, and looked to the grass at her feet.

They must have given Alice a hard time . . . and with despair Pippa remembered one of the tests—the Lord's Prayer.

Oh, Alice, she thought. *Who accused you? Who accused any of us?* But perhaps sweet Alice had passed their absurd tests, after all. Pippa could only pray.

"These are the seven accused witches of this village," Hopkins's voice rang out over the heads of the crowd. "They have been watched and tested. Some have confessed. But others . . ." he glared down at Pippa, ". . . have refused to admit to their crimes, in spite of evidence of imps and of Devil's marks upon their skin. So there is a final ordeal to which they must submit, and for which I need your help as witnesses." Hopkins nodded at the constable. "They will be swum in the pond. This recreates the process of baptism. If they sink, they be innocent of the crime of witchcraft, and be freed. If the water rejects them, and they float, guilt is thus proven."

Pippa turned with slow eyes toward the duck pond. How pretty it was, how gentle the ripples on its surface . . . but it was deep. Deep enough to drown in, for the Renshaws' oldest boy had drowned there many years ago. The parents of the Vale always took care to watch their children around that pond's waters and, in the winter when it froze over, to test the ice before the children were allowed to play.

But most people float in water, her mind protested. She did not know how to swim, and she supposed they would not untie her arms. Sink, and be innocent, and drown today. Float, and be guilty, and be hanged later.

She searched for Hugh among the eyes of her neighbors turned against her, but she could not see him. He was perhaps at the back of the crowd, unwilling to speak out against it. *If you love me, help me,* she implored. But he was not there.

What if Hugh had decided that Pippa had unfairly bewitched him all those years ago? What if he had run from her in fear, like her other neighbors?

Then she saw him, standing straight and tall. Her eyes tunneled on the feminine hand on his elbow. *Elizabeth Yates,* she thought, locking eyes with Sybil's sister and reading their haughty victory. Elizabeth stood as if she owned Hugh, and now she did, for Pippa had been dropped, damaged. She could almost hear Elizabeth's whispers into Hugh's ear, the poisonous tendrils of suspicion, the suggestion of "Are you *sure* you're not bewitched? Is there not something very *strange* about that Pippa Wylde?"

Pippa's heart turned to stone, cold at the knowledge that Hugh, her *love*, her enchanted childhood husband, had turned against her and gone into the arms of a scheming other.

Winifred muttered a prayer, Lillibet mouthed a charm, Sybil hummed to herself, Ashley teetered on unsteady feet, the Buckett women whispered filthy words and curses. They were all strung along the same rope like cattle, dragged up the embankment along the grassy edge of the pond. Pippa saw that Alice hung back, held at the elbows by the constable. It did not look like she would be swum and Pippa wondered why.

"Untie them," ordered Hopkins, "so that if one be innocent, they affect not the outcomes of the others' ordeals!"

Two men seized Joan Buckett by the legs and heaved her into the pond.

She shrieked like a bird, twisting and turning about in a terrible melee. Her great splashing flung water droplets into the crowd, edged up as they were to the pond to watch, and Pippa felt a few sprinkles on her own nose. The sky too was getting ready to rain down on them—several chillier drops hit her uncovered head from above.

For all her fussing, Joan Buckett did not sink, and the men hauled her out of the water. The villagers cheered and jeered and old Joan was led to the caged cart. Pippa felt sick. She wondered if this was divine retribution upon her for misusing the power of magic. If only Joan had the money to defend herself . . .

Next came Anne Buckett, and the evidence against her was

so heavy to begin with that Pippa wondered why they bothered. She was as much a spectacle as her mother, screeching and hollering and floating.

Then it was Sybil's turn, and Pippa bit back a cry as the rough hands of two men took hold of Sybil's fragile frame. She was so light that she flew through the air, far out into the middle of the pond, and twisted and turned, her hair and her petticoats flashing pale beneath the surface . . . but her head remained above water.

"She floats!" came the cry. "A witch, a witch!"

There was something so vicious in the sea of familiar voices. From the way they looked at Sybil, she was no longer the daughter of their minister, but a stranger. Something had turned in their minds and the ranks were closed.

The Reverend did not acknowledge his daughter, and Catherine and Elizabeth stared ahead, calm as though this were a matter of simple justice.

Sybil was an abandoned child as she was led, shivering, to the cart.

Winifred was next. She remained dignified even when tossed into the pond, and although she could not help her natural reaction of trying to swim, she did so with a certain grace. It did not change the evidence: she floated, and lived, and was declared guilty. Several families cheered on, for the Radcliffs had money, and that was always a source of jealousy for some. Again Pippa wondered who had planted the accusation.

Elizabeth Yates had shunned Winifred, it seemed. Winifred's former friend stood without pity, and her hard features even held a trace of anger.

Winifred's mother and sister looked on, stony-faced.

They too had closed ranks.

Old Man Ash, bawling at the injustice, floated. No surprise, for he was light as a feather and drank more than he ate.

As she watched, and as the fear grew inside of her, Pippa

started to think of how she might make herself sink, and wondered how long a person could hold their breath if they tried.

"Lillibet," she whimpered, as her tired, abused mother was yanked away from her, and thrown into the water by a man she'd healed of pleurisy, and another for whom she'd fixed a broken leg, and delivered as a baby.

A diminutive cry was silenced as Lillibet's head was dunked under the water. She struggled with the bindings on her hands and feet, bending over and then stretching out again, trying to keep her mouth above the rippling waves. Pippa's heart seized when she heard Lillibet's choking and gasping as water crept down her airway.

How long should it last? At what point was floating or sinking determined? It seemed to be up to the discretion of Hopkins, whose eyes were not on Lillibet in the water, but on Pippa's face to see her reaction.

Hatred rose in her throat like bile.

"She floats," he said with a casual flick of his hand. "Take her away."

Lillibet could hardly walk and her silver hair was plastered to her head. Water ran down the aged cracks of her face . . . wrinkles that had not been noticeable the previous week.

"Think of the rocks in the brook," Lillibet whispered on her way past Pippa.

Rocks in the brook. Pippa was breathing hard, afraid to go into the water hog-tied, afraid she would drown. *But then you'll go straight to Heaven!* said a mocking voice in her head.

Hands grabbed her and before she had time to even cry out, her petticoats were flapping around her legs and with a deafening splash, she was immersed. *Rocks in the brook.*

Insight struck her. She must be the rock. Taking one last, deep breath, filling her lungs, she did not struggle against the water or the ropes but curled herself into a tight ball.

She sank.

The noise, the insults, even the sprinkles of rain . . . all fell away as she went down. The weight of her clothing helped. She opened her eyes to see the flashing skin of a fish, and the waving tentacles of pond grass, and a few glittering things in the mud at the bottom—coins for luck, or long-lost trinkets. Slowly she let her breath escape in a column of bubbles. She sank further still. Her toes touched bottom and she wriggled them in the slime.

Glancing up, she could see the wavering figure of Hopkins peering in, his cape and hat and boots forming a distinct silhouette. He was waiting.

And she was out of breath.

Hold, she thought, *hold.* The rush of energy was seeping away. Her muscles and mind screamed for air. Darkness edged at her vision. A burning pain exploded outward from her chest. *Breathe!* The water that had been a sanctuary for a few seconds was now the enemy. She tried to relax herself and unbend her legs so she would rise up, but still she hovered far below the surface. They must see that she had sunk. They must pull her up soon . . . but the rope was left slack.

It was no good.

She bent her knees and with all the force of her growing panic, she sprung upwards off the bottom of the pond. Up, up, and with a tremendous splash Pippa was flung almost entirely out of the water like a leaping fish. She gasped and the air was sweet nectar, filling her with red life, and she fell back into the water.

The rope tightened and she was dragged out of the water.

"How interesting," said Hopkins.

The crowd was silent, avid with the drama.

Hopkins's eyes wandered over her as she stood wet and dripping in front of him. For a few beats he looked lost in some private memory. Then he spoke. "She attempted to sink . . . but see how the water ejected her very body!" He shook a finger.

"Attempt not to trick God! He has spurned you and cast you out of the water!"

Winded, Pippa shook her head, for there was not yet enough breath in her lungs to speak her piece.

"Yes! Yes! Guilty!" screamed the mob.

She did not know their faces.

As she was led toward the cart, Pippa thought she heard someone cry "No!" over the din . . . it was lost in the chaos. She also saw Hopkins accept a large bag of coinage from the Reverend. The witch-finder did not look back at the condemned as he walked toward his horse with the grey imp heeling at his boots.

"Oh, Pippa," said Lillibet when they were in the cage together, and leaned her head on Pippa's shoulder.

"Alice?" Sybil said, leaning over.

But Alice was still next to the constable, staring at the ground, tears rolling down her face. The cart was locked without her.

"Get on!" said the driver, and with a lurch, the Vale rolled away behind them.

The journey northward was full of bumps and bruises. The cart did not stop except for the driver to relieve himself on the side of the road. He drank constantly from a jug of ale that rested on the seat next to him and so it was no wonder that he needed to stop every half of an hour.

It was a miserable group held captive in the back. Pippa took tiny naps, overcome by exhaustion and soaking wet from the pond, and then from the rain that unleashed upon them. She was with her friend and her mother and that was enough for now. Perhaps they were a coven after all, although missing one member.

On the other side of the cage, Anne and Joan Buckett

huddled together, staring with bloodshot eyes at the others. Winifred sat curled into a forlorn ball. Old Man Ash was passed out on the bed of the cart, his bones seeming to rattle with every rock beneath the wheels. For all that, he looked comfortable and Pippa envied his ability to sleep through it.

She was so famished that she'd forgotten what normal hunger was like. Her appetite had descended into a hard lump at the base of her stomach. At least her thirst was quenched by the sky—she tilted her head up and caught the rain on her tongue.

"How long did they watch you?" she asked Winifred. She was curious how Winifred, so refined, so upstanding, so well-dressed, had been degraded to her level.

"One night," Winifred said. "Until my imp came along in the morning. A *field mouse*," she added with derision.

"Has your imp a name?" Sybil asked.

Winifred looked at her, confused.

"She's teasing you," said Pippa, although she was not sure.

"How about Lip?" Sybil suggested. She hummed to herself.

"They came with no warning," said Winifred. "Middle of the afternoon. I thought the accusing was done."

"Someone must have come forward, but I can't imagine who would hold such a grudge against you," said Pippa.

"Nor I." She sighed. "Seems that the accusation is enough."

"Ye should a' been more generous," rasped Joan Buckett from her corner.

"You!" Pippa lunged at her. "Was it you who accused her? Any of us?" Masked by her aggression was the fear that Joan would find out her secret, and tell the court how Pippa and Ash had conspired to steal from her.

"I was more than generous with you, for all your ingratitude," Winifred added to Joan.

Joan laughed. "Like them men'd listen to an old witch like me. 'Twaren't me. Hold them wild horses in ye, Pippa Wylde."

"It wasn't them," said Sybil. Her voice was, as always, clear and musical and so very out of place in the dripping wooden cage. She leaned back against the slats and closed her eyes.

"I wonder why Alice is not with us," said Pippa. "They did not swim her, either."

Sybil bit her lip. "Did they make you recite the Lord's Prayer?"

"Yes . . . I can't imagine how she passed that test. I hate to think her speech was evidence enough to those witch-finders."

"But she not be with us now," said Lillibet. "I can't help but pray they've let her go." Then she muttered, low so only Pippa could hear her, "Alice was innocent, and I am not."

"What?" Pippa whispered.

"'Tis punishment," Lillibet murmured. "We brought this on ourselves. My . . . fault . . ."

"What do you mean?"

Lowering her voice even further, Lillibet said, "For what we did. What I did. Sarah Ford. I never should have meddled . . . my fault, I brought God's punishment onto you. I'm sorry . . ."

Pippa glanced around to make sure the others weren't paying attention. "No! Lillibet, no, that was not your fault," said Pippa, but the possibility of retribution was a fresh concern. As you sow, so shall you reap, she thought, and was this the reaping of the murder of an unborn child? That had been Sarah Ford's mistake, her decision. God couldn't be angry at the scissors that cut the thread. Yet . . . here they were, stripped of home and position and safety. A tear slipped down Pippa's cheek, merging with the raindrops that already soaked her skin.

Pippa could not forget how Lillibet had confessed on her behalf. Noble as it was, there was little chance Pippa would escape the same fate. There were none to vouch for her character in Bury St. Edmunds, and none to listen to her. And if there was a divine hand in this, the life of a cunning-woman and her daughter in exchange for the seed of life they'd helped to destroy . . . Pippa could not escape. Despair leaked into her heart.

She had the rare ache of missing her father, John Wylde, who would have been able to protect them. If he'd been alive, Lillibet would never have had to use her cunning magic at all. They would not have needed Sarah Ford's fee. They would have been safe and rich.

Pippa took her mother's hand.

They hit a hard rock and the cart groaned at the seams. Despite the damp clinging of her petticoats and the grittiness of pond water in her hair and in the cracks of her toes, her eyes fell shut. But there was no mistaking the nightmare that would follow, the evil end of their journey: the gaol at Bury St. Edmunds.

The Gaol

It was a hot, stinking day in the town of Chelmsford and a massive crowd gathered at the main square. Looming above their heads, a gallows had been built of wood and metal and rope. Caught in the throng, Matthew Hopkins tugged at his collar. It felt like the collective body heat was contributing to the temperature.

As he moved, Hopkins received his share of attention. People nudged and whispered to each other; the fingers of little children pointed at him. "There goes the Witch-finder General. Matthew Hopkins 'imself."

Two days previous, he'd testified in his first major trial. He'd given evidence against most of the women scheduled to hang this day. The raving, hot, drunken crowds had hushed to hear his voice. The trial jury, a collection of freeholders, farmers, and merchants, had agreed with all his results. He'd been nervous at first, but had reminded himself that he was God's lawyer. *Name the witches. Name them, and be free.*

He'd like that cranky old lawyer in Ipswich to see him now. Wearing a quiet smile, he moved through the packed bodies, knowing that he had done God's will. All around him, the audience was settling in with bread, ale, cheese, sausages, and a ravenous appetite for the death about to be served.

Not everyone was enthusiastic, however. A man could be heard grumbling to his partner. "Costing 'em a pretty penny to have this hullabaloo. The town don't have much to spare as it is, and who's to pay for the incarceration of all these witches? Pounds, I heard, been racked up in costs."

His friend said, "Small price to pay for the ridding of witches. They cause more trouble out of prison than in it."

"If they be witches at all, and not poor ignorant women," said the man.

A skeptic, thought Hopkins. They were in the minority. Most people had reached the conclusion that witchcraft was real, and it behooved them to pay the witch-finders to sniff them out. What, indeed, was the price of an immortal soul?

He spotted a narrow stair against a building and stepped up out of the masses. Sighing with relief when he was several feet above everyone else, he waited for the first group of the condemned to appear.

The crowd roared, the cheers beginning at the edge and moving like a great wave to each throat . . . there was the procession of prisoners in carts . . . soldiers guarded the way, shoving bystanders out of the way so the doomed cargo could get to the gallows.

Hopkins noticed the hangman marching back and forth on the high platform, checking the integrity of the knots dangling from the beam. He wore a black hood made of thin wool that covered his face. *A job for a strong Christian,* thought Hopkins, feeling a momentary affinity with the hangman, for both men carried the burden of justice on their shoulders.

At the base of the platform the witches were blindfolded and led up the stairs. Their lips were moving, some of them, but their last words were lost in the noise of a thousand free, redeemed people. It was just as well. Witches were prone to throw curses when they were at the end of their rope.

One of the women was being half-dragged up the stairs because she had only one leg: the widow Elizabeth Clarke. She did not frighten Hopkins anymore. She was just a wretched old woman who had sold herself to Satan. This was a mercy killing as far as Hopkins was concerned. The only thing that surprised him was that she was still alive after so many months in prison.

A thunderous cheer rose up as the final noose in the row was tightened around Clarke's throat. She wavered and wobbled on that single leg of hers.

Even above the multitude, Hopkins heard the simultaneous crack of five necks as the doors were loosed beneath the feet of the condemned. They jerked and swung. The crowd screamed its approval.

He pretended that it didn't affect him.

Yet, as he watched the drunken sway of the hanged witches' feet, a persistent crawling sensation tickled his gut. It was he, Matthew Hopkins, the Witch-finder General, who had put these women in their place . . . he who had brought them to their death.

He took in the hot, excited faces of the mob, saw the sick pleasure that twisted them into howling imps themselves. *This is not for your entertainment!* He burned with annoyance at the crowd.

His deepest spiritual quest had turned into a mere spectacle on an idle summer's day. None of these common people knew the dangers he faced, the evil he confronted, the battles he fought. Not for the first time in his life, Hopkins felt trivial and small, as if he were the only one who understood the stakes, a lone voice shouting against a gale.

The sun grew higher in the sky as he lingered on the steps above the square, caught up in his thoughts. It took thirty minutes for the witches to hang until dead. In the interim between new batches, the people milled about, gossiping and eating and fighting. The thrill was gone from the discolored bodies that swung from the gallows. His dissatisfaction grew.

You can stop.

The thought came out of nowhere. It was clear, calm. Hopkins regarded it. His eyes lifted up to the blue sky. Perhaps he hadn't meant for it to go this far. He'd never seen a person hanged before. He'd never even seen a person die before this day. Every woman who walked across that platform to the waiting noose was there on *his* testimony. They were the sacrifices to his self-purification. *Sacrifices? But the Lord gave up His own Son that no blood sacrifice would ever again be required.*

As though there was an imp on one shoulder and an angel on the other, two parts of Hopkins began to argue.

One voice said, *This has gone far enough. Give up now. Let the rest go free.*

The other voice said, *Witches meet in the trees and the dark places. We will consume you. Smack, our lips go. Smack and spack.*

The problem was that Hopkins couldn't decide who was the angel and who was the imp.

His mind turned to the heavy money sack resting in his hearth at home in Mistley. This witch-finding was a business. It was his work. How could he turn away from it?

The girl was innocent, and you knew it.

The vague image of a fair, unworldly girl floated in his head. He couldn't pin down the particulars, but she was in a bad place, a dark place, because of him.

You can set us free.

Another face, with darker hair, with crackling hazel eyes that matched those of her mother. There were other ways to save Philippa's soul. He could explain to her the wickedness of her ways. Even . . . if he dared . . . with gentleness and patience and the tender touch of hands, he could bring her back into the Puritan fold.

Hopkins stood up too fast and the blood swirled in his head. He could go to Bury St. Edmunds. He could propose a different approach, where he preached to the accused and brought them back to God's flock. The witches could be rehabilitated, made to repent, and with hard work, become pure once more. Pure like him, not bad like him. He could recant on his evidence. Say it was a mistake. Say that their names were not in the Devil's Register, after all. He could bring Pippa home, tuck her under his wing, show her, touch her. They could go to the New World together, to his brother's parish in Massachusetts, and leave their mistakes behind. Pippa might grow to appreciate him, to *love* him, they could have *special time* . . . He could do all of these things.

Let us go, said the voice.

Before the next round of trials he would speak to the magistrate and have the women released. At least, he would have a few released, the important ones. He shivered to think of Lillibet Wylde free to roam the land and curse him . . . but not if he was in the New World. She couldn't reach him there.

There were arrangements to make, ship's schedules to inspect, and in a haze of excitement he rode for home that very night with Elspeth at his side.

THE WORLD WAS MADE of hard edges. Her soft bright hair had dimmed and gone brittle. Sybil's fingers skimmed across the sharp crescent of her clavicle that jutted out from beneath her filthy bodice. If things kept on like this, her very bones would be starved out of her body.

Next to her was another pile of bones—a woman collapsed in upon herself. The sole indication that she lived was the motion of two fingers, idly picking at lice in her petticoat. The woman's name was Mary and she came from a hamlet called Combs, near Stowmarket. Last week, when Mary was still able to speak, she'd told Sybil about the day Matthew Hopkins had arrived, and how she had been accused and watched and pricked. It was like speaking into a mirror, down to the pained eyes and the mouth cracked at the corners.

Sybil had lost track of the days and nights. There was no such thing as sunshine here. Time was measured by when they were fed cold gruel, a slop unfit for swine. Sybil found it difficult to swallow with the maggots and bits of gravel, so she'd opted for a voluntary fast.

"Fasting," Pippa had whispered to her, the ghost of a laugh in her voice.

It was what drew Sybil to Pippa like she was a flame: that undaunted spirit. Every day they spent in the gaol, Pippa grew more infuriated. Sybil didn't know where her friend found the energy for anger.

Lillibet, however, was not well.

The sleeplessness, the dehydration, and the brutal swimming had not been good for Pippa's mother. The longer Lillibet went on like this—eyes glazed, lips cracked, hands shaking—the deeper Sybil's worry for her.

The cell in which they lived was the size of a cottage and it held, at last count, forty-two women. Pippa had taken to naming them by that old sheep rhyme: "*Yan, Tan, Tethera, Pethera* . . ." They were women, but their humanity seeped away with every hour they waited. They wallowed in their own stink and in the common stink of others. The smell was a layered chorus of excrement, decay, dirt, grime, sweat, fever, blood . . . with a high note of fear.

It made Sybil eager for a trial, eager even for a death that would release her from this place. If she went to Hell, it could not be as bad as this. At least Hell, she imagined, had plenty of space to move about in one's torment, unlike this cell where she knocked up against an elbow on one side and a rib on another.

She slid down the wall to sit in the only open space, beside

Winifred Radcliff. The rich girl had been quiet so far. Her fine black wool dress was fraying. Sybil noticed the slight dimple on Winifred's cheek that meant she was biting her mouth, perhaps to keep from screaming. The gleam of a tear lurked in the corner of her eye. Her fingers clutched at the rough floor.

Despite Winifred's past snobbery, Sybil could not help feeling sorry for her. It could not be easy to be brought so low, so quickly. And Elizabeth had abandoned Winifred in her hour of need. *See the kind of friend my sister can be,* thought Sybil.

On Winifred's other side, Pippa passed the water gourd with some reluctance. "Here, have a sip."

Winifred took a choking gulp of the prison water that tasted of decay, of spittle, of minerals and dirt. "Thank you," she said. Her voice was throaty and scratched. "Here, Miss Yates," she said, passing it on to Sybil.

Sybil took the gourd and tilted her head. "You can call me Sybil, if you like."

"Oh," said Winifred. "Sybil." She dabbed her mouth with the edge of her sleeve. "How long do you think we'll be here?"

"Only God knows," said Pippa.

They fell silent amidst the coughing and low murmurs of the other women. Then Winifred spoke again. "I wonder what they're saying back home about us."

"Nothing good," Pippa snorted.

Winifred opened up into the conversation. "All of us accused had grudges against us. I don't believe there ever were witches in the Vale. Too many stood to benefit from this."

"Who had a grudge against you?" Sybil asked.

Winifred took a deep breath. "It's all over now. I may as well tell you."

A long moment passed and Pippa said, "Well?"

"I almost accused you," Winifred said to Pippa.

Pippa's eyes tightened, but she said nothing.

"Almost?" said Sybil.

"Yes, almost. I thought about it, but I didn't. You see . . . I'm in a rather precarious situation, and I thought that by making an accusation, it would make me look better. But I couldn't bring myself to do it, not after seeing those wretched Buckett women, who may be scandalous, but deserve not hanging over it. Mostly I just wanted the witch-finders to leave the Vale. They were disrupting everything. And so I spoke with Elizabeth, and we . . . quarreled. I suppose I do have an enemy."

"What happened?" asked Sybil gently. She understood how it was to quarrel with Elizabeth.

"I told her that she was taking it too far. I urged her to act with restraint, to not accuse unless she was certain, and how the witch-finders said they would dismiss frivolous charges. And then she said that I wasn't a good Puritan, that I cared more for fine clothes than proper morals." Winifred picked at her cuffs. "Perhaps she was right. Before this, my life was about pearls and lace and who spoke to whom after church and the new style of bonnets. But in the heat of our quarrel I didn't think about that. Instead I told her that she cared not for other people, to go so far as to accuse her own sister—" Winifred broke off, looking chagrined.

"I already knew that," Sybil said. "Go ahead."

"Anyway, it ended when Lizzie called me pretentious and chubby. I told her that she was vindictive, spiteful, and spotty-faced."

Pippa laughed and even Sybil had to smile, thinking of the look that must have earned from Elizabeth.

"It was quite a scene," said Winifred.

"I'm glad you told her that," said Sybil. "I would never have the courage!"

Winifred sobered. "Then they came and watched me in my garden, with their needles and . . . I've done everything to deserve this. I haven't been a good person. I know that. If that be witchcraft, to keep an ill tongue, then I'm guilty after all. But I still cannot believe Lizzie would accuse me of this, just because of that one quarrel. That's beyond cruel." She lowered her eyes, brow furrowed in thought.

Pippa looked at Winifred with new warmth. Sybil knew what Pippa thought: an accusation of witchcraft might just be worth telling off Elizabeth Yates. Sybil's thoughts formed in a different direction. Her eyes fluttered as she pieced it together. "Oh!" she blurted. "You mean about Thomas. Perhaps someone suspected your politics and wanted revenge?"

Winifred's eyes widened. When she finally spoke, her voice was low and wooden. "What do you know about my brother?"

"Oh, that he's away," Sybil said airily. "That he's with the army. The other army. He told me before he left."

"Why would he do that?" Winifred demanded. "Why would he tell *you* such a thing?"

"You didn't know?" Sybil said. She'd always thought Winifred at least suspected it. "Tom is going to marry me when he returns. So you're going to be my sister someday."

"What? What?" Winifred turned to glare at Pippa, who had a knowing smile on her face. "Did you know all this, as well?"

"Yes," Sybil answered for her. "He used to kiss me in your garden. It was very nice. And I love your garden, with all the pretty roses and the lavender."

Winifred straightened back against the wall, eyes turned upward. Her head shook back and forth. It was a long time before she said anything, until finally she seemed to pull herself together and looked into Sybil's eyes. "You like the roses, then?"

Sybil laughed. "Yes, the white ones most especially."

"They're my favorites, too." Winifred gave a tiny smile.

"So, do you believe that someone found out about Tom?" asked Pippa.

Winifred hiccupped, but answered, "It makes a kind of

sense."

"None others knew, though," Sybil assured her in a whisper. "Just your family, and my sisters."

"Your *sisters*?" Winifred said. "Elizabeth! That mean-spirited harpy *would*—"

"No, she means her spirit sisters," Pippa interrupted. "Me and Alice. Good God, no one would tell Elizabeth anything so sensitive!"

"Oh," said Winifred, mollified. "But Alice, your other friend, where is she?"

"In another gaol, I imagine," said Sybil, closing her eyes, trying to see with her mind's eye. Alice's face floated there, her tender mouth frowning, her eyes full of pain. "I pray she keeps well."

Winifred's eyes narrowed. "Are you certain she's trustworthy?"

"Of course!" said Pippa, offended. "It's Elizabeth you have to worry about." Her mouth twisted. "Now she's got exactly what she wants."

"Hugh Felton?" asked Winifred.

"His choice is made," said Pippa. "He chose *her*."

This pained Sybil, too. She knew what it was like to be forgotten. She would never forget the cold look on Elizabeth's face during the ordeal at the pond.

"We were always friends," Pippa said of Hugh, a plaintive note coloring the air.

Winifred admitted, "I did hear from my mother that he was betrothed to someone. He'd said as much himself. I did not realize it was . . ."

"Elizabeth," said Sybil, most sorry.

"I don't hold it against *you*," said Pippa, reaching across Winifred's lap to squeeze Sybil's hand. "We cannot choose our family." She extricated her other arm from around Lillibet's sleeping form and clasped Winifred's arm. "And as for you, I pray that whoever accused you is made to pay."

"Thank you," said Winifred, straightening her soiled bodice. "Shall we pray together?"

"I think we should," said Sybil, and they all clasped their hands and bowed their heads in silence.

THROUGH THE GLOOM SYBIL saw that Pippa had awoken from a nap and was playing a game of scratch with Winifred on the floor. They had folded their legs together to make a square foot of space. Now that they were friends, Sybil remembered how Winnie—as they'd been calling her—had visited during her fever. Now that Winnie was thrust into this situation, Sybil was impressed with her steady mood and her ladylike manner, untainted even in this cave of suffering.

As Sybil swam across the sea of limbs and bodies to get to her friends, a claw gripped her arm. "Christ rose to save us," said the crinkled voice of an old woman. No one knew her name, for she had been one of the first in this cell and spoke nonsense most of the time. "We rejected Christ. Die, speckle, die!"

Christ rose under the hill, thought Sybil, and pried her arm away from the scary old hag.

"Ho! Watch where you're puttin' them feet!" someone said. There was no avoiding it, but Sybil felt bad nevertheless.

"Hello, darling," said Winifred. She stretched her legs out as best she could and pulled Sybil into her lap as though she were a small child. "Lord, Sybil, you must start eating! You're as a feather."

"I'm not hungry," Sybil said. "I've been giving my ration to Joan Buckett. She's poorly, more than me."

"I order you to stop that nonsense," said Winifred. She was herself weak, Sybil could tell, and her throaty voice sounded much less compelling than normal.

"She's right, Syb," said Pippa. With a thin hand she petted Sybil's hair. "You must keep up your strength."

"All right," said Sybil, although she knew, and her friends did not, that there was no reason to keep her strength. In the precious moments of sleep that she carved for herself amidst the coughing and stuttering, she had been having a recurrent dream. In the dream she was walking through the forest, *their* forest, and there was a clearing up ahead filled with white flowers. Every time she slept she drew closer to the meadow. When she reached it, she knew there would be some sort of ending. This did not frighten her much.

She looked toward Lillibet on the other side of Pippa. "How does she do?"

Pippa's face was shadowed. "Time will tell."

"I would pray for willow to ease her pain," said Winifred, "if there were any hope of attaining it."

"Or valerian," said Pippa.

Sybil looked more closely at Lillibet. She was half-reclined against the rough stone wall and a deep wrinkle seemed to cleave her forehead in two. She'd been suffering headaches for the last day and the muscles on her jaw and neck were stiff and twitching. A thin sheen of fever afflicted her skin. It was difficult to tell if Lillibet's color was normal, for everyone here was malnourished and pale as a fish's underbelly.

"Get, get!" Winifred snapped, brushing at a large mangy rat that threatened them. "Filthy creature!"

"Me imp," crooned a woman a few feet away. She was called Margery and openly declared herself as belonging to Satan. "Come to me, Bucky Tom!"

"Be quiet, you old fool," said Pippa, who had argued with Margery on the first day and called her a fake. "It's just a rat." Nevertheless she helped Winifred turn it around towards Margery. "Eat it, if you like!"

Sybil whispered, "Do you believe Margery's really a witch

as she says?"

"No," said Pippa.

"She does seem a bit confused," said Winifred.

Across the cell, in a different corner, a woman convulsed and groaned. Her feverish murmurs were a steady stream beneath the general noise. She had been fevered for three days and had the dreaded lump on her neck.

"Gaol rot," muttered a woman nearby. She was part of the newest group of prisoners brought from Bury's hinterlands.

"What's that, gaol rot?" Winifred asked her.

"She been in here too long," said the woman, chewing on a piece of straw picked up from the floor. "Me husband died of such a rot two years ago."

"Your name is Anne?" Sybil said.

The woman peered at her, startled. "Why, yes, Anne Alderman. How'd you know, child?"

The name had occurred to Sybil in a flash of knowing, as things often did, but there was no explaining this so she shrugged.

"Ah, you be usin' witchcraft!" said Anne.

"No," said Pippa, placing a hand on Sybil's shoulder and smiling. "She's just cunning."

"Cunning-folk, then?" Anne asked.

"Minister's daughter," replied Sybil, and Anne laughed hard for a few seconds.

"No other cunning-folk been accused, you must be the only ones," said Anne. "I reckon most of them had the good sense to stay away from all this. In our village it's a cunning-man and he even helped to watch the witches." She shook her head.

"You said your husband was imprisoned?" Winifred asked.

"That's right. For a'listenin' to the preachings of Bishop Laud, and then giving such sermons hisself. He weren't no minister, mind you, but he was listened to by some. They accused him of being a Royalist and then he came here to this very gaol." She spat into her hands and rubbed them together. "I been here before to visit 'im. But he died before any trial ever started." She nodded across at the sick woman. "Looks like nothin's changed."

"You were accused as a witch?" Pippa asked.

"That's right. Me husband used to have cattle, see, but I had to sell some on account of having no more money. I kept the best milkers for meself, as any sensible person would, but the beasts I sold to me neighbor . . . two fell sick and thrashing, and died. He accused me of bewitching them."

"Did you?" asked Winifred.

"No, 'course not! At least . . . I don't think I did. Maybe I had some ill thoughts toward that neighbor, for the price was less than fair to me."

"Perhaps he feels guilty for cheating you," said Sybil, "and tried to justify it by calling you a witch. Then he wouldn't have to look at you every day and be reminded."

"Hmm," said Anne. "I believe you be a minister's daughter. Your language is good." She poked Winifred. "So's yours."

"She's not supposed to be here," said Sybil. "I don't think she'll be here for much longer."

"What do you mean?" Winifred asked with unease.

"You won't die of gaol fever," said Sybil. "I mean . . . I don't know. I just feel something will happen."

As she said it, there was a clang and a shout from the corridor. The way brightened as several men with lamps entered, bringing with them a chained group of men and women. The gaol-keeper was there, looking exasperated. All the times Sybil had seen him, he looked exasperated. It was the hassled look of a cattle farmer with too many livestock in the pen.

Every woman in the cell ceased her speech or humming or moaning to watch. Sometimes the guards told them news. There was one guard in particular, a round young man with most of his teeth missing, who usually passed along the prison gossip. He was with the keeper now.

"No room in here," said Winifred as she watched the prisoners parade past the bars.

The keeper said the same thing as he raised his lamp, shining a light into the chaos of the cell, and then shaking his head to move on. "I got a hundred in here as is, we're beyond capacity," the keeper told Bucktooth, the head of the guard, a cruel man with protruding front teeth. "Put them in the solitary cells." He laughed as though this concept were funny. Sybil had not seen the solitary cells—including the men's cell where they'd put Old Man Ash—but she could imagine they were overcrowded too. "The next lot after these, send them on to Ipswich."

Sybil closed her eyes and thought about Ipswich, another city in Suffolk, and remembered that dream storm that had swept through her home, that hungry dream worm . . . how it must have visited hamlets, villages, and towns all over the land. Hundreds accused . . . she opened her eyes to see them. They were mussed, hair encrusted with dirt, and clothing stale, and faces without hope.

Even in prison, women would be women. Small cliques had formed within the cell—some of the women already old friends, others new acquaintances forged within a common misery, like their Winnie.

"Ugh," said Winifred, picking a flea off her sleeve. It jumped off in the direction of a mother and daughter huddled next to her.

Sybil tilted her head so her eyes were at the level of the hunched, curled bodies around her. *A flea feast,* she thought, smiling, for she could see dozens of other fleas hopping about from one person to the next. At least something was having a good time. *Is this the nature of torment?* Sybil wondered. *That one party suffers and another celebrates?* She could still see the gleam of needles and the matching gleam in the eyes of the search-women.

Some minutes or hours later, the gossipy guard brought a cart with a large tureen of gruel. "Get out your bowls," he called. There was a scramble as the women reached into their pockets or under their knees for the small wooden bowls. Most stood up and formed the queue so that the guard could slop two ladlefuls into each woman's bowl. "Stay there, I'll get yours," Pippa told Lillibet, holding both bowls in her hand.

When a prisoner died, her bowl became precious property, at least for a few feedings before the guards noticed the lifeless body. Then the guards demanded the return of the bowl, too, for there was a rule of one serving per prisoner.

Staring down into the cloudy, lukewarm liquid in her own bowl, Sybil decided there was slight difference between drinking it and fasting on purpose, so at Winifred's insistence she drank down the broth. A tense gag threatened to reject it. She coughed and wiped her mouth. "A tasty brew," she said. "Like stewed saliva."

Pippa choked on her own mouthful and then laughed after swallowing.

The foul stuff seemed to form a whirlpool in Sybil's gut. She groaned and curled into a tired ball on the floor.

"Rest for awhile," Winifred agreed.

From the floor Sybil watched as Pippa attempted to feed Lillibet without success.

"Ah, me head," was all Lillibet could say through clenched teeth. "I'm . . . so tired . . . canna' swallow . . ."

"Take a bit of soup, Lillibet, please?" Pippa said, edging the bowl up to her mother's lips, trying to force open the unyielding jaw.

Sybil was reminded of the throbbing headache of her own fever and wondered if Lillibet had something similar.

"Come back to bite ye now," said Anne Buckett to Pippa.

Anne was crawling past them to where she lived on the other side of the crowd.

Pippa did not dignify that with a response.

The cold hand of fatigue crept upon Sybil. She closed her eyes and the pained murmurings around her faded in and out. The last thing she heard before falling asleep was Lillibet hissing, "Can't open me jaw." There was some vague alarm associated with this, but Sybil couldn't think of what it might be.

AFTER A LONG SLEEP, ANOTHER feeding, and a recitation of her daily prayers, Sybil felt better. It must be the addition of the gruel into her diet—disgusting food was better than no food, according to her stomach. "I feel quite fine," she said to Winifred.

"Unfair," said Winifred, "you made yourself worse off at the beginning so you could start eating now. Your body has been offered hope. Mine is just falling down." She placed her hands on an abdomen grown frighteningly thin in just a few weeks. Winifred had been the plumpest of them. "But then," she said just as Sybil thought it, "I had much more to spare than you did. 'Tis more extreme for me . . . but I think more dangerous for you."

"Did Jesus not fast for forty days?" Sybil said. "I might do the same."

"This counts as a fast," said Winifred. "That gruel is little better than the juice from meat, and a bit of fat floating in it." She sighed. "My strawberries must be ripe now . . ."

Sybil could not hear or see it, but she knew that a tear had formed in Winifred's eye as she thought about the garden of which she was so fond.

The unquenchable thirst for a large, ripe red strawberry danced in Sybil's mind and she thought she might cry too. *Oh, Lord, release me from this prison of a body,* she thought, for it was her body to which she was a slave. Her hunger, her cold, her deprivation . . . the dank cell was nothing to compare to her body's invisible chains.

"Sybil. Winnie."

It was Pippa, picking her way across the floor with a cup of water. "Help me hold her head."

Lillibet was pale. At times, out of the corner of her eye, Sybil would see a flash of a white light above Lillibet's head, or a moving shadow across her body. Something was very wrong.

Pippa dropped brackish water into her mother's mouth, and the girls helped the old woman stretch out on the floor. Lillibet's arms and legs twitched, and her hands curled into tight fists.

"'Ey!" protested Margery, who was jostled out of the way. "Watch yourselves or I'll curse ye."

"Be quiet," said Winifred.

Hissing at them, Margery crawled over to harass a different part of the cell.

Lillibet's face was frozen in an expression of surprise. Her jaw and throat were hard to the touch.

Then, with a violence that made the shadows tremble, Lillibet arched upward, her spine bent like the curve of a yew-branch bow. Her agitating muscles rippled under her skin. Her jaw was locked into a sardonic smile and a low whine escaped her throat.

"A demon!" cried a woman nearby.

"She be possessed, cursed!"

"Satan has come for us!"

"Do something!" Winifred said, reaching out toward Lillibet.

Sybil remained still. To witness such pain made her want to disappear.

Just as abruptly as the fit began, Lillibet slumped back down, motionless. Pippa hovered over her mother, her face panicked. "She's a-fevered," said Pippa, desperate hand on Lillibet's forehead. "I know not what's wrong! I know not what to do."

Lillibet was silent. There was no improvement, no motion in that inflexible jaw. For an hour they waited, hoping for some sign, some instruction from the ailing wise woman.

They took turns watching over her.

Later that day, or night, or dawn, or dusk, there was a treat: the guards tossed several large loaves of old bread into the cell. This happened on occasion and it was left to the women to divvy it up. The process was unfair, for the weakest could not fight over it, and the bullies got the largest share.

The guard rattled a stick along the bars and the bread was flung into the sea of outstretched hands and starving, quivering mouths. Violence erupted—fingernails were made into claws, elbows into weapons, feet and hands clambering over each other and reaching for the prize.

Fortunately for the Vale sisters, Pippa was in the thick of it, hollering. She emerged from beneath a pile of bony bodies with half of a loaf tucked slyly into a fold of her skirt. "Here," she whispered, dividing the bread into three equal pieces.

"What about Lillibet?" Sybil asked.

"She can't open her mouth to swallow," said Pippa, looking upset. "Besides, fever's not to be fed."

"That's right," said Winifred. "Sybil, you didn't eat anything solid for five days during your fever."

"I had a fever for five days?" Sybil asked, for she'd never quite had a grasp on how long it had lasted.

"Longer, but you were on the mend when Martha began feeding you porridge," said Winifred.

They fell silent at the mention of treacherous people from home. Martha had been the one to catch Ursula. Sybil chewed on the bread, trying not to think of their pet raven and what might have become of her. Although the bread was dry and crumbly and made of cheap mullet wheat, it expanded in her stomach and made her feel almost satisfied.

"Thank you, Pippa."

"I know what you're thinking," said Pippa. "About Ursula."

Sybil swallowed. "Yes, I worry for her. She's just a bird. But she was a friend."

"Worry not," said Winifred. She'd been told all about Ursula when the girls compared imps. "After you were accused, I heard that Martha brought the bird to that pigeon coop the Renshaws keep." Quiet Will Renshaw bred carrier pigeons. "Will wouldn't say anything, he'd take pity on a lame bird and be sure she's fed at least. Until we get home."

Sybil squeaked with happiness. "Oh, bless you, Winnie!"

"Until we get home," said Pippa, finishing her bread.

Sybil kept thinking of Ursula, turning over a picture of the bird in her head, holding it close like a blanket to soothe her. Her fingers itched for a needle and thread and fine white piece of cotton. She would like to embroider something, a black bird, and a border of thorns and twisted vines, all in black to match. Black and white. She closed her eyes to see the stark contrast . . . not like this gaol, which was dim and brown and dirty.

When she opened her eyes again, the keeper was at their cell, flanked by two guards. There was a man, a civilian with them . . . a man Sybil recognized.

"Winifred Radcliff!" the keeper called.

All around, women stirred and began to sit up.

"Have the trials begun?" someone asked.

"Winifred Radcliff!"

"Winnie!" Sybil shook her sleeping friend's shoulder.

"Mmm?" Winifred raised her head and rubbed her eyes. "What is—*Papa!*" She stood up so fast that she had to cling to the wall to avoid toppling over. Sybil knew what that was like—the rush of blood to the head.

"Go, go!" Pippa nudged her.

Winifred was pushed through the crowd by their fellow prisoners.

"Papa!" Winifred reached her arms through the bars and clung to Mr. Radcliff's clean lapel. He looked very serious.

"Daughter. You are to come home with me at once."

"I—what?"

"Your charges have been dropped. Come, child, come out of there."

Oh, thank you, Almighty Father, thought Sybil. Some angel had tugged on a thread, and that thread had pulled another, and somehow Winifred was free. She collapsed against Pippa in joy, feeling almost as though she was freed, too.

Winifred turned to them, but the keeper yanked her out of the cell so as not to keep the door open. Sybil didn't know why. *We poor creatures are not capable of rebellion.* She felt Pippa's hard, jubilant clasp on her hand and thought, *None but one, anyway.*

Winifred said, "Wait!" but she was whisked away and Sybil hoped she never returned. It sparked a little hope . . . perhaps her father, too, would come for his daughter. Perhaps the Reverend would realize that she was his own child and that he'd made an error in judgment. Sybil settled in to wait. She traced a lacework pattern into the dirty floor with her fingernail.

The Dissolving World

The indolent air of mid-August did not reach inside the gaol. It held a different kind of heat—Pippa sometimes had the odd sensation that Hell itself was nearby, and that if she pulled away some kind of veil, she would see it. The shadows played tricks on her. Her mother had often said that idle hands did the work of the Devil, and that an idle mind did the same. A hundred breaths were held, waiting for trial.

There was a heavy weight on Pippa's lap. It was Lillibet's head, for she was sliding towards death, and Pippa knew there was no stopping it. The sentence was written: lethargic weakness punctuated by terrifying spasms. Lillibet's jaw would not relax, not even to eat or breathe, and her lips were pulled back in a helpless snarl. Every so often, her entire body would lift off the floor, twisting up as though lifted by demons, the contortions so wild that several rib bones and a vertebrae had snapped. The other prisoners stayed away from the cursed one, the possessed one.

The fever had taken Lillibet's mind a few days ago, just after Winifred was released. Now she mumbled nonsense, when she was able to speak at all.

Pippa was tormented with the thought of the herbs that might save Lillibet, the rest and care that might cure her. And if she'd not been so weakened in body and spirit by the cruel tests of the witch-finders, she might have fought it off. Pippa used a gentle touch to soothe Lillibet's brow. All she could give her mother was her presence and her prayers.

Two days ago, in her disappearing voice, Sybil had asked Pippa what ailed Lillibet, if it was what they feared.

"I've not seen it before," Pippa said, "not in the flesh. But I know it to be the lockjaw." The very word was a death-knell in this place with no treatment, no ointments to relax the clenched muscles. Sybil had shuddered and Pippa ordered her not to touch Lillibet, not even in comfort. "You're too weak. It might be a curse. I would not want you to be afflicted."

It was impossible not to touch and be touched in this cell, however. Three or four others also suffered from plague, a disease of incarceration. The first woman who'd caught it had died a week ago. Pippa wondered if all of them might die before coming to trial.

With every thin, rough breath that Lillibet took, Pippa felt her own will to live draining away. In . . . *gasp* . . . and out. That breath was a clock winding down to nothing. *The whole world might do this,* Pippa thought, *drain away like Lillibet.* She began to wonder about the great fiery battles in the Book of Revelation, the Apocalypse, and she began to doubt they would ever come. This was the way things ended, in fever and in mindless suffering, in broken bones and disintegration. If God was order, then Satan was chaos, and from where Pippa sat, Satan was winning.

There was nothing to be done about lockjaw, but it was not always fatal. If the blood could be kept pure and the humors in balance with the use of herbs, recovery was possible. But in a body already ravaged by starvation and torture . . . Lillibet's light was gone. Her hands were claws and her bones were cracked by the ferocious supernatural writhing of her own muscles. There was a liquid sound in her lungs, which meant the infection had moved into dangerous areas of her body.

What was more, Lillibet seemed to know. She'd known at the first sign of stiff jaw before being yanked into oblivion by the fever.

And there was *nothing* Pippa could do.

Sybil crept up, tiptoeing around the field of arms and legs, holding onto the wall for support. She was so thin she could have been swept away by a breeze . . . not that there was any fresh air down in this pit. "Shall we pray over her?"

"All we can do," said Pippa, bitterness a poison in her mouth.

"Shh," said Sybil, "Quiet your thoughts. She has taught you well. Death is not the end of things, but the beginning of new life."

Grief seized Pippa's heart in a vise, warped it in a mockery of Lillibet's own twisting, and she sobbed. Once, twice, three times she cried out for her mother. Sybil watched with impassive gentleness.

"That's it, Pippa. You must accept what you cannot fight."

Her vision blurred by tears, Pippa looked at Sybil and wondered how she had become so wise . . . that she, who was like a song on the wind, could pin down the very essence of the thing.

"Let us pray," said Sybil, clasping her tiny hands together and bowing her head.

Pippa recited with her the prayer for the sick. "Oh, Father of mercies, God of all comfort, our only help in time of need . . . We humbly beseech Thee . . . relieve Thy sick servant for whom our prayers are desired . . . Grant that she may dwell with Thee in life everlasting . . ."

Throughout it all could be heard Lillibet's failing breath.

"She is sanctified," said Sybil after the prayer. "She will go to a place better than this."

Pippa watched the slight rise and fall of her mother's tense chest. Lillibet had been hollowed out.

Sybil said, "Every breath must die so that another can begin."

Pippa closed her eyes. Perhaps they were all but a breath inside the mind of God. Perhaps death was that moment of release, when the lungs contracted to fill anew. She thought of all that Lillibet had taught her, and was sorry she could not have learned more. She was sorry how badly she'd botched her life before the trials, that she'd ever disappointed Lillibet with her silly and unthinking ways.

"But you've seen the death of my father, your husband," Pippa whispered to Lillibet. "You would not want me to grieve the coming of your winter, and your rest."

As the hours dragged by and Pippa waited and prayed, she could be almost grateful that her mother would not suffer the indignity of a public execution. This way it was almost a natural death.

And then she would remember the utter destruction of her home and safety. Lillibet was going without her. And then the despair would rear up, seizing her, breaking her into pieces as the curse had done with Lillibet.

"Oh, no, it's Bucktooth," said Sybil, nodding at the nasty-faced guard at the bars. On occasion he liked to take a woman out of the pen and beat her, and sometimes drag her somewhere else, after which she would return a shattered creature. It was why Sybil and Pippa stayed toward the back, even if it meant they were last to get a ration of food or water.

When a woman reached a hand around the bars, begging for water, Bucktooth swung his club at her, and with a nauseating crunch and a high-pitched howl of pain, her fingers were smashed.

Pippa could feel the weight of the building and the earth above her head. She was in a different kind of cave here. If her spirit was a flame, it was being snuffed out by that swinging club in Bucktooth's hand . . . by the hands that tossed her into a pond . . . by the bodkins and needles that pricked her skin. She closed her eyes. "Sybil, I have something to tell you."

Sybil tilted her head to listen.

"If . . . in case . . . well, I think you're the one most likely to survive this. I should have told Winnie. If I'd known she would be released, I would have." With a deep breath, and an apology to Lillibet who'd sworn her to secrecy, she whispered, "There is a special place in our woods."

Sybil's wide eyes reflected the torchlight from the corridor. Pippa knew it was right to tell Sybil how to reach the cave, about the mark on the rowan tree, how to move the stone and crawl inside, and of the treasures that could be found there. She said it was a safe place. "If we be accused of witchcraft, then perhaps they truly covet our knowledge." If Pippa was going to hang for what she knew, than she wanted to be worthy of it. That cave *was* special and it could not be left to decay.

Sybil, with a touch of her usual flightiness, said, "'Tis no surprise to me. All sorts of things can hide beneath the hair of a leaf." She blinked at Pippa. "The secret is safe with me."

"Thank you," said Pippa. She felt she could follow Lillibet into the shadow lands. There was not much else to live for. *He's dropped me, he's forgotten me*, she thought about Hugh Felton. *If it was a small chance before, 'tis impossible now. He thinks of me as I am: a low failure, a wretch. He must believe I did bewitch him.* He hadn't come to save her, to speak for her, and she knew what that meant. She was never his, as much as she wanted to be. Now the one thing that had made her stand out to Hugh— her spirit—was dust on the ground.

Like a cat chasing its tail, such thoughts went round and round in her head, and still Lillibet's thin breath grew thinner, and her eyes dimmer in the gloom.

A SPASM WOKE PIPPA from a listless sleep. "Lillibet!" she said, hovering over her mother's face. "Oh, Lillibet. Please be at peace. I can stand it no more . . . please, *please* . . . oh Lord God, please!"

Lillibet's limbs stiffened, and then were limp again as the pulses of disease did their last work. Her mouth was a grinning rictus. With broken fingers, Lillibet grasped the folds of Pippa's petticoat and lifted herself halfway to a sitting position. Her eyes were fierce with inner concentration.

"Let me go," Lillibet rasped. "Release me."

For a terrible moment Pippa thought her mother truly was possessed, that it was more than disease and fever. But then . . . by a miracle, Lillibet's jaw moved, and she spoke around her rigid tongue.

"John. John."

Through her tears, Pippa said, "Papa—your husband—is waiting for you. He's there."

"Pippa. Let me go. You go and live." A small smile lifted the bleeding corners of Lillibet's mouth—a sight so gruesome it was almost beautiful. "The Death Crone comes for us all. I will go, and dawn will follow the night." With a final determined wince, Lillibet said, "Listen close." She breathed in short, shallow pants. "Take me head when I be dead. Keep it in the cave. Then I shall always be with you. *Take me head when I be dead.*"

Pippa's mouth fell open.

Lillibet giggled a girlish laugh through her teeth. "Funny, yeah? They not be expecting that!"

A bubble of laughter escaped through Pippa's weeping. Of all the things . . . struck dumb, she could but nod at Lillibet.

"Good girl," said Lillibet. Her head fell backward onto Pippa's cradling arm. Her breathing was erratic, labored, as her own body tightened against itself, suffocating her. Something seemed to lift away . . . and then it was just a ruined corpse with a mouth that gaped like a cavern. Lillibet's eyes were empty windows and with shaking fingers, Pippa closed the lids over them.

"Farewell, Lillibet," she managed to say, before falling against the wall. Her own eyes were suddenly dry of tears. She was hollowed out, too.

Several hours later, Pippa and Sybil took Lillibet's bowl and discussed what to do. Pippa didn't know what the gaol did with the bodies of accused witches and so she crawled over to Anne Alderman to ask her.

"Isn't hallowed ground, if you be worried about tha'," said Anne. "Accused don't mean guilty, so I believe a blessing still be said . . . but, the grave is common. Behind the prison and near to the tanning pits."

"What happened to your husband's body?"

"That be how I know. Had to sign for it, and he was buried at the plot at home." Anne peered over Pippa's shoulder at Lillibet's slumped figure. "She died, then?"

Pippa nodded.

"Sorry. But unless you got someone outside to take 'er body, she'll go to the common ground. 'Tis an open pit, horrible stench this time of year, and the birds go for the pickin's."

Pippa crawled back to Sybil. "They'll toss her in the common grave."

"And she wanted you to take her skull?"

Pippa would have expected fragile Sybil to be shocked by this request, but Sybil seemed to think it perfectly normal. "'Tis what she said."

"Hmm. You'll want to take the rest of her body, too." Sybil fingered the button on Lillibet's petticoat. It was dull pewter.

With deft fingers she tugged on the threads and detached it. "I have an idea. Rub this button against the wall and make the edge sharp."

"Why?"

"We've got to have a way to find her body amongst the others. So we give her a necklace." Sybil parted a small section of her long hair and began to weave it into a braid. "Make that sharp enough to saw off this hair of mine."

"Oh!" said Pippa, understanding. She filed the edge of the button on the rough stone. Soon the curved edge was thin and sharp enough to cut skin. She flicked the edge of her thumb on it and wondered if it could help her escape.

Sybil smiled sweetly and took the button. With a sawing motion she cut off the long plait of hair from the roots of her scalp. The rope of gold fell into her hands and she tied the ends together in a firm, expert knot. "Here. Lift her head for me."

With gentle hands Pippa raised the head of what had once been Lillibet. It did not look human anymore, and like no one she recognized. Still, the body acquired a sort of dignity when Sybil graced the neck with the pale braid. The hair looked fresh against the taut grey skin. Sybil tucked it beneath the collar and patted it once.

"There. Now you have something to look for."

"Thank you, Sybil." Pippa wasn't sure what she would have done without her friend. She leaned back. "Do we tell the guards now?"

"I'll tell the round one," she said. "*Not* Bucktooth."

"Lord, no."

When the fat guard came on his round, Sybil, who was waiting at the bars, flagged him over. In the suffering hush of the cell, Pippa could hear her words clearly. "A woman died. Of the lockjaw."

"Fine," said the round boy, who did not have the hard eyes of a man yet. "It'll be collected. Who was it?"

"Her name was Elizabeth Wylde."

"Fine." The boy leaned over. "Anything else?"

"No . . ." said Sybil.

He licked his lips. At first Pippa thought he was going to say something fresh toward Sybil, but it turned out his interest was gossip. "The assizes are set for a week from now. That's when the trials start. But they be trying to get them done fast, for the King's army is marching this way."

Sybil turned toward the corner where Pippa waited, and nodded at her.

Pippa's spine stiffened.

"The girls in here think you're sweet," Sybil said to the guard in a faux whisper.

The guard shook his head at her, but seemed chuffed nonetheless.

Another pair of guards arrived for Lillibet's body and her bowl. She was passed across the cell and dropped onto a wooden board. Pippa watched her mother go. Every part of her ached.

Sybil picked her way across and collapsed next to Pippa. "The trials are almost here."

"I don't believe you," said Anne Buckett. "We ain't never gettin' out of here."

Pippa kept her distance from the Buckett women, for every time she looked at Joan Buckett, she thought of her own mistakes. She knew she was not responsible for Joan—the hag was bound to have been accused. Still, Pippa couldn't help but wonder if she herself was being punished by God for misusing the cunning ways. She wished she could go back in time to wield herself with utmost care and wisdom and to act as Lillibet had done. No ridiculous quests to find illicit treasure for drunken old soldiers.

I wonder where he is, she thought of Old Ash. He'd been taken to a different cell for men. He could be on the other side of the wall that had eighty-two stone bricks, for Pippa had counted them many times.

"Anything to get out of here," said a woman, speaking of the trials.

"Straight to the gallows, you'll go," said someone else.

"Worry not," Pippa whispered to Sybil, and they retreated against the wall. She curled up and closed her eyes and imagined that she was in Lillibet's cave in the forest. She could feel the darkness around her like she was a rabbit in its burrow. She could see the warm flickering of a fire and could smell the dust of the books, the dried green of the herbs, the clear mineral water that dripped from the seam in the rock. There were rubies in the cave.

ONE OF THE GUARDS ANNOUNCED when it was Sunday, so that they might spend their time in prayer. Pippa could not pray and could not care anymore. She just lay in one place and arose once for the cold slop of food in her bowl, and Sybil's. They took turns fetching it for one another.

Pippa could feel the poisons of this place in her body. She had not had her monthly cycle, and her digestive processes seemed to have ceased as well. Hunger had congealed into a dull ache in her stomach. Where once she would have gulped down the gruel and stale bread straight away, now she was indifferent and often waited hours before bothering to eat.

Sybil looked more like a skeleton than a person. Her eyes were huge in her face, and her skin was almost translucent. Her blond hair hung as a matted curtain down her back. There was bone but no flesh.

The numb silence was broken when Bucktooth called for her by name.

"Pippa, don't go!"

"I care not," she told Sybil, and lifted herself off the floor. If the guard wanted to force her, nothing would stop him, and it was no difference to her.

Bucktooth leered at her, but did not open the door. Instead he said, "I been told to give this to ye." He passed her a parcel wrapped in cloth.

Pippa looked down at the solid thing in her hands. "Who sent this?"

Bucktooth didn't answer, but gave her a gap-toothed grin before sauntering away.

Tip-toeing back across the women, Pippa reached Sybil and they unwrapped the package together. Pippa's fingers were her eyes in the dark, and she knew she felt the soft hairs on a strawberry.

"We're saved," said Sybil, biting down onto a berry with a small moan.

Their unknown benefactor had packed a dozen fresh strawberries, two meat pies, a loaf of rich white bread, a chilled roll of butter with cress, and even a few ripe lemons. The girls huddled over the treasure so it wouldn't be discovered by the others. It would cause a riot.

"It must be Winifred," said Sybil. "She grows strawberries in her garden."

"Bless her," said Pippa, taking a small bite of meat pie. Every night she had dreams about food, only for her appetite to vanish upon waking. *This is real*, she told herself, and took her second bite with a renewed hunger.

Slowly and quietly they ate the pies. Sybil offered the last third of hers to Anne Alderman. Anne said, "I used to bring me husband things when he was here. God bless you, Sybil Yates. And your friend."

Pippa's stomach protested at the sudden riches. She knew to save the rest for later, but she could not resist a ripe strawberry. She held it in her hand as though it were that ruby in the cave. The taste of its red juice on her tongue was more than delicious; it was a smuggled piece of home. But who had sent the gift? Most likely it was Winifred . . . but Pippa dared to wonder if it had been Hugh Felton. Either way, she wasn't forgotten. Someone was thinking of her.

She and Sybil ate half a lemon each, and Pippa used the rind to scrub the skin of her face, sighing at the fresh scent and feel of it.

"Philippa Wylde!"

It was Bucktooth again. Pippa gave Sybil's hand a squeeze and stood up. "Perhaps we're being released."

"It cannot be long now," said Sybil with a tremor.

Pippa went to the guard, and to her surprise he unlocked the cell and yanked her out. "Ye've got a visitor. An important man." Bucktooth eyed her speculatively.

Hugh. Pippa reached up and smoothed her hair. There was nothing to be done about the way she smelled, but she hoped Hugh would forgive that. She was led down the row of packed cells, up the narrow stairs, then ushered into a tiny office.

At first Pippa was caught by a square of sunlight. It came from a small window that pierced the regular stone of the wall. It had been weeks since she'd seen such a bright, beautiful thing. The tantalizing smell of clean outside air made her lean forward.

As her sight adjusted, she noticed the figure of a tall man, his back to her. There was no hint of the gold of Hugh Felton's hair or the summer's brown of his hands.

Pippa turned to flee but the door was closed and locked behind her.

"Miss Wylde," said Matthew Hopkins. He spun on his heel. There was a flash of white at his throat, an expensive collar. There was a different kind of gleam in his eyes.

Pippa backed up until she hit the desk behind her. Bitter disappointment filled her eyes with tears. "What do you want?" she croaked.

"Did you receive the parcel I sent to you?"

Pippa gaped, unable to believe it.

"I trust it was adequate to renew your strength. The gaol is too conservative with rations, I think."

Pippa felt a lump in her stomach. A part of her wished she hadn't eaten that food, not after learning its source. Incredulous, she said, "'Tis *your* fault I'm here!"

"That's not true," Hopkins said. "Your own sin brought you here. But believe me, I have no wish to see you die without a fair trial."

Pippa sputtered—for herself, for Lillibet already dead, for the absurd notion of fairness in the world. "Oh," she said sarcastically, "I suppose you wish to see us all properly convicted! Hanged by our little throats until dead!"

Hopkins let out his breath and averted his gaze.

Pippa stared. She'd been right. He *liked* it. Something in the base of her mind tightened in fear. "What do you want?" she asked again in a low voice.

He approached her and Pippa drew back further, but he moved past to sit in the chair next to the desk. He placed his hands firmly on his knees. They were trembling.

"Sit," said Hopkins, nodding at the floor in front of him.

"I'll stand."

There was a long moment, the space between them drawn out like the awkward quiver of an off-key note.

"I need you to confess," Hopkins blurted.

"To what?"

"To being a witch. I need you to admit to it." There was something almost plaintive in his voice.

Pippa couldn't believe he was back for this. She was incarcerated already. Had he not done enough? The thought bubbled up quick and certain: *He's not close to being finished. He wants you dead.*

She stared at his hands. They were beefy, strong-looking. It occurred to her that she might be in real physical danger from him—and for the first time in weeks, she was glad there was an armed guard on the other side of the door.

Pippa felt Hopkins's hungry eyes fixed on her. It made her feel like an animal caught in a trap, and he was the hunter. Not only did he want her accused and hanged as a witch . . . he wanted her to declare it, to admit it. There was some role he wanted her to play.

She wouldn't do it. "I told you before. I am no witch."

Hopkins clutched his knees. "I have a—an idea—a notion to—free you. And your mother, and your friends from the Vale."

Pippa almost cried out that her mother was dead, but thought better of it. Hopkins was afraid of Lillibet. It was better if he thought she was alive. "Free us?"

"Only if you confess."

"You make no sense."

Hopkins's jaw moved in frustration. "God allows forgiveness of even the worst sins. Does He not?"

"I know not about God, but I shall never forgive you."

"Forgive *me*? My dear girl, you are the—"

"Witch, yes, I know."

Hopkins leaned forward. "So you admit it?"

Pippa couldn't understand why he was so ardent about wanting her particular confession, but the hair on the back of her neck prickled. She looked at the floor. "What if I did? Why must you hear it from my own mouth?"

"Confession is part of the Lord's plan. It would cleanse your soul. When you do, we can leave this place—"

"*We?*"

"—and go to the Americas. Your mother would have to stay here, of course."

Pippa, weakened by fear and grief, didn't quite understand what he was proposing except that he wanted to control her again. Steal her from her own life and into whatever sickness played inside his mind. To the Americas? *Naked savages,* she thought, and a laugh of hysterical fear hovered at the back of her throat.

"You know," said Hopkins, looking past her shoulder into some reverie of his own, voice growing soft and almost seductive, "just because the mother is a witch . . . we can overcome the stain. We can purge it. *Wring* it out of our souls."

All Pippa could think of was Lillibet, ravaged by the lockjaw. Rotting now in a mass grave.

Hopkins had done it.

"My mother is dead!" Pippa cried. "Bastard! Thief!"

She almost lunged for Hopkins's throat but she saw something in his eyes that frightened her back. It was shining and wanting.

It told her that if she continued, things would turn ugly for her.

Shaking, she turned instead, pounded on the door, and yelled for the guard. The door opened.

"We're done here," said Hopkins, standing and brushing his trousers straight. "For now." He walked out without another look at Pippa.

WALKING THE STREETS OF Bury St. Edmunds, Hopkins felt dissatisfaction with the way things had gone with Philippa. She hadn't understood him. All she'd done, the dirty creature, was cry about her mother. Didn't she know that she was claimed by the Devil? Unsettled, he walked hard toward the inn where he'd secured rooms for himself and John Stearne.

Already the festival atmosphere was beginning in the city. There were hordes of people eating and drinking outside of the pubs. Farmers were arriving in carts with their families, ready to go to court and sue their neighbors over boundaries or bull rights.

Hopkins arrived at the inn, a three-story building with expensive glass windows. In this busy time he was fortunate to have a private chamber in one of the nicer establishments. In no mood for socializing, he ordered his dinner to be taken in his room.

Upstairs, he pulled off his boots. The miserable smell of the gaol had affected him, a headache creeping at his temples. He went to the window to close the curtains and his fingers brushed the rope tie.

If only Philippa had known what he wanted of her. He was tired, so tired. He wanted to stop, but he needed Philippa to admit they were disgusting, that they needed to be punished by each other, and so turn to the Lord's straight true way. As it was, she was still trying to trick him with protests of innocence. He clenched the rope in his fist.

A knock on the door interrupted. "Your dinner, sir."

"Come in."

The serving woman smiled at him. Her eyes were clear, sparkling brown. Like *hers*, the maid, the harlot, the pitiful excuse for a woman who had birthed him. *Deborah*. Memories clawed their way up and his head throbbed in one great spasm.

Hopkins started backward. "Leave me," he stammered.

The woman dipped and exited, leaving the tray of food. Hopkins approached it . . . and could not help remembering.

"'How can there be peace,' Jehu replied, 'as long as all the idolatry and witchcraft of your mother Jezebel abound?'" Matthew Hopkins, fifteen, sat on the stone wall and murmured aloud from the thick Bible. His hands clutched the top of the book and his eyes darted upward to glare at his house. Through the open kitchen door, he could see the generous outline of Deborah as she prepared the evening meal.

Behind him, the sun grew dim and pale, slipping closer to

the edge of the sky. The light was not enough to read by and so Matthew hopped off the ledge, closed the Bible, and walked across the yard.

"Matthew," said Deborah, popping her head out, her eyebrows in a lovely arch over her brown eyes. "Be a darling and toss me that basket of carrots." She pointed at the lean-to shelter. Inside was a small bunch of fresh-picked carrots, a shock of orange against black.

He stared at her from the gloom. How he wanted to make her pay for everything she'd done, her warped love that broke his father, that broke him. As he looked at her pale outstretched hand, other memories surfaced of their special times together. How those hands had been so pleasing to him, bathing him, holding him, and then . . .

"Matty, the carrots," said Deborah again. "Are you a'right?"

He reached over, seized the handle of the basket, and thrust it at her.

"Get washed up," she said, turning away and shaking her head. "That boy's got so odd," she murmured, but he heard her.

He knew her whisperings and charms.

In the hour before dinner, he thought of something he could do. Deborah had a special chest in her small servant's room. She kept the chest locked at all times.

Matthew crept into the kitchen, and while Deborah's back was turned to him as she peeled the carrots, he plucked a small knife from its hanging-place. He slipped it into the cuff of his sleeve and backed out, then climbed to the third floor attic where Deborah kept her quarters.

The chest was a pretty object, painted with flowers and animals, the colors fading. Its lock was sturdy. At first Matthew tried to pick it with the knife, but it wouldn't budge. He glared at the box—this is where she keeps the tools of her craft, he thought—and stabbed the wood with the knife. It left a tiny mark.

He smiled. He began scoring the chest, slashing at the flowers, *drawing x's through the eyes of the animals, taking his revenge.*

"Matty! What are you about?"

Deborah was at the door, red mouth open in surprise.

Matthew dropped the knife and it clattered to the floor. She was going to curse him now. His life was over. He would die in a shaking fit as she lifted her finger to point at him.

"You're a witch!" *he blurted.*

Deborah strode across the room and made to grab him. "Ye're a little hellion to say and do such things! That's me family chest!"

Matthew flailed at her approach, his awkward young arms hitting her as best he could—in the face, across her breasts, her upper arms.

"Stop that!" *she shrieked.* "Stop it!"

He kept hitting her. He was still small for his age, but what he lacked in strength he made up for with passion. "Jezebel," *he gasped.*

Deborah was powerful. She put her arms up to block his blows. Somehow, her hands ended up around his neck.

"I ought to throttle ye," *she hissed, and began to squeeze.*

It wasn't painful, but rather firm. Matthew had slight trouble breathing, but then came a giddy rush of mischief and excitement. And something else . . . down there. Thrilling and peculiar feelings twisted through his gut. She is a witch, Father said so, she knows Satan's tricks to bind us, to tie us up—*and he knew that she rode the Devil's human form, lay with him, went to him in the night.*

Deborah released him. "You're a bad boy, Matthew." *She placed those* sweet white cloying choking *hands on her hips.* "Get out before I take a switch to ye. And don't think I won't tell your father what you've done."

Matthew swallowed against the rising force inside him. This was his birth mother—his mother!*—and she was evil to make him feel such things. He felt sick at himself, just as he had when he'd learned he was born of a witch.*

That evening, as his family sat together and his father said the blessing, Matthew clung to the prayer with all his force, his forehead creased in concentration. "Lord bless us and keep us . . ." Keep me, oh Lord, keep her away from us . . . *the prayer turned into something else* . . . Flat on my back, Satan is a woman, I am helpless, she rides me until I die, her hands around my throat . . . *He choked aloud, his face burning, and he was grateful for the low candlelight as his elder brother sent him an acerbic look.*

Matthew was terrified to take a bite of the ham, glazed as it was in Deborah's honey and herbs. He watched as his father's wife cut a delicate piece and raised it to her lips, chewed, and swallowed. He waited. When the rest of the family was halfway through their meal he finally mustered the courage to cut, and chew, and swallow.

The meat was pink and sweet.

THE MEAL HOPKINS HAD BEEN served at the inn was ham, of course. He didn't touch it. Instead he went to his bed and laid back, placing a pillow over his face, enjoying the cool heaviness of the cloth against his skin.

Images flashed across his mind's eye, of Deborah and their special time, of Philippa bathing in the forest pool, and that same witch this afternoon in the gaol, decrepit and dirty inside and out. The embarrassed blood in his cheeks tingled; he thought they might stain permanently.

How had he ever thought a woman innocent? How had he ever thought one could be redeemed?

He had almost succumbed to Satan's temptation—to quit, to free the witches, to unleash the lustful, shameful part of himself. *If they go free, I will never be.* Shaking, Hopkins resolved to never question his path again. *Too close.*

In a few days, a fresh round of trials would begin and his testimony would send their necks to be cracked, his sin to be cleansed. He breathed cool air through the pillow. His thoughts turned to something more pleasant: he needed to think about opening an account with a goldsmith banker in London. If he continued to earn such wages for his work, he would soon have a fortune to worry about.

THE CACOPHONY OF THE CROWD had been a dull rumble from inside the jail. When Pippa, Sybil, and the other unfortunates were hauled out of the cell where they'd languished, it was into a different world. Bury St. Edmunds was overrun with soldiers, witnesses, magistrates, prisoners, merchants, and the curious. Their feet and voices brimmed with excitement and fear. For those not directly involved in the assizes or in the army, it was entertainment on a long summer day.

The soldiers, in red coats and the rounded helmets of the Parliamentarian forces, were on high alert, for the King's army was indeed marching on nearby Cambridge.

One step ahead, two back again, thought Pippa. Her hands gripped the wooden slats of the prison cart.

Her cheeks were wet with tears, for she hadn't seen the full sun in weeks. The searing light felt like a thousand tiny cuts on her eyes. The noise, too, was overwhelming. Pippa would have thought so even on a normal day, used to the gentle quiet of the countryside as she was, but today it was like being tossed into a seething cauldron of humanity. She was almost grateful for the prison cart that separated her from the street.

Although not a word had yet been spoken, Pippa was already resigned to her conviction. Her sympathetic witnesses were either accused themselves, dead, or had dropped her like a hot stone—like Hugh. A dart of anger punctured her indifference for a moment. *He's either too dim to see that I was in danger, or he never cared about me from the beginning.* She sighed. There was nothing she could do about it, or about him.

She was in this alone.

Of course, there was Sybil, sitting next to her. *It must be worse for her.* It was Sybil's own father who'd abandoned her to rot. But they couldn't convict a minister's daughter . . . could they?

In ill news for Sybil, Pippa overheard a conversation between two rough-dressed men walking alongside the cart. From the sounds, they lived here in Bury and were attending the witch trials much as they would a sporting event. They spoke about a minister, a Reverend Lowes, who was on trial today for witchcraft. Pippa's heart sank. No one was immune.

"Now there's a wretch," said one of the men, nudging his friend and pointing at Pippa. She felt like a freak in a side show.

"She's an old hag, really," said the other, snorting. "Witches make they-selves look poorly, so you take pity on them . . . then they git you!" He punched his friend and they veered off toward a pub.

The cart waited in traffic for what seemed like hours before it lurched forward and then stopped behind the courthouse. Pippa saw little of the building, for she was shackled and prodded forward, and had to keep her eyes on her feet to keep from stumbling. She saw a clean-swept floor and then she was sitting on a bench between Sybil and Joan Buckett, in a low-beamed room full of other chained individuals. They heard from another prisoner that Ash Potter had died during his incarceration.

Pippa was ashamed to feel relief. The truth about Joan Buckett's stolen money would never be revealed in court, and Pippa would hang as a witch and not a petty thief.

Along the sides of the room, clerks ran with stacks of paper, looking twice as hassled as the gaol-keeper ever had. There was little talk amongst the prisoners, for what more could be said? This was happening to Pippa and she was no agent in her own fate. Was this what was meant by surrender to God? She closed her eyes and felt the first pins and needles of panic in her fingers. She might die tomorrow. This was the end, this dusty, smelly, crowded, foreign room. The apathy that had protected her in gaol ebbed away in the face of this excitement.

"My nerves cannot take this," she whispered to Sybil.

"I know," said Sybil. "Just . . . surrender, I suppose. Fret not over what we cannot change."

"We could pray."

Sybil began, "Oh Heavenly Father, be with us now and at the hour of our deaths . . ."

"Not aloud! And not that." Pippa was beginning to have sore feelings toward the God of church. "Something . . . older . . . I know not . . . something about us, not about Heaven. We're far from that right now."

"Not so far as you believe," said Sybil, smiling. "All right. I'll think on it." She closed her eyes and her lips moved. "Earth and air, fire and water . . . fathers, sons, mothers, daughters . . ."

Pippa repeated Sybil's phrase over and over in her head, taking whatever comfort it might give. *Earth and air, fire and water. Fathers, sons, mothers, daughters.* Everything there was, and everything there had ever been.

A bucket of water and a ladle was passed around and she drank. It tasted gritty, like prison water. Pippa's thoughts were an endless circle of worry and fear. What would happen in the courtroom? What would they decide? She knew it was false hope, a chance like the eye of a needle, but she couldn't help but pray she might be the exception . . . that the jury would listen to her, would see her innocence.

Looking down at her grubby hands, she didn't feel innocent. There was nothing respectable about her appearance. She was no better than Anne and Joan Buckett—pitiful, desperate. Willing to do and say anything to save her own skin.

The knot in her stomach turned and twisted. Tears gathered and she pushed them back, telling herself to hold on for the sake of her friend. She had to be strong for Sybil. Even so, a few tears managed to escape her control, hot tracks down her dirty face, and Pippa felt ashamed of herself for being so scared.

The accused were taken in groups of five and not seen again. They disappeared through a wooden door in the corner of the room and up some stairs. From the outside, Pippa could hear a milling crowd, an occasional bout of shouting or clapping, and the echoing strains of song-sellers and the honking voices of food vendors.

Another roar from above. The mob was its own beast, many minds acting as one, like a swarm of bees.

The godly, thought Pippa.

"Philippa Wylde."

That was her name. There was a clerk standing nearby. A thrill of terror ran down her spine. *Oh Jesus, save me, save me, save me . . .* Victim, accused . . . was there a difference? She stood up. She turned to Sybil, whose name had also been called, and found her friend's face calm but body shaking.

They ascended the stair beyond the door and entered the large courtroom. Pigeons flew about the rafters above, a menace to the sea of heads below. Pippa rummaged through the multitude of faces, looking for someone friendly, someone she knew, but they blurred together. She almost caught on a man with dark eyes and a beard in the front row . . . but couldn't bear to look at *him.* The murderer who used law as his weapon.

She was led into the dock with the other four accused. A wooden half-wall divided them from the rest of the courtroom, and at the head of the room was a long table covered with a cloth. There sat the grand jury, all serious-looking men dressed as officials. There was also a chair on a wooden stand—for witnesses, she assumed—and a great many clerks writing things down.

A man wearing bright purple robes spoke, projecting his rich voice across the room. "The following are charged with the heinous crime of witchcraft. Katherine Tooly, of Westleton;

Anne Buckett, of the Vale; Joan Buckett, of the same; Sybil Yates, of the same, and Philippa Wylde, of the same." He cleared his throat and addressed the row of jurors. "Let it be known these are charges most serious. Take each case on its merits, and by evidence alone. A charge is not guilt. Wretched they may be, but not damned, unless by proof they are discovered to be guilty."

This speech made Pippa feel a bit better, but from his manner the man in purple said this as a matter of routine before each arraignment.

First on the dock was Katherine Tooly. Asked how she pled, she answered "Not guilty."

"Witnesses come forward for Katherine Tooly, accused of bewitching a neighbor's cow and for the selling of poisoned milk."

A clerk called out a name and a man in farmer's clothes stepped up to the empty chair. He told the court of how Katherine—a middle-aged woman with a sad face—had done him wrong over the years through magical workings. With each point, the public cheered, booed, or shouted. They had their own measures of justice. One of the jurors asked, "Be there a confession on her part?"

"Yes," said the man in purple, flipping through a stack of papers and handing over a scrap upon which Katherine had been forced to confess.

It was shocking how little time Katherine Tooly's case was allowed. Anne Buckett was next.

Pippa sat up straight in her chair, for it was Robert Pye who took the stand against Anne. It made Pippa want to cry to see someone from home. Pye told the story of how Anne had bewitched his son Francis.

Knowing as she did that the curse on the Pye family was not Anne's doing, Pippa's heart was heavy. *Oh, Lillibet. If only I'd followed your direction.*

She noticed that her name was omitted from Pye's testimony. He said nothing of how she'd helped "break" the spell.

Then again, that was cunning-magic, and might condemn her as well as help her. The court could even reprimand Pye and his wife for turning to that instead of prayer.

"The court calls Master John Stearne."

When Stearne took the stand and told the court of Anne Buckett's confession and the result of her swimming ordeal, something black twisted inside of Pippa. Stearne's reedy voice told thin lies.

Still, Anne's verdict was plain from the look on the jurors' faces.

Next was Anne's mother Joan, against whom Stearne also testified. Joan looked the part of the witch with the magnificent wart on her nose, her greying puff of hair, and her rough voice. Again Pippa prayed her thanks that Joan didn't know who had stolen from her. Instead the old woman seemed to be quite mad, and she was unrepentant. When the man in purple asked how she pled, she said "Guilty," with clear relish.

The crowd drew back in their seats, hushed and enthralled.

As with Anne, the jurors were convinced of Joan's guilt, and the man in purple waved his hand at the clerk to get on with it.

"Sybil Yates, please stand. How do you plead?"

Sybil, clear and angelic, said, "Not guilty."

MATTHEW HOPKINS SUPPRESSED A YAWN and fanned himself with his hat. *Lord, but this chamber is hot,* he thought. Although it was gratifying to speak his piece in court, it was uncomfortable. Sweat coursed down between his shoulder blades and gathered in the pits of his folded knees. Summer was his favorite season because it offered the longest hours of daylight, but he didn't appreciate the lack of proper ventilation in the court at Bury St. Edmunds. Mosquitoes and flies buzzed in the air, and the circulation from outside was hampered by the narrowness of the windows. The room smelled of cloth dampened by sweat, of the dusty odor of a city in summer, of yeasty ale-breath. Hopkins wiped his forehead with his handkerchief.

At present, John Stearne was testifying against the witches from the Vale, that back country hamlet. The older woman with the rat's nest of hair had actually pled guilty. *I knew I was right about her,* he thought. *About all of them. Especially—*

But he cut himself off there. He had to stay alert and focused.

This trial was different from his first at Chelmsford. The Bury magistrates and the sergeant, Godbold—dressed in the official purple robes—had been less than enthusiastic about the number of witchcraft cases flooding their chamber. It meant the assizes would go on for days in order to get through the hundreds of accused witches. *Perhaps we did our job too well for them,* thought Hopkins disagreeably. *Would they let such evil go unpunished?*

Godbold in particular had been skeptical of the ordeals used by Hopkins and Stearne, hinting to the grand jury that they were too harsh and yielded questionable results. Hopkins was gratified that old Joan Buckett had stated her guilt in addition to Stearne's testimony. It made him look more believable.

With a frown Hopkins regarded the jury. They were not as zealous or dedicated as he would have hoped. The costs of incarcerating over one hundred and fifty accused witches was outweighing the rightful fear of their craft. Already one of the magistrates had complained to him that many of the smaller villages could not afford the prison debt. Hopkins had replied, affronted, that it was not his fault that a plague of witchcraft was upon the land.

The magistrate had also hinted, and not very subtly, that Hopkins himself was out for profit, mentioning that at twenty shillings per interrogation, and hundreds accused . . . Hopkins coughed into his fist and shifted in his chair, trying to calm his anger. It not *his* fault that God's work paid well.

The magistrate didn't know the things he knew.

Sybil Yates was up and so was Hopkins, testifying against her. He nodded at the other witnesses ready to speak against the changeling girl.

At first Hopkins did not recognize Sybil, for her eyes were large and sad inside her head. The gaol had not gone easy on her and she seemed to have shrunk in size and age. She could have passed for a child. Harmless, innocent . . . *Have no sympathy, suffer her not*! he warned the jury in his head.

Her pure voice said, "Not guilty."

But Hopkins had her confession, the one she'd signed herself. He smiled and stood and took the stand. He'd been sworn-in many trials ago to tell the truth as he knew it. "I have proof in the form of a confession signed by Miss Yates." He handed it over to Godbold, and a clerk entered it as evidence. Hopkins told of how Sybil had boasted of reciting the Lord's Prayer backwards, how the search-women had found an unnatural mole near the girl's privy parts, and most shockingly, of the raven imp which had come into the room during the watching.

"The raven, black as the night, came straight to her," Hopkins addressed the crowd as much as the jury. "Then . . . it was quite terrible, from what I was told . . . the bird opened its mouth and *spoke*."

Gasps blossomed across the room.

"What did the bird *say*?" asked a magistrate, who was also a minister.

"It said—in the girl's very own voice, like an echo—her name. Sybil. 'Twas the surest case of an imp I've seen in my considerable experience."

A muttering of dread rumbled through the crowd. The slight figure of Sybil, who was eerily calm, had taken on the quality of a witch at last. Hopkins avoided looking to the left of her, where Philippa Wylde sat. He could feel her eyes on him.

"Thank you, Master Hopkins. The next witness is the Reverend Peter Yates." The clerk paused and whispered to someone. "He is the girl's father."

Hopkins sat down in the front row and watched Reverend Yates ascend. From the way he licked his lips, he was nervous. Hopkins hoped he wouldn't back out now.

Sworn in, Yates sat down and began to speak. "The girl was born eighteen years ago. My wife died during the birth after refusing the midwifery of the town's cunning-woman, Lillibet Wylde. Elizabeth."

Godbold asked, "Elizabeth Wylde?"

A clerk shouted out, "Dead!"

"Go on, Reverend Yates," Godbold said.

"I believe the midwife, who was also a witch and accused by this court—is she dead?"

"Dead!" shouted the clerk.

"Yes. So. The midwife bewitched my wife and caused her death. The child, Sybil, was never normal."

"Are you saying that your child herself is bewitched, sir? If so, that be victimhood, and not for her to be tried for witchcraft," said another jurist.

"No! What I say is—I'm loathe to speak of it, even after all these years—I say that girl," he pointed at Sybil, "is not my own daughter. She is a changeling, a creature of Satan, planted in my own home!"

The crowd was justly horrified.

Sybil's eyes blinked, wide and beguiling. Her lip quivered. "Papa?"

Yates lowered his pointing finger and turned his face away. "You see, your honors, she came to us with . . . with a caul over her face. A veil, an unholy sight it was."

The drama reverberated through all those present. Hopkins

shuddered at the thought of a child born with no face. That was the surest witchcraft of all. As he looked at Sybil, he imagined her veiled, approaching him, and was glad he'd already given his testimony.

"She is not my own child by my wife. She is a creature of the Devil." Yates stood down, staring at the hat that he turned in his hands, over and over.

"Next witness, Elizabeth Yates!"

The prim figure of the Reverend's eldest stood and climbed up to the witness chair. Her hair was coiffed and her clothing spotless. She looked every bit the godly woman and Hopkins wondered why he couldn't feel attracted to someone like that, someone who would make a fine wife.

"I have witnessed terrible things of Sybil," Elizabeth told the court. "All her life she has been strange. But it was this very summer when she revealed her evil pact to me. She fell ill with what she claimed was the marsh fever. But I walked in upon her one night and she was conversing with a spirit, some terrible presence. I could see nothing, but her eyes were aglow with the talk."

The courtroom was hushed, on edge to hear what came next.

"She then told me a nonsense rhyme. After, I suspected trickery, and we moved her bed . . ." Elizabeth paused and held a hand to her mouth. "There were Satanic symbols written beneath her bed, on the floor, where she thought none could find them."

"Dear God," said a magistrate.

"What was more, Sybil confessed herself to be part of a coven. The leader was her." Elizabeth raised her finger to point at Pippa. The eyes of the crowd followed the line of her finger and registered Pippa with her dark hair, haunted eyes, and cheekbones chiseled by hunger. "They wrote the evil symbols on the floor."

"What did the symbols look like?"

Elizabeth paused, as though thinking. Hopkins was proud of her performance. He and Stearne had coached her on how best to convince the jury. "Pagan. One was a spiral. The other was the Devil's star. And then there was a magic square made of words. It must have taken great knowledge of the black arts to remember nonsensical letters like that."

"Proof, you are saying, of Satan's direct influence?"

"Yes, your honor," said Elizabeth. "Sybil is not normal, not human. She knows too much—as though she can read a mind. One dreadful night, she claimed to speak to the ghost of my dear departed mother. From the start was she corrupted, and she has showed us power not given by God!"

"Thank you, Miss Yates."

Elizabeth stood down, looking pleased with herself.

"Are there any other witnesses to offer proof?" called Godbold.

"Yes, sir, one," said Hopkins. He nodded at the girl who stared at him with the eyes of a terrified doe in the forest. "*Go,*" he mouthed at her.

Alice Baxter stood and approached the witness stand.

The Pigeon in the Rafters

Pippa felt the blood drain from her face. *No.* She was unable to believe who was standing against them. Alice was like a stranger and refused to look in the direction of her or Sybil. Her hands shook and clutched onto a tattered handkerchief, the epitome of a country girl—unfashionable, terrified, and humble in her brown wool. *But she's me sister.* Then a wild hope took hold of Pippa—perhaps Alice would tell them there were no witches in the Vale!

Sybil reached over for Pippa's hand.

"Let the court be aware, the girl has a speech impediment," said Matthew Hopkins, speaking to the man in purple. "Patience is needed, but her testimony is both sound and full."

"Very well," said the man in purple, who sounded anything but patient.

Alice began to speak. "I h-have s-s-sinned," she said. "Th-th-there be w-witches in the Vale, and I w-w-was . . . I was . . . part of them."

"You must be more specific," said a magistrate. "You will not be prosecuted, but only if you tell the truth, Alice Baxter.

Tell us everything that you said and did, and who the witches are."

Alice nodded and stared at the wooden floor in front of her. "W-We went into the w-w-woods. There the D-D-Devil himself took m-me stutter away. I c-could speak as all you here t-today. 'Twas s-s-sometimes at night, s-sometimes in the day, and w-w-we lit fires. D-Danced about them, ch-ch-chanting old things."

At first the court had been disorderly, having not the patience to decipher Alice's stuttering. But they had grown silent, aware of this precious peek into the lives of witches. Pippa could not believe her ears. Alice had never done evil magic! None of them had. *Tell them, please, Alice. He has poisoned your mind.* She dared a look at Hopkins, who was intent on his witness as though willing her to say damning things.

"The w-w-witches were as accused," said Alice. "Lillibet Wylde. She w-was the elder wh-wh-wh-who brought us in. Pippa Wylde. W-Winnie Radcliff. And S-S-Sybil Yates." A lone tear dropped from Alice's left eye.

"Radcliff?" asked the man in purple, rummaging through a stack of papers.

"Winifred Radcliff. Dropped charges, not enough physical evidence," called a clerk.

"Fine," said a magistrate, "it seems this is the nest of them." He gestured at the young women in the dock.

It was as though the floor had fallen out from beneath Pippa's feet. There would be no recovering from this treachery. Everything she'd ever told her friends to keep quiet . . . there was quiet Alice, airing it against her. This was the end. There was no point trying to rise in a world so determined to snuff her out. If the witch-finders had turned Alice's kind heart, then no one was safe.

Alice's painfully slow speech told the court further things— about how the girls, mainly Pippa and Sybil, had cast spells, and called out incantations, and kept imps, and observed the old sabbats, and worshipped Satan in the forest. That she, Alice, had been dragged into it as an unwilling participant and how she'd never cast a spell herself. *False witness,* thought Pippa, recollecting Alice's full participation in their games, and the time she'd crafted herself a charm to sweeten cow's milk.

"I be very s-s-s-sorry," Alice said. "I knew n-not wh-wh-what I did. Every day I pray to God th-that He forgives me."

"You have done your duty here today," said a magistrate gently. "Is there anything else you can tell us about these witches?"

Alice held her handkerchief over her mouth. Not once had she raised her eyes to Pippa. "I-I've told you all I w-witnessed."

"You may return to your seat."

Alice was led by a clerk away from the stand.

"If there be no more witnesses against Sybil Yates, the court will move to the case of Philippa Wylde," said the man in purple. "Since they are related in deed and Satanic pact, the court will consider all testimony as thus related. Finally, does Sybil Yates have anything to say for herself?" He swiveled toward the dock.

Sybil, still holding Pippa's hand, managed to stand up. "I have only to say that I am no witch, and have no pact with Satan. My confession was forced from me, and I say now it was false. I have committed no crime that God Himself would condemn."

"Do not presume to speak for God!" a magistrate thundered at her.

Sybil's lips quivered and she sat down.

"She holds to her original plea," said the purple-robed sergeant with a sigh. "Next! Philippa Wylde. Stand up."

Pippa stood. Her knees wobbled.

"How do you plead?"

For one lunatic moment Pippa considered screaming her

guilt, cursing the chamber, going unrepentant to a death already carved in stone. Lillibet had warned her that the world might consider them witches. If knowledge was evil, then she was evil, and let the rest of them be damned. Her eyes scanned the crowd. Their faces were leering, hostile . . . But she felt a squeeze of pressure from Sybil's hand and held true. "Not guilty," she said, and sat.

"Very well," again sighed the man in purple. "You have already been found out by Alice Baxter, and accused by association by Elizabeth Yates. Let the next witness come forward."

Pippa sneered at Goodman Charles Ford, wife of Mary, father of wayward Sarah. He sat down, holding his hat in his hands, and was sworn to tell the truth.

"She cursed me daughter," said Ford, pointing at Pippa. "I have proof of her witchery. She and her mother be conspirators. Me daughter went to them for a headache, for Lillibet Wylde was known for her remedies as a midwife. But instead, they cursed me Sarah, and gave her a poisoned tea."

"What happened when your daughter drank this tea?"

Ford glared at Pippa. "Sarah could not move for many days. She fell into fits, vomiting, and became so weak she could not work. Also, me wife tells me that she . . . bled, as a female bleeds . . . for two weeks."

The court gasped as one.

Pippa was helpless to say what had really happened. If she told the truth about Sarah Ford, and told ignorant Charles how his own daughter had fallen with child and then asked for a miscarriage, Pippa herself—and possibly Sarah—could be charged with murder. *That* sort of knowledge of life's secrets would be the highest proof of witchcraft. Boxed in to silence, Pippa slumped in her chair.

"Do you deny that you gave Sarah Ford a poisoned tea?" she was asked.

"No, I do not deny it," she whispered.

Charles Ford took a seat. Pippa did not look up at who was next. She was already damned. She didn't care who else wanted to perjure themselves on her account.

"The court calls Matthew Hopkins, the Witch-finder General."

Her head snapped up.

"Thank you, your honors," said Hopkins. His voice was practiced as brushed velvet. "It was under my observation that the witch Philippa Wylde was watched, and my search-women pricked her. She has been a difficult case, for the Devil has given her unusual strength, and she refused to admit her guilt up until the last." Hopkins turned to look at Pippa. His black eyes locked on hers.

Like a flint on stone, a spark flared in Pippa's core. Her back straightened and her head was level. She stared straight back at Hopkins. Hatred for him was a living creature inside her, flooding her with new life.

Hopkins looked away first. He said, a slight waver in his voice, "She never confessed, but the ordeals showed guilt nonetheless. A most dramatic incident occurred when she was swum in the common pond."

"Hopkins, I'm warning you," said one of the magistrates. "This swimming business is too harsh. Witches should be brought to confess out of spiritual fear, not mortal fear."

"I agree!" said Hopkins. "But in this case, the swimming ordeal was a true test of a woman who defied all goodness. Any of the witnesses would tell you."

"Noted. Go on."

"There was nothing to make her sink or swim," said Hopkins, "only her own conscience. At first, she pulled a trick. She had weighted herself down to sink. And down she went, into the pond." He paused, allowing the jury to imagine the scene for themselves. "And then, with a supernatural force, as though God Himself were pushing her out, she was launched full out of the water! Into the air she did fly, for the pure waters of baptism had rejected her."

A shocked murmur rippled through the jury and the watching crowd alike.

"I never seen the likes of that!"

"Proof was had," added the distinctive whine of John Stearne. "I saw it with my very eyes!"

"That is compelling evidence," said a magistrate.

Hopkins bowed. "There is also the matter of her birth. I have on good authority that Philippa Wylde, like Sybil Yates, was born unnatural. The mother, Elizabeth Wylde, was in her old age when she conceived and carried Philippa. A woman who yearned for a child, and had been denied by God, did turn to Satan to grant her wish. And so she lay with the Devil and he did give her this spawn, and to this she admitted. She signed a confession, and described in detail the names of their imps 'Eli Pilly' and 'Yewberry,' and was found to have the Devil's teats . . . it creates a clear picture of the evil pact in this family."

"He lies!" Pippa called out. She glanced at the magistrate who'd reprimanded Hopkins for the swimming ordeal. "It is as you say, your honor. He tortures and brings forth false confessions. And *I* never confessed, for *I* am not guilty!"

This created a storm of shouting and jeering from the chamber. Many people grinned, enjoying the spectacle of debate.

Hopkins took a threatening step toward her. "You cannot hide behind words," he hissed. "There are a hundred witnesses to see you cast forth from the pond." He turned to the jury. "She disrespects this very court!"

"Enough," said the sergeant. "A clerk informs me there is a witness who wishes to speak."

To Pippa's utter surprise, the farmer Robert Pye stepped up again. He'd spoken out once against Anne Buckett. Would he tell the jury how Pippa had used magic to try to undo the curse? White magic was black magic in the eyes of this court.

Pye was quiet and had to speak louder to be heard over the excited crowd. "Anne Buckett cursed me boy, Francis." This reminded everyone who he was; in the stream of witnesses and accusations, it was easy to grow confused. "But it was Pippa Wylde and her mother Lillibet who helped Francis recover. Lillibet made health tonics for the boy, and she attended the birth of me own daughter, a healthy girl," he smiled, "and Pippa, too, was being trained in the healing use of plants."

The man in purple narrowed his eyes. "But you say she used magic to cure magic?"

Pye paused. Pippa stared at him in a silent plea to make something up. He said, "No . . . she gave him a concoction of herbs to soothe his mind. It was simple, really, no magic. Just tender care from God's own creation. That be all I have to say." Pye stood down without being asked to leave.

"One character witness does not erase the overwhelming evidence!" said Hopkins, spitting.

"There is one more character witness," said a familiar voice that made Pippa's heart stop.

An impossible voice.

Hugh Felton stood on the edge of the crowd, holding his hat in hand. He wore his finest coat and breeches and boots befitting a baronet's son. His gold-brown hair shone, and his clear blue eyes were like the freedom of a summer's day. Pippa blinked. He *was* there, she didn't imagine him.

"Who are you?" Hopkins sneered.

"I would like to speak as a witness. My name is already recorded by the clerk," said Hugh. He walked forward and glanced at Pippa. It was a splinter of a second, but it was full of promise. Something lifted in her chest. She supposed it was hope. Yet, she was ashamed for her bedraggled appearance in front of Hugh. She couldn't bear to think this would be his last impression of her—dull, dirty, starving. *I'm not bright for you anymore,* she thought, and almost cried. Her pulse hammered as she waited for what Hugh would say about her. Would he tell the court that she, a wicked child, had cast spells on him to make him love her?

She felt the comforting squeeze of Sybil's hand on hers.

Hugh was sworn-in by the clerk and took a seat. "I come to testify that Philippa Wylde is no witch, but a trained healer and midwife. I expect she will receive her license, if her mother has indeed died. There is no doctor or apothecary in the Vale," he addressed the jury, "for we are too small a place for that. Furthermore, I testify as to her character, and the character of her late parents. Miss Wylde's father, John Wylde, was a close friend of my father Sir John Felton, and an honorable yeoman. He married a midwife, not a witch. It is likewise impossible that his daughter Philippa is one."

"What is your relationship to her?" Hopkins asked.

"Master Hopkins," said a magistrate, "you are not asking the questions, we are." He turned to Hugh. "Sir?"

Pippa couldn't breathe.

"She is my betrothed," said Hugh. His eyes were steady on Pippa, holding her up, erasing her fears with those four simple words.

Her mind fell back to their first and last kiss, when he'd said he wanted her. Was that what he'd meant? Had Hugh considered them betrothed this entire time? *Daft*, thought Pippa, *insufferable, silent, presumptuous man*!

Hugh's back was straight as a sword as he continued. "I am a pious man, son of Sir John Felton who is both a baronet . . . and a generous patron to our parish and to the parish here in Bury." Hugh's mouth quirked and he glanced at the magistrate who was dressed in the cloth of a minister.

"Noted," said the sergeant.

"She is no witch," Hugh repeated, and stood down.

"I have more to say!" said Hopkins.

"We have no more time," said the sergeant. "We must

deliberate now, there are scores more of *your* accused to get through, Hopkins."

There was a murmur of assent from the jury and the crowd. They had grown impatient and were salivating for the next group. Pippa felt something tug at her chains—"Stand up, move!" she was told—and they were led out of the room and into a small antechamber off to the side. It was bare of all furniture and had white-washed walls. Two soldiers with mean-looking guns stood at attention on either side of the door.

When the wooden door slammed shut, they could not hear what was happening in the big chamber, and all five women huddled over. Pippa was shaking. Now that Hugh had spoken for her, she could love him without reserve. Even if she died, she would take his love with her . . . but she *wanted* to live, wanted it with every sinew and fiber in her body, wanted to cling on with her crumbling fingernails and never let go. It made her dizzy with fear to think she might lose that life.

"I don't know why they bother to talk about it," grumbled Joan Buckett. "We're to the gallows."

Katherine Tooly sobbed into her skirt.

Their waiting time stretched into an eternity. Life was paused here, in this antechamber, this limbo. Pippa's mind seesawed between hope and despair, between confidence and crisis. All-powerful Matthew Hopkins had ripped her life away from her, so it was probable the court would listen to him.

"Everything's all right," Sybil whispered, a film of tears clouding her pale eyes. "We will shed these chains somehow."

She was right. Hanging would be preferable to the gaol. Pippa tried not to think of the gallows that had been constructed for them—high, sturdy, made of oak. She tried not to think of what it would be like to die blindfolded.

They waited.

On the other side of the door, the grand jury discussed among themselves the testimony they'd heard. Pippa wondered about those who held her life in their hands. Men, powerful, educated, religious. She was none of those things.

They would convict her.

So what if they do? A small voice was in her head. It sounded a great deal like Lillibet. *You know death is not the end.*

"But it is!" she said in a whisper that did not escape her throat.

You will be all right. This will pass, as all things do.

Pippa couldn't shake the feeling that she was in the throes of a terrible dream. It had to end sometime. She looked at Sybil and felt admiration for her friend's calm. Sybil's eyes were closed and her mouth was a sweet arc that showed no sign of pain. Always in her own Heavenly world, Sybil was.

A fist pounded on the door and Pippa's stomach lurched.

The door to the courtroom opened and they were led back into the fray. The jury was a line of solemn faces, expressionless, pitiless. The public audience was hushed and eager to hear the verdicts. The man in purple robes filled the room with his official stance and by the paper in his hands. On that paper was written their fate.

He spoke. "The jury has deliberated and the verdicts are returned."

Lightning crackled through Pippa's veins. Her nerves were in shreds. It was difficult to breathe.

"Katherine Tooly: guilty."

The audience crowed with delight.

"Anne Buckett: guilty."

A louder cheer.

"Joan Buckett: guilty."

This was no surprise. Joan spat on the floor and shook her fierce head of hair.

Pippa was so tense that she could not move to see the faces down the row.

"Sybil Yates: guilty."

A tremor shook the courtroom. The blood daughter of a Puritan minister . . . but it was nothing to the tremor in Pippa's heart. Sybil did not move in the seat next to her, but stared up at one of the pigeons misplaced in the rafters. Her eyes moved this way and that. Everything seemed black, except for the light in Sybil's eyes.

Then, it was her turn. "Philippa Wylde: not guilty."

She was startled back to attention. Did her ears deceive her? But no, the crowd was shocked as well, and whispered and commented and stared at her. She found Hugh's face several rows in. He looked too relieved to even manage a smile, but his lips were moving in a prayer.

I'm free, she thought, not quite believing it.

"I protest!" shouted a voice.

Pippa saw Matthew Hopkins, red in the face and standing up to wave a fist.

"This is a mistake! She is the guiltiest of them all! I've seen her! I *know* her! She is Satan's own creature!" He began to cough violently.

"Master Hopkins!" the sergeant said. "Sit down! This is the jury's decision."

"But I have proof! Test her again, watch her again, there can be no doubt . . ."

"Hopkins," said the gravelly voice of one of the magistrates, "if you do not *sit down*, you will be held in contempt!"

Hopkins's mouth twitched with rage, his fingers drummed along the rim of his hat, but he eased back down into his chair.

The purple sergeant cleared his throat. "The sentences are thus: the guilty are to be hanged from the neck until dead. The innocent—Miss Wylde—you are free to go."

Someone was fumbling at Pippa's hands with a key. The shackles fell off and she felt bereft. "Sybil," she murmured, "Sybil!"

"Pippa!"

All around them was chaos. Soldiers were at the doors, the convicted were being dragged away, and Sybil was three steps away, and then four. The clerk was shouting down the stairs for the next group to be brought up. The public audience was standing, shouting, coming and going. Pippa didn't know what to do. And Sybil was being taken away from her.

"Sybil!" she shouted, and plunged past a heavy-bodied soldier. She gripped Sybil's arms. "I-I don't know what to do. I'm so sorry."

"Don't leave me," Sybil said, looking just as bewildered. "Please. Don't leave me, Pippa."

"I won't! I'll speak to someone, I—"

Someone had Pippa by the elbows from behind. "Stand aside, miss! No civilians allowed down there."

The prisoners were being pulled through a door by their chained hands. Sybil turned and looked over her shoulder. A wisp of fair hair seemed to float on an invisible wind. Her shining eyes were full of fear, and sadness, and love.

"Oh, Sybil," Pippa choked, watching until Sybil was gone. Turning once in a circle, she was surrounded by people and all alone. The faces of strangers swam in front of her face. *What do I do? Where am I? Sybil!* She was paralyzed.

"This way. Philippa Wylde, this way!" It was a clerk, a small and nervous man, and he wanted her to sign a piece of paper.

"What is it?" she asked with suspicion. She thought it was a trick by Hopkins to get her to confess to something. She skimmed the words and realized it was some sort of release.

"Your freedom," said the clerk. "States that you was found not guilty and released."

"Oh," said Pippa, taking the feather pen with a shaking hand and signing. It was hardly legible. From the tip of the feather, a fat drop of ink fell next to her name, spreading outward in a dark circle, grazing her signature. A blot on her name.

She was shuffled off to the side, down some stairs, and out

the doors in a stream of people. Some looked at her with disdain, for she was filthy, in rags, with unkempt hair and the desperate air of a beggar. How would she get home? Where *was* home? The Vale was not what it used to be, not to be trusted.

"Pippa! *Pippa*!" Hugh was in front of her, holding her hands. "Oh, Pippa, you're here, you're safe." He peered down at her.

She could not quite pin him down. He was a wavering figure, one she'd dreamed in the gaol but never imagined she'd see again.

"Are you well?" he asked.

There was no answer to such a question.

"Philippa, dear. Come with me." That was Hugh's mother. What was her name? *Constance.* Constance Felton. The last time Pippa had seen her, Lady Felton had complimented her on her spirited reading. Indeed.

"You must be exhausted. Come along, dear, come." A motherly hand guided her shoulders out of the crowds and along a side street. "We'll be driving home now, the light is long in the day and my husband's horses are swift."

Pippa wanted to say, *I can't leave Sybil,* but she found that her voice did not work the way it should. She did not even register the houses rolling past her vision as they walked, the shops, the large and impressive structures of an ancient town. Hugh was steadfast by her side, and she soaked up the strength of his nearness like a snake basking on a warm rock.

"Here, the carriage." Lady Felton was a woman with the easy manners of the gentry. She did not seem to mind, or even notice, Pippa's state of degradation. She handed over a cup of ale. "Drink this."

The bitter, fuzzy taste of it was almost foreign. It revived her from her confusion, though. "Thank you," she said.

"Hugh, help her up."

Hugh took her hand, and with the other hand on her waist,

lifted her up into the carriage. It was a small open vehicle with fine wheels and a cushioned seat. Lady Felton climbed up next to her. They had a driver, a man from the Vale that Pippa recognized.

There was also a second cart behind them. Pippa turned to look at it and wonder what was bundled in the back.

"I signed for your mother's body," said Hugh gently. "We'll take her home."

Pippa blinked. "I thought she was in—in a—left in the mass grave."

"She was," said Lady Felton, "but we had her brought out and prepared for a home burial."

It would have cost them, Pippa knew, and not just money but the taint of dealing with the gaol, the record of signing for a prisoner's body. She could not begin to thank them.

"'Tis all right," said Lady Felton as if knowing Pippa's thoughts. "Here, have a bit to eat." She handed Pippa a stack of biscuits wrapped in cloth.

Hugh climbed up next to the driver and the cart started forward. The wheels turned, bearing Pippa through Bury St. Edmunds, away from the assizes and the gaol and away from Sybil.

She bit down on a biscuit. It had sugar in it. It crumbled in her mouth.

A fly hovered around her face for a few minutes and then moved along.

She was shaking, so Lady Felton placed a steadying hand on her knee.

"He truly loves you, coming all the way up here to speak for you," Lady Felton said. She tilted her head ruefully. "I don't know you well, Miss Wylde, but you must be something special."

Pippa could not see Hugh's face, but from behind she saw that the tips of his ears were bright red.

Lady Felton continued, "I always said you were a good girl, your honorable father's daughter. Now we see that you are, and always were, innocent of all this."

Innocent. Pippa knew better. She was sullied, her faith shattered. The filth of the gaol clung to her. The word "witch" would follow her forever. Innocent was before the cruel invasion of a pricking bodkin, the prodding hands that defiled her in search of guilt. How could she ever be innocent again? But she offered a tiny smile to Lady Felton, hoping for silence.

Many miles later, Pippa turned around in her seat and looked across fields at the distant silhouette of the ruins of St. Edmund's Abbey. The gentle sounds of the countryside surrounded her, but her ears still echoed with the brutal voices of the court, the gaol-keepers, the guards, the witch-finders. She did not feel safe. Any moment they would race after her on horses. Hopkins would use that devilish grey dog of his to track her down.

I need to be in the cave, she thought. The thought was paramount—it swelled into a physical longing to be shut away inside the earth. Closing her eyes against her fear, she thought of the refuge in the forest that had once been Lillibet's, and that she had now inherited.

Closer, closer, with every turn of the wheels.

THE SUN WAS TOUCHING the edge of the western horizon when they rounded the bend, topped the hill, and descended into the Vale. Thin columns of smoke rose as the women inside their cottages prepared evening meals. Pippa's heart seized. She realized that home was not a place, it was a time. She wanted to return to the time before Matthew Hopkins had found her. The Vale was foreign to her now—or perhaps she was foreign to it.

"We'll take you home," said Hugh over his shoulder.

He didn't understand. He *couldn't.*

"Thank you," said Pippa.

Lady Felton looked at her with sympathy. "Hugh tried to keep an eye on the place for you—at least the inside. We couldn't do much about the pig and chickens."

"Stolen?"

"I'm sorry."

"There are worse things," she said vaguely. It was too bad about Eli the pig. He would have made fine bacon someday.

The crossroads, the roundabout, the inn . . . all were unchanged in form. The front of the white church looked menacing, the cross black and the church white, all contrast and no compassion. She didn't know how she could ever walk through those doors again. And she turned away from the pond, remembering the view from beneath the water, the shadow of the witch-finder playing over its surface as he waited for her to drown.

She was grateful that the crossroads was not busy this time of day. The only person about was Will Renshaw, sweeping the front stone of the inn, and he tipped his hat when she was let out of the cart at the beginning of the footpath. In her torn, dirty clothes, she felt naked as a babe—no personal effects, nothing to show for her time in prison except for the red welts around her wrists and an itchy case of head lice.

The path home was difficult in her weakened state. The incline was steep, but Hugh and Lady Felton aided her, and she was surprised to see a group of laborers standing in her yard with shovels.

"The Reverend won't allow Lillibet to be buried on the church grounds," said Hugh with a touch of anger in his voice. "I told him—"

"No, she would have preferred this," said Pippa. She turned and saw the slight shrouded form of her mother's body being carried up the path. "Under the yew tree."

The laborers began digging. Their work was hindered by

the stubborn roots of the yew, and Pippa murmured for them to be careful and not hurt the tree. They stopped when the hole was about four feet deep.

It was unconsecrated ground, and there was no service, and Pippa was glad for it. She didn't think she could stand to hear what passed as holy words these days.

Lillibet's wrapped form was smaller than Pippa remembered. She went to pull back the shroud but Hugh stopped her.

"You don't want to see her like that," he said. "The undertaker said she'd been exposed to the elements."

She's rotted away, thought Pippa, and wanted to cry. "How do you know it to be her?"

Hugh reached into a fold of the shroud cloth and pulled out a shining loop of braided hair. "She had this about her neck. I thought you would want it."

"Sybil," said Pippa, taking the braid with trembling fingers and thinking of her friend, who would spend this night imprisoned without hope.

Lillibet was laid in the grave and covered with soft scoops of earth. Pippa watched, while Hugh and his mother kept a respectful distance. The laborers finished, patting down the disturbed ground with the backs of their shovels, and filed away, murmuring their condolences.

Pippa put a hand to her face and discovered that her tears had dried. There was a shadow against the setting sun and she looked up to Hugh.

"I'll come round tomorrow," he said. "Winifred Radcliff will be glad to see you returned, as well." His brow furrowed. "Pippa—do you want me to fetch her? She said they'd have you at their house."

Touched as she was by Hugh's felicity, she wanted to lick her wounds alone. "No, tomorrow would be better." She tried to smile at him. She hated how her teeth were loose in her gums from malnourishment. "Hugh Felton, you're a good man."

"I'm sorry I didn't come sooner," he said. "I realized not how bad it would become. How bad it was. I never dreamt . . . I'm so sorry. This should never have gone so far."

"I wish I would have known your feelings. It would have given me comfort in the gaol."

Hugh winced. "Did you not know that I love you?"

"No!"

"You've always been mine, Pippa, since we were children. You must know that."

"You never told me. How could I know, when you walk around with other girls, never making me an offer?" This was not going the way Pippa wanted. She didn't have the energy for this fight. Marriage seemed like the least important thing in the world at this moment. All she wanted was to sleep, to be absorbed into the ground.

"I thought it was understood." Hugh took off his hat and rubbed his forehead in frustration. "Pippa, say you'll marry me. I'll take care of you. Your father would have wanted it—your mother, too. Please marry me."

Numbly, Pippa felt this was the cloak to cover the gaping holes in her life. Hugh had saved her from hanging. What else was left? She was too exhausted to think about what she wanted. She owed him an answer. She owed him a yes.

"Yes, Hugh. I will."

"Thank you," he said, grasping her hand, holding back the kiss she knew he wanted to give. His mother was watching. "God keep you. I'll return here tomorrow morning."

Pippa nodded, but couldn't muster a return. She hushed the inner voice that warned her there *was* more to life than this simple solution; that Lillibet's dying words had demanded courage, not compromise.

The sky was blood red behind the silhouette of her ruined cottage. It was shocking how bare the thatch had become, and how many weeds had sprouted in the garden, and how much dust and dirt had built up around the door. The windows were blank, empty, as Lillibet's eyes had been when she died. They stared accusingly at her.

I cannot be here tonight. She pushed open the door and in the gloom, saw that someone had stolen their store of grain and the barrel of ale. The herb cabinet was untouched; fear of witchery had kept the thieves away from that. The yard was quiet, for the animals were indeed gone.

Turning toward Lillibet's bed, her heart sank to see the locked chest had vanished. With it had gone the pencil drawings her father had made of her mother and his own self-portraits, Lillibet's amber and jet brooch, a Roman coin, and Lillibet's mother's fine-tooth comb made of bone and silver. At any other time this loss would have Pippa in a rage. Now, it was just one more thing.

She went to the wall and pulled away the loose stone. She half-expected their savings to be gone, but discovered that the money satchel was safe. Someone had scoured the fireplace, looking for the cottage hiding-place, but had been disappointed. She dragged the sack out and counted the shillings, pennies, and farthings that added up to just under one pound. The summer had been profitable after Sarah Ford, and with a coil of fresh guilt, Pippa remembered that she would never need to pay Joan Buckett now.

Pippa scratched her head furiously. She had to get out of her grimy dress. Climbing the ladder to her loft, she saw her blue petticoat and bodice intact. She dragged her fresh clothes down, then walked out to the brook and filled a bucket with water. Inside the cottage, heedless of the water that splashed around, she stripped off and scrubbed her skin and hair with the horsehair brush and a bar of lavender soap. The accumulated dirt was released layer after layer.

Frowning, Pippa would have to brew something complicated to kill the lice in her hair, so she would save that for later.

Tomorrow she would go to the Radcliffs', for she and Winifred needed to discuss their business in Bury St. Edmunds. Sybil was still there. They had to save her before the unthinkable happened.

The Feltons had given her part of their picnic, a half-loaf of bread and some goat's cheese, and she placed it in a satchel with the household savings and the braid of Sybil's hair. She hoped that the forest would welcome her, and that she would find her way.

The door was left open behind her and she walked fast through the fields, into the trees that swallowed her up, down the pathways that she knew and loved. The air was warm and clean. Every breath was a relief and as the trees swayed around her, the edge of panic that had stalked her for so many weeks began to ebb away. She pretended that Lillibet was one step ahead of her, leading the way to the cave as she had done before. Pippa followed.

Her hands felt the smooth bark of the rowan tree. The grooves of the symbol were a greeting beneath her fingers. "One, two, three, four . . ." she counted the paces into the thicket.

Pausing, hearing nothing but the forest, she scrabbled at the rock and it rolled aside. *In,* she thought, *safe, home.* The vines and ferns and leaves brushed at her face as she crawled into the hole. The match on the ledge was struck and a candle's flame flared. Pippa yanked the holding-stone out of the groove and the boulder slid closed.

When she emerged through the tunnel and into the main cave, she found herself in the sanctuary where her imagination had gone during the worst times in the gaol. The water trickled pure and clear. The ruby in the pool was a glinting drop of heart's blood. The herbs were in order, the books lined in a row, the fire pit charred with the remains of centuries past. Then, something different.

There was Lillibet's chest, unlocked, resting on the floor. Pippa opened it and saw its contents in order. Her fingers touched the heirloom comb. *Lillibet must have brought it here when the witch-finders came,* she thought. *She knew what would happen.*

Pippa gathered the items from the chest in a small pile and placed Sybil's braid on top. She laid down next to her history, the remaining tokens of her previous life, and blew out the candle. All was silent except for the soft plinking of her tears that hit the cave floor.

14

The Last Dance

The assizes were a time of gratification for Hopkins, strong in his renewed purpose. The first day had been spoiled by the acquittal of Philippa Wylde, but Hopkins tried not to think of *that creature*, to maintain a larger perspective. He could find a way to take care of her someday. The convictions were rolling in. This was his work. The size of these trials was all due to him. He'd suffered no further hiccups in his resolve. The witches were being named, the witches were being hanged.

One by one, he was purging his soul of evil's claim.

Today the Reverend John Lowes, a notorious witch, had been convicted. Hopkins had given the damning testimony. Every day he was more feared, more respected. He'd spoken to an old friend high in Cromwell's intelligence service who had hinted that when the liberator Cromwell won the war, Matthew Hopkins—once a clerk, once a humble fingerman for Parliament—might be awarded a higher post. If witches were an infestation here in Puritan East Anglia, he could but imagine the corruption in the rest of the country.

Witch-finder General, by appointment of Parliament. None

could doubt his piety or competence again. He would have the power of the State behind him, permission to destroy Philippa and then the rest of them.

When he exited the courthouse and people moved out of the way for him, Hopkins's chest filled with the sweet air of power. He wanted to submit, and so he must dominate. Control over the fates of others meant he was in control of his inner self. "Hopkins," they whispered. "The Witch-finder General!" And they shrank away in respect for his deeds, just as they had in Chelmsford.

"Here, boy, come back tomorrow," he said to the youth he'd paid to watch Elspeth while he was in court. He had an income of over two hundred pounds from the summer's witch-hunts. Luxuries were suddenly within reach.

The boy handed over the rope on which Elspeth was tied and Hopkins patted her head. She waggled the stump of her tail in greeting.

Bury St. Edmunds was closing up the day's business. Curtains were being drawn across windows, merchandise packed away in the stalls. Already the pubs were overflowing with men, and the lewd women who frequented such places. Hopkins winced when he saw an aging barmaid with a large bobbling bosom. She giggled and swatted at a soldier who was as wiry as she was fat.

If it were up to him, such behavior would be punishable, too.

"Ho, Matt."

Rounding his thoughts away from the barmaid, he forced a smile. "John. A long day!"

Stearne nodded energetically. "God's work we've done today."

They walked together down a shadowed main street. The alleys were already in twilight, but the sky was still bright above them. Hopkins watched as two wives in humble dark dresses walked with their farmer husbands. Then he glanced through the latticed windows of a pub. "Tell me, Stearne," he said. "What is it like to be married?"

Stearne pondered for a split second. "'Tis a good thing, of course. When the woman is pious, the marriage is indeed blessed. Why, Hopkins? Are you thinking of taking a wife?"

"I suppose," said Hopkins. He knew that it was part of his Biblical duty to rule over a wife and children, but women were dangerously weak. He was proof of that. Besides . . . when he thought of marital duties . . . he knew that his tastes were so defiled by the witch's womb, so immoral that no Christian woman could or would ever be able to rouse him.

Helpless, hopeless, you have no choice. A woman hovers above him, and says, "What I would do to you!" He lays flat below her, and says, "What I would do for you!" The woman wears the witch's face.

Stop it! he thought. Biting the tender skin on the inside of his cheek, he tried to look as though contemplating philosophy. To Stearne he said, "Do you not worry about the lesser moral quality of women? In the generality, I mean, not your own wife."

"As long as she submits to your moral authority, and you take full responsibility for guiding her thoughts in the direction of Heaven, then I've found no trouble."

"And you have a child, as well."

"Yes, women are needed for that," said Stearne, amusement playing at his lips. "Listen. Do not let our work taint your view of marriage. You see how godly wives have helped us—searched, and watched, and been the first to denounce their wayward sisters."

Hopkins nodded, but he could not muster any enthusiasm for the idea of a pious wife. "I suspect that God may have other plans for me."

"Ah, adventure!" said Stearne. "'Tis true you would be

pinned down by a wife now. You know I cannot venture too far from home. Women are as dogs—discipline, and a husband's presence, is an absolute necessity." He paused to knuckle-rub Elspeth's head. "You, Hopkins . . . you should wait until your situation in life is less movable."

"It would have been if I'd stayed at the Thorn Inn, stayed in Mistley," said Hopkins. "But that would be to reject my calling. I would not do that."

"This is just the beginning for you," said Stearne, gesturing up at the sky.

"You give good advice, friend," said Hopkins. He shook Stearne's hand and they parted. Stearne was finished with his testimony and would wake early the next day to ride south toward home.

Hopkins, however, would stay until the end of the executions. High level connections made here could benefit his work in the future.

He turned a corner and walked toward his lodgings, fixing after a pint of ale. Elspeth trotted alongside him. The pub there was frequented by magistrates, gentry, and wealthy businessmen—a subdued drinking-hole without any fat wenches lolling about.

Inside, however, there was an air of emergency. A group of patrons huddled around a piece of paper. The barkeep nodded and said, "Master Hopkins," then turned back to the group.

Removing his hat and keeping Elspeth at heel, he said, "What's the word?"

One of the men, a wealthy farmer, said, "The King's army is very near to Cambridge!"

Hopkins frowned and turned away. He had no fear of the war, but was irritated that the King might interrupt the course of justice. With armies moving so close, the trials might be suspended or dissolved, and Hopkins suddenly wondered what might happen if hundreds of known witches were loosed on the streets, all blaming *him* for their prison time.

He coughed and shivered.

"The army's being called up, all able-bodied," said another patron. "Muster's being called tomorrow."

"Dear God! This is dreadful!"

"You don't suppose the King will succeed? What if Bury goes under siege?"

"Lord bless the New Model Army, may they stave off this menace . . ."

"This means they'll have to hurry the assizes," said the farmer. He looked unhappy; his case must not have been heard yet.

Troubled, Hopkins retreated up the stairs with Elspeth and settled in for an early night. Tomorrow was the last day of the trials. After that, the hangings. Then he would be out of Bury and, he decided, back home to lay low at the Thorn Inn for awhile. He was too important to be caught up in the earthly battle as the armies clashed so near to him.

When his head hit the soft down pillow, the tilted angle made him start to cough.

"*Hep the hackle*," said a voice, but he was too exhausted to listen.

HOPKINS AWOKE TO THE SOUND of marching in the street. Pulling aside the curtain, he saw a company of soldiers in formation, on their way out of town to meet the rest of the army. There were never enough soldiers, especially not with hundreds of witches to guard. Most of the accused—the ones brought from the larger gaol at Ipswich—were locked in a tithe barn until they could be convicted and then hanged.

When he emerged, his beard trimmed and his hat secure on his head, the streets were in a clamor of panic. The townspeople ran this way and that, some leaving, others arriving. A woman dragged her two children by the hands down the street, saying, "Say farewell to your papa, pray for 'im!" A minister hurried past clutching a Bible. Then came a cart loaded with prisoners—women, drab and dirty. One or two spat words at him, but he paid no heed.

They had no power here in the city of men.

At the corner of a stone and timber-framed building, a boy held pamphlets, shouting out the news of the approaching army. The sheaf of papers were distributed quickly to the many people hungry for information. Hopkins picked one up, but it was nothing he didn't know. The King was on his way. The army was called up. All good Parliamentarians should join the fight. Hopkins folded the paper and tucked it away in his pocket.

"Praise God that the witches are being punished," he overheard a man say to his wife. "God will see that we are faithful folk. He will have mercy on us and save us from a battle."

The eyes of the good people looked for something to blame, and Hopkins had found the root cause of this strife: witches. *I ought to mention that witches often work as Catholics and Royalists,* he thought. The more he did his work, the more of Satan's footprints he found in the world.

This is a war of the spirit, Hopkins thought, *and the witches are casualties on the* other *side. Satan's side.* The harder he fought, the more leverage he would have to get into the Heaven that might otherwise turn him away. Chest puffed, he walked into the assizes.

THE JOURNEY BACK TO Bury St. Edmunds was made with urgency and on horseback. Pippa and Winifred rode alongside Hugh, whose father had business interests in Bury, and they would be staying overnight at the home of a family called Proctor.

"There are no public rooms to be had in Bury," said Hugh

as they cantered along the road northward. "And now the King approaches Cambridge . . . Roger is joining the Roundheads."

"Your brother?" Pippa asked. Roger Felton was a boy roughly her own age who liked to play football. The thought of him fighting in a battle made her nervous.

"I would, as well," Hugh said, "but that my father cannot risk the both of us dying. One must stay to help run the estate." He sounded irked about this, but Pippa knew what truly bothered him: that it was politically expedient for his brother to fight for a cause that he didn't much believe in. She, however, was glad Hugh would stay out it.

"We shall pray for Roger," said Winifred.

Pippa wondered if Roger Felton and Thomas Radcliff, on opposite sides, would find each other. But no, she remembered, Tom was further west, defending the royal interests in Wiltshire. Sybil's speaking of it seemed an age ago. War and politics and strife . . . all were miniscule in comparison to the very real danger in Suffolk. Matthew Hopkins. The imminent hangings.

Pippa watched Hugh's back as he rode ahead of her. His thighs gripped the horse in an easy seat—he was a fine horseman. Were it not for him, her betrothed, she would be in a grim cell with Sybil, awaiting her own death. She could still scarcely believe her escape had been real.

Thank the Lord he came to his senses, she thought. The problem with Hugh was that he gave other people a greater benefit of the doubt than they deserved. He'd even considered himself friendly with the likes of Elizabeth Yates. The golden-edged life of the gentry had not prepared Hugh for the boldness of Matthew Hopkins.

The journey that had taken so long in the lumbering prison cart was hours shorter this time. From a distance the abbey's tower pierced the sky and the sun's overhead angle created reflections off the shingled roofs and clocks. It looked almost idyllic, but Pippa's stomach tightened as they grew closer. There were crowds and judges who'd wanted to hurt her.

Their plan to save Sybil *had* to work. Winifred's father had bribed the magistrate to secure her release . . . the same magistrate that Hugh would demand to see this afternoon. "What did your father say to get the court to release you?" Pippa asked Winifred.

Hugh slowed his horse alongside to listen.

"My father paid bail," said Winifred, "and then . . . well . . . he knows someone who knows this magistrate, who had a gambling debt that was suddenly paid. I asked him to do the same for you and Sybil. But the debt wasn't large enough, and we're not rich enough." She bit her lip. "He didn't just bring money. He made heavy hints, promises even, about future donations to the man's political campaigns. It was . . . difficult for Father to do."

Pippa could imagine Mr. Radcliff would have been hard-pressed to promise support to a Parliamentarian. But he'd been desperate, willing to do anything to get his daughter back and restore their good name.

"How much was it?" Hugh asked. A large sum of money was tucked into his jacket's secret inner pocket. Pippa prayed it was enough.

"I think several pounds," said Winifred. Their plan rested on details. "I feel terrible knowing that Father might have gotten us all out, but he knew not that I'd found friends in that dreadful place."

"Not your fault," said Pippa, leaning over to squeeze Winnie's arm.

"We'll restore Sybil to freedom," said Hugh. His jaw was hard. Perhaps he felt guilty for not acting sooner. "I'll be as forceful as I dare with the magistrate. I'll try more than one. I don't care. I'll go to them all until I find one to listen. If they won't release her immediately, perhaps I can bargain for a delay, give us some time."

"I just hope the assizes aren't so busy that he won't take your audience," said Winifred.

"He will," said Hugh. "He'd *better*. You two, worry not. We'll save her."

Traffic grew heavy. They were entering Bury St. Edmunds. Hugh led the way through the outskirts and then into the dense city center. The color red was everywhere—the red cross of St. George on flags, the crimson of uniforms, the deep russet of dried blood on the stones near a butcher's shop.

They emerged into a sector with houses that were old but spacious and made of stone. Hugh stopped at a blue door. "The Proctors," he said. "Close to my family in business. Mr. Proctor is a tradesman in fine leathers and buys from our cattle stock on occasion."

A maid opened the door, dressed in the apron and cap for kitchen work. Bowing, she opened the door wide. Pippa was glad to be wearing her good black church dress.

Mrs. Proctor was a city matron in very fine clothing, at least to Pippa's country eye. She was fat, and wore a grey silk bodice and petticoat trimmed in black rope. Her lace collar was so large as to cover her shoulders down to her elbows. A ready smile made Pippa feel at ease.

Pippa mimicked Winifred's manners and dipped a greeting.

"Here to watch the assizes, are you?" Mrs. Proctor asked Winifred and Pippa.

Pippa realized that Hugh, in his message to them, had told the Proctors nothing about the circumstances . . . that she had been chained and under the boot of that very entertaining court. She was grateful that Hugh hadn't advertised her shame.

She and Winifred were shown up the stairwell to a spare bedroom with a thick down mattress—they would share. The sooner they went to sleep, the sooner the morning would come, and in the morning, Sybil was scheduled to hang.

"Let us accompany Hugh to the magistrate," Pippa said. "I don't believe I can stand waiting here."

Winifred agreed.

They walked with Hugh to the grand rectory where the magistrate—a minister—lived. As of this afternoon the assizes were finished, and the juries recessed. The swirling crowds had thinned on this street. There were no public spectacles of death to be had here.

Hugh said, "Await me. I'll not return until it's settled." He disappeared through the rectory's gate and into the yard obscured by high hedges. Pippa and Winifred sank down onto a stone ledge, hands clasped. Pippa's stomach did somersaults. Could they be about to get Sybil back? Would Hugh emerge with relief and victory on his face, the same expression he'd worn when Pippa had been released?

Next to her, Winifred sighed. "With every thought, I'm praying for her."

"As am I."

Turning with a sudden eagerness, Winifred said, "The King's army is moving this way."

Pippa looked into Winifred's bright eyes. "Yes, I believe so . . . plenty of Roundhead soldiers running about, worried over something."

"And my brother Tom is with the King's army." Winifred was breathless. "Pippa! What if we could get word to him somehow? What if the King chose to take Bury instead of Cambridge, and they put off the hangings? If the King had any idea what was happening here, he might do it! Tom could take Sybil far away, to someplace safe! I know he would!"

Pippa's hope was suddenly ignited. "Armies. The war. If it came here . . . with Tom . . . yes!"

"We could send a rider with the message," Winifred was saying. "Across the lines."

"Explain what's happened with the trials. We should tell

him that even his own sister was accused."

"That he must convince the King to come to Bury."

"This could work, Winnie!"

"I'm quite certain they'll delay the executions, what with the armies so close. They couldn't possibly go on with this, not with a battle about to happen," Winifred said, sounding quite sure of herself.

"If Hugh can win a small delay . . ."

"Enough to bring Tom and the cavalry behind him."

Pippa closed her eyes, imagining it. Dashing Thomas Radcliff in his royal cavalry uniform, riding in and rescuing Sybil, lifting her onto the back of his horse . . . the witch-finders and the crowds and the magistrates fleeing from Bury in a panic . . . herself chanting the rites of protection around Sybil and Tom as they escaped to the west.

"Oh," said Winifred, in an altered voice.

Pippa opened her eyes to see Hugh emerging from the rectory. His face was full of bad news. *No*, said a meek voice in her head. *Please, no.*

Hugh stood in front of them, silent for a few moments. Neither of the girls wanted to ask the question for fear of the answer. "I tried," he said at last, hands limp at his sides. "I . . . tried, I begged, even, but he would not listen."

"This cannot be!" Winifred said, indignant. "He must listen! Did you offer him the bribe?"

"Winnie," cautioned Pippa. "You know he did." She turned to look up at Hugh. "But we cannot give her up!"

"There is nothing for it," said Hugh. "The magistrate said that because of the impending battle, they're hanging all those convicted, beginning at dawn tomorrow. There will be no delay, no special cases." He paused. "Not even for ten guineas."

Winifred gasped at the outrageous amount.

"He was unmoved," said Hugh. "In fact, he had the gall to lecture me! He said that I couldn't be hoping to marry every single accused witch from the Vale. He cared nothing for her innocence. 'No room for exceptions,' he said, not even blameless victims. I swear, I will find a way to end him . . ."

"'Tis all right," said Pippa, reaching forward and grasping Hugh's elbow. "You did all you could." Her hopes deflated and the future stretched awful and empty in front of her. If the hangings were at dawn, there was no army that could get here fast enough to stop it.

"'Tis as though they want a sacrifice," Winifred whispered. "Kill these witches, and perhaps God will save them from the King, from the dreadful war that they themselves created. They're no better than heathens!"

Pippa agreed, though for different reasons.

As they walked together toward the Proctor home, Pippa felt her fighting spirit leak away. Her legs were rubbery and her mind confused. Most of all, she felt like laying her head upon a pillow, or perhaps upon Hugh's strong chest, and sleeping for a very long time.

The money in her purse jingled and she remembered that she needed to go to the market. Perhaps it would distract her from the dreadful news of Sybil.

"Leave me at the market, I have an errand," Pippa said. Hugh and Winifred looked at her with concern. She would have kept their company, but she was embarrassed about needing the ointment to kill the rest of the lice in her hair. "Please, I must do it alone. It won't take but a short time."

Hugh warned that if she wasn't returned by the top of the hour, he would come looking for her, and Pippa was glad for it. The city was full of darker men, the ones who hunted her, the ones she dreaded to see ever again.

"Worry not," Pippa said, as much to herself as to Hugh, and she stole into the crowded marketplace.

The paths of good and evil intersected by accident at the corner of Northgate Street and Looms Lane. Matthew Hopkins was looking down at Elspeth and the brim of his hat blocked his view ahead, so he nearly collided with her.

"Watch yourself!" he snapped at the slight figure who stopped short in front of him.

Met with silence, he looked up and saw vigorous distress in a pair of hazel eyes.

"You," Philippa Wylde choked. Then she turned on her heel and fled down a narrow path between two leaning buildings.

"Stop, witch!" he cried, unsure what he was doing, what terrible string tugged him to run after her. Elspeth growled and took off after Philippa. He called the dog to heel but the animal paid him no mind.

Hopkins was winded after a few paces of running in the stuffy heat of the alleyway. Breathing hard, he placed his hands on his knees and paused. In the murky light he could hear Elspeth's low growling. He edged past a scaffold and found his greyhound, bent in a guardian stance, and Philippa cornered.

Her face was stark. He drank in her unveiled expression. This was what he'd always wanted, to make witches fear him, to make people fear and respect him, so that they might never guess his inner weakness. Perhaps now the balance was reversed: she feared *him*, and he had power over her. This was not like the other times in the forest, or the cottage, or the gaol, or at the trials. There was nothing to hold him back now. There was no one to protect her. *I am the Witch-finder General,* he told himself, and stepped towards Pippa.

"Elspeth, heel," he told his dog quietly.

Elspeth retreated to stand next to Hopkins.

"You dare to stay in Bury?" he said.

Pippa shook her head.

"I can accuse you again," he said. "I can tell the court that you cursed me here, now. You give me the evil eye."

"No," she whispered. "No."

He chuckled. "You beg me to hold your innocence?"

"No," she said, but her voice was unsure. "I mean, you cannot accuse me again."

Hopkins was startled. That man of hers must have told her that the assizes were over-full, that she was safe for the time being. *How vexing.* "You do not fool me, Philippa Wylde. Your name is on the Devil's Register."

"What Register? Has he a list of us?"

"Of your sisters in evil? Why, yes," he said.

There was a gleam of realization in her eye, although it was edged out by her dilated pupils and her obvious agitation. Her breath came in quick pants. The tips of her fingernails had turned white, so hard were they pressed against the wall behind her, and her head was tilted back to expose the curve of her neck. He took another step toward her. The heady rush of blood through his body told him that he was not afraid . . . that he was thrilled to feel no fear of her . . . that he had all the power.

"Approach me not," she said.

Hopkins laughed. "Do you think I would touch you now? Pollute my soul with your trickery? No," he sneered down at her, for he was much taller, "you are a hag, in the league of Satan, and I do disdain you."

"You're wrong," she breathed, "there never was any league of witches! You're mad, deluded, seeing terrors all around. A-feared of your own shadow, you are!"

"Your lies will not sway me," he said. He took another step. Elspeth growled again.

"A-feared of *women* you are!" Philippa said, triumphant despite the way her limbs trembled.

Something dark and angry unraveled inside Hopkins. Philippa's mocking voice merged with all the rest, the voices that haunted, the voices that whispered, *Blackie, sackie, darkie, smite. I'll suck your bones for the rest of the night!* He licked his lips, staring, lost in the cauldron-holes that were Pippa's eyes. *Sator rotas, lime and own us. Feather and tar them all.* He tried to cling to the slippery tendril that was his faith, his God . . . The abyss gazed back at him . . . The abyss had a voice. *Garden snake, Eve-ning snake. Take me, slake me.*

Satan was in her.

Unknowing, out of control, he lunged forward and placed his hands on either side of Pippa's face. His face was inches from hers; he could smell lavender on her skin. He wondered what she tasted like, her parted lips, the shadow of the tongue behind her teeth.

His voice was demented, a stranger to his own self. "*Nearest, dearest, take me, slake me. What I would do for you.*"

"Who are you?" She was a thin line of strength, of bone.

She should know . . . Satan herself had taken hold of them . . . Hopkins saw the flames of Hell reflected in her eyes.

With a finger he traced the line of her gaunt cheek, then pressed a hard knuckle into the hollow of her white throat. "*My delicate firebrand-darling,*" he whispered.

"You're insane," she whispered back.

"No . . ." He pressed his body against hers and clamped his mouth down upon her lips. He was pleased with what he found, thrusting his tongue inside her weak open mouth, feeling her struggle against him. He was equally trapped, drawn forward to explore her obscene softness, grazing her tongue with his own. He felt a special thrill when her breath shortened to animal gasps of terror.

At the end of the alley, something crashed and clattered, and Hopkins turned to look. A cat slunk along the wall, having knocked over a bucket.

Pippa took the broken moment and slid down the wall, ducking underneath his arms that entrapped her, and backed away from him. "You're mad. Stay away from me. Stay away!"

She was tense as a spooked horse and ready to bolt.

Hopkins snapped-to, returned to himself. He gazed back at her. "You *are* a witch," he breathed. "My Lord God." His heart pounded from what had just happened. Satan had indwelled him. He had spoken in the voice of that imp, that Devil, that dark thing who tried to capture him at every step of the way. *I will not allow this curse,* he thought. "Run," he told Pippa. "Run, away from me, for I have God on my side! I will hunt you always! You will fear me *forever*!"

She needed no further encouragement and turned, tearing down the alleyway and leaping over a pile of bricks to escape.

He had wrestled with the Devil, that *scritch scratch* man, that *firebrand* woman, and won.

Hopkins glanced down at Elspeth, who whined back at him. "Do you feel like supper?" he asked. They set off toward the Dog and Partridge, where he was meeting two local politicians for a meal. The pub was renowned for good sausages.

THE FIRST TINGE OF A SCARLET SUN bloomed in the east, to match the soldiers' coats, the blood, the anxiety in Bury St. Edmunds. Pippa stirred on the feather mattress. Next to her, Winifred snored softly. The window—real glass—was closed off by a wooden shutter, but Pippa could see the changing color of the sky through a crack. It gave the Proctors' guest bedroom an unsettled light.

It was time to get dressed. An early rooster called, and then came the clacking hooves of a horse passing by on the street, and then the clang of a pan in a kitchen somewhere. The noises of a large town were unusual to Pippa. She edged out from beneath the down-filled bedclothes. Peeking through the window, she shuddered at the sky, for bands of vermilion clouds blocked the eastern horizon.

The deadly sun would follow close behind them.

Pippa went to the washstand and brushed her teeth thoroughly, trying not to remember her encounter yesterday with the witch-finder. She rinsed and spat into the bowl, feeling her mouth would never be clean.

She hadn't told Hugh about Matthew Hopkins. Nor would she. It would infuriate him and he might set out for ill-advised revenge. She couldn't risk him in a duel—not when he was all she had left. She swallowed the sick feeling aroused by the memory of Hopkins's touch . . . and felt grateful to Hugh for having kissed her first.

Glancing at Winifred still sleeping, Pippa's mouth twisted at the thought of their powerlessness. They three young people had no defense against the sinister powers that held Bury St. Edmunds in thrall of witches and armies. For Sybil they had tried and that was all that could be said. And so, on that red Wednesday morning, Pippa tied her petticoats, buttoned her bodice, and fixed her collar with a difficult errand in front of her. Today she would watch her friend, her sister, die.

With a gentle hand she shook Winifred awake. "'Tis dawn."

"Oh, Lord," said Winifred, pulling the blanket inward, and then sitting upright with tired, blinking eyes. "God Almighty be with us. I don't want to watch, Pippa."

"Nor I."

"But we must," said Winifred. "We must be strong for her. We must make certain that she sees us and knows we love her." She unhooked her clothes from the wall peg and dressed for the event in somber black.

As Pippa pulled her hair into a bun, it seemed that time itself was her enemy. Every moment was a tick closer to *that moment*. How could she have any thought at all, except for Sybil? She was on the lip of a cliff, staring down into a kind of grief that should be reserved for the old and careworn. For Lillibet, who had in her own way prepared Pippa for her own eventual death. Lillibet was good that way. She never did shy away from beginnings or endings.

But Sybil was a child. It went against nature for her to die this way. There was no preparation for it except to tie the strings on her linen cap.

To lace up her shoes.

To straighten her collar.

To reach into a pocket and feel the spiny, glossy edge of a feather.

To walk out the door with Winifred.

They met Hugh in the downstairs hallway. He too was dressed all in black except for the white of his shirt and the silver buckle on his rounded hat. His blue eyes were blackened too, for his pupils were dilated in the dim light before the dawn. "It's set for the market square," he said.

Pippa knew that. She'd seen the gallows being readied yesterday, just before taking the wrong corner and running into Matthew Hopkins. She shivered and moved closer to Hugh. She dreaded the thought of going anywhere alone again. *He* might find her. He was the dark man.

They were not the only ones to make an early start. Already the day had the air of a festival. Townspeople and country folk had arisen to watch and cheer the executions. Later the people would drink enough ale to forget about the heat and the approaching battle. Hugh, Pippa, and Winifred joined the steady stream of chattering spectators. As a river to the lowest point, the crowd converged on Cornhill Square and settled in with their breakfasts. The yeasty smell of fresh bread and beer hung in the air.

Glancing about, Pippa asked, "From where will the cart come?"

"I hear they're kept in the barn that way," said Hugh, pointing down a wide street.

"Then let us choose a place near the cart's path," said Winifred. She whispered to Pippa, "Do you have it?"

"Yes," said Pippa. She took the feather from her pocket and showed Winifred.

"Ursula?"

She nodded.

"It was good for Martha to leave her with Will Renshaw's pigeons. He scarce noticed the addition."

Pippa's stomach growled. It seemed wrong that she should be hungry when she might have been killed this morning. Hunger was for life, for vitality, and Pippa felt anything but.

Winifred, however, had no such reservations and pulled out a cloth-wrapped loaf of fresh honey bread. Breaking off a piece, she offered it to Hugh, who murmured thanks.

Pippa accepted a torn piece of bread in spite of herself. It was fluffy and white and sweet. Again it seemed wrong that it should taste so good.

The square was congested with bystanders, spilling over into the streets nearby. Sellers of food, of drink, and of pamphlets spread amongst them. One woman with a cloak full of cheap pewter spoons and forks showed her wares to Winifred, who shook her head. Some yards away, a man preached and others formed a circle around him to listen. "The abomination be cast out of our midst and the witches sent to Hell! Pray, and in your hearts know the pure love of God. Follow Him in all ways and He will show you mercy . . ." In the other direction, a song-seller crooned, and not very well: "*Now I remain in a world apart, but my heart remains in captivity . . .*"

Faces appeared at open windows and children climbed on stairs, ladders, railings, and roofs for a clear view. The gallows were built high and strong, well above the heads of the crowd. Constructed of solid fens oak, the simple structure was a long beam from which were suspended five lengths of rope. They were to be knotted at the last minute, for sometimes children dared to play on the gallows and could not be chanced to stick a head in.

The two framed sides were the brace for the beam and also supported a platform with five trapdoors on which the doomed would stand. These had a rope mechanism that, when pulled, would release them. A steep stair-ladder led the way up to the high platform.

Pippa could not keep her eyes off the ropes that dangled like dead snakes in the morning breeze.

When the stained red of the sun first burned their faces from above the rooflines, there was movement on the gallows and an excited murmur grew in a thousand throats. It was the hangman, the supervisor of the proceedings. He wore a thin black veil over his face. Pippa wondered who he was, and whether he had children, or a mother. The man stopped at each rope and with expert quick motions, made nooses of all.

After the hangman came a company of soldiers. When the hangings were done they would likely rendezvous at Cambridge. There was a rushed look to their young faces, as if they wanted to hurry this unsavory duty and rejoin their comrades to fight a clearer enemy in the King

The throng cheered them, the first proper roar of the day.

In a triumvirate of silence, Pippa and Hugh and Winifred waited.

From down the street, the distinct creaking of a cart could be heard, heralded by the shouts and taunts of a pack of feral children. Pippa's gut twisted, tight like the nooses. She wondered if Matthew Hopkins was in the crowd.

"There!" shouted one of the mob. "The witches!" A mighty cheer arose that made the ground rumble.

"God be with us now," murmured Winifred. "God be with Sybil."

Pippa hoped so.

There was a large number on the hanging roster, at least twenty souls according to a pamphlet Hugh held in his hand, including witches and a couple of thieves. There were two carts to hold them. Over a sea of heads Pippa could see the swaying vehicles, their wooden wheels turning and turning towards fate. She was on her tiptoes, waiting for the cart to come closer so she could find Sybil.

"Is her father here?" Hugh asked.

"The Reverend? Doubtful," said Pippa. Her thoughts toward the village church and its minister burned like acid.

The carts entered the square and the mass of people split apart to allow them through. Pippa and Winifred elbowed their way against the surge. Pippa did not bother to excuse herself as she pushed and shoved; there was nothing polite about this morning.

"Soldiers," said Winifred in her ear.

"Oh, no." There were indeed soldiers around the carts, as much to deter the passions of the crowd as to prevent the prisoners' escape. "We have to get past them!"

Stepping on toes, and getting stepped on themselves, Pippa and Winifred kept moving to intercept the path of the carts.

"There! There!" Pippa said. She was taller than Winifred and could see the lank blond of Sybil's hair. She was in the second cart.

On sight of her dear friend, Pippa no longer cared about any old soldiers in her way. She yanked Winifred through a gap in the crowd and stumbled up to the cart. "Sybil! Sybil!"

Sybil's luminous eyes turned to her. "Pippa! And Winnie!" She smiled at them.

Pippa's heart cracked open to see her.

"You there!" a soldier warned, menacing them with the end of his musket.

"Give us one moment," said Winifred to the soldier in the haughty voice reserved for servants. She turned to Sybil. "Oh, darling Sybil, we're so sorry . . . I know not what to say . . . We tried everything, to bribe the magistrate, Hugh offered him ten guineas for you, and no one would relent . . . I would do anything . . ."

"Be not sorry for me," said Sybil. "There are better worlds than this one." There was a purity to her prominent cheekbones and pale eyes and filthy clothing that made Pippa think she was halfway in Heaven already.

Innocent, she's innocent, thought Pippa, reaching through the thick wooden slats to grasp one of Sybil's bound hands. Winifred took the other. They walked alongside the cart.

"Back!" said the soldier.

"Hush, or I'll speak to your commander!" Winifred returned.

The soldier was not sure what to do with a strident woman of Winifred's class, and so he turned back to the crowd.

"Here, Sybil, I brought you something." Pippa reached into her pocket and found Ursula's feather. She passed it through the bars.

In the morning's light the feather was black and red and azure and violet, a nighttime's rainbow, a million girlish secrets. Sybil held it with white bony fingers. "Ursula," she whispered.

"A gift from her," said Pippa.

Winifred was crying.

A lone tear dropped from Sybil's eye, too, but it was not sad somehow. Instead it gleamed lustrous like the feather. "Goodbye," she said, as though stepping out the door to buy a new spool of thread. "A merry parting!"

"A merry parting," agreed Pippa, so stifled with tears she could hardly speak.

"God bless you, Sybil, oh, God bless!" Winifred cried as their hands were wrenched apart by a knot of people, and by the cart's implacable motion toward the gallows.

Pippa saw Sybil tuck the feather into her hand, clenching a fist tight around it. Then she was swallowed by the rowdy multitude. Standing bereft with Winifred, she made her way slowly back toward Hugh's tall figure halfway across the square.

Another mighty thunderclap rolled through the crowd as the first five were led up the ladder; Sybil was not among them. The condemned were blindfolded with black cloths. A great hush across the square followed them in case there were any last confessions, condemnations, or pleadings. All five women remained silent. Another woman's voice could be heard from the cart, exhorting God to have mercy, that she was the lone innocent amongst these witches. "Please," came her thin cry, "Oh, the Almighty Lord will embrace me! I am as the Israelite cast in the land of magical Egypt, and I fear not the reckoning of God!" There were some rumblings of sympathy for her.

Pippa had more sympathy for the silent ones. They would not dignify this awful thing with words.

Appalled, fascinated, Pippa watched the hangman move off the platform. She could not see him move the mechanism for the doors, but—with a swing and a violent "snap"—the five living people dropped and met the ends of their ropes. Pippa jerked when it happened. So did many of the spectators around her.

One of the hanging women was motionless. The rest, Pippa realized with a shock, were still alive. Their feet did an airborne jig. Their mouths opened and closed like fish. The skin bloomed purple and red, and their tongues swelled, and their hands clenched and unclenched.

"How long does it take?" Winifred whimpered. "How long?"

It took a long time.

Then, when all had ceased their convulsions and swayed in stiff circles, the ropes were released and they tumbled to the ground beneath the gallows.

In the intermission, the crowd chattered and drank ale and bought fresh pies.

"When will it stop?" Pippa asked when the ropes had been used twice, and a third group was up. Sybil was still in the cart.

Along the current row of condemned, Pippa recognized Anne Alderman from the gaol. There was also a man in the attire of a minister.

"John Lowes," said Hugh, nodding toward the gallows. "He was known to preach in favor of Bishop Laud." Hugh's face had gone quite pale. "I . . . I've never seen anyone die before. And I said nothing to stop it. It was my responsibility to speak and I was silent . . ."

"I fear responsibility is beyond any of us," said Pippa.

"I am certainly forming new opinions of earthly justice," said Hugh.

Snap.

The bilious lump in Pippa's stomach tensed again as the dead bodies were released onto the growing heap below. *I don't want to watch, I can't watch, I won't.* Breathing hard and fast, she stared at a spot of mud on a shoe, four feet over.

Winifred's hands were clasped in prayer. Nearby a rough-hewn woman with a snaggletooth said, "Stop that prayin'! Don't you know they're witches? Ha!" She took a large bite out of a loaf of rye bread and spat a seed on the ground.

Pippa twitched as though she'd been struck.

A tiny figure was climbing the ladder. It was Sybil, clenching a fist. Her other hand was splayed outward, guiding her along. She was led by the hangman to the middle rope, between two grimy men, the thieves. The hangman forced Sybil's head forward. The rope was fastened and tightened. She raised her head and tilted it this way and that. It was as though she could see past the blindfold, or inside her own eyelids to a world of her own. A better world than this.

A strong breeze lifted the hairs on Pippa's neck. On the western wind was the scent of an afternoon rain that Sybil would not live to see.

Overhead, drawn by the juices of fresh death, an unkindness of ravens flocked in the sky, rasping. Pippa knew Sybil must hear them, because even from this distance she could see the slender arc of a smile.

Some in the crowd must have caught their breath at Sybil's delicate beauty. Some must have wondered if she was a misplaced child, caught by unfortunate accident.

Or, perhaps the crowd was mindless and intent in their fear, like animals, not knowing friend from foe. Godly was another uniform.

None of Pippa's racing thoughts could stop the hangman from descending the stairs and walking to his station.

Oh, Lord God, let her neck break, let her suffer not.

The floor was released and Sybil fell, fell, and her neck did not break. Her feet jumped and skipped and hopped the way she had uncounted times in the forest. It was her last dance, her death-dance.

Go, Sybil, leave!

Sybil suffered first. But after that eternity of shaking, her hand unclenched and a glossy black feather was seen to float downward and settle in the dust.

The Skull in the Hollow

The spectacle had taken most of the morning. They did not stay to see Sybil cut down. That which had made her their friend was long-gone. They had no standing to claim her body, which only the living father could do.

Deep sickness fell upon them as they walked toward the Proctors' home. Hugh would not speak, Winifred was crying, and every time Pippa blinked she saw a row of broken silhouettes swinging against the restless sky. The rumble of the mob was behind them.

It surprised Pippa when Hugh's fingers clasped her own, in public, but the streets were empty of watching eyes. Most everyone was at the hangings. She clutched his hand in return.

Mrs. Proctor, who had accounts to settle in her husband's ledgers and no time to waste on capital punishment, waved them in. At first she did not notice their grim mood. "We have cold meats for dinner today, and Hugh, our boy Samuel wishes to accompany you to see about the lamb leather. Sam will take over the business someday and it would do him good, if you mind him not . . . Your father, Hugh, has fine such herds... Why, what be the matter?" Mrs. Proctor looked from one to the next.

"'Tis nothing," said Winifred, her voice sodden. "We happened by Cornhill Square."

"Oh, you've not seen a hanging before," said Mrs. Proctor, bustling with sympathy. "A cup of tea will cure you. East India Company. Mr. Proctor buys it in London."

Pippa took a bitter sip of the expensive tea. India tea was rare and only Winifred had tasted it before. They sat facing each other, their tears obscured by the gentle coils of steam. She could hardly meet Winifred's eyes, fearing that she would see the echo of what she'd just witnessed. Instead she bowed her head and looked into the cup and saw the glimmering reflection of her own nose, her own mouth, as she raised her cup and touched the liquid blackness to her lips. Her heartbeat was slow and pained, carrying a weight that she was certain would never leave her.

Mrs. Proctor did not seem to mind their strange silence, or more likely, she didn't understand it. A woman whose husband could afford India tea would never imagine such a thing as Pippa and Winifred had shared.

"Of course young Samuel may come with me on my errands, if he pleases," said Hugh with an odd tightness. He too refused to meet glances with Pippa and Winifred. It was as though they had become strangers to one another. Hugh took slow, deliberate sips of his tea.

The smooth white of such fine porcelain reminded Pippa of polished bone. It clinked and she was lost again inside her own thoughts. *"Take me head when I be dead." Lillibet gave me instructions. Sybil's hair is about her throat. A rope about both their throats... how did she know? Oh Lord... Lillibet, Sybil...*

They were scheduled to ride back to the Vale at four o'clock and according to the lantern clock on the Proctors' mantle, it was noon.

"Excuse me, Mrs. Proctor, but my head is aching," said Winifred. "The tea did help."

"Of course, dear. Lay thyself down for a nap, I'll have Prudence close the shutters in the room for you."

Pippa said, "Thank you, Mrs. Proctor, for the tea. I've never tasted anything like it." It was a day full of new and bleak things. "I'll take a rest as well."

"Yes," agreed Mrs. Proctor, "this heat does no good for the constitution."

When Pippa and Winifred had their shoes off and they were side by side on the bed, Winifred murmured, "Nothing will ever be the same."

"No," said Pippa, "it won't."

"I cannot think of it. I . . . I cannot think."

Pippa lifted herself up. There were two washcloths hanging on a rail near the basin of clear water. She dipped a cloth in and wrung it out. The water was cool. "Here," she said, folding it into a band and placing it over Winifred's eyes.

"Thank you," said Winifred, but then she was sobbing again. "'Tis my own blindfold."

Pippa squeezed her eyes closed against the analogy. She was torn between curling up with Winifred to cry out her grief, and avoiding any reminder of it. If only she wasn't in a city. She craved the quiet of the fields and the forest, to be safe from what lurked amongst men.

The Proctors had a garden. That would have to do. At least Pippa could see the sky and await the journey home. "I'm going to sit in the garden for a spell," she said. "Rest, Winnie. I'll be back soon."

Winifred nodded feebly and held the washcloth tight over her temples.

As quietly as she could, Pippa laced her shoes and went outside. She stared up at the clouds, but all she saw was the face of the reaper of death. A rain shower hit her face, but all she felt was the hot cascade of tears.

Later that afternoon, they left for home, a miserable caravan of three plodding through the streets crowded with soldiers and drunken civilians, and then into the open countryside. Pippa swayed in her saddle, rolling around with the horse's motion, unaccustomed to so much riding. The rain had passed and the sun was bright in the sky; at this time of year, it would not set for many hours.

Pippa wished it were night. Then she would not have to look at Hugh and Winifred, or see the inconstant horizon, the road that spun sickeningly in front of her. Her stomach felt too light, too buoyant. She wanted the blanket of summer's darkness to protect her from these wide-open spaces.

Hanging, swinging, swaying.

All at once, the trotting of the horse was too much, and the empty country fields and road were a dizzy blur. She reined the animal to a halt, swung her legs around, and dismounted in a clumsy heap. Hugh barely had time to say, "Pippa?" before she swaggered upright, stumbled into the holly hedgerow, and vomited in the dirt.

ONLY THE STRAWBERRIES HAD BEEN saved in Winifred's garden, and that was because her sister Jane liked strawberries and could be bothered to tend them. Everything else had been chewed on by rabbits, or eaten by insects, or baked in the sun, or drowned in the corners because the ditches were not kept clear. The healing herbs were brown and wilted on their stems. No one had harvested them. Their house-woman had unearthed several of the carrots and radishes, but they had not been ripe yet, and the rest were rotten. It was quite shocking how quickly a garden could deteriorate without the care of a conscious soul.

The blazing, overheated summer had faded into a pleasant autumn. Winifred had regained weight under the watchful eye of her mother. "It would be best for you to marry soon," said Mrs. Radcliff, "for with a husband you might settle down and forget this nonsense."

"This nonsense" was how Mrs. Radcliff referred to the witch hunts.

Winifred thought it would be years before she felt ready to be married. She barely felt like herself anymore, let alone capable of choosing a husband. It was September, and her main priority was to harvest what could be saved from her garden, trim back the rest, and weed out the noxious plants that had taken root there.

She had a special miniature scythe made of silver. It was a sharp, shining curve that was ideal for the precise work Winifred had in mind. *It took too long to get back here,* she thought, looking around her garden. For weeks she'd been unable to venture into what had been her favorite place. She kept thinking of the search-women and their invasions. This was where they'd watched her. This was the garden where she'd lost her innocence.

Life at the Radcliff house had become subdued for other reasons. The summer's battles revealed a losing streak for the King. They'd heard nothing from Thomas for months, no letters and no word of his health and whereabouts. Thinking on it, Winifred realized it had been almost a year since they received word of him. That didn't seem right.

She remembered how things had gone the night before. Her cousin Jonas Martin, the Bible printer, had visited for dinner along with Elizabeth and Catherine Yates. For two unbearable hours Winifred had listened to Elizabeth harp on about the moral qualities of various neighbors, and Jonas had mentioned victories of the New Model Army, to Catherine's encouraging nods. He was now courting Catherine Yates and she'd taken on his Parliamentarian politics.

Jonas and Mr. Radcliff had gone to the study for an uneasy

smoke, giving Elizabeth the chance to start on about the witch trials.

"'Tis truly a shame you were wrongfully accused, Winifred. There is such a stigma attached to it, you know not how many times I've had to explain it away, seeing as we're friends. You ought to think of the Americas. There at least the influences are pure and free from the stain of it. Even though you were innocent, unlike my poor father's changeling child—"

Winifred had been simmering low all evening. It took a great deal to ignite her temper, but listening to the words "pure" and "free" and "innocent" issuing from Elizabeth's lips . . . to hear of Sybil . . . something erupted inside of her and she could not contain it. "You have no right!" she'd shouted. She'd stood up and shaken a finger in Elizabeth's face. "You have no idea, you have nothing but your pale imitation of a life! You judgmental, pock-marked *spinster*! Judge not, lest ye be judged!"

"Winifred!" their mother had gasped. Jane's eyes were the size of saucers.

Unable to tolerate it, Winifred had thrown her cloth napkin to the floor and run upstairs.

In her garden now, she sighed and pushed away the memory. The bridge was burned. She need not ever keep company with Elizabeth Yates again.

The day was warm and sunny, and it was the time of the grain harvest. Winifred wielded her blade without passion. Out came the tangled knot of collapsed fennel. Out came the nettle weeds near the roses. Out came the heads of stunted cabbage. Their leaves were full of holes.

Winifred tossed it all into a compost pile in the center of the yard. That would have to do over the winter. Come next spring she would use the material to spread out new beds for flowers and vegetables.

Sighing, she saw that the entire bush of white roses would have to be pulled.

With swift strikes, she untangled the roots and yanked upward. It left a hole in the ground. Winifred stared down into the bare earth and thought of Sybil and, connected to her dead friend, her brother Tom. That absence, too, was a hole in her heart, an ache that never quite seemed to diminish. Every day she thought about it less and less . . . but she still thought about it.

Taking a deep breath, Winifred pushed the earth back into place to cover the pit left by the white roses. Someday, Sybil would not be the first thing she thought of when she woke up in the morning. Someday, Sybil would not be the last thing she thought of before falling asleep. It was, like the dead garden, being sorted out.

Through the hole in the fence she could see the figure of a young woman carrying a milk pail. She narrowed her eyes. Alice Baxter did not speak anymore, not even in stutters.

Winifred did not care. She did not allow for a lying weakling who'd betrayed her friends. Besides, the Baxters' farm was not prospering. Fluctuations in the price of wool and the rising quality of Flemish weavers meant that it was more difficult for them to break even on their herds. Alice was on a downward slope. *I was right about that one*, she thought. *A common girl who ought never to open her crooked mouth again.* Winifred would remain with her own set that included the Feltons and now Pippa.

Winifred's snobbery could not explain the volcanic rise of anger whenever she saw Alice, though. The Bible taught forgiveness. Winifred was unsure if she would ever forgive. It was easier to gloss it over with class consciousness.

"Just shows that weakness is born and bred," she muttered to herself as she pulled out a stinging nettle with bare hands. "Those girls did wrong to befriend her."

Alice, almost past the fence, seemed to pause in her step, but then continued on.

Winifred turned to a patch of dead lavender. It still smelled nice despite its condition. She might be able to rescue the blooms, ground them up, use them to make scented water or frosting for a cake.

With a wooden fork she pushed the dead weeds into a heavy, compact pile. She frowned as something half-buried glinted in the light. She pushed aside the dirt and then gave a pained cry. A drop of blood oozed from the tip of her finger. The thing was sharp, pointed . . . it had pricked her.

It was a needle. There was only one time a needle could have been dropped here. It was from the search-women who had—

But she couldn't finish the thought.

Using a handkerchief from her apron pocket, Winifred wrapped up the needle and walked through the house to the front.

"Winifred? Are you alright?" Her mother was in the parlor.

She didn't stop. There was but one thing to do with the offal of that time, that storm, that *nonsense*. She went out the front door and walked calmly toward the forest, careful that none saw her, wanting to be alone.

Winifred craved solitude often. Family meals were a strain with her grim father, her listless mother, and Jane's chattering as though nothing bad had ever happened. Tom's absence was heavy upon her parents, worse every day that passed without word of him.

A cool breeze moved through the woods and along the path Winifred took to her favorite oak. The oak was hers. It was masculine, or so she felt, and it had huge roots and soft earth beneath it. His arms were heavy and embracing. He was thick in the trunk, thin in the foliage, like an old balding gentleman with a large belly. Winifred sat upright against the base of the tree and dug her fingers straight down into the earth on either side. She cried.

She had been crying these days, too, and that always alone.

Sniffling, she scraped a hole in the earth, and kept scraping until her hands were black and she'd reached the soft, always-moist roots of the oak. Reaching into her pocket, she took the handkerchief and shook it. The needle tumbled out into the hole. Winifred squeezed out a last drop of blood from her finger and flung it in with the needle. Then she covered it up again. "Take it," she implored the oak. "Take my pain. Hold my injury. You have the strength I do not."

Winifred flung herself onto the curve of a root and lay there until her sobs turned into deep, even breathing. It was so very peaceful here. She understood that just as the earth was bruised in the winter, and seemed to die, it was a necessary part of the cycle. The dead remains of her garden would make an excellent spread in half a year. *I'm grown up,* she realized. *This is my cycle.* And just as she buried some things, and allowed them to decay, she needed to accept what had happened to her.

As she drank in the power of the oak, she remembered one of the Psalms of David. She whispered, "The Lord is the strength of my life. Of whom shall I be afraid?"

The leaves of a nearby ash were already tinged yellow on the tips. The earth was moving on. So must she. This was all just a summer's fever. It would pass. Sybil had died in a fever, a disease of the spirit that turned men's minds against the innocent. It was a force of nature.

Still, there were people to be held to account.

Wiping her nose, Winifred decided she would be quite all right. There was no need to wallow in self-pity. *Get on with things,* she thought. *Start with readying that garden for the winter's first frost. It will come in a month or two.*

She walked out of the forest with a different mind guiding her footsteps. On the way home she passed the Wylde-Wood Cottage. A plume of smoke rose from the chimney. The thatch had been repaired on the roof, but Pippa had not yet weeded the yard. Even the yew tree looked ill-kempt with decayed red berries scattered around its base and a patch of upturned earth where Lillibet had been buried.

Pressing her lips together, Winifred marched up to the door and knocked. "Pippa!"

It had been several days since she'd spoken with her friend. It was an odd thing, but Pippa reminded her of everything: the gaol, the terror, the hanging. She suspected Pippa felt the same way about her. There was much gravity in their friendship now. *Still*, thought Winifred, *someone must do something about this yard.* "Pippa!"

The door swung open. "Hello, Winnie." Pippa's hair was tied back and her face was shiny. "I'm just finishing up. Come in."

The cottage smelled of herbs and vapors. On the table were three or four open books, and something was boiling over the fire. All the shutters were closed. "What are you doing in here?"

"Lice," said Pippa, scratching her head with great drama.

"You didn't seem to be itching before."

"I got out the live ones. Now it's them nits come back to pester me." She glanced into her potion. "This should kill the last of them, then I'll comb them out."

"Oh," said Winifred. "Well. I've come to tell you that I'm going to weed your garden. I cannot look at it anymore."

Pippa grinned at her. "It bothers you that much? I'm sorry. I haven't time."

"I don't shy from hard work, long as it be in the natural out-of-doors," said Winifred. She glanced into one of the open books. "Midwifery?"

Pippa nodded. "I'll be damned if I let that Isabel Moore get the license. She couldn't midwife a field mouse."

Winifred said, "She couldn't nurse my mouse *imp*!" This made them laugh, something Winifred hadn't experienced in awhile. Wiping her eyes, she said, "'Tis so mean!"

"'Tis so true!"

"Pippa, I've been thinking." Winifred sat down on a wooden stool. "How are you? About . . . you know?"

Pippa shrugged. "Well enough. Day by day. The Feltons have been a help."

After Hugh Felton had so forcefully spoken for Pippa at her trial, all of Suffolk knew of their betrothal. The Feltons would hear nothing against their son marrying the daughter of an honorable yeoman, even if that daughter had been accused of witchcraft. Besides, the worth of the family had been raised in compensation when young Roger joined the Roundheads, the New Model Army. *Once she marries Felton,* Winifred thought, *she'll be untouchable. As wealthy as we Radcliffs are, and her children will be titled, no less.* Witness to Hugh and Pippa's obvious attraction, Winifred wondered how she could have ever thought Hugh would marry Elizabeth Yates.

"He is a good choice for you," said Winifred. "When will you marry?"

"In the spring," said Pippa.

"Then we will be the strongest families in the Vale."

"What are you thinking of, Winnie?"

"I'm thinking we must do something to make sure this never happens again," she said. "These witch-hunts. Do you believe Matthew Hopkins will stop? Already the village is in debt for our incarcerations. The parish's common fund is gone, paid to the witch-finders! And that doesn't account for the spiritual debt. An innocent was . . ." Winifred still could not quite say it. Perhaps next year she could pronounce what had happened to Sybil. "Truth be told, I suspect *all* of the accused are innocent."

"Hopkins believes there's a list of witches," said Pippa. "He thinks Satan has a *list* of all his witches and their imps. That we—the guilty—signed our names to it and made a contract."

"You cannot be serious."

"From his own lips."

"When did you speak with him?"

Pippa looked at the ground and her hands trembled. "In Bury."

With a noise of disgust, Winifred said, "This is what I speak of. He will not stop. There is nothing to be done about him . . . but we must make a pact, you and I. Someday we will be the matriarchs of this village. We must guide its morals and make it a safe place."

"A pact . . ." said Pippa.

"Yes! That we ourselves will maintain our good fortunes and become the guardians of the Vale. Someday we will have daughters. Someday the witch-finders will return."

Pippa knelt on the floor across from Winifred. "I see what you mean. But will we make this something official? Like a rule?"

"That's it!" said Winifred, relieved that Pippa had given words to what she was feeling. "That's just it! Once you're married, and I'm married to a powerful man—for I would take no other—then we need local parish laws that prohibit a witch hunt. As for you and me . . ." she fixed her jaw in a stubborn way, "We're a different sort of sisterhood, for we are all that survive. That Baxter girl—she's nothing to you anymore. She's not your sister and never was. Let me have that place in your heart."

"You are dear to my heart, and always should have been. And as for my former sister . . ." Pippa spat on the dirt floor.

"If you marry Hugh, you must stop spitting on floors," Winifred teased.

With a smile Pippa said, "I'm learning. So. Shall we shake hands?"

"No," said Winifred, glancing around and finding Lillibet's Bible on a shelf. She took it from its place. "We swear on this." They laid their hands across it. "We swear to God that this village shall be a place of safety for as long as we live. We swear that no superstition ever takes the place of God's justice. We swear that no man or woman or child will be accused of witchcraft here again."

Pippa added, "We swear that all things pagan and Christian exist under God, and nothing shall threaten the cunning ways."

Winifred felt better. If they could not take lessons from all of this, then it truly was in vain. But her friendship with Pippa had been tested and found worthy. Now they might use it for good.

"Besides," said Winifred, shaking her head, "there really is no such thing as witchcraft."

Pippa's eyes slid over to her and her coy smile was pure Lillibet.

THE LIGHT ARRIVED AND PIPPA'S eyes opened on the morning of a very important day. She was on her back in her loft. It was cold, and a heavy woolen blanket wrapped her from head to toe. Although Lillibet's bed was more comfortable, she could not occupy it just yet. She felt unworthy. Pippa sat up, shivering with the cold air that invaded her sleep's cocoon.

The coals in the hearth were prodded into life and a kettle of water set over the new fire. Pippa drew her cloak over her nightclothes and went outside to use the privy. Although it was not comfortable, there was something clean about the chilly countryside air. She never took it for granted anymore, not after the time in the gaol. She was still slimmer than was healthy but she was eating properly.

Mist clung to the ground and swirled around Pippa's feet. It was thick as custard. It reminded her that things were not always as they appeared.

She drew a full bucket of water from the brook and carried it inside. She planned on bathing later. It was too cold now to take full dips in the swimming-hole or the tub. Winter lurked—the time of sponge baths, or no baths.

Her breakfast was simple porridge with milk and a touch of honey. Routine was a weak remedy for the hole in Pippa's life. She had lost herself. She could not walk past the church without becoming nauseated. The pond gave her tingles of panic. Even this cottage was a challenge; half an ear was always listening for Lillibet's instructions or for Sybil's song-like greeting.

She had not seen Hugh for a week. They did not have as much to speak about as they once had. She had changed while he had not.

From across the valley, Pippa could hear the first messy task of the morning. It was the slaughter. It was the time of screaming and of sacrifice. A cow was being killed on one of the farms and there was its last hollow cry. Its hooves would be ground into powder. The best meat would be sold, or served at the table. Tougher meats would be torn into strips and dried in an oven. The hide would be sold as leather.

Something was dying inside her, too. This summer had been the end of her girlhood. Now it was time to step up to her own messy tasks.

She opened the shutters on the kitchen window that looked to the forest. The clinging fog was clearing away to reveal the tangle of trees. The leaves were aflame: red, brown, gold, orange. Lillibet had always told her, "The October harvest is the most important. In the old days it was a fire festival. The people would throw a dummy man made of straw onto the bonfires and they would eat the meat from their herds."

The meat was still eaten, but fires were civilized and contained in stone hearths, minded by goodwives and servants. There was no dancing in this land now except at the end of a rope.

Children still threw the effigy in the fire, though. They dressed him up as a Catholic. The Reverend always gave a sermon about how God had saved Parliament from the evil demon Guy Fawkes forty years ago. Pippa recounted how Fawkes had danced, too, and wondered if he was to be the new god of chaos, set afire when the air turned cold.

Truth be told, she didn't know what she was doing today. All she knew was that it was All Soul's—*another* Catholic festival—and she must go to the cave. She must come to terms with death. She would pray, or speak, or light her own tiny fire.

She poured the wooden bucket of water into the cauldron so it would heat up. Despite her general sense of numbness, there was no way she was taking a cold bath.

"Tan-a-dik!" said Ursula from her perch in the corner.

Pippa had taken custody of the bird, and Ursula spent her days on a wooden rail, speaking up on occasion and eating the remnants of Pippa's meals. Pippa wished she had the courage to take Ursula on her shoulder for walks but the bird was identified as an imp. Widow Moore, or Goody Brewer—whom Pippa refused to acknowledge, even though she was her nearest neighbor—or Goody Ford would say something. All pleasures were forced underground.

Ursula spoke in Sybil's voice, a near-perfect mimicry that always caught Pippa off her guard.

The water was warm, almost hot. Her bare skin puckered in the chilly air. "Brrr," she said.

"Rrrr," agreed Ursula.

Using an absorbent towel-cloth and the lavender soap, she cleansed herself from head to toe. The bruises were gone. Her hair was at last returning to its former gloss and volume. The lice were long-gone, and so was the grime, but still Pippa never felt clean.

She hoped tonight would change all that. There must be an answer in Lillibet's books.

At noon she took a thin meal of broth. That was all she would eat for the rest of the day; her plan included a small fast.

Aloud she said,

"*The fire bites, the fire bites, the fire bites.*
Hogs turn over it, hogs turn over it, hogs turn over it.
The Father with thee, the Son with me, Holy Ghost between us both to be."

Then she spat over her left shoulder into the hearth fire, and again over her right shoulder, and then faced forward to spit a third time. Her saliva created a hissing steam. Pippa wasn't sure what the charm would do, except that Lillibet used to say it before she took one of her half-day cleansing fasts.

What do I do with myself? she wondered as she sat beneath the yew tree that afternoon. She was sewing a pair of house slippers of leather lined with rabbit's fur to last her through the winter. The yard felt empty, for it was silent of animals and Winifred had cleared it of weeds.

From where she sat, she could see down the way to the village common. There was the sharp ridgepole of a roof, the Green Man—*The Charter Inn*, she reminded herself—where she would never again see Old Man Ashley nursing a pint and talking about the war. The innkeeper's son, Will Renshaw, was engaged to Susan, the girl who'd come to Lillibet for a husband charm. Lillibet's magic was still doing its work in the world.

Moving on, Pippa could see the plain cross on top of the church, where the Reverend Yates preached every Sunday, and next to the church his house. The curtains of Sybil's window hung straight and untouched, guarding an empty bedroom.

The reverie was a lump in her throat.

A figure was moving toward the Yateses' front door: Elizabeth Yates, judging from the humble cloth, the prissy walk, the sneering angle of the head with its plain cap. She was living fine and proper and attended church and Bible study. So did her sister Catherine, betrothed to a Bible printer.

There was the Moores' house, and Widow Moore had been a watcher.

There was the very edge of a field belonging to Goodman Ford, who'd testified against her, and where his wife must think on the glory days of pricking witches.

There was the Radcliffs' house, the place of secrets, the unexpected friend.

Pye's hill, and it seemed like forever ago that she'd raced up that hill, trying to reverse a hex, trying to impress Lillibet.

Her eyes trailed along the opposite ridge that cradled the Vale and she noticed an empty field, where Baxter's herd of sheep ought to have been. Pippa had successfully avoided seeing Alice since the—*betrayal,* her mind offered—the trial and she was in no mood to be taken unawares, like she had been in Bury when she ran into Matthew Hopkins and he'd chased her down the alley.

She pricked herself with the thick needle and jumped.

A-feared of me own shadow! Once, she had made a wish on this very tree behind her, in the days when she was bold and green. She glanced up at the tattered remnants of the red ribbon she'd tied on the branch on that summer's full moon. It looked faded, like she was.

Delicate firebrand-darling. That was what Hopkins had called her. The sour clench of fear turned her stomach every time she thought of him, thought of her powerlessness on that day. She was flat on the ground and could take no more.

The woods were a presence at her back. The yew tree groaned once when a crisp breeze moved.

The sun was setting and the slippers were finished. She put her needle safely away and felt the inside of the shoes—soft, warm. They would keep her feet toasty. She wiggled her toes inside her old shoes and tapped them on the ground.

Something tapped back.

Pippa jumped up and peered at the ground beneath her. She'd been sitting near the tree's ropy trunk. Lillibet's grave was a few yards away, marked with a cross of pebbles. Pippa knelt and swept her hands over the ground. She brushed something with her hand, something smooth and round just beneath the surface, like a stone.

A white-yellow stone.

It couldn't be. Pippa scrabbled at the dirt and uncovered the thing, blood pounding through her, because this was important. This was a sign.

The roots of the yew tree had wound themselves through Lillibet's buried body and drawn her skull toward the trunk. The tree's gentle brown death-fingers clutched the skull by the nose-hole, the eye-holes, the place where her neck had been. Decay had done its work quickly, leaving the clean bone, and Pippa touched it reverently. It was almost waxy, and shone in the thin October light.

It had come to the surface for her.

Pippa looked up into the dense branches of the yew, knowing that the tree had taken nourishment from what was left of Lillibet, knowing it had transfigured her into its own eternal growth.

"Thank you," she whispered to the tree as her digging loosened the roots' hold on the skull, and Lillibet's head was given up to her for safekeeping.

Take me head when I be dead. Pippa shook her head at her mother's incredible foresight. How had she known?

Pippa would have to ask for herself. She tucked the clean skull into her skirts and took it inside. She would use it tonight.

The sun began its daily decease in a cold burst of orange light. Pippa cleaned the kitchen without being tempted to eat anything. A few months ago she would have been complaining of starvation, with so little in her stomach, but she had learned the hard way to quiet her pangs. To ignore them. *My spirit is starved,* she thought. She was tired all the time.

"I'll see you in the morning, maybe," she told Ursula.

The bird looked at her with a knowing eye.

"I cannot go on this way. I must find me power," she said. Ursula bobbed her head and ruffled her feathers.

The sun vanished behind the woods. For a startling moment, the tops of the trees were consumed in red. Pippa doused the fire in the hearth. It would be a disaster to lose the cottage to a careless spark. She packed a skin-sack of water, a blanket, and carefully wrapped Lillibet's head in a clean kitchen cloth. Then she approached Ursula. "May I have another feather?"

Ursula was docile as Pippa's hands ran along her lame wing. A feather was released just as before. "Thank you, girl!" She fed Ursula a live cricket from the jar she kept in the kitchen.

"Thank you, girl!" said Ursula.

The door was closed behind her and the nebulous edges of twilight were perfect for concealing her path. Few were brave enough to be outside on this night, for superstitions were stubborn. The mist had returned, as though a veil were cast over the hard earth. There was no moon in the sky, for it was horned and dying, and would not rise until past midnight.

The woods were silent and waiting. Even the animals did not stir. It was time to disappear into hibernation. Pippa arrived at the cave's hidden entrance and the rolling boulder seemed hushed, too. "Shhh," she whispered to herself.

There would be found rubies of wisdom.

She crawled in and placed her blanket, water, and Lillibet's head in the tunnel. She took a few moments to collect kindling. The twigs were dry and snapped easily in her hand—perfect for a fire. Some large wood pieces were already inside for later.

Ensconced within, Pippa took a sip of her water and pulled out one of the grimoires. She turned page after page. It was a printed book, *The Key of Solomon*, and it contained some very complicated magic. Necromancy, the invocation of demons . . . Pippa put it away. She did not feel up to that sort of thing.

There was that smaller book bound in indigo leather—the

one Lillibet had caressed. The pages were thick, as though the binding was homemade, and the letters were handwritten. She opened to a page that said, "The Healing Fever."

Using her finger to guide her along, Pippa read aloud. "The Healing Fever. To see the truth of all things." Next to this passage was an illustration of a mushroom—Pippa had seen them growing in the cow pastures—and the words, "Fairy's cap." A warning seemed scrawled in the margin, and she read, "Not to be eaten every day, or on church days, or but twice every year." She paused. "Hmm."

She leaned over and set Lillibet's skull on the floor across from her. It shone in the flames, a pure deadly white. "Is this the thing to do?" she asked the skull.

It did not reply.

"Lillibet, you were an odd duck," she said.

Her fingers tapped along the many jars and bottles in the cave. There it was—a glass with a ribbon wrapped around it. The ribbon was labeled, "Fairy's cap." The mushrooms inside were dried and brown, long and thin. Pippa took the jar and shook out a handful. The heads of the mushrooms were conical, like a hat. "Hmm!"

A fraction of her old courage returned. Shrugging, she ate one.

"Show me the truth," she said, and ate another, and another.

They had a mild, nutty taste, like a dry wafer.

"Show me the truth."

She ate all five of them, because she knew where to find more, and because she wanted the truth.

She wrapped the shining rope of Sybil's hair twice around her wrist, like a bracelet.

The book was unclear as to what she might expect from eating old mushrooms. Taking another sip of water, she stoked her fire and added a larger piece of wood. The kindling had caught well. She felt like she ought to pray, but the Bible was not among Lillibet's books here. Instead she watched the way the fire glinted off the surface of the tiny pool, and the way the ruby down there wavered and winked.

Her mood lifted. A pleasant numb tingling started in her legs and arms. She had an urge to laugh. A few minutes later, she did.

Then she found Ursula's feather and tossed it into the fire. It sizzled and hissed and threw a golden spark.

The handwritten book had a charm written on the corner of a page. The words were difficult to make out, for they were nonsense. It took her a long time to read them aloud, to form the words, for her mind had wings and it swooped this way and that. The stroke of every letter was a long thread and her eyes followed their path on the page, wondering where they would lead her.

"*Sun et Siphereth by the love of Jesus Christ does Jehovah stay, Jeh Jeh Jeh, The Dryads play, Kam a-Umi, Nalgah, present the loom, weave the scorpio, Have mercy, God the All, I am, Will I am, our ward does Thomas gard.*"

The page was square and her fingernail was round. It took a long time to move her hand. She followed the words to where they would lead her. "*By the love of Jesus Christ. The Dryads play.*"

Time melted. Her mind skipped a pace. It skipped forward, it danced backward. Nothing in the world existed except the book. The book. Everything was in the Book.

Her eyes swung toward the fire. A spider crawled through it. It folded its eight legs and rested beneath a blazing log. The flame was bright as the sun, glowing and soft, an orange rose at the center of the universe. Liquid silver ran down the forked branches of a stag's antlers and landed in the coals.

She was in the heart of the world. The fire beat a drum and the chamber pulsed, in and out, breathe in and breathe out. The world was warm, the world was melting, she was fevered.

What did I eat?

She laughed and laughed. The fire peeled away the skin of the deer. The smoke lifted and was whisked away into the night. Looking up, she saw through rock and root, through leaf and branch, through air and to the stars that pulsed with the same great orange heartbeat.

Crackle and burst. The sound of sizzling meat. The sound of burning feathers. The sound of a thousand tiny births and deaths.

She melted and became the cave. She was the mind and the earth was her body. For many long years she stared at the face of the Green Man, who gazed back at her from inside a pulsing coal. He blinked and then he was . . . *Jesus Christ Jehovah does the Dryad play?* He had a long white beard and kind eyes. He blinked. *He sees me, He sees me,* and it was gazing into Winifred's looking-glass. *You are the same man, you are the same thing*, she realized. *I am you and you are me. God the All.* The face was Hugh. He blinked. She smiled at him, happy to see him here inside the great mind.

The book was heavy on her lap and she set it aside for a better look at the fire. It was the center of the universe.

The book had the names of the witches in it.

The man in the fire blinked at her, and she was in a dark place, she was sliding down . . . down . . . she was lost in a black vein and she was frightened. A heart's attack. The man in the fire was Matthew Hopkins. There was his sharp beard, there were his fanatic's eyes with red on the rims.

Looping downward, and again, caught inside an endless knot. She was back in the gaol. Lillibet lifted into the air, spine arched, muscles kinked and twitching, eyes wide, grotesque mouth pulled into a laughing grimace. Matthew Hopkins stared at her and she was captured. There were ropes around her wrists and she tugged at them, frantic, crying. Screaming. Wailing. Tugging.

Tight, too tight, I can't move, I can't breathe. She was dying.

There was a rope around her neck. She tugged. The world dropped from beneath. There was nothing solid and she swung. She hung.

"*Witch*," he said. "*Choke me.*"

There was no way out. She would die in this place, in this black pit, in this dark *dark* foul filthy place. Nothing was familiar. The ink blot shadows chased her. A word on a page, a name on a roster, *guilty guilty guilty.* She had not slept in months. He would find her, that face in the fire. She had signed her name "Philippa W." and she was on the Devil's Register.

"That not be your name," said the skull sitting on the floor. "You have no name."

A thousand names. The many-named. With great effort she turned away from the fire and crawled toward the skull, and yet did not move. The earth spun beneath her. She was a pendulum. Tick, tock. The lantern clock.

There was something important about that skull. Who was it? Something came forward out of the blank sockets. The light of the stars was inside. There was a twin universe, another orange flame, another heart. She recognized the eyes that turned and looked at her. They were familiar.

Lillibet, she remembered. Lillibet was here. That was her skull. The thought dropped like an anchor to the racing, raving mind, and she was yanked back into the cave—*cave, orange flame, Lillibet is dead and I ate mushrooms and I'm in the cave*—and she settled in to watch and listen.

"You are a witch," said the skull. "As was I. Seek not to change your nature."

"*I am a witch,*" her mind repeated.

"No one can harm you as long as you are here."

"*Here in the cave. Here in the orange heart of the universe.*"

The flames licked and teased and danced. She watched them and learned the steps. It was time for more fuel. It was time for another leg of deer. Another leg of wood. Her hands clutched a log and placed it on a crisscross. Cross the T, cross on the church, black on white. The church of men had no place here. This was a deeper place of worship.

This was the pulsing center inside of her. The fire was life and she must feed.

For too long the fire had starved and choked, been beaten and prodded and pricked by needles. For too long had it been a coal sputtering in the darkness.

The skull smiled at her proudly.

"You control what happens to you. *Sun et Siphereth.*"

Lillibet was not dead. She was laid to rest here in the center of all things. She was eaten by the fire of life, bones that rested and fluttered at the base of the orange bloom, the bones of a thousand people, hung and drowned and prodded and pricked, but now resting on the floor of the cave. They were dead. The fire was alive. It consumed and it grew. Her heart was dancing and drumming and pounding to its crackle, its sparkle.

Narrowing her eyes, she saw *his* face again. Hopkins. He was here in the heart of all things. But he had no power here.

I fear you not. Her thought was the force of a dragon's breath, a dragon's head, a dragon's tail that twitched in the coals. *You have no permission to harm me. I fear you not. You will fear me. I am the thousand-named.* She blinked and the face was the Green Man again, leaves circling and crowning his brow. He watched her from the forest, from behind the trees. He hid behind a glossy mulberry bush.

Her mind wheeled and twirled and then was still, clear as the crystals in the pool.

Fairy caps indeed, she thought, and laughed, for this was euphoria, and she knew the answer to every question ever asked.

Why did this happen to me? she asked.

"You only believe it happened to you, and that it was bad. But you asked for this very thing."

The answer was a red ribbon tied around the branch of a yew. The answer was a rope that bound her hands, a rope that bound her neck.

The leering faces and the binding ropes had been real once, and real twice here in the cave. She understood. The only thing that had changed was her mind. It had wheeled and twirled and was now still.

She felt as though she could swallow that fire and it would make her stronger. This was the burning-bright knowledge that was forbidden. It was too much power but not for her. She gripped the end of a burning branch and lifted it out of the fire. She held it aloft and the smoke made patterned smudges on the rocks. She grinned to match Lillibet, resting on the floor.

In this dazzling faceted sobriety, Pippa knew why. *I have seen your face, and I am not afraid,* she said to the shadows and the ink blots and the ropes. *I am a witch and I have seen what there is to see.* The responsibility was feather-light. No more a burden than Ursula, resting on her shoulders, digging in with a good solid claw to remind her of her power.

The faces were still there—all of them. The bones still rested in their bleached thousands. The flames danced a happy jig, the outlawed kind. But none could condemn this fire burning bright. They could but drive it underground for awhile and it would emerge once more.

She understood too what Lillibet had been. No church woman, but a wise woman, and one who knew that Pippa's final initiation must be to confront Death, to take it by the hair, to unearth its beautiful, laughing face. She reached over and rubbed the top of the smooth pearled skull.

At last, at last, Pippa knew who she was.

16

The Pond at Mistley

A nightmare afflicted Matthew Hopkins, and he tossed and turned in yet another strange bed. When he startled himself awake, he discovered beads of sweat on his brow that had already cooled, and it made him shiver. Elspeth was curled into a tight, heat-conserving ball at the foot of his bed. She was his only constant in these dreary days.

The infestation of witches along Suffolk's coastline was worse than he had hoped. They worked in clusters, in covens and in conspiracy, seven or eight or thirteen in one place. In the small villages and towns that edged the sea, witches often used the elements to wreak destruction on their neighbors. Hopkins had been troubled by stories of vast storms that sucked boats and houses into the water. One man had told of an elderly neighbor, a *witch,* who coveted his family. Then a great storm had arisen and swallowed his fishing boat and his two sons.

When Hopkins interrogated the woman, she'd taken some persuading, but eventually confessed to the entire deed and named three imps: Weedling, Eppie, and Yellow John. She had been hanged along with two others.

A meager light tinged the sky to the southeast. The sun would rise, and Hopkins knew it must be near eight in the morning. He rose out of bed and pulled the top wool blanket with him. Yawning, he sat down at the desk and lit the candle there.

So many inn rooms were alike, and yet they were all different—and none were home. It was also more difficult to ward off the nightmares and the whispers. This was an engaging life but sometimes he yearned for the familiarity of his house in Mistley.

Then again, he thought, *when I feel the urge, hear the whispers, it means there are witches nearby.* With the astounding success of the past year, Hopkins knew that he had a real gift. God had given him the ear to the ground to hear the witches. He no longer tried to shush the fell voices in the corners. Instead he embraced them, listened to their directions, followed them to their source, the warty and straggled women, the cunning men, the fallen souls.

Someday, when all the land was purged and Matthew Hopkins was the national Witch-finder General, the voices might be silenced.

As long as I feel it, the witches conspire. Where there is smoke, there also be fire. He smiled grimly to himself and held his glass ink-well over the candle's flame. The ink had frozen overnight. With the other hand he opened the shutter a crack. The North Sea was a slate mirror. Ice had collected along the seams of the window. It was a most unfriendly sight.

Turning to his pages, Hopkins wrote some notes about the activities of witches in this area. He was planning a master's manuscript to rival *Daemonologie*. Even King James I had not the experience he did, with scores of convictions, searchings and ordeals. Hopkins knew what worked and what did not.

He tapped off a fat drop of ink and put quill to paper. He must address the problem of swimming ordeals. In this weather, it was too harsh to swim a suspected witch, for guilty or innocent she would die of the cold water. There must be a different way to use the purity of water to produce a reaction.

He remembered reading about a technique used on the Continent in which a cloth is placed on the face and water poured over top.

"If the suspect twitches and screams and believes to be drowning, they reject their own baptism," Hopkins said aloud, scratching notes. "If they take the water with faith and welcome, they are likewise pure of guilt."

That would surely satisfy the naysayers.

Later in the day, after eating a hearty breakfast of eggs and sausage and bread fried in butter, Hopkins attended the town's trial. Three witches were convicted and hung.

It was too long a wait for assizes and no one wanted to pay gaoler's fees for months on end, and so some villages had taken to homespun trials. Hopkins preferred this form of justice, for it meant relief was instant. It had become a routine . . . a ritual . . . a purge.

After the witches were hanged and the villagers felt better—the relief after a vomit—Hopkins was paid. He commanded heavy fees now. Witch hunting was a monumental responsibility. When there were complaints about the cost, often running into the pounds, Hopkins always suggested the villages cut the pay for local search-women. After all, *they* had the benefit of living with the purified results. No witches. They should be grateful to him.

Then it was packing up, settling his bar debts, and moving on. He was drinking more ale than he should, but it was the only way to help him sleep and to reduce his cough. His lungs rattled in this freezing weather.

Mary Phillips, his loyal search-woman, said, "Why do you not seek an apothecary?"

"Because the power of prayer is the best medicine," said

Hopkins. Apothecaries were too close to cunning-folk and herbalists for his comfort. They might know his name and poison him.

Mary Phillips always fussed and worried over him. The Widow Phillips had no sons of her own and she took a motherly pride in Hopkins. Mary was the ideal—pious, stern, a whole-hearted believer in their task. She never complained about being summoned from her home in Manningtree for her skills as a search-woman.

Today, though, Hopkins was alone on the road with his horse and with Elspeth. A frozen prickly hedge to his left guided the road across a flat, marshy land. Their progress was inhibited by the crunchy slush. Elspeth's paws were mud all the way up to her joints.

He coughed into his hand, and he wheezed, and he cleared his throat with a prayer to the Almighty. This was his job, he did it gladly, and soon the dappled white of a village appeared around a bend. Smoke hung in the sky and blended with the low clouds.

He had not been here before. He wrapped the loose reins tight around his wrists, tight, pinching. How good that would feel. He could almost hear the Friday whispers.

Yes, there were witches ahead.

The day before her wedding and with some discomfort, Pippa thought about what was to come. Not Hugh—no, she was glad of him—but of the necessary formality in the church. Most people in the Vale got married in the church with Reverend Yates conducting the ceremony. It was natural and convenient to do so.

Pippa, however, had not set foot in that church since the events of last summer, and so she had insisted that they be married at the fine stone parish church in Lavenham.

This was the last night she would spend in the cottage where she'd grown up. Once she married, it would stay in the family as Sir John Felton's property, and she planned on knocking out the back wall and replacing it with a large barn-type door. It would allow a flood of natural light from the south. She would receive customers here, pregnant women, and would still brew and sell medicines here. Traditions were long to change, and the folk were used to going to Lillibet Wylde's place for a remedy.

Besides, the Felton manor was too far from the crossroads, and it was not proper to invite in a stream of ailing people. Sir John was suffering from consumption and fading fast. His health demanded that Hugh and Pippa live at the manor, for it was accepted that Sir John would pass on soon. They would make it their home from the start.

"Ready?" she asked Ursula.

The raven said nothing, but was obedient and climbed onto Pippa's shoulder when she held out her arm.

Her most important possessions were in the small trunk that rested, open, on the floor. It contained everything that she needed for her new life—her father's drawings, Lillibet's brooch, the antique comb, her savings in coins, and a valuable piece of parchment, rolled up and tied with a red ribbon.

Pippa took it out and unrolled it. Her letters had improved after a winter of poring over the books from the cave and she could read it with ease. She smiled. It was her midwife's license, arrived in March.

"Hallo!"

She turned to see Winifred wearing a dove-grey dress and snowy white collar, face framed by a fashionable diadem cap.

"Good morning!"

"Are you ready?" Winifred asked.

"Yes," said Pippa.

"Yes," said Ursula in Sybil's voice.

Winifred laughed. "I'm excited for you." She sat in the

rocking chair near the cold hearth. "Tomorrow will be a happy occasion. But, Pippa, are you certain of marrying on May Day?"

"Quite," said Pippa. "It's a rubbish superstition, no marriage on May Day. I suspect it might be the best day to marry, and it be kept from us."

Winifred groaned. "I had to abide the company of Elizabeth Yates last night. My mother hosted a gathering, a dinner and then Bible discussion."

"Sounds a thrill."

"Oh, it truly was! For good or ill, Elizabeth is engaged to a man from Stowmarket. A strong Puritan, and training to be a minister."

"That's fitting," said Pippa. She hoped that marriage would take Elizabeth away from the Vale. She was like a tenacious weed, always popping up to cause trouble.

"There be talk that he could take over from the Reverend Yates," said Winifred, familiar with the look on Pippa's face. "You know Elizabeth doesn't want to leave here. She hates us too well."

Pippa could only laugh, for she had won Hugh Felton. Elizabeth Yates might hate her forever because of it, but she was a small-minded creature and Pippa had no time for her. "So when can we expect *that* happy match?"

Winifred's mouth tilted up. "Certainly not until after you and Hugh have been married. She was spitting last night about it. She's convinced that you're so weak in moral character that you'll run off with a pack of demons and leave pious Hugh behind."

Pippa laughed, hard and strong. It was almost a cackle. "She thinks I'm a witch still?"

Winifred winked. "She knows no difference between white and black magic."

"She wouldn't," said Pippa.

"My father was in Stowmarket recently, on business." Winifred paused. "He says that the witch-finders have been there."

Her words drifted in the air longer than they should have. Pippa did not know what to say at first. She was surprised at her own lack of reaction. "Oh," she said at last.

"They're still doing . . . that. Father brought home a pamphlet about hangings along the coast during the winter. *He* was involved, Matthew Hopkins."

"I'd like to see them try it again here," said Pippa with a humorless grin.

Winifred looked frightened. "Pippa, look not like that, it's wicked."

"Wicked, wicked me."

"They cannot continue like this," said Winifred. "The witch-finders, I mean. They'll bankrupt the countryside. We might be safe here, but the rest of the country remains in their grasp. The only reason they get on with it is because the royal justice courts are disbanded. If there was some order, it would cease. Oh, but I wish this war would end!"

"I know," said Pippa, who did not know much about politics, but that word had arrived about Thomas Radcliff just before Christmas. He had been dead for the better part of a year, perishing of battle fever following a wound. Mr. Radcliff's hair had turned white at the news.

While sorrowful on behalf of her friend, Pippa was glad that Sybil hadn't arrived all alone in Heaven . . . that Tom had been waiting for her.

Winifred, still thinking of the witch-finders, said, "What do we do?"

"Let us wait," said Pippa. She understood the value of patience and timing much better now. To everything there was a season, and Matthew Hopkins's reaping would come. On the equinox of spring she had done scrying with the obsidian glass bowl in the cave. She'd seen her hand in his fate. "Perhaps at some future time, you and I will know what there is to be done about Hopkins."

"You're right," said Winifred, who had natural patience, where Pippa's was learned.

It reminded her, though. "How is the Reverend Yates?" She had not attended church since before the Vale trials.

"Aged. Worn. There is nothing wrong with him specifically, but there seems a great weight upon his shoulders."

"Good."

"Be not bitter toward him, Pippa. He is a victim of wrong thinking. I'm quite certain he regrets what he said and did."

"Do any of them regret it? Or would they do it again?" she wondered aloud.

"Here's your cap," said Winifred, holding out the folded white linen.

"No, I'll wear me hair free today," said Pippa. It was her last unbound day. "Ready!"

They walked out the door. Ursula was still perched on Pippa's shoulder. She took the bird with her now about the village, a spark in her eye that dared anyone to say a word against it. If she were destitute and in rags, the young boys might have thrown stones at her and called her a witch again. As it was, she wore fine thin wools, and too many depended on her for their herbs and teas and charms to find husbands.

It was a bursting, lively day and the deep cloying scent of flowers caressed the valley. Clouds were puffs of white meringue in the sky. Along the way they picked colorful wild blooms from alongside the footpath and gathered them into a cheerful bouquet. "She'll like this," said Winifred.

They turned onto the main road and past the crossroads. When they passed the ducks at the pond, Ursula ruffled her feathers at them and Pippa giggled, for it tickled her neck. She was no longer distressed by the pond. She was also no longer afraid of the church, despite her distaste for its sermons and its minister.

Winifred opened the iron gate into the graveyard.

There was a small, fresh mound of earth near the entrance—the Moores' fourth and youngest child, who'd died of fever. They passed by the new and the old graves and crossed to the very back of the burial ground.

A headstone adorning a grave was set at a diagonal to the rest of the orderly rows, for it had been dubious to bury Sybil there at all.

Winifred laid the flowers down and Pippa allowed the raven onto the ground to walk about in freedom.

Ursula pursued an earthworm that wriggled near the stone's edge.

"I'm getting married tomorrow," Pippa told Sybil. "To Hugh. I'm certain you already know that, for you can see from Heaven above. Tell Winifred who she's to marry!"

"No, don't!" Winifred said. "I wish not to know!"

"An older man, I think, and very rich," said Pippa, looking archly at her friend.

"We miss you, Sybil," said Winifred.

Unbeknownst to either of the girls, the Reverend had been in Bury at the time of Sybil's hanging, although he did not see it himself. He'd been there to pay for and retrieve her body. Because she was a convicted witch, she'd been buried at this strange angle, and there was a rumor that she was face-down with a stake driven through her, to prevent her rising on the Day of Judgment. Still, it seemed that after her conviction the Reverend had begun to change his feelings toward his daughter . . . reason, or guilt, or even love.

The grass was greener over Sybil's grave, and at the foot grew a thick cluster of ground ivy with tiny bright purple flowers.

Every week, on a Friday, Pippa and Winifred visited. Sometimes there was already a bouquet, left by someone else in the Vale who missed Sybil, too.

"I never realized how much work was involved in packing a household," said Pippa as they walked beneath the shade of the graveyard's yew trees on their way out. "It will take me the whole of the day."

"Do you need help? I have chores for my mother but perhaps after . . ."

"No, I'm organizing as I go. Thank you anyway, I—" Pippa stopped. There was a figure at the gate with a handful of daffodils.

"Just keep walking," said Winifred.

Pippa's face was neutral, blank as white stone, and they passed Alice Baxter without trouble. Alice was little seen in the village, except for delivering milk on occasion, and no one had heard her speak since the day in court. Some said she'd been cursed by Satan himself for betrayal; others thought it was the crushing guilt of false witness.

Alice lowered her eyes and backed away from Winifred and Pippa. She said nothing, not even a stutter, and half-turned until they were gone.

"She's in church all the time," said Winifred.

"Her own mind will punish her suitably," said Pippa, on the brink of feeling sorry for her former friend, for she knew the trapdoors of the mind.

"Ah, well," said Winifred, sighing in that pragmatic way of hers, with no reason to hold a grudge against an inferior person.

The rest of the day was taken up with Pippa in her cottage cleaning the table, folding the blankets and linens with herbs to repel moths and insects, and then bathing and washing her hair. These were the things that ought to be done with a mother or a grandmother or a sister, but she had none of these and so she did them in lively solitude.

"Sybil," said Ursula from the corner.

Pippa looked up. *Sybil*, she agreed. Then she smiled, because along the left side of her face she felt a strange sort of warmth, an unseen light.

For the wedding ceremony the next day, she would wear a fine black silk bodice and petticoat. It had once been Winifred's and the skirt had been too short for Pippa, so they'd improvised with a contrasting black band of wool around the bottom to make up the difference. She could not afford a new collar and so she'd stitched a black bird and flowers on the corner of her white church collar. The flowers had sharp petals because Pippa was impatient with the precise stitching associated with smooth curves . . . even if it was for her own wedding.

After bathing indoors she allowed her hair to dry in natural waves. It would be styled into loops the next morning.

Nothing much would change, she reflected. She would still live in the Vale, but in the Feltons' old and lovely manor. It was fitted with modern conveniences and had a pleasant rambling quality, with large latticed windows, strong timbers, and stonework around the doors. Climbing vines gave it the look of the forest. Pippa was already determined to commission the carved image of the Green Man somewhere on the premises.

She drank a mug of birch wine. She'd made it on her own this year. Goody Brewer had not uttered a peep about it. With the wine she ate a bread roll and a slice of ham and a handful of green beans, cooked in lemon water. The longest winter of her life was over, finally, and now she would start something new and wonderful.

It was that magical time of the evening when the world was pale blue and the shadows were indigo. The farmers in the fields would be bringing in their herds for the night.

In the corner Ursula said, "Thank you, girl."

"Shhh," said Pippa.

There were footsteps on the path outside and the gate swung open. She sniffed the air. Her heart beat faster—that drum, that great fire—and she smiled. She'd asked Hugh to come around. She wanted to speak with him, to make sure this was for the right purpose, and that her changing life was lined up with her precious inner self. She owed him a debt for helping her out of the witch trials, and for lifting her out of a life of certain hardship, but those were obligations and not reasons.

"Pippa?" Hugh's voice was so deep and so vibrant that it made her knees weak.

"Hello," she said, pulling open the door. "Walk with me for awhile? Just along the field."

"You're not about to change your mind, are you?"

"No . . . are you?"

"No."

They left the cottage in semi-darkness. They walked together across the narrow wooden plank that bridged the musical brook. Hugh led the way. Pippa thought of how much had happened, and was yet to happen. A life together loomed ahead of them. That future was a physical pull over her.

Was it the future she wanted?

"Hugh," she began, hoping there was no trace of trouble in her voice. "Before we go ahead with this, there are things about which I need to be sure."

She could feel his frown in the darkness. "No matter what's happened to you, Pippa, I love you. I'll be your husband. I care not for any history that might come between us."

"'Tis not that," she said. How could she explain that it was not the accusation of witchcraft that disturbed her? That she had taken control of that word, *witch*, and that was what she had become? "You know that my family is cunning. I need to know that you won't force me away from what I am."

To her shock, Hugh laughed. "Have you any idea why I love you? Or have you just taken it for granted?"

"Well, I . . ."

"Pippa." Hugh stopped and held her face in his hands.

He loomed over her. "I *know* what you are. It is your cunning that I love most about you. From that day when we were children—when you enchanted me in the forest—oh, don't think I'm ignorant of what you did! You bewitched me, and gladly was I bewitched, and from that day on, as you grew up to be so beautiful, you were special to me and different from any other girl I could ever be in company with."

"But, Hugh, I mean it. I am truly . . . there are powers that you cannot know, things I can never share with you."

"I mind it not," he whispered. "In fact, I like you better for it. And after your terrible ordeals, you fear nothing. Now, you're a sight to behold!" He smiled, then sobered. "I confess, for a short time, I did wonder. I was not sure that you were on the side of godliness. Right after you were accused I—I hesitated, thinking perhaps those men were right. But when you were taken away, Pippa, this village was empty to me, and I decided I cared not what you were. You could not belong to the Devil, for you belong to me.

"I do not pretend to know your mysteries, but that matters not. I may have wealth and land and title, but without you I have no spirit."

Pippa unclenched the breath she'd been holding. He had saved her during the trials, of course, and had always been an upstanding person. But with his society and wealth, her position would be made safe, and that was what a man should do for her. Pippa knew she was lucky such a man existed in her village, or else she would have gone through life a lonely woman, scrapping out an existence, never secure enough in body to be expressive in that spirit he loved so much. "Thank you, Hugh. You are a good man."

Relaxing, they began to walk again. They passed a glowing cloud of fireflies. It was the first day of summer and the countryside gave them a soft welcome. The last weight of worry had vanished from Pippa's shoulders and now she felt buoyant, floating on a tide of joy, with Hugh beside her. Her thoughts turned to the next day and she giggled.

"What's funny?" he asked, and gave a quick smile.

"I don't know," she said. "I just can't believe tomorrow we'll be married."

"The village can't stop reminding me," said Hugh. "My mother, going on, and the lads all teasing me, and my father—he gave me an excruciating speech."

"About what?"

"About my duties as a husband." He arched an eyebrow at her.

"*Oh!*" Pippa laughed. She found it rather embarrassing that the whole world—at least, the whole of the Vale—knew and would be speculating on her initiation into the ranks of wifedom. If one thing bothered Pippa anymore, it was the imposition of others onto her free will. She didn't want to follow other people's rules. She wanted mischievous secrets to fill up her smile.

She looked up at Hugh, at his strong profile, and at the thin curve of a moon that glowed in the sky beyond. It was a growing moon. She had used her books in the cave to discover the best astrological alignment for a marriage and it happened to coincide with tonight, May Eve. The most fertile time of the year.

Poor man next to her. There were many things he would never know. Some things, she could show him.

"Hugh," she said, and her voice had changed. The night was in her breath. She reached out and with a bold hand that darted forward, she touched the tips of his fingers with her own. They laced together for an instant, for an invitation. She stepped away and headed toward the forest.

Hugh was so good, so virtuous, and she was unsure if he would follow her on this primitive errand. But when she glanced back over her shoulder, she saw that he was near behind her.

Along the way, she flung off her shoes and left them near a blooming hawthorn bush. Wild blood hummed in her veins and, laughing, she began to run away from him.

His low chuckle echoed and he was chasing her.

Pippa felt her mouth go dry. There was no going back now. She was falling forward into a hot, dark place, and a few paces later the forest embraced her in thick shadows. The ground was springy and warm beneath her bare feet. Winding through, she passed near the brook, close to the marked tree and the cave, and beyond to the grove of apple trees.

Hugh moved through the forest in pursuit, his footsteps swift and sure. He did not conceal from the trees his presence, his intention.

The muscles in Pippa's legs grew weak when she saw the hanging blossoms of the apple trees. They were the color of silver roses in the deep twilight and they beckoned her into their circle. The grass in the grove was a soft carpet. When she felt Hugh step behind her, when his strong arms encircled her at the waist, she almost collapsed. His hands moved across her abdomen, feeling through the cotton of her bodice, and then to the apex of her thighs. Pippa laughed through her closed smile, a sultry and ancient invocation.

"This is wrong," Hugh whispered in the darkness. "We're not married yet."

A flash of anger arose. "This is our marriage," she said. "This is the way of things."

"But the ceremony, the church . . ."

"This is the church of trees and God's creatures," she said. "This is our church." Her voice was low and commanding, for she wanted to wait no longer.

It was not Hugh's fault that he succumbed without further concessions to morality or society. It was the oldest of celebrations and they were outside of themselves. Cast aside, lost in the night, Hugh leaned over and kissed Pippa on the neck, moving his lips to her collarbone and pushing aside the fabric.

They sank to the ground as one, shedding laces and cloth, hands flashing and finding each other. Pippa was spinning with the new sensations that shimmered across her skin and then, a few moments later, deep inside her. Hugh kissed her on the mouth when they were joined and she sighed against his lips. The trees and the wind seemed to sigh, too.

All was put to rights in the apple grove in the forest. She married him that night and was happy.

LAST MONTH, MATTHEW HOPKINS had been told that he did not have long to live. "Consumption," said the old doctor in Colchester. "You must rest if you hope to recover. I can bleed you with—"

"No," Hopkins had told him. It was enough of a compromise to see the doctor at all. For a long time he had felt his lungs shiver but had not wanted to believe he was seriously ill. Then, in early July, he had awakened to coughing and when he placed his white handkerchief over his mouth, there were spots of bright red blood that spelled his doom.

It was now August. It had been over two years since Hopkins had begun his quest and he was no closer to finishing it. *Two years ago,* he mused, *I was in Bury St. Edmunds, giving evidence against all those witches.* He had been quite the success. He'd refurbished the interior of the Thorn Inn and hired new help that baked bread every morning. He wore the finest imported silks and leathers, donated money to the parish, and still had more money than he knew how to spend.

On the bedroom wall of his cottage, the beams were decorated with hundreds of tiny etched crosses. They marched in rows outward from the original two . . . pale against the stain of the wood, each one proudly scratched, tiny figures with arms outstretched, a necropolis of tribute to his work.

Satan, however, was always there. Where one witch was named and hanged, another one sprang up to take her place, like the many-headed Hydra, and Hopkins felt fevered with the effort of finding them all. He felt a battle raging for his very soul. He was terrified that he had not done well enough . . . that he would go straight to Hell when he died because he had not punished all of the witches. The lure of their choke-hold had not vanished . . . if anything, it had gotten worse. Meanwhile John Stearne was fighting the good fight north of here, edging the prosecutions closer to Cambridge. Hopkins thought of his friend with fondness and some envy of his better health. He buttoned his waistcoat.

He was preparing to go to St. Mary's church, his own parish, because of a mysterious letter.

> Dear Friend, Master Hopkins,
> I fear to give my name to you, for I am also a-feared of the witches' curse. I write to you from a most grievous position. A supernatural plague is rotting here in Manningtree yet again. Whether this be nature or witchcraft I know not. I call upon you to investigate, and choke it out where it be found. If you do not, I fear that God himself will punish us for such wickedness in our midst.

There had been no signature, but instead a verse from the Psalms: "*The angel of the Lord encampeth round about them that fear him, and delivereth them.*"

Hopkins had been nursing his pleuristic cough, but had jumped out of bed at the word. This, he was convinced, could cure him. Clearly Satan had turned more women to his malefic cause.

Lord God Almighty, he'd prayed, *if You return me my health, I would do Your holy work in this land, and remit to find more witchcraft in Manningtree, and then beyond. I want to smell them. Oh, God, I did doubt Your plan, and for that I am most humbly sorry . . . Make me well and I will do well . . . in lust was I born, my sorry self . . . she touched me, and I liked it . . . ripple of flesh, sinful in Death . . . Lord, Heavenly Father, in You I do pray . . . slay . . . scry, die . . . Jesus, please . . .*

This had been followed by an unusual burst of energy and a respite from the worst of the coughing. It was a sign. He still felt overheated and faint around the edges, but he figured that was from the weather. It was an ill month, August, for it bred the worst of disease. If Hopkins could survive August, then he was sure he would live for much longer.

The previous January, the very esteemed astrologer William Lilly had visited the Thorn Inn, much to Hopkins's thrill. Over mugs of spiced ale, Lilly—a thin man with intense, deep-set blue eyes—had given horary predictions to Hopkins about his life and work. He replayed the astrologer's words in his mind. "So will there be lasting impact of your work upon the world, and stories written about you, from the way that Mercury aspects Saturn. Beware the danger of Leo's sun, for Mars and Venus are joined against you here. I foresee a problem with your breathing."

Frowning, Hopkins recalled that Lilly had not given advice as to how he might improve his breathing. But then, the astrologer had not told him he would die. He would have said so, if that were meant to be.

No, no, work to be done, thought Hopkins. He readied his things in the main room of the inn, sparing a moment to admire the glassware he'd imported from Italy.

A cloud of flies attacked a loaf of honeyed bread on the table.

On the bar, a stack of printed manuscripts was bound with twine. The top sheet read *The Discovery of Witches,* and below that, *by Matthew Hopkins, Witch-finder.* It was his book, shorter than he would have liked, but he'd been under pressure to answer his critics. He already had a more detailed work in mind and hoped that a reputable publisher would bank on him.

The way to the church was not far. He and Elspeth passed fields and trees and scattered homes. To his right, the River Stour was a flat brown expanse edged with mudflats.

As he arrived at the church he started to cough again and his anxiety grew. He must find the witches, begin the trials, so that the Lord would see his dedication and take away his cough.

The landscape spun once, then twice. The church's tower seemed dizzying in its height. Elspeth was panting, her tongue dry and hot. "Water for the hound," he ordered a small boy standing nearby. He tossed a coin in the boy's direction.

"Yes, Master Hopkins," said the child.

It was hot and he was covered in a film of dust. Even over such a short distance the summer's grime managed to cling. He dipped his handkerchief—spotted with rust bloodstains—into Elspeth's water bowl and dabbed his neck and brow.

A farmer with a magnificent beard approached and asked him, "Master Hopkins?"

"Yes."

"There be a gathering at the church. They're waiting for you. More talk of witches 'round here." The man shuddered. "A gallows has already been built."

"Really!" Hopkins was impressed.

He walked toward the church and saw a small gallows set up across the field, near Mistley Pond. That made sense. It was easier and cheaper to hang a witch on the spot than to bother with the gaol. Hopkins had learned that villagers were less likely to become annoyed with him if their problem could be disposed of in the heat of the moment. He fingered the empty velvet satchel in his pocket. It was large enough to hold his fee even if it were given in many small coins.

A stream of people was on the approach to St. Mary's. Many of them Hopkins recognized, for they were his own neighbors. They held a familiar look: fear, curiosity, suspicion, ready to be incited on this slow summer's day; they were ready to convict. He wondered who had been dabbling in the dark arts this time.

He tossed the boy another penny and ordered him to watch Elspeth while he was inside.

The church was packed from aisle to aisle. Hopkins had the sort of fame by now that drew crowds. The people whispered amongst themselves. In times of such distress, it was the quiet sanctity of their parish church to which they turned. It was one of the few places where a public accusation might be made without fear of immediate supernatural reprisal from the witch herself.

In all, thought Hopkins, *a fine idea to have the inquest here today.* Someone in this congregation had sent him the mysterious plea. He straightened his Dutch collar and marched up the center aisle. *It would be better if Mary Phillips were here to assist me,* he thought, *but I must meet the Devil on my own today, it would seem.* He wondered why she had not come, for she lived in neighboring Manningtree.

A cough rose from his liquid lungs and tickled the back of his throat. He swallowed it down.

Parishioners were still filing into the church. It was a tall, cool cavern against the midday's beating sun. It was also dim inside, which Hopkins appreciated. Too much light made him sneeze.

In the congested center aisle on the way to the altar, Hopkins almost collided with a solid man dressed in clothes finer than his. "Pardon," said the man, turning.

"Ah!" said Hopkins, for he recognized him. It was the Honorable Robert Spring, of Lavenham, who had studied at Cambridge with his own brother Thomas Hopkins. The Spring family was wealthy and prominent from the wool trade and were deep into Suffolk politics. He wondered what Robert Spring was doing here in Mistley. It seemed odd.

At Spring's side was a chestnut-haired young lady with a clean, attractive face. Hopkins knew her from somewhere. She looked at him for a frank moment and then lowered her eyes. On her arm she carried a closed wooden basket. This, too, was an unusual detail . . . it was not the sort of day for a picnic and they were of the class who had servants to carry their personal effects. *Where do I know you?* Hopkins searched his memory and finally decided that the young woman may have lived in a village where he'd hunted witches. It was disturbing how they all ran together over time . . . names and faces a blur of guilt or innocence. This one had likely given testimony against a neighbor. She had the look of a solid citizen.

"My betrothed," said Spring, without offering her name.

Hopkins noticed that Spring held in his hand a copy of *The Discovery of Witches*. "You have read my work!" he said, flattered.

"Indeed I have."

"What brings you to humble Mistley, sir?" Hopkins asked.

Spring gave a tight smile, almost condescending. "Business."

"Ah," said Hopkins. Why was he so unsettled? Bowing, he shrugged off the whiff of danger that accompanied Spring's presence. It must be that Sir William Spring, Robert's elder brother, was the High Sheriff of Suffolk and recently elected Member of Parliament. It always put Hopkins on edge to be around men with powerful connections.

Perhaps Robert Spring is here to observe my skill, report back to his brother in Parliament, and they will offer me a high office! Yes, that made sense. He smiled and bowed once more and continued up the aisle.

When Hopkins stepped up to the altar, the congregation quieted, and he did not need to shout in a voice weakened by fever.

He raised both hands. "Godly people, my own neighbors," he said. "A terrible ill *does* afflict you. I have on good authority that Satan is working amongst you. Witchcraft has returned here. If there are any who know of such activity, speak now, for you are safe within these walls!"

There was a muffled silence. A few coughs, the clearing of throats, but no one spoke.

"Fear not reprisal! I will find any malfeasance and identify the witches responsible."

A man raised a timid hand. "Er, um . . . eh . . ."

"Stand, sir, fear not." Wearied already, Hopkins pressed his handkerchief to his mouth.

"Me cow fell with a seizure," the man said. "I believe it to be witchcraft."

"Do you have a neighbor with a grudge against you? Remember, they are likely to be women of the lewd variety, and do have imps, creatures under their command."

The man scratched his head. "Well . . . I suppose me third cousin always had 'er eye on that particular cow."

"Ah," said Hopkins. His energy was draining away. Desperate, he scrambled for something to say . . . perhaps he was bewitched himself! He must find her . . . find it . . . He scanned the restless crowd. There was a key here. There was someone in this church that stuck in his mind like a thorn. The staring faces were like a long paragraph, and he was skimming for that one important word amongst them.

That word was *witch*.

The recognition hit him like a hammer, like the very *malleus maleficarum*, and his left knee weakened.

Robert Spring. Next to him was his betrothed—*Winifred Radcliff*, his memory finally reminded him—and next to her was the *witch*.

Philippa was more beautiful than ever and dressed in the distinguished cloth of a well-married woman. Her skin was luminous and healthy. Her face had regained its strong lines after her incarceration. Most of her hair was properly set beneath an expensive diadem cap, but there was one wild tendril that had escaped. It twisted like a dark serpent behind her ear and grazed the top of her shoulder. A pair of rose lips curved an evil smile. Her eyes pinned him.

"Witch!" he screamed, pointing at Philippa. "That woman is a witch!"

The crowd gasped and heads swiveled to see where he pointed.

"She dares to defile God's church," Hopkins shouted.

But no one shouted agreement. Instead they stared at *him* with vague, stupid puzzlement.

Can't you see, she has bewitched you all . . .

He heard her voice in his mind.

Philippa the witch stood up. Hopkins noticed a man sitting to her left, the same nobleman who had spoken at her trial. He must be her husband now.

All eyes were on her.

"Matthew Hopkins," said Pippa, and her voice rang clear and strong through the church. "I, Lady Philippa Felton, am an upright woman and I will answer your charge with the voice of truth."

"You speak naught but lies!" he hissed.

She shook her head. That wild tendril of hair dangled and danced. Most in the audience were captivated by her, Hopkins could see. She gave the illusion of loveliness, the glamour of health. *Hag.*

"How is it that you, Matthew Hopkins, are so well able to find a witch?" she asked. "Who has given you this knowledge?"

"God!" he said.

"Nay, I say that it is Satan who has told you. You have enriched yourself. You bear the manner of a cursed man, one who has sold himself for worldly possession."

Hopkins suddenly regretted the fine thin silk waistcoat and breeches he wore. "No," he gasped. The cough was returning. His voice was clogged with the pleurisy. On his own tongue he could smell onions.

"Oh, yes. Torture innocent women no more with your ordeals! How could any man claim to know the ways of the Devil, unless he himself be devoted to Satan? How could you, with such *effect*, find so many witches in a mere two years? I say you are the evil influence that menaces our towns and villages. Good people, see how misfortune follows where Matthew Hopkins goes!'

"God will punish you most grievously," Hopkins warned.

"God will forgive me for my human sins more readily than He will forgive your evil! *You* are the witch. It is *you* who was given the register of witches by Satan himself. It is not with the help of God but with the aid of the Devil that you have found fellow witches!"

"I do not—I reject these outrageous—spurious—" Hopkins began to cough. He had no breath left. Her words echoed his own fears, his own deep suspicion that he was borne and owned by witches . . . she had come to claim his head at last . . . had he been working for Satan all along? *Am I a witch?* In a blinding flash of fear he realized that he'd been hearing their voices and they'd driven him forward. He had abused his body in atrocious ways, and had taken pleasure in it. Did that not make him *one of them*? Blinking away the wellspring of tears, he tried to believe that *I am in church, I am safe, I do God's work*. His lungs screamed in agony. Bloody sputum erupted into his handkerchief. "She's bewitched me with illness!" He took a shuddering breath and screamed, "Kill her! She is a witch! *Kill her!*"

The men in the crowd were standing up. Hugh Felton, Philippa's husband, was one of them. "No, Hopkins," he said loudly. "*You* are the witch. And that greyhound of yours is your imp."

"That's right!" said another man. "He has that dog at his heels, dotes on her, suckles her no doubt!"

"Witch! He is a witch!" someone else shouted.

The light of blood shone in a hundred pairs of eyes.

The tide of them turned like a beast upon Hopkins.

"Swim 'is self in the pond!" a grinning old woman suggested with a cackle.

Hands clutched him and he cried out. He was swept out of the church, half-carried and half-dragged. "No! No! I can't—I haven't—!" His traitorous lungs did not allow any more protest. They bubbled and spasmed in his chest. He was without a voice.

As a pair of angry yeomen dragged him by the elbows toward the pond, he passed near Philippa walking out of the church. In fact, she glided as though floating. On her shoulder was that dastardly raven. *Where did that come from?* It was her spirit familiar! He tried to point at the imp, but a rope had materialized from somewhere and his hands were bound behind him.

The beady-eyed bird said "Sybil," in the tone of an ethereal girl, that minister's crazy daughter who had hanged. He heard it.

The raven's word was lost amidst the eager shouts of the mob.

"Swim him! Toss him into the pond!"

"He's a witch!"

"I been ill since he started his hunts! He's bewitched us all into killing!"

For a terrifying moment Hopkins hovered in the air as a dozen strong arms heaved him into the pond. The murky water rushed at his face and then he was submerged with a mighty splash. He did not know how to swim. Thrashing and gasping, he swallowed water on the first breath, and it seared his throat and mixed with the consumptive phlegm in his lungs. *Oh God, oh God, oh God* . . . Black spots swarmed in his vision like twitching flies, the vanguards of a torment that beckoned, a witch with her legs akimbo . . . Hell was coming, Hell was here . . .

In the stolen moments when his head was above water, he could see the grinning, awful faces that lined the edge of Mistley's pond, and he could hear them shouting, "He floats! He floats!"

It did not feel like floating to him.

He was dragged out of the water and onto the grassy bank. He moaned with fear. "No . . ."

"He's a witch!"

"The ordeal proves it!"

"Hang the fellow!"

"We need a long rope."

"Here, right here!"

"Up," ordered a voice and Hopkins was hoisted up by his underarms.

Someone had tied an inexpert noose and attached it to the gallows. It was empty, a gaping eye of rope waiting for his neck.

"Enough of your witchery," a man whispered in his ear.

Hopkins's last words were a violent, blood-speckled cough. The red of his own lung tissue edged his mouth and teeth. All of these people were under a spell. His work was unaccomplished. He hadn't had enough time to name the witches, to destroy them, to break their hold over him, could not God save His own servant? He twitched weakly, knowing he was about to die, and nowhere near ready for it. *He* was bad, *he* was the witch, *they* had discovered him . . . he had tried so hard to be good.

A hand shoved him up the ladder and onto the narrow platform of the gallows.

Elspeth's frantic whine punctured his fear; a man had the

greyhound on a lead, choking her, leading her toward the gallows, toward her master.

Across the heads, he could see Philippa standing in the background with the black raven on her shoulder, her arm linked with her husband's. She raised her other hand at him and made the Devil's sign: two horned fingers that waggled at him, claiming him. He saw how well she had laid her spider's trap. *Witch,* he tried to say, but his head was already through the rope.

Beside him, Elspeth was strung up, and she gasped and thrashed.

Oh God, no, God, no . . .

Black and red and terror blossomed in his vision. His feet scrambled to find a surface but there was nothing but space beneath him. The rope held him, it hugged his throat in a deadly embrace . . . faces drifted and swiveled in front of him . . . for a thousand years he struggled . . . the last thing he felt was the trickle of warm urine down his expensive silk, and then a twisted, humiliating lust that made him stiffen in his wet breeches *in front of all these people*, and the white-hot fist in his lungs that squeezed, and squeezed, and squeezed.

Epilogue

An old woman and a young girl spirited through a wood at dusk. The currents of a gentle wind parted the green branches in front of them. The deep countryside was full of life on this warm spring day. The girl was smiling, for she was excited, and had been told of a great secret that was hidden in these woods. Her hair was fixed in curls that bounced with every step.

The older woman wore a green hunting costume with a long jacket that billowed out behind her. From the way the skirts moved, she had foregone the usual layers of petticoats and her feet were bare underneath the expensive fabric. Her hair was the same dark shade as her granddaughter's, except for a long streak of lunar white that began at the peak of her forehead and tumbled down in a side curl.

All the world was silent except for the feet on the path, the distant song of the brook, and the rustling of squirrels who scrambled for a hide. Night was approaching and the owls would be on the hunt. People did not often tarry in these woods. They were rumored to be haunted.

"Pip," said the child, for that was what everyone called her grandmother, "why did you tell Mama that we were visiting Mr. Pye's new calf? That's the other way from here."

"Your mother doesn't know about this place. This knowledge comes through your father's side." Pippa smiled, remembering how Lillibet had done this thing for her.

"This place? Everyone knows about the woods!" Her tone was quiet, for she'd been told this errand was a great secret.

"Not where I will take you, Beth. No one knows about it except for me, and now, you."

"Oh!"

Beth Felton adored her grandmother. She loved how Pip did not talk down to her as most adults did. Just because she was nine years old did not make her stupid—even the Bible said, *"And a little child shall lead them."* But Pip wasn't like other adults. She made ribald comments and drank wine and sang happy songs. Beth knew that her father's parents were wealthy—they lived in the manor—and so could do just about whatever they pleased.

Pippa stopped next to a tree. She almost blended into its shadow. Kneeling, she took Beth's hand. "You will swear an oath to me now. What I am about to show you, you will never reveal to another soul, except your own daughter or granddaughter."

Beth's eyes widened. Feeling most solemn, and privileged that her grandmother trusted her so much, she nodded. "I swear to keep the secret."

"You are a strong and wise girl," said Pippa. "Now, feel here, along the tree . . ."

Old, papery hands guided small, white hands along the trunk. The wind whispered along with Pippa as she counted off the paces for Beth. The ferns and the branches swayed. In this hollow, the very earth seemed to open for them, the good witch and her granddaughter.

"Shhh, now, here is the way, and in we go . . . I will teach you everything here . . ."

Historical Note

For generations, a hidden history has been passed along, the kind of knowledge that grows beneath the notice of churches and governments. The practitioners of folk magic depicted in this tale, the cunning-folk, the wise women, the Christian witches, were—and still are—real in England. The man who hunted them, Matthew Hopkins, was real. Although some of the characters in this story are fictional, their experience was real.

Since 2003, archaeological excavations in Cornwall, England have revealed a surviving pagan history, a ritual site where a circle of swan skins were buried for reasons unknown, by persons unknown. The site was dated to the 1640s, the same era as this story. Other archaeological evidence of what the English call cunning magic includes charms inscribed on paper and over doorways of cottages; shoes and bottles and nails buried beneath hearthstones; and court records of the business transactions of these cunning-folk, men and women who earned a living by casting spells. Their world was magical, and it is a part of history.

Matthew Hopkins, the infamous "Witch-finder General," was the leader of a sudden and brutal witch craze that swept through the eastern counties of England during the 1640s, while the civil war between King and Parliament raged. I have elaborated on his character and family history in ways that would surely infuriate him; however, I have tried to weave my story without contradicting what is known about his personal history. Indeed, very little is recorded of Hopkins's life before and after the two years of his activity, only that he was a young Puritan man with legal inclinations, and died in August 1647, buried at Mistley.

Many historians believe that because the civil war had effectively dissolved the King's courts of justice in pro-Parliament areas, this left a power vacuum where local magistrates were able to take justice into their own hands. In a world where witchcraft was real, disease rife, and the country at war, it was all too easy to seek a supernatural explanation for the ills afflicting England. It was the perfect opportunity for Matthew Hopkins to seek witches and secure hundreds of dubious convictions in so short a time.

Witch hunts elsewhere in Europe, such as France and Germany, were on a low simmer for hundreds of years. In England the pattern was different: they were a flash fever, a sudden and violent outbreak, and then there were none for many years.

During the 1640s, it was Matthew Hopkins who instigated one of these terrible fevers that ended as suddenly as it began, with as many as three hundred women and men as victims of the noose.

Acknowledgments

For research I am indebted to the following historians and authors:

Davies, Owen. *Popular Magic: Cunning Folk in English History* (Hambledon Continuum, 2003)

Durschmied, Erik. *Whores of the Devil: Witch-Hunts and Witch-Trials* (Sutton Publishing, 2005)

Gaskill, Malcolm. *Witchfinders: A Seventeenth Century English Tragedy* (John Murray, 2005)

Godbeer, Richard. *The Devil's Dominion: Magic and Religion in Early New England* (Cambridge University Press, 1992)

Hopkins, Matthew. *The Discovery of Witches* (1647)

Jackson, Louise. "Witches, Wives, and Mothers." *Women's History Review* (1995) Vol. 4, No. 1

Orme, Nicholas. *Medieval Children* (Yale University Press, 2003)

Ryken, Leland. *Worldly Saints: Puritans As They Really Were* (Zondervan Publishing House, 1986)

Scot, Reginald. *The Discoverie of Witchcraft* (1584)

Sharpe, James. *Instruments of Darkness: Witchcraft in Early Modern England* (University of Pennsylvania Press, 1997)

Valiente, Doreen. *Where Witchcraft Lives* (Aquarian Press, 1962)

Any factual or historical errors are my own.

Photo by Patrick Gallaway

Morgana Gallaway is also the author of *The Nightingale*. She splits her time between Arizona and Texas.

Find her on the web at
www.morganagallaway.com

CPSIA information can be obtained at www.ICGtesting.com
Printed in the USA
LVOW08s2054020714

392722LV00006B/677/P